THE GIRLS FROM ALEXANDRIA

CAROL COOPER

ABOUT THE AUTHOR

Carol Cooper is a doctor, journalist, and author.

Born in London, she was only a few months old when her cosmopolitan family took her to live in Egypt. She returned to the UK at eighteen and went to Cambridge University where she studied medicine and her fellow students.

Following a string of popular health books as well as an award-winning medical textbook, Carol turned to writing fiction. Her first two novels are contemporary tales set in London. Ever a believer in writing what you know, she mined the rich material of her childhood for *The Girls from Alexandria*.

Carol lives with her husband in Cambridge and Hampstead. She has three grown-up sons and three stepchildren.

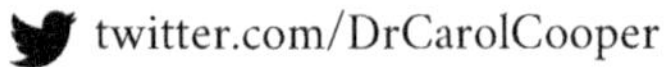

ALSO BY CAROL COOPER

NOVELS

Hampstead Fever

One Night at the Jacaranda

NON-FICTION

Twins & Multiple Births — The Essential Parenting Guide from Pregnancy to Adulthood

Baby Essentials

Pregnancy Essentials

Your Clever Baby

Baby Milestones

The Baby & Child Question & Answer Book

Surviving at Work

CO-AUTHORED NON-FICTION

General Practice Cases at a Glance

General Practice at a Glance

Twins

Growing Up! A Parent's Guide to Childhood

Johnson's Mother & Baby

THE GIRLS FROM ALEXANDRIA

CAROL COOPER

This is a work of fiction. All characters and events in this work, other than those clearly in the public domain, are entirely fictitious. Any resemblance to any persons, living or dead, is entirely coincidental.

Print Edition ISBN 978-0-99-545142-1

Cover Design By: Emma Rogers

Cover Images © Shutterstock

Second Edition, 2022, Hardwick Press

First published in Great Britain in 2021 by Agora Books

For Muriel

1

NOW

They drilled into my brain. No wonder my head throbs.

I dare to touch my forehead, inching across a mammoth bandage until my fingers reach the very top. They said they might remove a flap of skull. Did they, in the end? And what have they done with my piece of bone? They could have lost it.

Funny how the minute you step into a hospital, it's always *they* and *them*. I'm stuck in here where there's no choice but to trust them. Well, they'd better figure out what's wrong with me before it's too late.

I clutch the sheet, twisting its edge in my fingers. My tongue is dry and wooden, and all I've got is the plastic glass by my bed with tepid water, hopeless for a parched mouth. What wouldn't I give for a cold lemonade served to Simone and me beside the mimosa tree in Alexandria? I imagine Rashida calling me, '*Nadia, my heart, my soul. I made lemonade for you.'* Here in the ward, the grimy windows don't open, and the suffocating heat makes my head worse in every way. I may never get out.

I picture them splitting my skull apart with a saw that scatters bone dust in its wake. Did the surgeon sink fathoms down into my brain, deep into the catacombs of memory, obliterating the very things I need to cling on to? The pulse in my temple gallops at the thought. They might even think up more tests to do. You can't put anything past them.

They. Who are *they*? And who, for that matter, are we? That question goes back to my childhood, even to my parents' childhood, yet still I have no answer.

From my bed, I see right into the corridor. There goes the man in a beanie hat thing again, as he does several times a day. To the prayer room, I guess. The name for his hat won't come for the moment. No surprise. I've begun to struggle with even simple words. The man keeps adjusting that hat as he strides down the corridor. Must know exactly where he's headed. Lucky him. The other day, I found myself at the butcher's when I'd meant to collect a book from the library.

A *taqiyah*. There's the word for his hat.

There's no *muezzin* in British hospitals, but the man must heed an internal clock, just as a mechanism within my head reproduces the crash of the waves against the rocks; next door's cockerel; a stray dog barking; the hooves of an exhausted donkey labouring up the hill; impatient klaxons at the crossroads; the fruity voice of Umm Kulthum on the radio; the penetrating call of the *roba bikya* man as he trawls the neighbourhood for junk; the tram that hurtles from one gloriously named station to the next, shifting its heavy human cargo through Chatby, Camp Caesar, Ibrahimeyya, Cleopatra, Sporting, Sidi Gaber, Roushdy, Glymenopoulo, and San

Stefano; and, through it all, Rashida's shrill demand for someone to bring her a knife that is both sharp and clean for a change.

The nurse in the dark-blue tunic and squeaky shoes is back, dragging a machine on wheels to do what she calls the obs. It checks my pulse, temperature, and blood pressure, while she fits a little clip on to my index finger to measure oxygen. I'm surprised there's oxygen left in this stifling ward, let alone any of it reaching the tip of my finger.

'All right, Nadia?' The nurse's voice suggests minimal interest in the answer.

I don't need a machine to know that my heart is bouncing all over the place. My mouth is still a wad of felt, so I focus on the nurse and tap the plastic thing that's empty.

'I'll refill your jug in a moment.' In one slick movement, the nurse rolls up the blood-pressure cuff and tucks it back into the wheeled machine.

'You remind me of someone,' I add, but the nurse and her equipment have already moved on to the next patient.

I know what I need to do. Now, more than ever, I must find my sister. For that, I'll need all my faculties and every memory I can dredge up. I check inside my head. What did they take? Memories are fragile when you are seventy years old. Seventy! I can't afford to lose any more of them, not when remembering the past might help with the here and now. You haven't a hope of understanding the present unless you understand the past. Miss Brownlee taught me that at the English Girls' College, all those years ago.

If I close my eyes, I see the ribbon of Corniche all the way from the harbour to Montazah Palace. A blue parasol with a white fringe. Mother in a huge scarf, her face shaded from the sun. Father studying *Al Ahram*. My frilly cotton swimsuit with straps that cut into my shoulders. Simone and I digging down to wet sand. A huge block of ice that only Abdou could lift.

ALEXANDRIA, JUNE 1953

It seemed unfair that one of our servants, usually Abdou because he was stronger than toothless old Ibrahim, had to lug a block of ice to the beach cabin, break it up with a pick to keep our drinks cool, then spend his time looking after us instead of enjoying himself. Displaying one gold tooth, he always said, *'Maalish.'* It means *never mind.*

Once our deckchairs and parasol were up, Father installed himself behind an Arabic newspaper while Mother read *La Réforme Illustrée,* paying special attention to the accounts of who had worn what at whose party. I squinted against the sun and made out the date in the top right corner of *Al Ahram.* ١٩٥٣ may look like 1907 gone wrong, but it's Arabic for 1953.

Here, the sea was deep azure in colour. How could grown-ups not want to fling themselves into the waves and go for a swim, or just jump in and out of the sparkling foam, as Simone and I did for hours? Called Sidi Bishr Two, this beach had a string of cabins all along the edge, many of them belonging to our friends. Uncle Selim, who wasn't a real uncle, didn't have a cabin of his own. Instead he would join us and lounge on a chair in his white trousers, straw hat, and special shoes. *Handmade in England,* he reminded us. His glasses were so dark that I couldn't tell if he was looking at my swimsuit or at something else. In haste, I threw a towel around me and went back to building sandcastles, which pleased me and which everyone else ignored.

Today my aunts, who were very real, arrived wearing matching scarves. Even if they had seen Mother less than an hour previously, they always found something to talk about, rattling away in the usual mix of French and Arabic, with some English words sprinkled on top. Everyone we knew spoke at least three languages. You were hardly Alexandrian if you didn't talk with your hands and leap constantly from one language to another, mid-sentence or not. Rashida, the Lebanese *da-da* whose job was to look after Simone and me, rarely came to the beach. She was too busy at home doing essential things like stuffing vine leaves and praying to St Anthony.

Along to the East rose the rocky outcrop of the automobile club, while across the sea in front of me lay countries like England where many of my schoolteachers and schoolfriends came from.

'Yorkshire's over there, where Miss Brownlee was born,' I informed Simone.

'You're pointing straight at Cyprus.'

Being two years older than me, Simone knew everything. She taught me how to make sandcastles almost as tall as hers. She was a better swimmer than me too, and boasted that she could have swum out to the little island if she'd wanted to, just as older boys did to show off. It was less than a mile, she said. I hoped she wouldn't try. Even at the age of seven, I was afraid of losing her. Without her, I was bound to fade and perish like a newspaper in the sun. I knew I would.

Although it was June, it wasn't hot. Even when it was baking downtown, a stiff breeze from the sea swept the shore, the very same breeze that kept Alexandria at the perfect temperature and made you unaware that you were getting burnt. Every so often, Mother looked up from her *Réforme*

Illustrée and called out, '*Ton chapeau*, Nadia,' to remind me to put my pink sun hat back on. My swimsuit was still wet, but my shoulders already tingled. I got a cold Spathis from Abdou's icebox and pressed the bottle on to my hot skin before I downed the fizzy drink.

Simone sat drawing under the parasol. 'Look. There goes Zouzou again.'

Zouzou strolled up and down, chewing Chiclets and wiggling her bottom in yet another swimsuit. She was part Italian, part Egyptian, and maybe part French or Austrian. In Alex, it was normal for everyone to be part something, with all the parts jumbled up.

'Don't stare,' Simone hissed.

It was impossible not to stare. Zouzou was unbelievably old, maybe thirty, and she chewed gum with a wide painted mouth like the film stars at the Rialto. Simone and I made fun of Zouzou, but, at bathtime, I once caught Simone trying to perfect the exact same hip wiggle.

When I next looked up from my sandcastle, Mother was still deep in conversation with her sisters and Father had nodded off. Simone's sketch pad was still under the parasol, but she wasn't. She wasn't by the water's edge either. She wasn't anywhere. Blood drained from my face. In fact, it drained from my entire body.

I jumped up and bellowed, 'Simone!'

Several boys splashed in the water nearby, fighting over an inflatable mattress. Simone was nowhere to be seen. I felt sick.

'What is it, *chérie*?' Mother asked.

'Simone's gone. Simone!' I yelled again.

Mother was up, spinning her head around. 'When did you last see her?'

'I don't know. Just a moment ago. Simone!' It was when Zouzou went by, wasn't it? My heart was beating all over the place except, it seemed, in the one spot where it was meant to beat.

Father was wide awake and interrogating people, while Mother's sisters were in a state of high agitation, flailing their arms about like windmills.

'Anything could have happened to her,' one of my aunts said, which I realised already. I knew Simone would try to swim out to the island. Scanning the sea, I couldn't see her at all.

'There's a *shaweesh* up on the Corniche,' Mother told Father. 'We should ask him.'

Yes, I thought. A policeman might be able to find a missing girl. Unless she'd already drowned.

Father rushed off to find the *shaweesh* while Abdou hitched up his long *galabeyya* so he could race up and down the sand in search of Simone. By now, a cluster of people on the beach were randomly throwing out suggestions. I silently promised I would give St Anthony twenty piasters if we found my sister. Then, instead of standing there doing nothing, I too scampered up the steps to the Corniche. The usual vendors punctuated the pavement, yelling about their pretzels, soft drinks, and nuts. '*Soodani wa lib*,' they cried, to sell people peanuts and roasted watermelon seeds. I ignored them all today, even my favourite vendor who cooked ears of corn on a makeshift grill that he fanned with a piece of cardboard.

There was Father, clutching Simone's hand! He was red and sweaty, and she was staring at her feet. Although I couldn't hear everything he said, I reckoned he was ticking her off.

'I only wanted an ice cream!' she moaned.

'You're too young to go off on your own,' he said. '*Ça ne se fait pas*. It's not done.'

I'd never seen Father look so scared. When Mother got to

Simone, she hugged her tight and spoke softly, but then, she never did shriek like some other mothers. I don't think she got cross with Simone about the ice cream, even though we were never allowed the stuff because she didn't want us catching typhoid. I guess Mother was just relieved, like me.

Our parents decided we should go. I usually protested about leaving the beach, even when the sun had made my skin feel tight all over, but this time I was ready for home. Once Abdou had loaded up our things, we piled into the big Ford, with my heart still pounding like a road drill. Father claimed not to be superstitious, but everyone in Egypt believes in the Evil Eye, so we too had blue stones dangling from the rear-view mirror. They protected against the Eye and other drivers. I suppose they'd protected Simone.

The windscreen had a visor that was meant to keep out the sun but didn't. Simone and I sat together in the back and squirmed to stop the hot seat welding itself to our thighs. We were silent as Father drove. Simone didn't tell me why she'd wanted an ice cream that badly, and I looked out of the window instead of letting on that she'd scared me more than halfway to death.

As the sun dipped lower on our drive along the Corniche, it painted building after building a glowing orange. The breeze came off the sea more strongly now. In vacant lots, boys in pyjamas flew their kites or kicked a ball around. I never saw girls with kites or footballs.

Come sunset, the sky turned every shade of pink, purple, and red. As the last slice of the sun sank, there was a momentary green flash. You had to be quick to see it. The flash was when you could make a wish, in the instant before the sun dropped like a rock into the sea and the sky suddenly turned dark. I usually had a lot of wishes to fit into that brief moment.

Today I made just one wish under my breath, repeating it to myself until I felt the words meld with the sound of our tyres on the tarmac. It was my biggest wish of all, never, ever, to lose Simone. I would have squeezed her hand if she'd let me.

NOW

The lights have been dimmed for the night. I lie back on the pillow and tell myself my head is fine, yet pain ricochets around my skull, blending with a thousand thoughts. Simone did disappear years later, of course. I still don't know why, and I need to find her.

Did Uncle Selim have anything to do with it? He was always looking at girls or young women — to what purpose I never grasped. Even as I force myself to concentrate, my mind slips deeper into fog. I daren't let myself doze off, though, in case they do something to me while I'm asleep.

'Shame there's no family.' The voice comes from the counter at the top of the ward, where two nurses sit.

There are rummaging sounds. 'Yeah, isn't it?'

The nurses take turns choosing chocolates from a purple drum that sits on the counter. The one who hunts for green triangles has curly hair and reminds me of someone from school. Name escapes me. The other nurse must be shorter. Just the crown of her fair head is visible.

I smell oranges. The woman in the bed opposite has put down her *Daily Express* and left a pile of peelings next to it on her bed table. We patients are supposed to be resting, but it is never quiet here. There are sighs, creaks, mutterings, and the occasional loud noise that makes me flinch.

At the counter, another sweet wrapper is crumpled and tossed aside. 'No children, then?'

'Nope. Lives alone, too.'

A pause. 'Needs someone to look after her, don't she?'

'Yeah. Especially if she has another seizure.'

My heart beats a tattoo. Although I don't remember a seizure, another one could come along and kill me before I track down Simone.

'Wonder if she had visitors today?'

'Doubt it,' the other nurse says. 'No family, see.'

I clench my fists. I do have family. I do. Just not here and now.

'What'll happen to her then?'

'Dunno. There are places, though. You know, for people who don't have rellies.'

This sends my head spinning into orbit, and I have to cling on to the bedframe to stop it. Places like that smell of pee and Brussels sprouts. I've seen them on the TV. I forget the name for that type of programme, but they're real life, not soap operas, and those stories are true. In the Middle East, elderly relatives are treated with respect, while here in England they lock their old folk up and leave them to rot in so-called care homes that are nothing like a real home and where nobody cares.

'How long she been here now?'

I strain to catch the answer, but the voices are subdued, and there's digging in the tin. The whispers take me back decades, to lying in bed at night while, in the kitchenette next door, Mother and Rashida muttered things that children were not meant to hear. If I did catch anything, it has long since slipped from my grasp.

The blonde nurse sighs. 'Anyway. Looks like me and Rick

are finished. We'll go on shagging, though, till one of us finds someone else.'

I know about finding, or at least about looking. In my hunt for Simone, I don't know where to look, and I can't even move from my bed. I've searched before. I used newspapers, adverts, and detectives. Now I can't imagine how to find her.

2

ALEXANDRIA, APRIL 1952

Blood dripping from my knee, I got up from the gravel path and kept running to the north side of the garden where nobody would find me. There, I crouched between the shrubs and the air-raid shelter. The shelter hadn't been used since I was born, of course. I arrived nearly a year after the end of the Second World War. I licked my finger then rubbed my knee clean to prevent lockjaw. When she wasn't worrying about typhoid and TB, Mother fretted about the dangers of tetanus.

Rashida called out, 'Nadia, where are you, my heart, my soul?'

I ignored her and observed a lizard as it scurried over a rock. Despite the scent of jasmine and stephanotis, this part of the garden gave me the creeps. Sometimes I'd get the urge to do *caca* and would have to rush back to the house, buttocks clenched.

Rashida called out again. 'Come, *ya habibti*. There are 'Beek Frean' for you!'

I budged only to tickle a plant that obligingly folds its little fronds when you stroke it. Rashida always called me her beloved. Even adding the promise of Peek Frean biscuits could not lure me out. I had seen the assembled relatives and spotted a small cane chair beneath the mimosa tree. That meant only one thing. A visit from my cousin Victor. Victor would pinch me and pull my pigtails. Once, he put something down the back of my dress and told me it was itching powder. It was only earth, but still I squirmed and wriggled away from him.

'He's a toad,' Simone always said.

Last time, she had persuaded Victor to leave me alone, though we had to contend with him bleating for hours afterwards about his sprained elbow. Today, however, Simone was out playing with friends, and I had to fend for myself.

Rashida coaxed me out in the end. I dragged my feet towards the main lawn and the usual circle of chairs in which sat Mother, Victor's mother, Tante Georgette, Tante Joséphine, Tantes Zahra and Magda from my Father's side of the family, and Uncle Selim who wasn't on anybody's side but his own.

Mother poured out Rashida's special lemonade while her sisters Georgette and Joséphine sipped coffee noisily. As always, Tante Georgette used a fan. Her fanning movements were so extravagant that she produced more heat than she lost. They beckoned me, calling me *trésor, trésor*. Yes, I was everyone's little treasure, to be hugged and cooed over, to be covered with Tante Georgette's lipstick and have my cheeks scraped by the bristles on Tante Magda's chin.

Tante Zahra wore one of her towelling turbans to hide the fact that she was too old to have any hair. She burped as she greeted me. *Aérophagie* is when you accidentally swallow air when eating, though I suspected Tante Zahra did it on purpose. Apart from wind, it caused lots of other trouble. Tante Zahra clutched her chest as she described the full gamut of symptoms that she'd had for at least fifty years, *parole de dieu*. She had tried everything and sadly there was no cure. *Maalish!* Elders deserve respect no matter how much they belch.

With one leg over the other, Uncle Selim sat as if he lived here. Next to him was a man with a fez, possibly Victor's uncle. And there was Victor, grinning at me from the cane chair under the tree. It was exactly the same as the other chairs, except that it was the right size for two children if they liked each other, which of course we didn't.

Rashida was right. A box of Peek Frean biscuits sat on the table. She couldn't pronounce Peek as there is no P in Arabic. There is no V either, as it happens. To make up for it, however, Arabic has two Hs, two Ss, two Ts, two Ks, a Kha, a Ghain, and several other letters that can easily make you fetch up your tonsils.

I inspected the contents of the box and chose a square biscuit with pink icing. Victor had a habit of licking a couple of biscuits first before rejecting them and grabbing another one. Victor wasn't just my revolting first cousin. He was also my fiancé. Although I was only six, people said that we were to be married. It may have been a joke, but I was taking no chances. I sat as far away as possible.

'*Comme il est beau!*' his mother exclaimed, and others joined in the chorus. Quite how Victor could qualify as handsome was a mystery. Had they not spotted that his head was like a sugar bowl with handles sticking out at each side? When his eyes widened and his grin turned lopsided, I knew he was about to pull another prank.

I perched beside him on the chair and immediately turned

away to study the bed of nasturtiums next to me, the monkey puzzle tree by the garage, the swing, the dovecote, the trellis with the grapevine on it, the bougainvillea over the gate, and pretty much anything that wasn't Victor.

He twisted to take up even more of the cane seat. 'A flower has fallen on your head,' he said, poised to pluck it from my hair.

'*Comme il est gentil*,' went Tante Magda.

I glowered. Victor wasn't at all *gentil*. He only wanted to pick off stray mimosa petals so he could yank out my hair. Once, without anyone noticing, he had made off with practically a fistful in his mitt.

The grown-ups went back to discussing the heat, the scandalous cost of everything, and the superiority of Alexandria over anywhere else in the world. Tante Zahra talked animatedly about her *aérophagie*, which made her swallow more air than ever, only to bring it up noisily with every sentence. My mother gave the latest bulletin on her gall bladder, then Victor's mother reminded everyone that she had the worst heart murmur in Alex, and it would be miracle if she saw out the year.

Selim clicked his silver cigarette case open and shut as he told a stupid tale about King Farouk. The whole world was in revolt, apparently, though it didn't look that way to me. 'According to His Majesty,' Selim said, 'soon there will only be five kings left: the King of Hearts, the King of Spades, the King of Diamonds, the King of Clubs, and the King of England.'

Everyone found this hilarious. Silly them. Didn't they even know that England had just got itself a Queen?

As the man with the fez began a story, the breeze picked up. The next thing I knew, Tante Magda screamed. Her straw hat had gone. She bellowed as one of the *suffragis* scurried to bring it back. She couldn't have been without her hat for more than a couple of seconds, but she had howled as though caught without her knickers.

The man with a fez sipped coffee noisily and continued. 'At least a *tarboush* stays on the head, *mish kida*? Even though as a hat it is completely useless. It neither keeps off the sun, nor the rain, nor does it keep the ears warm in winter. It is like a flowerpot, that is all. You cannot even use it to hide from people you want to avoid.' He displayed a gold tooth as he enjoyed his own wit. Despite the *tarboush*'s inadequacies, I wasn't surprised he wore one. His fez made him look as superior as the man whose profile was on all the coins.

'There is no breeze at all in Cairo,' someone said.

'Already it is as hot as an oven there. And it's only April,' Mother said.

This was the cue for another discussion about Cairo and its evident inferiority to Alex. 'We have the perfect climate in Alex,' Tante Georgette said as she continued to fan herself frantically.

Mother agreed. She wasn't going to admit that year-round humidity in Alex made her hair frizzy and clogged up the salt cellars. 'One doesn't want to be vulgar, *chérie*, but Cairo is a cesspit.'

Tante Joséphine glanced at Victor and me on the cane chair and couldn't help exclaiming, '*Les petits choux*.'

I couldn't for the life of me see how my cousin and I looked like little cabbages, but I tried not to scowl. Nobody approved of girls scowling. Victor dug me in the ribs with his elbow, and I returned the favour. If all boys were like Victor, I would have nothing to do with them.

'I will become a priest,' I told my reflection in the bedroom mirror that evening as I arranged a strip of white cardboard around my neck. The cardboard, cut from a box of *petits fours* from Fluckiger, sawed into my neck. Perhaps that was why priests stood as straight as a stair rod.

Simone came in after her bath and burst my bubble. 'You can't become a priest, silly. You're a girl.'

'What?' I hadn't thought of this before, though admittedly I had yet to see a girl priest.

'Only men are priests.' She refused to say more.

Perhaps I would ask Mariam in the morning. Either that, or I would sit and think. I did a lot of thinking while I watched Mariam.

Nobody in Egypt had a washing machine in 1952. They had someone like Mariam. Here she was, as on every Thursday, dealing with our mountains of sheets, towels, and clothes. Mariam boiled water in huge metal tubs on the roof of our house and scrubbed the laundry by hand with *savon de Marseille* until it had that special smell that you couldn't mistake for anything else.

While Simone was at school, I loved being there with Mariam and the tubs of foaming water, which she stirred with a wooden stick. Sometimes she added a wonder powder. Instead of turning the clothes blue, it made them dazzling white.

Mariam's shapeless robe got wet down the front while she laundered, and her hair escaped from her scarf and formed curls around her face. Her arms had amazing strength, being washing machine and mangle all in one, but her bowed legs caused her endless pain, as she kept telling anyone who'd listen. I couldn't help staring at her feet. They were flat and leathery like the feet of the elephants at Nouzha Zoo. Unlike the elephants, she wore wooden clogs that clattered on the tiles.

Before long, the floor was awash with water and stray suds, and line upon line of washing flapped in the sea breeze that came up over the hill. Apart from a couple of rooms used for laundry, the roof was one flat terrace, and it was too hot for anything else. I tried to grow a plant there once. I brought it in a pot that dripped all the way up the stairs and placed it in a corner of the roof terrace. After that, I forgot to water it. Simone had predicted it would die. Honestly, she was so smart that she barely needed school.

Mariam whipped things off the line as soon as they were dry and heaved them to the ironing table by the fire. I watched her seize flat irons straight from the flames, holding each one with a thick pad of cloth to protect her hand. Then the smell of hot metal and seared cotton mingled with the sudsy scent.

Although I was too short to see over the side of the roof terrace, I heard the *roba bikya* man clatter by with his donkey and cart. He used a special voice to holler, '*Roba bikyaah!*' People would come out of their homes to give him old things they no longer wanted. I suppose he then found people who did want them.

If I stood on tiptoe in one corner of the terrace, I glimpsed the sea, and, if I craned my neck as well, I could see a flag. It was green with a white crescent moon and three stars held inside the crescent, like a hand cradling three bonbons. I could only have liked it more had the flag been pink with real bonbons.

Mariam wasn't in the mood for talking, so I made myself a tent by hanging a wet sheet across two washing lines and sat under it to think. The Phoenicians kept cool with tents like this. They lived thousands of years ago and were very clever, according to Father, which was no surprise since they were our ancestors.

We were Egyptian now, though, even if our origins were in Syria or Lebanon. I got Syria and Lebanon mixed up, as did everyone else. People still called us *shawam*, meaning from Syria, though the whole family had been right here in Alexandria for nearly a century. I was almost six years old before my parents explained it to me, and even then I suspected there was more that they were holding back. For one thing, if our family was Egyptian, then why did so many people call us *khawaga*? A *khawaga* is a foreigner. Sometimes respected, sometimes not, but never truly one of them.

Who are we?

The sheet on the line dried too fast to keep me cool for long. Phoenicians actually used woollen blankets, which stay damp longer than sheets. Father said it was to do with latent heat of evaporation. He was punching holes in a belt at the time. As he had just got this new gadget, he went about making holes in every leather thing that happened to be lying around.

There were no blankets hanging on our roof, just sheets, tablecloths, shirts, dresses, socks, hankies, a whole army of vests, and a few pairs of pants that belonged to Father.

Mariam had started on the last tub when I asked, 'When are you going to wash the blankets?'

'*Abadan!*' she replied. 'I never wash blankets. They are too heavy.'

I reflected. 'My blanket is very dirty.'

Mariam gave me a look without pausing from her scrubbing. 'It is as clean as the moon and as sweet as jasmine.'

'No, it isn't. I spilled *shorbat el toot* on it.' Mulberry juice was my favourite drink, but it had an alarming tendency to leap out of its glass. The dark red stain was still there, hidden for the time being under my teddy bear.

'You must be more careful, my darling. Blankets are too heavy even for Mariam to wash.'

'But what about the stain?'

'Then it will stay there. *Howa kida.*'

'*Howa kida,*' I repeated. It means *that's how it is.*

Mariam smiled. 'My soul, my heart. You and your sister are my favourite children.' She wiped her eyes with the hem of her robe and resumed scrubbing.

NOW

I grip the cool metal bedframe. Something bugs me. How could we have been Mariam's favourite children? She had a son. Mariam couldn't possibly prefer girls, especially not someone else's, to her own son. A boy was worth at least ten girls. Every Arab knew that. That explained the lack of girl priests, and a lot else besides.

Fi haga ghalat. There is something wrong. But what? It's exhausting trying to piece everything together when I don't even know which day I had the brain biopsy. Now I have to get the postcards before my mind gets even fuzzier. I'll ask Sheila to bring them the next time she comes. I check the clock on the ward. Honestly, time is so disjointed that I've no idea how long a minute is anymore. As I watch the second hand jerk forward, I hope its rhythmic movement will steady my breathing and help put things right. Another thing. My seizure needs explaining. I don't remember a seizure, but the doctors say I had one and that family history is paramount or something.

A woman down the end of the ward has a whole cluster of visitors who arrived with red and white cartons. The aroma of fried chicken fills the bay as they open the box and share it amongst themselves. The orange-eating woman with the *Daily Express* now has a husband and a bag full of grapes.

I lean back on the pillows, trying to shut out the smell of greasy chicken. My head, already wounded from the biopsy, aches from all the thinking. I pat the bandage. Hope there's still something inside that works.

When did all that fog get into my brain? Last winter, I think. I hadn't left the house for two weeks, and there I was outside the chemist, having forgotten why. Where was my list? I had tried my pockets then rummaged in my handbag, stepping aside as two people strolled by, fixated on their phones and using too much pavement. Men in hard hats loitered around a crater in the road. A child in a buggy spat the dummy from its mouth and wailed. My list was nowhere to be found. Sweating by then, I'd gazed up for inspiration. Just a new billboard with a semi-clad woman in some advert. No help at all. But a touch of confusion was normal with age, I'd told myself. No need for alarm. After everything I'd been through, it was hardly a surprise to find myself forgetting more than I ever learnt. Didn't everything, breasts included, go south after a while? It happened to everyone, even the woman on the billboard.

A patient shuffles past, steering her drip trolley on an erratic course while she holds the hospital gown together with her other hand. 'You should try a little walk yourself,' she tells me.

My smile is non-committal. The last time I tried to get out of bed, giddiness attacked me and made the floor swim.

Sheila still hasn't come to visit. Now the husband of the

orange-eating patient is flicking through the newspaper. I read from here that two bodies have been found near a canal in Manchester, their identities unknown.

Panic rises through my body and spreads out into my chest. According to the headline, both bodies are men, but that's not the point. There's still the possibility that a future dead body – or a past one – could be Simone. I've looked for Simone over the years, of course. The detective I used didn't rate his chances but took my money anyway. I've still got his bill somewhere. It's all his efforts produced. And now to think she might be dead.

I must calm down. With the ward full of visitors, nobody's looking in my direction. I contort my body to extract my bag. By each bed, there's a thing called a locker, though it doesn't lock. It's a wheeled cabinet with multiple openings, and whatever I need from inside it is always furthest away. I grab the bedframe with one hand and feel for my handbag with the other.

Under the folding umbrella in my bag lie a bottle of ginkgo biloba tablets and another of St John's wort. I can't recall when I last took them, but the woman in the health shop said they weren't to be stopped suddenly. Better have two pills of each. Make that three.

Before I shove the bag back, I retrieve my Nokia. Damn thing won't power on, no matter how hard I push the button. Needs its plugger, I expect.

'Nurse, nurse.' I'm aware of sounding pathetic.

'What, my lovely?' It is a cheery woman with a collection of spare chins that telescope when she speaks.

I can't find the words, so I display the charger.

She plugs it into the wall. 'There you are.'

'Thank you.'

The nurse has already gone.

The woman in the gown shuffles by in the other direction as she and her drip stand creep back to her bed. Laughter drifts in from the nurses' station in the corridor. A pager goes off. Phones ring. It's hot and my eyelids are heavy, but I force myself to stay awake. I don't want to find I'm somewhere even worse than here.

At last! The mobile has power. I dial my friend right away before the signal goes.

Sheila takes a while to answer. Probably tottered in from her garden. 'How are you faring today, Nadia?'

'Okay. Look, can you please bring something in for me? There's a big box full of postcards in my bedroom.'

'*No problemo,* sweetie.' There's a pause. 'You did ask me already.'

'I did? Well, I'm just checking.'

'Can it wait till tomorrow?'

'I suppose, but don't lose it, whatever you do.'

Here's someone to see me. I forget her name, but she's my GP. GP is short for General Practitioner, though this slim, British-Asian woman with straight hair down to her waist is as far removed as it is possible to get from Doctor Tadros, our family doctor in Alex.

'Hello, Mrs Wissa, I came in to see how you're getting on.'

Today she's practising how to smile, but I still don't trust her. She once wanted to send me to the Memory Clinic. As if anyone there would know how to sort out my purée of brain into which things drop, never to be found again. She even gave me a leaflet on dementia.

'How are you?' she asks.

'I'm all right.' I must be careful what I say.

Her brow puckers as it did when I couldn't answer questions in her consulting room.

'I don't need the Memory Clinic,' I had told her.

'You had trouble with the questions I asked.' She had observed me quizzically, then become insistent about a clinic referral. There was some protocol, apparently.

British doctors may sound reasonable, but they make an illness out of every little thing and, before you know it, you are in hospital having tests, swallowing dangerous drugs, and catching MRSA. There's no way I want that to happen, not before I find Simone. So I tried to keep calm and said, 'You have very kind eyes.' That was a blatant lie. The doctor had little marbles that kept darting to her computer screen. *Maalish!* Mother often said the same thing to people she couldn't stand.

In the end, I didn't go to the clinic. I had that seizure, they say, and wound up here.

Now my GP's saying, 'Your memory isn't quite what it was, is it?'

The GP is rude, and she's wrong to boot. My memory is exactly what it was. I remember things perfectly from the olden days. I can't even stop remembering them.

3

ALEXANDRIA, DECEMBER 1952

Instead of knees, Hamza had stumps wrapped in grey rags. He lived on our corner, but, thanks to a wheeled tray propelled with his knuckles, he sometimes begged downtown, too. Although I hadn't seen the accident, I knew Hamza's legs had got cruzzed. That was the word I used. Some said an ice truck had hit him, others were sure it was a tram, while my cousin Victor claimed it was a red car driven by King Farouk himself. I didn't believe him.

'Of course it's true,' Victor insisted. 'Bet you didn't even know that only the King is allowed to have red cars.'

I nodded even though it was news to me.

The long and the short of it was that, until I was seven, I wasn't allowed to cross the street on my own. 'Remember Hamza,' Rashida muttered.

I nodded sagely and allowed my hand to be gripped.

I had been preparing for my seventh birthday for years. On the twenty-fifth of January 1953, I would have reached *l'âge de raison*. At that point, I might even catch up with Simone who had reached the age of reason two whole years ahead of me and now crossed the street as if it was the easiest thing in the world. Maybe I'd become less clumsy when drinking *shorbat el toot*, too. Not that Mother ever called me clumsy. Her silence was enough.

Meanwhile, Rashida taught Simone and me how to make *kahk*. She used a dough made with stuff called *samna*. It was a kind of butter that she had done something to. *Kahk* went back to the time of the Pharaohs, Mother said. That's why everyone in Egypt has *kahk*. Muslims have *kahk* at the end of Ramadan every year, but Christians get to eat them for both Easter and Christmas. If only for that, it seemed worth being Christian, though praying like a Muslim intrigued me. I had studied our *suffragi* Abdou, as well as Hassan the gardener, and often did exactly the same as them on our bathmat when nobody was about.

Simone and I sat with Rashida and helped mould the date filling for *kahk*. Simone was way ahead of me, deftly rolling her date paste like plasticine into a long cylinder. 'See? Like a *zizi*,' she whispered. 'Bigger than Victor's.'

'How do you know?' I couldn't understand how Simone knew what Victor's *zizi* looked like, and luckily Rashida had understood nothing.

We then covered the filling with dough and crimped it with a special metal tool. It was tricky to pierce pretty little holes without making them so deep that the filling poked out, but I copied Simone until I got it right.

Rashida wore a cotton dress with buttons down the front, its belt knotted immediately below her massive bosom. Her headscarf was fringed with beads that danced about as she worked the dough. The scarf bore more than a passing resemblance to the covers that kept flies out of jugs and bowls. A cross and a medallion of the Virgin Mary hung from her neck, and she had half a dozen slim gold bangles on her wrist, the sum total of her wealth. She never took the bangles off, even when making *kahk*, so a jingling of bangles accompanied Rashida wherever she went. She could make big noises, too, especially when the kitchen boy just sat there looking idiotic.

Rashida never yelled at Simone or me. She gave us all the attention we wanted except for one hour in the evening when we had to shush for her to listen to her favourite *timsileyya* on the radio. The soap opera began with a wailing theme tune and continued with people shouting and sobbing in equal measure. You only had to listen a couple of times to figure out that the men yelled and the women cried.

Sometimes Rashida sat with a coffee in the upstairs kitchenette and looked at magazines that Mother gave her, moistening the tip of a finger to turn the pages from right to left. She pored over the pictures for hours, which was just as well, as she could neither read nor write.

I wanted Rashida to do one thing above all else, so I'd get bored waiting while she spent time on other things instead. It was even worse on days when she sent a letter to her family in South Lebanon. This was a serious business that happened once a month and took at least an hour and a half, plus a jug of homemade lemonade. Rashida placed two cane chairs and a table by the mimosa tree. Then Hassan the gardener sat cross-legged on one of the chairs in his baggy trousers. He rearranged his white sunhat with its frayed brim while Rashida installed herself opposite him. To help her concentrate, she pulled her headscarf low on her brow, which made the beads dangle from her eyebrows. The last letter from her brother had to be re-read and digested before Rashida dictated her reply.

'Tell my brother and his family that I am well, Allah be praised.'

Hassan smoothed out the sheets of airmail and licked his stubby blue pencil before applying it with some force to the paper.

The Good Lord didn't approve of gossiping, so Rashida never spread rumours or told tales. That didn't stop her from repeating the same rude story to me almost every bedtime. *Once upon a time, there was a teeny, tiny little girl whose every possession was tiny, and one day there came a thief to her little tiny house to steal her tiny little treasures.*

I lived for this story. All Rashida had to do was to begin with *Kan fi bint el nooneyya, 'andaha kul haga noonoo,* and from then on I was spellbound, even though I knew precisely how the tiny little girl would outwit the criminal by putting a cockerel in the rafters, a donkey behind the door, sharp nails in the wall, and a pail full of *caca* with a few gold coins scattered on top. Night after night, Rashida told me how the thief got kicked by the donkey, smeared *khara* all over his hands when he reached for the coins, then cut himself to ribbons by wiping them on the wall. I laughed manically every time she neared the end when the thief looked up to heaven and begged God for mercy. At that point, the cockerel peed in his mouth.

Rashida told other stories, too, like the one about a princess who was raised as a boy in order to please her father who naturally desired a son and heir. The snag was that this prince didn't have a *zizi,* as the king discovered one day in the bathroom.

I liked stories with a *zizi* in them, but not this one. 'It's unfair to girls,' I wailed.

'Why is it unfair, my heart, my soul?'

'Because she has to pretend to be a boy.'

'*Howa kida*.' Rashida did not grasp my point at all.

'I want *el bint el nooneyya* again.'

But it was time for bed, and no amount of begging would change that. After a final spray of Flit around the kitchenette, lest any flies or mosquitoes should dare reappear, Rashida arranged her hair into curlers topped with a hairnet tied at the front. The knot looked like the horn on a baby rhino, I always thought as she put me to bed. My bedroom had an icon of the Virgin Mary with Baby Jesus, while Rashida's bedroom was hung with pictures of St Anthony as well. You couldn't pray to anyone better than St Anthony if you had lost something.

Once I was in bed, Mother came to kiss me, brushing against me with her silk scarf and wrapping me in a haze of perfume. I never knew its name, but it was glamour, intelligence, and comfort all blended into in one scent.

The Christmas before I turned seven was celebrated as usual in our wood-panelled basement where a huge tree was installed in front of the mirror. Everything twinkled and sparkled with glass ornaments and real candles. Our relatives visited, and, to my great excitement, some of them brought parcels to put under our tree.

I watched Tante Zahra struggle out of her car and pat her green turban before walking towards the house as regally as age and *aérophagie* allowed. Then, before my eyes, she was gone, leaving just a splodge of bright green on the ground. Tante Zahra had melted. What other explanation could there be?

I must have screamed, or maybe my aunt did. At any rate, there was soon a crowd of us out on the path. I saw that a sizeable pit had opened up in the ground, and Tante Zahra was folded up inside it, visibly shocked but still burping.

'*Comment*? How? It's not possible!' Everyone agreed that nothing of the sort had ever happened before, *parole de dieu*.

I stared. The hole was deeper than any I'd ever dug at the beach. Tante Zahra waved her hands to be rescued, but it wasn't that simple. First the men had to agree on the depth of cavity and the solidity of its walls, while Mother enquired after Tante Zahra's legs, arms, head, and any other body parts that might conceivably have been injured. My aunt's claims to be unhurt astonished Mother, who proceeded to mention several people who'd died of a broken hip after far lesser falls. Why, someone she knew had fractured her femur merely while removing her knickers. '*Ses culottes, tu t'imagines!*'

Rashida crossed herself repeatedly and kissed the cross on her chain to encourage the Good Lord to get Tante Zahra out. In the end, Father and Abdou got a ladder, and Zahra emerged unharmed. I resolved to be careful, in case similar holes opened up without warning and the Good Lord found himself too busy to rescue me.

Santa Claus visited, too, and I sat on his lap facing outwards so my parents could take photos. He whispered in my ear. Of course I had been good all year. I nodded without looking directly at him. His eyes were funny, though I couldn't have said in what way. I might not have reached the age of reason yet, but, as I told Simone, I knew who I liked and who I didn't, and Santa Claus and my cousin Victor were both in the second category.

'*Whom* you like,' Simone corrected. 'I learned that at school.'

'*Whom* I like and *whom* I don't,' I repeated, even though it sounded wrong.

Simone said she was too old for Santa Claus. 'Besides, I don't like him either,' she said.

'Who is he, Simone? Who?'

I chased after her, but she raced off, leaving me with an uneasy feeling and unanswered questions.

4

NOW

When did Sheila say she would bring my postcards? I need to see them now instead of just sitting here, hot, thirsty, and nursing an aching head. There must be clues in those cards from Simone. When they were first delivered, I studied each one, but there's always something you miss the first time. I learned that at school.

My headache is from the biopsy, I expect. Not that they tell you anything here. I don't even know what pills the nurse is handing me now in a tiny paper cup. I do know they upset my stomach, and I'm making noises like Tante Zahra. Plus I'm dizzy, as if I've had a long swim in the sea.

Today's nurse is jolly with a beauty spot on her plump jaw, and she looks at me as if she's actually interested. That makes it hard to fling the tablets out or put them in my pocket. Could I hide them in a tissue? Everyone knows old women like to clutch a crumpled hankie or tissue in their fists. My nurse, however, waits until I down both tablets.

'I remember you,' I tell her when I've put down my water.

'That's right, love. I was on duty yesterday. Did your mobile charge up all right?'

'It did. Thank you.' I'd forgotten it was this nurse. Which bits of me have they taken? Which other memories have gone? They haven't actually gone, though, have they? More arrive all the time, like trains at Sidi Gaber. Like the trains, they quickly leave again, losing themselves in the distance.

Because the nurse is nice, I ask her what's happening to me.

'Try not to worry,' she says. 'Doctor will be here soon.'

As if that'll help. I told them all about the chemist and my missing list, and they couldn't have cared less.

'Anything else you need?' the nurse says.

'Nothing, thanks.' I want my sister, but I don't tell her that. Even St Anthony couldn't find Simone, and he can find anything, even the bright pink handbag that Rashida once left on a tram on her day off. If my favourite saint couldn't bring my sister back, I'm sure the nurse can't help.

ALEXANDRIA, MAY 1956

My aunts greeted me from their landing. '*Trésor, trésor,*' they called, their voices cascading down the stairwell. To them, Simone and I were always treasures, as the whole neighbourhood must have realised.

The staircase had an iron handrail that I barely touched as I raced up to their fourth-floor apartment. Tante Georgette was wiry, while Joséphine was as fat and comforting as a collection of pillows. I couldn't imagine them living apart, but they must have done, once, when Tante Georgette was married.

My aunts had sombre oil paintings of elderly relatives that I had never met and never would because they were dead, as dead as Tante Georgette's husband with the walrus moustache. The corridor went all round the apartment, so I would run right through the apartment again and again, making myself dizzy in the process. They had a tall Sudanese *suffragi* whose teeth were gold at the back and not there at all at the front. Best of all, my aunts had a limitless supply of *pâtes de fruits,* cheese straws, and crystallised dates, none of them previously sampled by Victor. No matter what time of day it was, Simone and I were allowed to eat as much as we wanted. This was in sharp contrast to Mother's views on the heinous crime of snacking.

'We don't need to tell her,' Tante Georgette said. 'It will be our secret, *n'est ce pas*?'

Today I was visiting on my own, but it was always the same welcome with an onslaught of cheek-pinching and bright-pink kisses. I had the life squeezed out of my lungs while they exclaimed, *trésor, amour,* and *chérie,* and were astonished at how tall I had become, though I couldn't have grown that much in the last week. Tante Joséphine's jowls wobbled with excitement while Tante Georgette hugged me in a haze of rosy perfume and promised *loukoums*. Their other name is Turkish delight, and they were my absolute favourites.

Georgette pointed to the tea trolley in the corner, covered in doilies and laden with crystal bowls and pretty boxes. While I tucked in, my aunts said, '*Sahtayn*,' which means *two healths* in countries like Lebanon where stuffing yourself until you burst is deemed to be the healthiest thing you can do. Sometimes they offered me a giant *palmier* biscuit or *petits fours* from Baudrot. '*C'est un petit rien. Il glissera comme une lettre à la poste.*'

Alas, it was not always a little nothing, nor did it always slip down like a letter at the post office. Sometimes a pastry got royally stuck despite copious glasses of lemonade, and I would be sick.

'You'll be married before you know it.' Tante Georgette had been saying this since I was four. 'Don't forget. When you and Simone have children, Joséphine and I will help look after them.'

'If we're not working,' Joséphine warned.

I stared, unable to imagine my aunts doing any kind of work.

'*Mais oui, chérie,*' Tante Georgette said. 'One day my sister and I will have to find jobs.'

'One day very soon,' Tante Joséphine warned grimly. '*El dounya et-ghayar.*'

The world was changing? How? Here it was an eternal sunny afternoon, light spilling in through the massive windows as I enjoyed an abundance of *pâtes de fruits*.

Once I started school, my aunts wanted to know every single detail of my favourite subjects and the best teachers. They even asked about the English grammar I was learning. I took another *pâte de fruits* and made myself comfortable on the arm of the sofa, which was strictly forbidden at home. 'Do you know that *each other* means there are two people? They look at *each other* at breakfast means there are two people looking. But if you say they looked at *one another*, it means there must be at least three.'

Tante Georgette clapped her hands. 'Imagine that!' She then told me all about our ancestors who had lived in

Damascus during Ottoman rule. Back in the 1850s, mobs rampaged through districts like Bab Toma, forcing Christians to convert at knife point. When my aunts' grandfather refused, he was killed with a sword that carved a cross on to his chest and then went straight through his heart and out the other side. It was horrible and blood-curdling, and I yearned to hear more.

'*Mais tais-toi*,' Joséphine hissed. She added that her sister had far too much imagination.

Tante Georgette reluctantly changed the subject. 'Do you know that your great-grandmother came over from Syria at the age of thirteen — or was it twelve? — to marry great-grandfather?'

Mother never told us stories as fascinating as these.

'Of course, she had never met great-grandfather before. Because she was so young and so scared, poor thing, she threw up in the middle of the wedding right on to the priest's shoes. *Maalish!*'

The aunts wore scarves just as Mother did, but then Georgette would get warm, shed hers, and start fanning herself again.

'Don't get caught in a draught, *chérie*,' Tante Joséphine warned. 'You're so thin. You'll catch your death.' Joséphine always lived in fear of something, most often starvation, though she could have survived for years on her spare fat.

'I've never caught my death yet,' Tante Georgette replied.

'*Yiy!* The cook hasn't gone to the market yet.' Joséphine's chins trembled with anxiety. 'What will we eat tonight?'

'Don't worry about the market, *chérie*,' Georgette said. 'It's still early.'

'But we have no milk to make *labneh*.'

'The cook will get it later.'

'And we have run out of limes.'

Mother was due to collect me any minute. I gazed at a lone cheese straw on its glass plate.

'Take it, *chérie*,' Tante Georgette said, as she fanned herself again. 'We'll have more tomorrow.'

Joséphine shot her a glance. 'Tomorrow we may have nothing.'

'*Yom 'assal, yom bassal*.' One day honey, one day onions. You had to go with the ups and downs, Georgette meant.

Her sister disagreed. 'We have already run out of limes, you know.'

I left it. A single cheese straw would not sustain anyone for long, but it's the thought that counts.

'The day we have nothing, we'll go and live in Europe,' Georgette said.

'If we can get a visa.' Joséphine's lips set into a hard line.

NOW

I hope Sheila brings my box in soon. Age has changed my childhood pen pal, though she still likes rude jokes. As I see it, Sheila's hobbies are sex, money, and gardening. Her shoulders are sun-damaged from hours spent on her hands and knees in front of some shrub, a wicker basket at her side. Sheila falters when she gets up, blaming poor circulation. She also has a gin bottle in that basket.

More cosmopolitan than she once was, Sheila likes to pepper her conversation with foreign words. Apparently, the

Chelsea Flower Show is *molto* exciting, though to me it hardly sounds like a proper garden where Rashida picked vine leaves and Hassan swept with a palm under the sun of a thousand iron hammers.

I readjust my pillow to ease my throbbing head and try to stay awake as I wait for Sheila. There must be clues in Simone's postcards. What else did I miss, back then? I can't imagine how *el bint el nooneyya* relates to my sister disappearing, either, but the story reassured me that good would triumph, and that even little girls could get their way.

There's someone at my bedside. It isn't Sheila. My temple still thuds, so I budge only minimally from the pillow to study this new doctor. Perhaps it's the one the nice nurse mentioned. With his prominent ears, he bears a passing resemblance to Victor.

Without introduction, he announces that the brain biopsy is inconclusive. How can that be? I blink. In his starched white coat, he looks older than the other doctors here. He spends all of three seconds delivering his report, followed by five minutes telling an anecdote to the two younger colleagues who tagged along. They're a man and a woman with their hands clasped in front of them, nodding their heads like marionettes.

The story the consultant relates concerns a lung biopsy from long ago during his surgical training, when they'd cracked apart some poor old chap's ribs and chopped out a chunk of diseased lung, only to hear a week later from the lab that it showed end-stage changes that were typical of absolutely nothing. They'd only gone and sampled the wrong bit of lung; hence, they didn't have a diagnosis until the old boy's post mortem.

His retinue laughs while my thoughts race along with my heart. Does this mean I'm heading for a post mortem like the old man? I stretch my arm, but the consultant's sleeve is further than I think.

'Doctor,' I say, my tongue drier than ever. 'Do I need another biopsy?'

The doctors stare. I have dared speak! The consultant opens his mouth as if about to reply, but he only gives a fake smile before the little troupe moves on.

So the biopsy hasn't diagnosed anything. I will end up dead like the lung man, forgotten until entertainment is called for.

One of the nurses must know, but there is no nurse here to ask. A mountain of a person in the next bed is asleep, and the only sign of life is the woman opposite with her *Daily Express*. She has done the crossword and applied bright coral lipstick in a jaunty shape that has little in common with the contour of her lips. From a large bag in front of her, she is gorging on grapes, one swiftly followed by another.

'Grapes are good for the 'eart,' she says. 'You should get your family to bring some in for you.' She pops another grape into her mouth. 'I'm Pamela. What's your name?'

'Nadia.'

Pamela folds her newspaper. I can't see from here if the dead bodies from that Manchester canal have been identified. The front page is all about Princess Diana, who died at least fifteen years ago, at a guess. 'I read in here about grapes. They're giving me a CD version tomorrow,' Pamela continues. Her lipstick is smudged now.

'What's that?'

'Electric procedure. For me 'eart.'

'You've dropped some grapes on the floor,' I point out.

'It don't matter. I got loads more.'

I watch the errant fruit get squashed by feet coming and going. *Cruzzed*. That's the word.

'Nurse,' I call, when I see a blue tunic loom. I think it's the one who is shagging her ex-boyfriend.

'What is it, dear?'

My voice is as steady as I can make it, what with my heart careering about my chest. 'Am I going to have another biopsy?'

The nurse tilts her head. 'What makes you think that?'

'Because a doctor told me that the first one didn't give a result. Now I'm wondering if they need to do another one.'

The nurse pulls out a piece of paper from her pocket and studies it at length before replying. 'Don't you go worrying about that. Pretend it never happened, eh?' Then she beams and flits off somewhere.

Pretend it never happened? I know very well what happened and what didn't.

By visiting time, nobody has explained anything more, nor have they wiped the floor, which is now dark with dirt and littered with yet more grapes that are good for the heart.

I have a visitor! Sheila is wearing a grey and white striped blouse with mighty sleeves and a billowing neck ruffle. I have never seen such a garment on a seventy-year-old. I've only ever seen one in the school drama cupboard.

'*Ciao*, sweetie. Are they treating you well?'

Instead of telling her about my biopsy result and the old man's post mortem, I reply, 'Mustn't grumble.' English people always say that.

'Here's your precious box, old thing.'

I feel the weight of the box, the coolness of the metal, and the sharp edges of the lid. It is precisely as I remember. The box once contained biscuits and is mostly navy, except where it has worn off over the years. Inside, parcels of postcards lie tied up with ribbon and rick-rack, just as I had left them. My aunts had looked after my box carefully.

'Where shall I put it?' Sheila says.

I tap the top of the thing next to me.

'On the locker?' Sheila says.

Locker. That's it. 'Please.'

Sheila has done her nails. They match her newly purple hair which is the colour of a bruise. Must have got herself a new man. She launches into a monologue about wisteria and whitefly, but I have something more pressing to talk about. 'Suppose Simone is dead already?'

'What makes you think that?'

'They found two people dead in Manchester.'

'Oh, sweetie. I know, but those two in the canal were men. How can they be Simone?'

I shake my head. It's easier than trying to explain what I feel about these poor people. Perhaps they and their families lost touch, like Simone and me.

'Try not to worry.'

People should realise there's no point saying that.

When Sheila goes, I'm weary again and my head pulsates till I'm sure it will burst. I can't allow myself to doze for long, but I crave a little rest before delving into the magical tin box.

ALEXANDRIA, JULY 1952

The swing was in a shady spot by the dovecote. I sat on it and watched Rashida pick vine leaves, yanking each one off with more force than seemed necessary. Even though it would be another six months until I reached *l'âge de raison,* I knew things weren't right. People talked in hushed whispers instead of their usual voices, and they refused to explain a thing to me.

'What's going on, Rashida?'

She continued harvesting leaves in thick silence, so I went back upstairs to the little sitting room where my parents often sat. Father was in a white vest, as always, but he had a preoccupied air. Instead of taking appliances apart or punching holes in leather belts, he was listening to the news on the radio, one ear touching the speaker.

I asked Mother what was wrong. She replied with agitated hand movements that there was a frog in a pan of water, coming to the boil. I would have asked what she meant, but the phone in the hall rang, and she rushed to answer it.

After the call, Mother settled again in her favourite chair and resumed jabbing her canvas with a vicious needle. She was doing even more *petit point* than usual. I couldn't see any need for it, not when every table already had an embroidered cloth and every chest of drawers its runner. Where there wasn't *petit point*, there was tapestry in the form of chair backs, bell pulls, an armchair, and even a huge folding screen that did nothing except skulk in the corner of the dining room, looking sinister despite the fat pink roses stitched into it.

I approached and waited. Mother finally looked up and explained the difference between *petit point* and tapestry. I listened politely as I'd been brought up to do, but all I cared to know was why the phone rang so much.

Our telephone was a big black Bakelite thing on a table with, naturally, a *petit point* cloth. On the shelf below it sat a telephone directory with a *petit point* cover. When the phone rang, there were two *drings*, a pause, then two more *drings* which echoed throughout the house to command attention wherever we were. The telephone had to be answered solemnly and self-importantly, and the receiver had to be clasped with two hands in case there was a risk of it wriggling free. All conversations involved shouting, as if the other person was in Zagazig and telephones had yet to be invented. Despite all the shouting, though, I comprehended nothing. I did know, though, that a lot of the calls were from Cairo these days. The phone made a different *dring* if the call wasn't local.

'Trunk,' one of my parents would exclaim, and there'd be a race down the parquet corridor to pick up the receiver with even more haste than usual.

We had some relatives in Cairo. Why they had decided to become Cairenes was a mystery to me. It was even more of a mystery why they had taken to phoning so often.

I hung around doorways. I lurked outside rooms. I stayed awake after being put to bed. If the door of my bedroom was ajar, it let in a rectangle of light from the kitchenette where Rashida sat with magazines that she could not read. The jingling of bangles and the turning of pages usually soothed me to sleep, but Mother and Rashida had recently taken to whispering in the kitchenette. As soon as I got out of bed and tiptoed to the door, they would stop. Mother put on an innocent face, and Rashida assured me she was just saying her rosary.

Fi haga ghalat, I told Simone. She hadn't a clue either, but her hug made me feel better.

When the revolution came in late July, it took three days to unfold. It began in Cairo with soldiers in the streets, and, Mother told me, the announcement that the army had taken control of the country.

Things were changing. Rashida prayed even more fervently, kissing her cross and the medallion of St Anthony on the gold chain around her neck, yet refusing to say what was lost.

I was exactly six years, six months, and two days old when, on the twenty-seventh of July, Father told me that King Farouk had left Egypt the night before, fleeing on his yacht called the *Mahroussa*. It was my solemn duty to inform the dolls in my pram that the King had gone and that soldiers were now in charge.

5

ALEXANDRIA, JANUARY 1953

Despite reaching *l'âge de raison* that very day, I cried when I tumbled on to the gravel. I could reach my arm with my tongue, so I licked the coppery blood that oozed from the gash and told myself it would be all right, which is exactly what Simone would have told me. Then Mother dragged me to the bathroom to clean it. The soap and water stung, even though I tried to be brave. Rashida pacified me by saying my arm would heal beautifully, like jasmine, and that the new skin would be a gift from God. Actually, it went septic first, but it turned out all right in the end.

The rest of my birthday improved. I got a biro that wrote in four different colours and a chocolate cake from Baudrot, my favourite shop in the whole world because pretty much everything there was made of chocolate. That's how the age of reason began, but I still had much to learn.

Rashida taught me not to mind if I accidentally bit my

cheek while eating. She would say, '*Maalish*, my heart. It means you're going to get a present.' She also told me I should never wipe my bottom with a piece of bread, or God would turn me into a monkey. Until then, the possibility of putting bread to this use hadn't once entered my head. Now that she had mentioned it, I struggled to think of anything else.

For all the other things we needed to learn, Simone and I attended the English Girls' College. I learned to cover exercise books, though why they had to be protected with brown paper when they had perfectly good fronts and backs, I had no idea. Teachers said it was good preparation for being a grown-up. I couldn't see how.

I had a heavy wooden pencil case that smelled delicious but served little purpose, other than to hit people on the head. This I discovered one afternoon when Victor came to visit. Simone grabbed it from him, and I never let him near my things again.

The really grown-up thing was getting my first fountain pen, a serious writing instrument. After initial scratches that went right through the paper, I found to my delight that it wrote as nicely in Arabic as it did in English and French. However, within seconds of filling my new implement myself for the first time, I learned where it got its name. Simone lent me one of her school blouses. It was too big on me, but it gave me a lovely warm feeling. I had to hide my stained blouse until Thursday, when Mariam would be here. Underneath the wardrobe would do, as Simone agreed.

'And don't give yourself away by staring at it all the time,' she added.

I gave the wardrobe one last glance. 'Okay.'

Afterwards, we pushed dolls' prams round the garden together. I told myself not to step on any bit of path that looked as if it might open up. Soon, however, I forgot all about the dangers of dropping into a hole as Tante Zahra had. Walking about with Simone had to be the best bit of my day. We would have real babies at the same time, too, one day when we grew up. I didn't have to say it aloud because I could tell. We were best friends and always would be. I knew that as surely as I knew never to wipe my bottom with a piece of bread.

NOW

I untie the faded velvet ribbon from what looks the most recent bunch of postcards and fan a handful of them out on the bed table in front of me. They're from seemingly everywhere in Western Europe. Simone's messages were short and just signed *S x*. This card has the white cliffs of Dover.

Have fun at the beach, but be careful. S x

What did she mean? There were no cliffs at our beach. It must be one of those things. Metaphors or something. I used to know words.

A nurse comes over to straighten my bed. 'Not falling about today, are we, Mrs Wissa?'

'Of course not.'

'That's good.' The nurse adjusts the headrest.

'What makes you think I might fall?'

She kneads the pillow into shape. 'You took a nasty tumble out of bed the other day. Do you remember hurting your head?'

Silly nurses. They know nothing, though at least they don't hold out their palms constantly for *baksheesh* as they do in

Egypt. I touch my head again. They must have changed the bandage, because now I feel only a small dressing on my right temple.

'When did I fall out of bed?' Perhaps I can trick the nurse into admitting her lie if I focus on her eyes. They're pale blue like a goat's, though without a buttonhole slit across the middle.

'Two evenings ago.' The nurse looks straight back at me. The sign of an accomplished liar.

'I don't remember falling.'

She gives an indulgent smile. 'That's part of the problem, isn't it, Nadia?'

The nurse never asked if she could use my first name. Such liberties they take in hospitals. 'Did the fall delay my brain biopsy?'

The nurse shakes her head. 'No. You didn't have that biopsy you keep on about.'

'I didn't? But my head aches so much.'

'You misremembered, perhaps.'

I gaze into her goaty eyes and still can't decide if she's telling the truth. If I haven't had a brain biopsy, are there other things I've imagined, too? I lean back. The pillows are better now that the nurse pummelled them, but they still exude a synthetic aroma like everything else about this hospital bed.

The next appearance at my bedside is a doctor who says *Hello* and gives a name that I promptly forget. I notice a different nurse hovering by her side. The doctor folds her hands in front of her. 'You were talking to Nurse Emily about a biopsy,' the doctor says.

I stare. The doctor has very short hair dyed pink on only one side. Her glasses frames are decorated with little flowers, like a Laura Ashley fabric. How can anyone take her seriously? 'That's right. My brain biopsy.'

The doctor scribbles something. 'You didn't have a biopsy.'

'Of course not,' I say to indulge her. 'Then why did I think I had one?'

'We don't know exactly what's happening here. It might help to talk to family. Is there someone I can reach on the phone, perhaps?'

Blood booms through my head. 'I have a sister, but ...'

'But what?'

'I don't know where she is. Or how to get hold of her. I haven't seen her for fifty years, though I hope to find her soon.' I glance at the box. Perhaps I should make clear that I don't actually think my sister is inside the box.

The doctor tilts her head indulgently. 'You have a sister,' she says, in a tone used for humouring children.

'Yes, but I don't know where she is.' I show the doctor the postcard of Dover with Simone's signature. 'That's from her. See?'

'She has a friend called Sheila,' the nurse chips in, whereupon the doctor loses interest and makes to leave before I can explain that S is for Simone, not Sheila.

Why couldn't Simone have signed her full name? I study the message again.

Have fun at the beach, but be careful.

I have always been careful.

ALEXANDRIA, MAY 1953

Two bent hairpins. A pink comb with teeth missing. A torn hair net. A lid from a Kolynos toothpaste tube. One safety pin.

A coin worth five *millièmes.* A Gillette Blue blade with a rusty edge.

I had found all these treasures at bathtime. After drying myself, I used to reach as far as I could under the big white bathroom cupboard. It was disgustingly dirty there, Simone said. She wasn't about to go scavenging.

It wasn't disgusting, if you were careful to avoid the balls of dust. All this was treasure to add to my box. Mother's new diary had come in that little box, and Simone retrieved it for me, knowing that I'd love its shiny gold lid.

Now I lay on the bathroom floor, using the plastic back brush to check further under the cupboard. While I was busy getting myself dirty again, Simone admired her profile in the mirror, a towel piled high on her head in the manner of Nefertiti.

'Is it even worse,' I asked her, 'when you get to nine years old?'

'What do you mean?'

'Do grown-ups expect better behaviour than when you're seven?'

She stopped worshipping her reflection. 'They do. But they don't always get it. Remember last Easter?'

I did. As usual, the Greek Orthodox clergy were invited. The whole tribe had invaded our sitting room, with their long black robes, white beards, and massive crosses. To top it off, they wore ridiculous headdresses that I wasn't supposed to stare at, even when Simone whispered that one of them looked like Rasputin, whoever that was.

Lunch followed in the formal dining room. It had a mirror-topped table that reflected the vaulted ceiling so it looked like a tomb. Worse, on the wall in front of me hung a painting of a pile of fruit with a dead rabbit lying beside it.

A photographer took pictures for the newspaper. Simone

and I had to put on a camera face for ages, even though I was ravenous and Simone's tummy rumbled. Little girls should be seen and not heard. Ever, really. They were meant to stay in their place. A preparation for life as a woman, I could see that. Thus we stood still where we were told in our smocked dresses and frilly socks. I looked away from the rabbit.

Everyone had to kiss the Patriarch's ring, including Mother, whose hand was normally kissed by other people. Simone got introduced to the Patriarch before me. The holy man's beard had twitched as he rested his hand on her head. But, when presented with his ring, Simone refused point blank to put her lips anywhere near his fingers and ran out of the room. I would have followed her, had I been as brave.

6

MONTAZAH BEACH, ALEXANDRIA, JUNE 1957

Ralph was in a coma. He could have even died in his deckchair without anyone noticing. I had to check on him, which was why Simone and I were trudging across the sand to the other end of the beach.

'Ow!' I stopped to rub my bare foot. The stabbing pain was still there, and Simone was ignoring me. 'There's a pine needle in my foot.'

'They're casuarina trees. Not pines.'

'I forgot,' I fibbed. I was eleven and a half, and it was the first time I'd heard the word casuarina, but I didn't want Simone to think I was stupid. There were rows upon rows of these trees growing at Montazah, spilling in front of the beach cabins as well as planted behind them. The trunks were reddish-brown and their green fronds looked soft but broke off into short needles that went straight through your skin.

The revolution of 1952 had immediate consequences for

us and for most of the families we knew. With King Farouk in exile, the grounds of his palace at Montazah at the eastern tip of the Corniche became pleasure gardens and a large beach. From then on, we abandoned the beach at Sidi Bishr and rented a cabin at Montazah. That included Mother, Father, Simone, and me, plus Abdou and giant blocks of ice. If it wasn't too hot, Tantes Georgette and Joséphine would join us, as would Tante Zahra in her turban and Tante Magda with a scarf securely tied over her hat to stop it blowing away. Often there would be my cousin Victor. Our families no longer seemed keen on match-making, but Victor was even more nauseating now that he was armed with a camera. Although he had grown plump, that didn't stop him climbing trees to get a better vantage point for his photos.

'Peering down women's fronts.' Simone sniffed.

I sniffed too, even though I was a long way off having a front.

Other children popped round to play, or just to boast. Androulla bragged about being good at ballet, which she wasn't, and Zeinab claimed she could hold her breath underwater for four minutes. However, she refused to give a demonstration.

Alicia, who was between my age and Simone's, was sometimes there, in a pink swimsuit and a silly bow on her head. Her parents' cabin was right at the other end of the beach. I preferred Simone's company.

Our cabin smelled musty, and the key always stuck in the lock, but its window had flowery curtains that enabled me to change without being seen, and the concrete ledge outside made an excellent bench once Abdou arranged blue cushions on it.

The best thing was the beach itself, wide and closed off at each end. Simone and I were old enough to wander down to the sea on our own, out from the shelter of the casuarina trees and on to the hot sands that burned our feet until we reached the water. The sea here often had a strong current, though my parents, who rarely went into the water, seemed unaware of it.

There was Zouzou, cracking her chewing gum as she promenaded, her high-heeled mules going *click-click* on the concrete in front of the cabins. Meanwhile, her husband Ralph lay inert in a deckchair under the trees despite Dalida belting her heart out from the radio beside him.

I studied him as inconspicuously as I could before reporting back to Simone. 'He's alive.'

'Obviously,' she replied. 'Dead people don't breathe.'

Ralph never opened his eyes, though, so he probably missed Zouzou sauntering about the beach in a new swimsuit and even bigger sunglasses than last year.

With Simone, I was bold enough to lurk. People smoked, drank Stella beer, and played *tawlah* in the shade of the trees, slamming each piece on to the backgammon board as loudly as possible to intimidate their opponent. The men did, anyway, sitting at tables in tiny swimming trunks that made me want to stare then made me want to look away again. The women talked, leafed through magazines, and pacified young children who wailed when they fell on a broken seashell or got things in their feet. Casuarina needles. I rolled the words around in my mouth.

The *suffragis* served beer, lemonade, and things like falafel, tahini dip, hard-boiled eggs, radishes, pickles, and *wara' einab*. I guessed they made the stuffed vine leaves at home and brought them to be eaten cold. Some families had proper meals with rice and meat, and afterwards their *suffragi* would wash the dishes under the outside tap.

Every time I passed by the cabin belonging to Monsieur and Madame Amin, Madame was giving the same monologue.

She and her husband were back from the US where their daughter now lived, and the flight was *izay el zift*. That means lousy, and it was Madame Amin's favourite phrase, especially when it came to anything that wasn't Alexandrian. The man in the next seat had stubbed out his cigarette on her little finger while she was sleeping, *look*! Even worse, the airline had lost her luggage. Madame Amin regularly reeled off the wonderful things that had been in her suitcase: umpteen new dresses, scores of beautiful new shoes, irreplaceable jewellery, and all the presents for her family in Chicago. The nicest presents in the world for her daughter, of course!

'Don't stare,' Simone said.

How could I help it? Madame Amin had a bust so ample that you could have rested a huge tray of *kobeyba* on it, and still have room to balance a tray of falafel.

With her hands, Madame Amin demonstrated the size of the case, the extent of her distress at being separated from it, the luxurious feel of her dresses, and the value of her missing jewels. 'On my mother's eyes, the finest gems ever!'

Her entourage variously went *maalish* or *ayoo*, and nobody could decide whether the Evil Eye or Air France was at fault for baggage going astray. With each retelling, Madame Amin added more items to her suitcase. Today she remembered a couple of brooches, which were family heirlooms. '*Tu t'imagines! Une fortune!*'

The conversation often broadened out to include other travel woes, from exit visas to currency restrictions, with rarely more than four words in any one language before switching to another. Secrets went back and forth.

'Don't tell anyone. Even I'm not supposed to know.'

'*Chérie*, you can tell me. I won't tell a soul, *parole de dieu*.'

By seven the next morning, you could guarantee that the whole of Alex would know.

I listened. There were always stories that grown-ups wanted you to believe, and others they didn't want you to know. There was a *comtesse* who wasn't actually a countess, surrounded by numerous men with very little hair but masses of money. The less hair, it seemed, the more money.

One of the men began, 'Listen. I will tell you a story I have never told before.'

'Bet you ten piasters he's told it a dozen times before,' Simone hissed in my ear.

Under another parasol sat an older man, resplendent with a shock of silver hair that he stroked with elegant hands. He wore a tiny pair of swimming briefs, a gold medallion nestling in white chest hair, and a black eye patch like a pirate. That was all.

'Don't stare,' Simone said.

'He lost his eye in a duel, you know.' I thought this far too exciting to keep to myself.

She gave me a withering look. 'Don't be silly. His operation went wrong.'

'How do you know?'

She wouldn't say.

'What operation?' I bounced up and down and pestered her until she told me it was cataracts. I had no idea what cataracts were, apart from something to do with the Nile, and she refused to enlighten me.

Uncle Selim didn't have a cabin at Montazah either. He hung around ours, watching through his sunglasses. Today he had brought a friend, and the two men sat side by side fiddling with their worry beads as they sipped lemonade. The mere sight of their cool glasses made me thirsty.

'I want some lemonade, too.' I grabbed a glass from the tray.

'That's *arak, ya humara.*'

Simone often called me a she-donkey. But how was I to know that the pale, cloudy liquid in the glasses was that alcoholic aniseed drink?

Even when Simone told me off, I loved being with her. Later that day, Simone told me about the *sawahel* who patrolled on camels at sunset. '*Sawahel* means they're from the coast, remember.'

'I know,' I said quickly before she called me a *humara* again. 'What do they do?'

'They stop smugglers coming in by boat.'

'What do people smuggle?'

'Drugs. Money. Lots of things.'

We didn't see the *sawahel* because we always went home before then. Simone told me that the *sawahel* were probably Sudanese. The theory was that, as they weren't Egyptian, they'd be less corruptible. '*Sawahel* is where the word *Swahili* comes from,' she added.

'What's *Swahili*?'

'A language.'

I wasn't sure whether to believe her. 'Say something in Swahili then.'

The next thing she said was not in Swahili. '*Il est louche.*'

I had no idea who was louche. '*Qui?*'

'Him.'

'Uncle Selim?'

She gave me a pitying glance. 'Of course.'

Sometimes Simone was far more than two years ahead of me. Today she had a new swimsuit, and she acted as if she had bosoms, which she didn't. Her bosoms were unchanged since the winter. I knew that for a fact.

The other day, Simone had been cradling her bosoms again in the bathroom. 'I want all the blood in my body to go *there*. To my chest.' She gave an experimental squeeze. 'I want them to be as big as Madame Amin's.' Although nothing could be that big unless it had fallen off a watermelon cart.

'When are you going to have a chest?' I asked.

Simone gazed optimistically at her vest. 'They're called bosoms.'

'Bosoms,' I repeated, trying out the word.

She studied the mirror. 'Oh, God, if I don't have bosoms in a year's time, I will simply die.'

I kept quiet. The only time Simone's chest wasn't actually concave was when she squeezed herself tight with her arms as she was doing now.

'Stop staring,' she said.

NOW

Fi haga ghalat. Something is wrong, I know it. Was it something said or done beneath the casuarina trees? To do with Ralph or Selim? And what about Alicia's cabin? Alicia wore a huge bow in her hair. She had been Simone's friend, so why had they stopped spending time together? The harder I try to recall, the more it slithers away. Spaghetti through the fingers, as Mother would say. Not that we were ever allowed to eat pasta with our fingers.

Maybe it was about smuggling. *Drugs. Money. Lots of things.*

I need my box from the locker, but I can only reach it if I get up, which I immediately discover I can't. How did my limbs become so useless? Normally bedrest makes you better. Doctor Tadros always said so. Yet now I'm so weary that I may never get up again. I lie back with a thump, knocking the water jug off the table.

I'm peering at the puddle on the floor when a new doctor

arrives. He wears a magnificent turban and is very hard to understand because he comes from Scotland. 'Do ye have falls?'

'Only if the pavement is icy.' I don't mention falling and dislocating my shoulder the summer after I arrived in England. I had only needed a quick anaesthetic for a little shoulder procedure that the A&E doctor described as taking literally three seconds, *bish, bash, bosh*.

Now the Scottish doctor points to my arm. 'How'd ye get these bruises on yer arum?'

I am surprised to see purplish patches, some the size of a plum, with a few fading to yellow. 'I don't know.'

The doctor summons a nurse to help me out of bed, which makes me dizzy. Then he tests my balance by getting me to stand with my eyes shut. He catches me. Next, with eyes open, I must walk along a line on the floor.

'Like this.' The doctor demonstrates, touching his heel to his toe with every step.

I sway to the right when I do the same. 'That often happens,' I say.

His furrowed brow tells me this isn't the right answer.

'It's because of a knee injury years ago. It was very icy on that ...' I know exactly where I fell, but the right word refuses to show up, even though I used it recently. Maybe even today. 'On that day,' I say finally.

The doctor is sceptical. 'We need tae look into that.'

Early evening. One of the two nurses has brought chocolate Hobnobs. They sit at their station and one of them says, 'It's not just the falls. She can't even find her way on her own.'

'Bit of a head case, poor thing.'

Head case? That jolts the life out of me. Are they going to put me in a padded cell, where I can fall and thrash about all I want without getting bruises? There's nobody to ask, so I sit there holding Simone's postcard of the Eiffel tower. It's a comfort to touch the surface of the card even though it's cracked and its wavy edges are peeling. I can feel the grooves Simone's biro made when she wrote her message all those years ago.

Take care of yourself, little sister. I'm fine and hope you are too. S x

Perhaps her messages are some kind of code.

Now I need to pee. Predictably, I must cross my legs and wait for a nurse to bring one of those *papier maché* bedpans, more suitable for making fancy dress hats than for toileting. It requires concentration to balance on the *papier maché* and wee at the same time. As a result, I forget to ask about anything. The nurse has gone now, bearing the pan in front of her like a salver.

It is like a foreign country here, where I'm lost and can't manage the language. People should make clear to me what's going on. It's only polite, and it needn't take long. I'm hardly asking them to spend a whole week explaining everything to me as I did for Sheila, back then.

ALEXANDRIA, JULY 1961

'Why are those women carrying pots on their heads?' Sheila asked as we drove through the outskirts of Alex.

'How else would they carry them without a cart or a car?'

'But they don't fall off!' my friend exclaimed. 'How do they do it?'

'I don't know.' Simone and I had often tried to emulate them, resulting only in Mother rushing in to see what we'd broken.

The trouble was well and truly under way by 1961. I didn't give Sheila the details, but then I barely understood all the nationalisations, sequestrations, and confiscations that Nasser had brought in. Besides, she was asking tons of other things, too. 'How come you and your family all have blue eyes?'

I explained that my parents' family originally came from Syria. 'A lot of Syrians have pale eyes. Alexander the Great went through there on his way here. They say his eyes were blue.'

Sheila sniggered. 'He must have had sex with practically everyone.'

'He wasn't on his own. There was his army as well.'

'Why does your family speak French instead of Egyptian?'

'It's called Arabic, not Egyptian.' Most of the people we knew spoke French at home, except for the Greeks and Italians. Although Father's grandparents had only spoken Arabic, French had become the language of the Middle East, as the French had been through here, too, and stayed a considerable time.

I had no idea what business Sheila's father had in Egypt, especially in 1961 when most foreigners had left, but it was a treat to have my pen pal turn into a real live friend for a week. She was a friend of my own rather than someone that Simone knew, too. Even better, she had a brother called Tom. She showed me a grainy black-and-white photo of a fair young man on a croquet lawn. Not nearly as handsome as the screen gods I swooned over at the Rialto and the Strand, but far more attainable, even if he was thousands of miles away.

'We'll be able to park nearby, *insh'Allah*,' Mother, said as she manoeuvred the Fiat past a lorry piled high with fruit.

'What does *insh'Allah* mean?'

'It means God willing.'

'Oh, I see.'

She didn't really see. Allah was required not just when parking spaces were scarce, but for anything in the future. You shouldn't even say you'd meet someone next Thursday at the Sporting Club without adding *insha Allah*.

We were outside a café when Sheila grabbed my arm and asked, 'Are those men queer?'

Two men in suits were greeting each other in a perfectly ordinary way by kissing on both cheeks.

'They're friends. Or relatives. One or the other.'

'Not queers, then?' She seemed disappointed.

Inside the café, waiters in white *galabeyyas* swanned around with trays.

'Why do they serve a glass of iced water with the coffee?' Sheila. asked

'Because cold water takes the bitter taste away.'

The waiters gave a big *salaam* as soon as anyone clicked their fingers. Mother waved and a tall waiter in a sash materialised immediately.

I explained to Sheila that the coffee could be made *sada* (bitter), *arriha* (mildly sweet) *ziyada* (very sweet), or *mazboot,* which means just right.

'Can't we have teas?' Sheila asked in that English voice that can carry all the way to Port Saïd and back.

'Shh!' *Teas* means bottom in Arabic.

When I told Sheila, she said it twice more in that same voice.

'What are they smoking?' Sheila. asked

They were *narghile,* known in English as hookahs or hubbly-bubblies. 'Like the caterpillar in *Alice in Wonderland*,' I explained.

'Oh, right. And what are they doing over there?'

Seriously, had she never seen *tawlah* before? Backgammon must be played with seriousness and just the right amount of aggression. Raised voices help subdue an opponent, regardless of any disparity in skill. Luck could be enhanced by shaking the dice at length, then blowing on to your closed fist before hurling the dice down in one angry movement, usually followed by an invocation to the Prophet, especially when the dice do not furnish the numbers you want. A massive slap of the palm to the forehead is in order if one of your pieces is taken. If you win a game, you smile widely. The loser smiles widely, too. Being good sports, Arabs smile a lot.

Some people played *tawlah* literally all day, seated at small marble tables with a glass of *arak* or a coffee, slurped noisily. I say people but it was only the men. Women mostly went to the Brazilian Coffee Stores in rue Cherif. Although the street was now named Salah Salem, everyone still called it rue Cherif.

Men who weren't engrossed in *tawlah* fiddled with strings of worry beads, clicking them rhythmically. The other hand often wielded a *menasha*, a fly whisk that looks like a horse's tail and probably once was. For serious battle with insects, though, nothing could match a plastic swatter or a rolled-up copy of *Al Ahram*.

I scanned the passers-by, hoping to point out Zouzou, who was, in my opinion, an unmissable sight. With luck, she might treat us to her favourite advice, which was that you shouldn't ever do it before you got married. But, after you got married, she'd often add, you could do it with anyone you liked.

'Look at that boy,' Sheila said. 'With the dreamy eyes.'

'Don't be silly. He's just a *mounadi*.'

'A *mounadi*?'

My explanation baffled Sheila. It seems she had never

heard of getting someone to look after a parked car in return for a few coins.

The *mounadi* was sitting on a doorstep, picking his feet. He was a lad of about fifteen, like us. Unlike us, he had probably been working on the street since he was an infant.

'Is that all he does all day?' Sheila asked as she checked her lipstick in the mirror.

Mother went spare if I wore make-up, so I only used a little pink gloss.

'I guess so,' I said.

As soon as we'd finished our coffees, I offered to tell Sheila her fortune in the bottom of the cup. The best things to find in your coffee grounds are a tree, which is a symbol of wealth, a ring because it means marriage, a bird, which is good news, and a letter, which just means a letter. It's even better if your cup sticks to the saucer, as it's a sure sign that someone loves you.

Sheila peered into the depths. 'Is that a heart in there?'

'It's more like a snake. See?' Snakes are not a good thing, and I immediately felt I'd been mean. 'But look over there, near the handle. At the big white area.'

'What is it?'

'It means your every wish will come true.'

'Then I'll wish for a cute boy. With bedroom eyes.' She licked her lips. 'I would French him.'

I didn't know what Frenching was until she explained later, when Mother wasn't around. For my part, I never told Sheila that a big white area in your coffee cup doesn't mean a dream coming true, but a calamity heading your way.

Mother drove to Mansheya Square.

'Wow.' Sheila craned her neck at the statue in the middle of the square. 'Such a big Arab on that horse.'

I pointed out that Mohammed Ali was actually Albanian, adding what I had learned at school. 'Modern Egypt began with Mohammed Ali, who was born in 1769.'

'How come, if he was Albanian?'

It was a mystery to me, too. How had Mohammed Ali been not only readily assimilated, but become ruler of Egypt? I thought of my great-grandparents whose only language was Arabic, yet were still considered foreigners. I shrugged. 'He didn't speak Arabic. That much I know. And he defeated the French.'

'With Nelson?'

I wasn't sure. 'He had lots of battles.'

'Was that a one-way street we just went up?' Sheila asked.

'It's too long the other way,' Mother explained.

On the way back to the house, I pointed out horse-drawn carriages on the Corniche. We called them *hantour*. Many had harnesses decorated with red pom-poms. A few horses rested with their heads plunged in sacks of feed. I wasn't sure if the smell was their feed or their poo. Sheila thought horses were jolly sweet, but all I knew was to keep well away from both ends.

My friend was amazed to see trams with as many passengers on the outside as the inside. Two barefoot boys ran after the tram to Bulkeley as it accelerated. One of them managed to leap on, but the other lad missed his footing and tumbled to the ground. *Maalish!* He jumped up and dusted himself off.

'Why do they do that?' Sheila asked.

'To catch the tram, of course.'

'But the tram already has people all over it. Like barnacles.'

'What are barnacles?' I asked.

When we got home, Simone had already come in from an afternoon with her friends, bringing with her a 45 rpm of 'Ya Mustafa'. It had the catchiest tune in the world, and Simone and I sang our hearts out along with the lyrics. Soon Sheila joined in the chorus, grabbing a hairbrush to use as a microphone. We played the disc over and over on Simone's little gramophone until we collapsed with the giggles.

'That's enough.' Simone shooed us out of her room.

'So where's that cousin you told me about?' Sheila asked.

'Victor? He's having his appendix out. Believe me, you've had a lucky escape.' I wondered how the doctors could locate his appendix in all that blubber.

7

NOW

The box Sheila brought me will help me find Simone, *insha Allah*. I open it again and smell the postcards. Shame Simone only sent cards, but letters were unreliable during the censorship. What had the regime hoped to find in private letters — a plot to overthrow Nasser, hints of a ruse to outwit land reforms, or warnings of former factory owners bent on revenge? I doubt they knew themselves, but that didn't stop them from opening and reading private correspondence.

I pick up a card of a London bus.

Keep your wits about you, and don't worry about me.

As if I haven't tried to hang on to my wits!

Some men are best avoided.

This is on a postcard of a boat on the Seine. Even if, by some miracle, I can put together all these clues, how am I to find Simone? I'm in no fit state to escape from here, and they still don't know what's wrong with me.

As if on cue, two doctors are here now. The woman is the Laura Ashley-glasses doctor from the other day. Although the man doctor is equally young, his blond hair is so thin that it barely covers his scalp, and he stands poker straight as if his spine is steel. Put him in a uniform and he'd look like a Nazi. Before I know it, he fires umpteen questions about falls and bruises, none of which I answer to his satisfaction.

Next, he wants me to squeeze his hands as tight as possible, then pull him towards me. 'Now push me away.'

I concentrate despite thirst and dizziness. 'Can I have some water?'

Fritz rolls his eyes and passes me my glass. 'All right. Have a sip then we'll continue.'

In the second test, I must touch the tip of my nose repeatedly with one finger, while going back and forth to the doctor's finger. It confuses me.

'Your nose,' the doctor says. 'Not mine.' He makes it even harder by moving his finger.

'Hey!' I tell him. 'That's cheating.'

After that, the doctor runs something across each of my soles. My leg jerks away despite myself. 'What was that?'

'My thumbnail.' The doctor fakes a smile. 'In the old days, a consultant neurologist would test the plantar reflexes with the key to his Bentley.'

'I don't mind what car you drive,' I tell him.

The Laura Ashley doctor wants me to subtract seven from 100. That's easy. After all, I had Mrs Naggar for maths.

'Ninety-two?'

'Take off another seven.'

I pause. 'Eighty-six.'

'Keep going.'

The doctor smiles encouragingly, but my arithmetic worsens. By the time I get to seventy-four, she decides to make me repeat a long sentence instead. I get flustered, and panic rises in my throat. 'Do I have dementia?' I've never dared ask before.

Dr Laura Ashley shakes her head without conviction. She and Fritz confer at the foot of my bed. That must mean I do have it, especially after the blows Victor once gave me with the wooden pencil box.

'So do I have it?'

Instead of replying, they mutter to each other. I pick up something that sounds like pseudo-dementia.

'What's that?' I ask. In all the years of being married to Fouad, one of the best doctors in Alexandria, I never once heard him or his colleagues mention *pseudo-dementia*.

'Well,' Fritz begins.

At last I'm going to get a proper answer. With every word, however, his explanation becomes more complicated until I have no idea what he's on about. Now he's talking about cows with five legs.

'That would be a very odd cow,' I point out.

He ignores my remark and embarks on questions on crying and looking forward to the future. He must think I'm depressed. How can I convince him that I'm not what the nurse calls 'a head case'?

'I am sad,' I reply carefully. 'But I'd be a lot better if I had my sister.'

He sounds cross. 'What sister?'

'My only sister. Simone.'

'You're just distressing yourself talking about a sister,' Laura Ashley says.

Before I can say anything, the man throws something else at me. 'We shall leave you in the capable hands of Ms Smits.'

'What for?'

'Psychometric testing.'

They leave before I can ask what that is. I'd have yelled after them if I'd dared.

ALEXANDRIA, JUNE 1957

Every morning, two things were the same. The cockerel next door was well into his raucous commentary, and Simone was arguing with Father, as could be heard from the other end of the house. Simone was probably eleven when the rows began, and the ritual was well established by 1957.

I could only conclude that she and Father held opposing opinions on everything, from the best way of tying shoelaces to the position of the planets in the solar system, a fact that could have been checked if only they'd calmed down and looked it up. Whatever the topic, their exchange of views always took place at full volume.

'*Mais non, Papa.*' Simone's voice carried better than the legendary singer Umm Kulthum's.

Today my sister insisted that girls were every bit as good as boys. I had no idea what Father replied, but Simone howled and doors were slammed, as was very clear despite the pillow I moulded over my head, a purely temporary remedy as the day was already hot.

I got up to find Mother in the corridor. She was waving her arms as she repeated her usual plea. '*Ne fais pas de drame.*'

It was too late by then. Both Father and Simone had already made quite a lot of drama.

NOW

I'm taken down a corridor in a wheelchair and put in a room. A moment later, Ms Smits breezes in, introduces herself, and installs herself opposite me. Her hair is in a severe bob, and those capable hands have short nails.

'Are you a psychiatrist?'

'I'm a clinical psychologist.' The first few questions are simple, like the date and my age. Then she displays a card with a drawing on it and smiles as if I'm an imbecile. 'What is this?'

It must be a trap. 'What do you mean, what is this?'

Ms Smits tilts her head. I suppose she means to look caring, but she reminds me of Tante Magda the time she had torticollis.

Finally I say, 'A table. *Une table. Una mesa.*'

Ms Smits's long face tells me that none of these answers fits the bill. Apparently I should have classified it, not defined it.

'Oh, I see. What *kind* of thing? Well, it is not an animal. It's a thing. A thing you find in a house.' Should I mention that one can eat outdoors as well?

Ms Smits now wants a list of things that are vehicles. 'As many examples as possible.' She has a stopwatch. 'Go.'

The words, alas, elude my grasp. Once familiar with an abundance of words in four languages, I can now barely summon up a single response. '*Hantour?*' I offer.

Ms Smits sighs and instructs me to draw a clock. Simone

was the arty one, not me, but I manage to sketch a passable outline of the travel clock I've had almost all my life.

'Just the clock face,' Ms Smits warns.

'But this is my clock. It's a Jaeger Le-Coultre from Switzerland. My sister has the exact same one. Hers is green.'

'I need the clock face. With the numbers.'

'My alarm clock doesn't have numbers. Just dots that shine in the dark.'

Ms Smits sighs again to suggest she has better things to do. 'Now, Mrs Wissa, how many legs does a horse have?'

This must be a trick question. Perhaps only the back legs are called legs, and the front ones something else? My brain may seize up now and again, but I know that, with the British, anything is possible, especially if it's to do with horses. 'It depends,' I reply.

Finally, I am wheeled back to the ward where there is a dismal sandwich waiting for me on the bed table. The label says cheese, but the taste does not. I'm not hungry anyway.

The *Daily Express* woman sleeps with her mouth open, and the woman who's the size of the Alps has turned over on to her side. The ward is quiet, but everything whirrs inside my head. The postcards must wait because my heart is also batting along, and I'm dizzy when I move even a little.

There's no chance to rest, however. Those doctors are back. Laura Ashley wants to know if there's depression or any other mental illness in my family.

'No.'

'There could be clues in your DNA, you see, so I want to know all about your immediate family. What about your mother and father?'

'My parents were absolutely normal.' I overlook Mother's obsession with typhoid germs in ice cream, *millefeuille* that spread food poisoning, and all her bonkers expressions. 'So was my sister, though I haven't seen her for fifty years. Can you help me find her?'

I swear she gives an exaggerated sigh. Then Fritz pitches in with the worst idea ever. 'We should be looking at antidepressants for you.'

Oh no! Antidepressants will befuddle me more.

'They can help a lot, though, as you may know, they can have one or two few side-effects.' He lists nausea, vomiting, feeling shaky or anxious, indigestion, loss of appetite, stomach ache, dizziness, insomnia, headache, diarrhoea, and reduced sex drive.

'But I have those already. Besides, nobody ever needed drugs for depression in my family. Least of all me.' My voice rises despite myself. I know I sound like a hot-headed Arab, or, worse, someone in need of strong medicine to calm them down, but how can I persuade him that these medicines are a terrible idea for me?

As usual, he and Laura Ashley aren't even listening. I'm still quaking as they flash their shallow smiles and leave me to my thoughts.

ALEXANDRIA, APRIL 1956

By the time I was ten, Alicia was the only person I knew who still wore a *fionka*. Every girl I knew had a bow on the back of her dress, especially if it was a party dress, but Alicia had another one in her hair. She was older than me. In actual fact, she was one week closer to Simone's age than mine. I had verified several times. Alicia was really Simone's friend, then, one afternoon, she invited me to her house.

Me. Not Simone.

I never thought Alicia was a very Arab name, but her looks were another matter. She looked as Lebanese as anything. Even more Arab was that *fionka* perched on top of her head. Either white or pink, the enormous stiff bow tilted to one side made her look exactly like an Easter egg from Baudrot.

'Daddy likes bows.' Her mouth was downturned.

I was puzzled. If my father had liked bows, I'd have been happy to wear them every day.

Their house was only two streets away from us. Simone had once told me that it had a nicer garden, with a pergola and a gazebo. I didn't want to ask what a gazebo was. Or a pergola, come to that. I could see for myself, though, that the house had a pink roof, a proper sloping one like pictures in books, not like our flat one.

I made the mistake of telling Mariam about Alicia's sloping pink roof, whereupon she had burst into tears. How could I possibly like it, when everyone knew you could only hang washing on a flat roof with a terrace like ours? If we moved house, it might have meant finding another family to go to on Thursdays.

Poor Mariam. From the pile of ironing, I grabbed one of Father's hankies and handed it to her. She dabbed her eyes and twisted the hankie, and still she went on weeping. I didn't know how to stop the flow, but luckily Simone arrived and put her arm around Mariam. I stood by uselessly for a bit before creeping away.

Simone was sniffy about Alicia's invitation. 'It won't be nearly as nice as you expect,' she said.

That didn't fool me. 'I want to see her house.'

'It's not worth the bother.'

'I don't believe you.' My sister was just envious that I was going to Alicia's house.

I cradled the impending joy and held it close for three long days. It was April, and I feared that the suffocating *khamseen* wind would smear the whole of Alex with fine sand and the smell of rancid butter, as it did this time every year. It cut visibility, made people cry, and would ruin my afternoon out.

In the end, though, the *khamseen* held off, and I went to Alicia's.

8

NOW

There's more to remember, I'm convinced of it. My tablets may help. I dive into my bag and take two more tablets, one of St John's wort and the other of ginkgo. They don't work right away, obviously. I am not that gaga.

My heart still races, and the water glass trembles in my hands. It's not just the prospect of antidepressants. There's something about those early morning quarrels I used to hear, back then.

When a nurse arrives, it's a relief to see she hasn't brought those dreaded antidepressants. 'You're going to have a scan. To look inside your head. It's called a CAT scan. There aren't any cats in it though,' she adds with a chuckle.

I know about CAT scans from being married to Fouad, though, in all honesty, there could be a whole menagerie and I wouldn't mind, as long as the scan sorts out the workings in my head. 'Do you know when it is?'

'No, love.' The nurse pats my bed and makes as if to leave.

I flap my fingers towards the hem of her tunic. 'Nurse. One more thing. What about my brain biopsy?'

She gives me a pitying smile. 'Now, Mrs Wissa. You already know about that, don't you?' This time, she really does go.

A CAT scan is a good thing, I tell myself as I survey the ward. It's unusually peaceful this morning. The vast mountain woman lies in the bed opposite, one hand poking out from the bedclothes. The mountain swells and snores rhythmically.

I study the card with the London bus again.

Keep your wits about you, and don't worry about me.

An uneasy feeling takes root in the middle of my chest as Pamela of the grapes gets out of bed and rummages for her lipstick. She plonks herself down on her chair, proceeds to paint her lips, then announces, 'I'm going home tomorrow.'

'Good for you,' someone says.

'Yeah. Aren't I lucky?' There is triumph in Pamela's voice, then she says, 'God, I need the loo.' Her face turns an odd colour, and she promptly topples sideways in her armchair.

Two nurses come running and a commotion follows. A red trolley is rolled in, the curtains are drawn, and several doctors gather around the bed.

Eventually the activity subsides. A nurse pulls a sheet over Pamela's head, as I see through a gap in the drapes. Pamela has died. There is another word for this. A very English word from long ago is right there, sitting on a shelf out of reach.

Fouad once had a patient who died like that. Mere days after an operation for infertility, the woman asked for a bedpan and collapsed on the spot. Pulmonary embolus, Fouad said. He gave me the medical explanation, which I understood not at all, because at the time I was sitting there wondering why I too couldn't have surgery to enable me to have a baby, though without a fatal clot on the lung afterward.

A knuckle of discomfort grows in the centre of my chest. I know this feeling.

ALEXANDRIA, APRIL 1956

I wore my new polka-dot dress the day I went to play with Alicia in her beautiful house that was so unlike ours. A *suffragi* opened the door while Alicia's father hovered right behind him, beaming down at me. Although I had met her father before, I had never noticed his very pink upper lip.

'Hello, Nadia.'

'Can Alicia and I go up on the roof?' I blurted out.

He stroked my hair. 'Come and talk to me first.'

He steered me into the sitting room and shut the glass door. It was hung with fabric so nobody could see through it.

'Where's Alicia?'

'She'll be down soon.'

He offered me a glass of water and a cherry-flavoured bonbon, then he took a yellow cigarette from a silver box, tapped it on the lid, and lit it. 'Pretty dress.' He made me pirouette in front of him as he blew smoke out of his nostrils.

Mademoiselle Violette had made me that dress. It was mauve with white spots, and I loved it. I didn't love it quite so much after he stood up behind me and held me close as the scent of his cologne and his cigarettes suffocated me, then put his hand beneath the fabric, about to reach into my Petit Bateau underpants despite my hands pressing the dress down and my head violently shaking a *No*. My heart was leaping out of my chest as I begged the guardian angel that I believed in to wing his way down and make Alicia's father change his mind, stop doing what he was about to do, which, whatever it was, felt revolting and wrong. Outside, the *roba bikya* man passed, yelling his head off in his eternal quest for old things.

A rustling noise from the hallway made him turn me around. His teeth, I then saw, were as yellow as his cigarettes. A gap showed when he drew back his lips, gleaming unnaturally pink beneath his moustache like the pet rabbit Simone had once had that only lived for a few weeks before something bad happened, leaving him lifeless in his hutch with his red eyes glazed over. I willed something bad to happen to Alicia's father right now.

Alicia bounced in. 'Papa! Where is my bicycle?'

He swiftly let go of my dress. 'There!' he said. 'There's no stain at all from your bonbon. I told you that you hadn't dropped it. Good girl.' The pink rabbity lips had gone, replaced by a thin line of mouth below his moustache.

I nodded vigorously. I was a good girl.

'Have another one,' he said.

I took the bonbon without touching his hand.

Rubbing my arm where he had grabbed it, I followed Alicia upstairs to her room. I tried to concentrate as she introduced me to all her dolls in turn, making one of them spin around just as I had a few minutes ago. 'This one is Mathilde, my favourite.'

'She's pretty,' I said. Nausea filled my chest.

Alicia wanted to undress the doll to show me her frilly underpants.

'I don't think Mathilde wants us to see her underpants.'

'How do you know?'

'Dolls like their pretty dresses. That's why they want to keep them on.' My stomach was churning and rubbing it made it no better.

'Want some lemonade?'

I nodded.

Alicia poured from a jug on the table. The lemonade was nothing like Rashida's. It tasted sour and made my jaw muscles clench. Now I felt a stone lodged in my throat, preventing the drink from going down, no matter how hard I gulped. I glanced out of the window on to the veranda below, with a multitude of flowers spilling out of their pots on to the tiles.

'Do you want to see the roof?' Alicia asked.

'I've got a tummy ache.'

'*Maman* keeps peppermint water in her bathroom.' Alicia's smile begged me to accept.

I didn't want their peppermint water. I wanted to go home.

Only on leaving Alicia's house, with her father hissing into my ear, did I learn that a good girl was someone who didn't tell people what grown-ups tried to do. I nodded emphatically again before accepting another cherry bonbon. As soon as I'd left the house, I spat it out in the shrubs by the gate.

Someone should have stopped him, but I had learnt to be a good girl. I said nothing.

NOW

The curtains are still almost closed around Pamela's bed, but, when a porter comes clanking on to the ward with a vast trolley, a nurse pulls the curtains around all the other beds. There are still gaps through which I glimpse that the porter's trolley, unconvincingly draped in a blanket, has substantial depth. The Go-to-Jesus cart, I once heard someone call it. I've no idea who or where.

Even when the porter wheels Pamela away, the massive woman mountain near me manages to sleep on. I never thought of snores as soothing, but at least they tell you the person has yet to shuffle off their mortal coil.

Now Pamela's bed is empty and a plastic bag of her belongings slumps on the floor by the nurses' station. Business continues. Pagers bleep. Phones ring. Crepe soles squeak on the vinyl floor.

It isn't the first time I've seen someone die, but this death won't let go of its grip on me. If that can happen to Pamela, who was well enough to walk about, apply lipstick, and be sent home, what might happen to me? In the middle of my ribcage lies a lead weight that I can't shift.

ALEXANDRIA, MARCH 1952

I had nearly reached the age of reason, but that didn't stop me stuffing another chunk torn from the orange-red sheet of *amar al deen* while Mother was out. The dried apricot paste, both citrussy and sweet, was my favourite treat of all. To make sure that Simone and I only ate a bit at a time, Mother kept the box in her boudoir under lock and key with valuables like used stamps and spare wrapping paper. Through waiting and spying, however, I discovered that the key to that cupboard was in Mother's embroidery box.

Now my fingers were sticky, and my cheeks crammed full of the chewy sweet stuff. Once you start something, it is hard to stop, especially when that something is *amar el deen.* I ripped off another hank from the sheet and took the long way back to my room to avoid Rashida.

The cramps started during lunch when Tante Georgette

and Tante Joséphine were there, sitting opposite my parents at our oval dining table.

'Why are you clutching your stomach?' Mother asked.

Simone raised her eyebrow, and Papa studied me over his glasses.

'No reason.' I rubbed my tummy but made it no better.

'She looks peaky,' Tante Georgette said.

'*Yiy*,' Tante Joséphine said. '*C'est une appendicite!*'

The pain in my belly intensified. I grabbed a piece of Syrian bread from the basket.

'*Va chercher le docteur Tadros!*' Joséphine urged my mother.

'Shut up, *chérie*,' Georgette said.

Today the bread was no help. The hurt in my tummy refused to be silenced, and now thunderous sounds started up. Mother stared at me. I'm sure she heard them from the far end of the table.

Pushing back my chair, I ran from the room. I only just reached *el beit el mayya* in time.

Simone comforted me. She took me to the bathroom next to the toilet, wiped my face with a wet flannel, and gave me something to drink. And, just as important, she covered up for me.

'You left the key in the door of *Maman*'s cupboard,' she whispered.

'Oh my God. I'm so stupid.' I groaned.

'It's okay. I've put it back. Nobody will know.'

A few days later, Mother seemed a touch surprised when she opened the box in her cupboard. 'Nadia. What's this?' she said.

I scratched my ear as Simone had taught me and pretended to know nothing.

9

NOW

The woman mountain stirs, shaking off her bedclothes to reveal a round face and stringy grey hair that hangs down to her shoulders. Once she manoeuvres herself upright, she gives me a meaningful look. 'Who will it be next, eh?'

'I don't know,' I manage to reply. She's talking about Pamela, but I've still got the nauseating sweetness on my tongue, and without warning I'm remembering something else that's not entirely pleasant.

Now I know why I avoided Alicia's family at Montazah. Even before the day I went to her house, I'd felt awkward walking past their cabin. I've tried not to think about it, but now I can't help remembering. Once, her father had got up to adjust the strap on my swimsuit. Another memory flashes up, a tense exchange I'd heard at home early one morning. *'I'm fed up with being a good girl!'* Simone had shouted.

My head hammers and I can't figure it out, so I resume my

study of the postcards. Simone sent me a selection of iconic views, often posted from elsewhere. This one shows that wooden bridge in Lucerne.

Sea even lovelier in Montazah, I'm sure.

What on earth did she mean?

The woman mountain is telling stories about people dying. I ignore her and try to concentrate. Why *IN* Montazah and not *AT*? When there's so little to go on, a tiny preposition could be vital. A code! Suppose I take the first letter of each word.

SELIM IS.

Simone was warning me about Uncle Selim! Selim is what, though? There is nothing more on the card, and the front isn't a sea. It's a lake. Perhaps another card will complete the sentence. I'm rooting around the box when lunch arrives. Swiftly, however, the tray with the plywood sandwich is whipped away from me and a nurse hangs a sign on my bed.

NIL BY MOUTH says the sign. In no time at all, a porter is here with a wheelchair.

The bumpy ride all the way to the scanning department jars my head at every turn. There are lots of turns. On arrival, a woman in a tunic greets me, checks my birth date, and says, 'Give me your arm.'

'What for?'

'For the cannula.'

'What's that for?'

'Omnipaque.' Her gimlet stare discourages further questions. Then she snaps on blue gloves as if I'm carrying leprosy and puts this needle thing into my arm. Once she secures it with tape, I'm sent into a room to lie just so inside a giant doughnut.

I've been hoping this scan will reveal what's wrong with me, but soon I feel so wretched that I no longer care. The injection they give me through the cannula makes me flushed and nauseated, which another woman says is entirely normal. Then I have the bizarre sensation of peeing without meaning to. That, too, is entirely normal, I'm told.

Luckily my box is still there when I get back to my bed, under my cardigan at the bottom of the locker. A nurse obliges by getting my box out and helping me put on my cardigan. She is a stocky woman with glowing cheeks and a mole somewhere in her multiple chins. 'And would you like something to eat?'

'Yes, please.' I stare at her lapel badge. 'Thank you, Deirdre. You're very nice.' This time I mean it.

Beaming, Deirdre goes off and leaves me to my postcards.

SELIM IS. But what is he?

ALEXANDRIA, MAY 1956

While Simone sketched in a pad, I sat under the blue parasol pretending to look out to sea. In reality, I was carrying out a top-secret assignment.

Uncle Selim studied his pocket watch before replacing it in his trouser pocket and grinning in my direction, which I pretended not to notice. His teeth were like ancient tombstones. He also had lizard eyes and looked 100 years old, and it was my mission to find out all about him. While I knew Selim wasn't a real uncle, nobody had ever explained where he came from. By now, I had spent nearly ten and a half years at the bottom rung of the ladder. On the other hand, I was, thanks to Enid Blyton books, an expert in detective work.

Uncle Selim was with us a lot of the time, especially at the beach, where he sometimes changed into khaki shorts of a type miles too long to be called shorts. In winter he wore a houndstooth jacket, which was the height of chic, according to Mother's *Réforme Illustrée*. In the evenings, he posed in a white linen jacket with a cigarette holder tucked into his pocket. I'd observed him long enough to work out that, on Fridays, he might wear a cravat, all of which I put down in a notebook using a special code of my own devising. A code is essential when sleuthing.

Uncle Selim's hat was called a panama, and his shoes were black-and-white lace-ups. He boasted that they were British and handmade, though to me they looked no different to the ones made by the shoemaker in rue Attarine. His moustache was the thinnest I'd ever seen, apart from David Niven's. Sometimes Uncle Selim carried a cane with a gold top in the shape of an elephant's head. I never examined it closely, as his hand was always resting on it, twitching slightly. I imagined his fingers coming towards me, doing things I understood even less than the things people said about him.

'Spiv,' Simone hissed as she abandoned her drawing and ambled down to the water. I followed to find out what she meant. If I couldn't understand her, then at least I could be her shadow. I literally walked in the shade she cast on the sand. All the same, I wasn't about to share my findings with her, let alone my secret code. For all I knew, my sister might be a spy, too. A proper detective cannot trust anybody.

I had an idea that my pretend uncle was in import-export, but people also talked of him being in transport, property, or insurance. Whatever his work was, he didn't seem to spend much time doing it, unlike Father, who was always either at his office in town or at his desk at home, shuffling papers.

'Papa, why do you have to work so hard?' I asked one evening after supper.

Although Papa often made a goofy face, especially when talking to Simone or me, he was very smart. He grinned and said work was good. He worked most of the time, stopping only to take apart toasters and clocks, regardless of whether they were broken.

That day, he'd had a business letter from Spain. My parents had no idea what all these words with little accents and marks meant, and neither did I. At ten years old, I only spoke three languages, which was nothing to brag about. Androulla and her family spoke at least four. There and then, I decided that I was at the perfect age to learn Spanish. It might even help with my secret code.

Without breaking from his work, Father smiled and said it was a lovely idea. Mother nodded absent-mindedly over her *petit point*.

The very next afternoon, when I was out with my parents, we saw Uncle Selim on the Corniche with a beautiful woman. She wore a yellow hat, sunglasses that pointed out at the corners, and a dress with flounces like a curtain. I wanted one exactly like hers.

Mother made a face as she said to Father, '*C'est une poupoule.*'

While I'd heard the word before, I wasn't sure what it meant, apart from not being at all the same as *poupée* which is French for doll.

Selim and the *poupoule* were arguing about something. Had they not been shouting and waving their arms about, they would have been the most dazzling couple I had ever seen.

Mother grabbed my hand and pulled me away with the promise of a pretzel from one of the vendors.

I never saw Uncle Selim with her again, nor did I see him with any other women, though he'd have had plenty of time for promenading with them on the Corniche since he never went to an office. Uncle Selim was still a mystery when, as luck would have it, we had to go to Europe again.

NOW

Poupoule. That means a prostitute. Same as *sharmouta* in Arabic. I search for the rest of the Selim clue among the postcards, but I get hopelessly confused. Missing lunch has made me light-headed.

Feeling better after tea and buttered toast, I decide to make a list. The only paper within reach is a hospital menu, so I use the back of it.

SELIM IS.

I add some of my symptoms:

Trouble concentrating, Thirst, and *Headache.*

That's not quite what I'm struggling to remember, though. There's something about Europe and those trips. Isn't there? I root around for another postcard. A town in Switzerland with bears. The name eludes me, but it's not Geneva and probably not Zurich either.

'How are you, lovely?' Nurse Deirdre is back with the obs machine.

'Muddling along.' It's the British thing to say, and the muddling bit is very true.

'Let's do your obs,' Deirdre says as the machine begins its noises. When she's done, she rolls up the blood pressure cuff while peering at my bed table. 'What have you got there?'

'Postcards.'

'Do you collect them then?'

'Not really. They're all from my sister.' My mouth is so dry that it clicks when I speak.

'This one's nice.'

It isn't, though. Now I remember the bears huddled in a dingy pit in the middle of Bern.

'Where does she live, your sister?'

'I don't know, but she's from Egypt originally. Like me.'

'I had an Egyptian boyfriend once,' Deirdre says. 'He had such lovely, dreamy eyes. When did you leave Egypt?'

'A while ago. My sister left even earlier. In 1967.'

The woman mountain pipes up. 'She ain't got a sister.'

'I do too,' I protest.

'You'll have to tell me more about your sister sometime,' Deirdre says as she leaves me a full jug of water. 'And Egypt and all the places she went.'

My eyes are swimming because this Deirdre is the only one who believes me about Simone. I send the tears back by concentrating on something else.

EUROPE, JUNE 1956

I never got the point of being dragged away from the seaside in the summer purely to dawdle around European cities, usually the same ones over and over, while Father took tiny pictures with his massive camera. Even the Eiffel Tower and Geneva's *jet d'eau* lost their appeal when Father insisted on Simone and me standing as straight as palm trees in front of them, and Mother kept telling us to stop squinting into the sun. On the plus side, I got a rest from Victor.

Our parents believed travel was an education. This was just as well, since we often ended up missing the beginning of term. It also meant missing the Cairenes, which was part of the plan. People from Cairo moaned about Alexandria the rest of the year every bit as much as we moaned about them and their city. In summer, however, hordes of them descended from trains, buses, and cars, bringing with them their children, their nannies, their cousins, their baskets, their suitcases, and their ruckus. The government, too, moved to Alex, and not an inch of beach was left. This is because the weather in Alexandria is perfect.

Europe was so different. Shops kept themselves to themselves instead of spilling out on to the pavement, and shopkeepers didn't hail down passers-by to lure them inside. Where were the beggars? And how come everything was tidy and clean when there were hardly any servants?

I enjoyed the changing of the guard at Buckingham Palace and the Swiss chocolate that our parents bribed us with, but Italy was a pain. It had mainly glass shops, and we saw every single one, with Mother warning us in each one not to touch anything. Why she dragged us into those places was a mystery.

We ate in restaurants where waiters wore smart black and white suits, not *galabeyyas*. Instead of rushing over with deep bows as soon as you clicked your fingers, staff strolled over as casually as they could manage. The food was dull and the meals were endless. I spent my time fashioning bread rolls into igloos with my thumb while waiting for the next course to arrive. There was no street food except in Beirut, which we passed through once. Lebanon may not be in Europe, but it is practically France, people say, especially if they're Lebanese.

It was a relief to get back to Alex, to the beach, sunshine, the lucky green flash on the horizon, and the sound of Rashida padding around in her slippers. Simone and I didn't mind the heat, but our parents did. Despite everything they claimed about the Alexandrian climate, they installed a Carrier air conditioning unit in their upstairs living room. It took up half the room and sounded like a plane taking off. Mother insisted it was only for Father, as she herself hated the thing. That didn't stop her sitting as close to it as she could.

Father lay down on the sofa in his vest and boxer shorts to leaf through papers and news magazines. Those and the radio kept him up to date, and we all had to be especially quiet when the news came on. Mother actually turned the air conditioner off to listen.

That was a waste of time. Nothing ever happened in Alex.

10

ALEXANDRIA, JULY 1956

It began on the twenty-sixth of July when I was ten and a half years old, or, as I preferred to put it, nearly eleven. The whole affair was about a canal and a dam.

President Gamal Abdel Nasser was a big man with a muscular jaw and impressive teeth that he showed all the time. That night in 1956 was the fourth anniversary of the revolution, and Nasser celebrated by giving a long speech right here in Alexandria, in Mansheya Square by that statue of Mohammed Ali Pasha wearing a turban and brandishing a sword as he sits on his horse.

Although I had no real opinion on our president, I enjoyed listening to him on the radio because I could understand his speeches. Unlike other important men who make themselves sound clever by using formal Arabic, Nasser spoke a colloquial language that every Egyptian could follow, even a child of not quite eleven. That, I thought, was much cleverer.

As usual when anything interesting happened, I was sent to bed instead of being allowed to stay up, so I missed the big speech. Mother told me about it the next morning, which was hardly the same thing. I relished the idea of Nasser brandishing his words like a sword, and I was especially sorry to have missed the firemen dispersing the crowds in Mansheya Square.

We were all in the upstairs living room by the air conditioning, which was on at full blast against the sweltering heat. Father and Mother told Simone and me that the Suez Canal now belonged to Egypt instead of France or Britain. That meant it would raise lots of money for Egypt and would pay to build a High Dam at Aswan. Mother actually put down her *petit point* during the conversation, so it must have been significant. It was a good thing that the Suez Canal had been nationalised, wasn't it? Unless you happened to be Britain or France, I supposed.

For a while after that, I forgot about canals and went back to puzzling over Uncle Selim. People at the beach murmured things about him behind his back, often using words I didn't understand even though they were in French. Selim kept a poetry book in his pocket. At least, someone said his slim volume was full of poems. I wanted to see for myself. At school we were encouraged to read and recite all kinds of poetry. Whenever I took an interest in Selim's book, however, his reptile eyes swivelled towards me, so I'd have to look away. I only glimpsed it once before he whisked the little book back into his breast pocket.

'Poetry and papyrus,' Tante Zahra scoffed between burps.

When term started, I consulted the encyclopaedia in the school library. Papyrus came from a plant in the Delta, though that did not enlighten me about Selim. For good measure, I looked up *palimpsest* as well, its entry not being far away. That was all about scraping something off a parchment to use it again. As it was in the same volume, I checked *parchment*, too. Turned out it came from animal hides. My research done for the day, I slammed the book shut, scattering dust into the sunlight.

As it turned out, I didn't get a chance to visit the school library for ages after that. In October, some countries got angry with Egypt for taking a canal that should have been Egyptian in the first place. Father and Mother did not fully explain it, and Rashida prayed more ardently than ever, muttering and whispering over her rosary. I thought I caught her saying that Egypt had been better under King Farouk, but, when I asked her to repeat it, she flatly refused.

In no time at all, France, Britain, and Israel all ganged up to declare war on Egypt. Abdou stuck blackout paper on all the windows, and every night we heard air-raid sirens and anti-aircraft guns. That's what Victor called them. With schools shut, he was in our garden more than ever. He told me that the guns were at Smouha, barely a few kilometres away, but I insisted that didn't scare me at all, *so there*.

Simone knew better. She hugged me and reassured me that everything would be all right. 'You can sleep in my room,' she said.

I padded into her room when the lights were out, leaving my teddy bear behind. Simone told me she had grown out of teddies, and I didn't want her to think I was still a baby. Of course, what with the guns and Simone's feet, I barely slept at all while sharing her bed, but at least there was the chance that some of her courage would rub off on to me in the night.

Our school didn't reopen till the New Year, by which time its name had become El Nasr Girls' College. There were new teachers, too. Miss Appleton, Miss Brownlee, and all the English staff had all gone, as had my English, French, and

Jewish friends. But Androulla, Zeinab, and most of my class were still there.

No more Marmite, Enid Blyton books, or 'Beek Frean' biscuits for us. Alexandria had changed.

NOW

A page from Selim's notebook swims to mind. It had no poetry. Just columns of figures and words. Telephone numbers, perhaps. If it was his address book, why be so sneaky? And why did Mother dislike him? Her face said it out loud even if she didn't.

I take the hospital menu and write on the back.

Selim's notebook. Numbers and maybe names.
SELIM IS what?
Mother disliked Selim.
Sleeping in Simone's room 1956.

I add *Palimpsests,* though I swear to God I've no idea why. As a young woman in a tunic approaches, I stuff the paper into my dressing gown pocket.

'I'm the physio,' she announces. 'And I'm going to help you get moving again.'

That's the best news I've had in ages. I resolve to do exactly as she says, even though it feels odd putting my feet where she instructs me to, and even odder when I take a few faltering steps.

After fifteen minutes or so, she congratulates me as if I'm a contender for the Olympics. 'Next time, we'll see how we get on walking down a corridor, shall we?'

'Yes, please.' My legs are shaking from the exertion, but I'm not going to moan. 'When will that be?'

'Later,' she says briskly.

I have no idea what *later* means. Time contracts and expands, as if it's adrift from its chronological moorings. No wonder events have become distorted in my mind. But some things I remember perfectly. Inside my brain, they are just the other day.

Now Fritz is here, with his scalp visible through his straw-blond hair. 'Mrs Wissa.'

I keep my voice tranquil as I fiddle with the paper folded inside my dressing gown pocket. 'Yes?'

'I can now tell you that your scan was normal.'

'I told you my falls were just from my bad knee.' I display my brightest smile to help him put the idea of antidepressants out of his mind.

'Have you ever taken any drugs?' he continues. 'I mean recreational drugs? Street drugs?'

'Of course not.'

He persists regardless. 'Cannabis, coke, anything like that?'

'No.' Of course he doesn't listen. They never do. I've tried to tell them something important, and they've rebuffed me so many times that I've now forgotten what it is. 'Can I lie down please? My head hurts.' I could add that even my back teeth hurt, but the *Inglizi* don't care for exaggeration.

When he's gone, I remember the scan result. It's good news, but it only goes so far. Isn't there normally a breakthrough in situations like this? That's only on TV, I suppose. I can't imagine anything good happening in real life.

ALEXANDRIA, FEBRUARY 1958

Winter is aptly named in Arabic. *Shita* by name, shit by nature, as Simone liked to say. It brought grey skies, angry spray from the sea, and often lashing storms. The palm trees on the Corniche were dishevelled, the vendors had gone, and there would be no green flash for months.

The only jollity was Christmas, with a fir tree and a nativity scene festooned with cotton wool. I doubted Bethlehem had snow, but we had lots of cotton. I was no longer a baby, and Uncle Selim could no longer fool me in a red outfit and a fake beard. I had even learned that the sleek black horses and golden carriages so often seen down rue Fouad were not transporting a princess, as I'd once believed, but a coffin.

In other ways, however, I was still naïve in February 1958. I was twelve and a bit years old when I got a period for the first time, an experience more horrid than a double detention from Mrs Naggar for not handing in my maths. Terrified, I ran to Simone and showed her my bloodstained underpants.

She put an arm around me. 'You're a woman now.' Then she ordered me to soak my underpants in the handbasin. 'Don't stand there with your mouth open. Run cold water while I get *savon de Marseille*.'

As well as soap, Simone found me a sanitary towel and a strange suspender belt thing. It was torture, that rough pad between my legs with its elasticated belt that sawed me in two where it disappeared between my buttocks. Simone said a period was called *the curse* in English. I could see why. While I scrubbed my underpants with a nailbrush, she explained what was going on.

My legs trembled. What horrors! Mother had not warned me that blood would gush out of me without notice at some future date, still less that it was set to happen every single month until I got incredibly old.

Simone dispensed advice along with the Aspro she fetched

me from Mother's cupboard. 'Don't ever wash blood stains in hot water. Use a hot water bottle for the cramps, and don't sit on marble floors or anything cold.'

'Will I get a scab when the curse stops?'

She gave me a withering look. 'How could you possibly have children if there's a scab?'

That was even scarier. I dug my nails into my palms. Simone said I was a woman now, but I didn't feel any different apart from the chafing between my thighs. All the same, it meant I could be with a man. I had only the vaguest idea as to how this worked, but I held on to the hope that my sister would explain it to me, and that eventually she and I would have babies at the same time.

Once dressed, I checked my reflection in the bathroom mirror, turning this way and that, then smoothed my hair over one eye and tilted my head as Zouzou did when talking to men. I still looked like a child.

Simone decided it was high time I learned how to walk properly.

'How can I, with this mattress between my legs?' I wailed. I looked less than ever like Rita Hayworth.

'Like this.' She swayed her hips, picking her way across the bathroom in her new shoes from Bata. They were pale pink with a small heel. The effect was slightly spoiled by her heavy ankles and her pleated school skirt.

I tried hard to emulate her.

'Not like that. Keep your thighs together and your toes pointed out. See?'

I wobbled as we walked in unison, step by careful step. 'The floor's slippery,' I whined. In truth, I was merely clumsy.

'You're walking like a polio victim. Here. Borrow these.'

The magical shoes more or less fitted me, with the aid of loo paper scrunched into them.

'Keep your toes out, and wiggle your bottom like Zouzou.' She gave a further demonstration, then sat on the edge of the roll-top bath and observed me as I shambled from one side of the room to the other, pausing only once for support. 'Much better. All you need is practice. Right. I want my shoes back now.'

Sisterly love only goes so far.

That whole year, I was marooned in no-man's-land. Often I couldn't go swimming because of the curse, though I sometimes managed, with reams of cotton wool, to wear shorts without the belt and pad contraption that showed through my clothes. I was too mature to make sandcastles or collect shells, yet too young to enjoy Domenico Modugno's songs and grown-up drinks like *arak*. And I still didn't understand all the stories that made adults laugh outside the cabins at the far end of Montazah under the trees.

11

NOW

My head throbs and I have stomach cramps. We never did get pregnant at the same time. I sigh, telling myself to snap out of it and do something useful.

I select another card from the box and study it for clues. Does *NEHSAWF* signify anything? The message itself is:

Not everyone has such a wonderful father.

Obviously, I've always known this, but there must be a hidden meaning. I jot down *Father was wonderful,* in case the answer pops up later.

When Deirdre comes in, she helps me out of bed. As she slides a pillow behind my back in the armchair, she says she's been thinking about my sister. 'There are community groups on Facebook,' she says.

I am not on Facebook. 'My face is too old for that.'

'Nonsense. Now, I found several groups that my friend Baher liked, but they're in Arabic. Would you like to borrow my spare iPad? The screen's cracked, but it still works.'

I wouldn't know how to use it, but it's so kind of her that I have to blink away a stinging feeling behind my eyes.

With Deirdre's iPad, I learn about Facebook. The first thing I look for there is our family name. There's an overwhelming number of people called Khoury, not including the ones spelled Khouri, but I recognise no photos. As Deirdre said, there are several Egyptian groups. The pictures of Alexandria jolt me back in time, with images of the Nabi Daniel mosque, the Cecil Hotel, and the beach at Montazah, of the exact same rocks I sat on. There's even a photo of the Greek Orthodox church.

My limbs tighten as Fritz strides towards me again, accompanied by a new doctor. From the glint in their eyes, they've got something in mind. Sure enough, they start quizzing me about deer, ticks, and forests.

'I've never been to a forest.' A few casuarina trees hardly count.

'Not even Richmond Park?'

'No.'

That doesn't stop his questions on fever, rashes, joint pains, heart problems, headaches, and memory trouble.

I shake my head. 'Only headache and trouble concentrating.'

The other man doctor says, 'Could still be Lyme disease. It's getting more common, with climate change.'

'Difficult to diagnose, though. I think we'll need an ELISA test.'

'Can it be cured?' To me, that's the most important thing about that Lyme's disease.

'Well,' the new doctor replies in a tone that is not encouraging.

Fritz has been thinking. 'Could be something else entirely, though. Mrs Wissa, do you know anyone with the same symptoms as you?'

'I don't think so.'

'Hmm,' Fritz says. 'You're an interesting patient.'

My heart sinks. Fouad always said it was dangerous to be an interesting patient. *'You get too many tests, and there is never any cure.'*

They confer quietly for a while before Fritz clears his throat. 'Are people telling you to do things?'

'No.' That's not strictly true. Everyone tells little girls what to do, and that doesn't change much when they grow up.

'What about your family?' the other doctor asks. 'Are there any mental health problems? Schizophrenia, psychosis, anything like that?'

This isn't going where I'd like. I pick at the bobbles on my fluffy blue dressing gown. 'No, but my sister might know more.'

'I didn't know she had a sister,' the new doctor says.

Fritz shoots him a glance. 'She doesn't.'

I clench my fist around the woollen bobbles I plucked. 'I do have a sister. She's called Simone. I just don't know where she is.'

The doctors mutter something I don't hear.

'I do have a sister,' I say, upping the volume. I'm still saying it as they walk off to their next victim.

I turn my pillow so the woman mountain can't see me cry. My sister was – *is* – real. She may have lorded over me, but she protected me, too. What can I do to make the doctors believe me?

ALEXANDRIA, SEPTEMBER 1955

As soon as the clergy had left and everything had gone back to normal, I had taken off the despicable smocked dress and had stuffed it under the giant wardrobe in my room, hoping it would soon be forgotten. Nobody looked there. The servants cleaned daily, sweeping the floors, beating the rugs out on the balcony, and washing the kitchen floor, but they always missed the space under the wardrobe, just as they missed bits in the bathroom.

I hadn't banked on the earthquake a few months later.

It was early on the twelfth of September and nobody was up yet. All the furniture in my room shook, including the wardrobe. Mother and Father rushed in, followed by Rashida.

We were uninjured and the house was still standing, but Father decided the wardrobe was unstable where it was, so he got Abdou to help him move it by half a metre or so. Abdou stared as if he'd never seen dust before while Mother went, 'What's this?', as if she'd never seen a smock crumpled up.

I tilted my head and scratched my ear exactly as I had learned from Simone. 'Don't know.'

NOW

Perhaps the clergy were responsible for Simone's departure. They'd been a strange lot, not even pretending to like women, though I can't see a connection.

'Look out,' the woman mountain says. 'Here comes Dracula.'

A woman with mousey hair is heading my way. She puts

down a large box, takes out needles and an array of tubes, then instructs me to make a fist for her. Her needle doesn't bother me like injections from Doctor Tadros used to. Dracula doesn't explain what all the little tubes of different colours are for. All she says is to keep my arm bent afterwards. She's too busy sticking labels on to things to pay attention to me. I expect the tests are for that New Forest disease. From what the doctors let slip, its symptoms can be almost anything in the book. I'm becoming indifferent as to what they find. I just want to find Simone.

Once Dracula has gone, there's no wi-fi left on the iPad. I look at postcards instead. This one is of Trafalgar Square. According to Simone,

The pigeons take everything.

I finger the grooves made with her biro, but they bring me no closer.

Then it's lunch, a dish of some whitish meat and a slice of dessert with the texture and the taste of Polyfilla.

'I'm on a special diet,' the new patient opposite announces. Her lunch looks much the same, only with more sticky labels all over it.

In Egypt, my most hated food was calves' brains. Even whole glasses of water couldn't wash down the wobbly white stuff. Mother and Rashida swore they were good for my brain, but I bet they were wrong. Our cousins next door ate brains, and they'd done nothing for Victor's intellect. *Molokheyya* made me gag, too. The glutinous green vegetables reeked of garlic and had the slime of a slug. Then, one spring, lamb took the top spot on my hate list.

I push my tray away and shudder.

ALEXANDRIA, APRIL 1954

It began when Eisenhower came to stay.

Mother and Father brought a lamb to live in the garden. It was a skittish thing with a little face that was always chewing. They put it in a big cage that, according to Rashida, had once housed pigeons. In the corner of the cage was a fragrant mound of clover. Berseem, they called it. The rest of the concrete floor quickly filled up with droppings.

Simone took no interest in the lamb, but I talked to him every day before and after school. That made him my lamb. I decided it was probably a boy, though it never stood still long enough for me to be sure. Apart from a dark bit beneath his tail, he was very white, and his pale eyes were like a photo I'd seen in Father's *Newsweek*. I named him Eisenhower. Even when I beckoned him as nicely as I could, Eisenhower skipped away unless I held out berseem for him.

One day, he wasn't there. The door of the cage was open, and his pile of berseem had gone. I searched the whole garden, including the air-raid shelter, in case he'd scoffed all his food and escaped. 'Eisenhower! Where are you, Eisenhower?' I called, promising him handfuls of fresh clover.

Unearthly screams pierced the air. Mother told me it was children playing across the street, but I had never heard our neighbours make sounds like these. Besides, these screams came from nearer home. I caught a glimpse of the kitchen boy with a slash of dark red across his apron and raced up to my room.

Mother tried the door, but I had locked it.

'Go away,' I cried, beating my pillow. I held my breath and hoped to die. In the corridor, Mother muttered something about omelettes and broken eggs.

Even though Rashida begged me, I refused to come out for lunch, but, eyes puffy and nostrils blocked, I emerged for macaroni cheese at supper.

The full horror arrived a day or two later on the feast of *sham el nessim*. It literally means *sniffing the breeze*, and everyone in Egypt celebrates it whether they're Christian, Muslim, or anything else. It's the spring festival, and food is very important. The grown-ups began by drinking *arak* and progressed to Gianaclis wine, while Simone and I had our usual ruby-red *shorbat el toot*. Hassan had tidied up the flower borders, put up four large tables, and erected striped poles with decorations on them so that we could eat in the garden at *sham el nessim*. I resolved not to spill or drop anything on my new dress, least of all my mulberry juice.

There were Mother's sisters Georgette and Joséphine, as well as Father's relatives Tante Zahra and Tante Magda. Unfortunately, my family had invited Victor and his parents as well. Dozens of relatives I had forgotten all about turned up, too. Perhaps they had come from Cairo specially to pinch my cheeks, smother me with lipstick, and marvel at how much I had grown.

Abdou came out of the kitchen with a massive silver dish piled high with rice, followed by toothless old Ibrahim carrying another even bigger platter.

'What's for lunch?' I whispered to Simone.

She gave me a look only an older sister could pull off. 'Lamb, stupid.'

It was all I could do to swallow a few mouthfuls of rice and vegetables without sobbing. I pushed my chair out and ran into the house, spilling my glass of *shorbat el toot* down my front.

NOW

Simone had cried too that *sham el nessim*. I'd put my arm around her and said, 'See? You love animals, too.'

What had she replied? Something about worrying more about the people she loved? The conversation has buried itself deep inside my head where I've no hope of unearthing it, let alone figuring out if it means anything. I could try a few more of my tablets, though, in truth, I only bought them because Sheila, a big fan of alternative medicine, had nagged me to do something to boost the brain. She'd said I'd become quite scatty in the last few weeks. 'But I know an excellent herbalist,' she'd added.

After some negotiation, I ended up browsing the shelves of a health shop with its magnesium, ginkgo, and a whole alphabet of vitamins. The woman there suggested testing my reflexes for allergies and toxins. I declined, though she talked me into buying St John's wort and some honey that tastes exactly like supermarket honey but costs ten times more. The health-shop woman congratulated me on my excellent choice, particularly in view of their special offer at the moment. I went home with two sizeable supplies of St John's wort along with the miraculous honey and a bulk deal of ginkgo biloba tablets which apparently have some amazing properties too.

There the tablets are, in my handbag. Must be a while since I took any. I swallow a few of St John's wort and two of the ginkgo before swiftly hiding my bag.

'Hello there, Mrs.' Deirdre is here now. She quickly creates a profile for me on Facebook. 'There. Now that the wi-fi is back, you can log on and post things. Like this.' There's a lot of screen jabbing involved.

I savour the photos again. Simone had saved me from the clutches of boys right there, on the beach at Montazah. Big horrible boys. I can't remember which ones. People said they were from Cairo. I didn't much like boys at the time, especially those who banded together and tried to drag me to the casuarinas behind the beach cabins. This time it wasn't needles in my foot that worried me most. Then Simone had appeared and shouted, 'Fire! Fire!' until they dispersed.

One boy at Montazah had been nice. I remember him.

12

ALEXANDRIA, SEPTEMBER 1961

'I'm not innocent anymore,' I announced. I had been dying to tell Simone but managed to wait until Rashida had cleared away the breakfast plates. Today I didn't turn my empty eggshell upside down in its cup. I was grown up now.

Unimpressed, Simone continued to sip her tea, so I said it again. 'I'm not innocent anymore.'

Simone put down her cup and examined her nails.

'Well?' I said.

She finally looked up. 'Let's hope you don't get pregnant.'

'Of course not! Tewfiq and I only kissed.' I felt deflated.

'Tewfiq?' Simone's devaluing response hung in the air for a moment as she resumed her analysis of a particularly fascinating cuticle. 'Did you want to kiss him?'

'Of course I did!' Tewfiq was my friend Zeinab's older brother and a pupil at Victoria College. He was quite tall now, his spots were better than they'd been last year, and, if you had an exceptionally vivid imagination, he had bedroom eyes. I decided not to share with Simone any of the details of those few minutes spent under the casuarina trees by the back of Madame Amin's cabin. I had hoped it would be like at the cinema, all jaw action and kissy noises. The reality was Tewfiq's hot breath, all pine nuts and olives. His scratchy chin. His tongue a hard twig against my teeth, which I supposed was Frenching. His body wriggling close. Something firm within his shorts, jabbing into my hip. Most of all, the fear of being seen by the Amins or one of the *suffragis* who might be rinsing dishes under the outside tap.

I was fifteen and it was 1961, notable for being a number that could be flipped through 180 degrees and yet would still read the same. A laborious calculation told me that this wouldn't happen again until sometime in the seventh millennium.

In other ways, 1961 was not that special. Father pottered about as usual, dismantling things after work and on Fridays, when the office was shut. He loved pulling random appliances apart every bit as much as he liked assaulting belts with his hole-punching gadget. Today he was less jolly than usual.

'What's the matter, Papa?'

Apparently, that man Nasser had decreed that capitalists were the enemy of the people. There had already been changes, as everyone knew. July 1961 had seen the nationalisation of Egypt's major department stores. Until then, shops like Hannaux, Salon Vert, and Au Rêve des Dames were as smart as stores in Paris or Beirut, and sold almost anything you could want. Now that the shops belonged to the government, their displays reeked of a Soviet uniformity. Shortages became the norm. Simone moaned that she could no longer get her favourite lipstick.

Mother retorted that nobody needed a lipstick at seventeen. 'It makes a nice Arab girl look like a *sharmouta*.' She thought anyone in visible makeup was a whore.

'*Merde!*' Simone said 'All my friends wear lipstick.'

'Don't you dare swear again,' Mother warned, while Father reminded us all that many people couldn't buy essentials like matches and toilet paper.

Luckily, friends often rang with the news that such-and-such shop had just got a shipment of toilet paper, so one raced there before they ran out again.

When Mother's *petit point* suffered through lack of suitable threads, she took to making bags instead, such as a completely unnecessary fabric bag for the hairdryer, and drawstring bags in which to pack stockings and shoes inside a suitcase, which we were unlikely to need now that getting visas had become difficult. Sometimes Mother amused herself by turning old bags into new, but the thread was poorer quality than it was. '*Merde*,' I heard her say when another length of cotton broke.

Simone contented herself with raising an eyebrow.

These days, Zouzou's outfits came from Egypt rather than France or Italy. A little seamstress like our Mademoiselle Violette could run fashionable clothes up very reasonably, and clever shoemakers knew how to make leather goods that were indistinguishable from the designer versions. Madame Amin had a fake Gucci bag. She made a show of reaching for a magazine inside it whenever she had an audience. It was often the same magazine as the previous month, minus articles that the official censor had decided to cut out because they were unacceptable to the regime.

I had never seen Madame Amin drink alcohol. One day at Montazah, however, she heaved herself out of her deckchair and returned from her cabin with an *arak* in hand. 'We are all,' she announced after downing a sizeable slug, 'going to hell in a *hantour*.' Everyone knew the horse-drawn buggies on the Corniche, but I had no idea what hell she meant.

Later, Father and Mother explained to me in hushed tones that entire businesses were being nationalised. Anyone who ran a company was in trouble. Anyone who owned more than 100 *feddans* of land was in trouble, too. People who got sequestrated were in especially big trouble because they lost all their assets and most of their freedoms.

'Are we going to be sequestrated?'

'I hope not,' Mother said.

'But we're capitalists, aren't we?'

Father gave me a whispered explanation. The gist of it was that his work mattered to people that mattered. 'Don't worry, little one.'

I tried not to. We had far less to worry about than many people, I reflected when Simone and I next got carted off to Mademoiselle Violette's. She had run up our clothes for years, in her workshop up two flights of unreliable steps. Everyone in Alex referred to their dressmaker as *little,* but Mademoiselle Violette was literally that, with quick movements that reminded me of a sparrow. Even when she was standing, I could easily see over her head. While Mother perched on a threadbare chair, I stood in front of a cheval mirror that had lost much of its silvering, as stock still as one can while someone sticks pins into you.

'One day I'll make your wedding dress,' she said.

Meanwhile, Mademoiselle Violette turned out dresses with modest hemlines and necklines that Mother considered becoming. If I was lucky, I got to choose the fabric, as when I pleaded for a bright yellow cotton and got a lugubrious shade of lilac.

I couldn't imagine the ritual at Mademoiselle Violette's ever changing, but other things did. The next time I was at the beach, I took another batch of pictures with my Brownie camera before people got whisked away in that *hantour*, as per Madame Amin's prophecy. I captured Zouzou sitting in front of someone's cabin, deep in conversation with a man who wasn't Ralph. Zouzou's luminous orange swimsuit shone out of the shadows, and it wasn't clear how the tiny brass buckle at the front could possibly keep it from coming adrift in the middle.

Like our friends, Simone and I untucked our blouses and tied the ends together to show off our midriffs. It was the height of chic, though Simone only did it when we got down to the water's edge, well away from the cabins. Summoning up all my artistic skills, I took glamorous shots of her posing on the rocks, her lips as much like Marilyn Monroe's as they could be without lipstick.

'Oh God. There's Victor,' she said.

'Where?'

'Over there. Don't stare.'

Too late.

'Hey, girls.' Victor waddled over. He had gained more weight, which he delighted in throwing around. 'Want to see my camera?'

I saw nothing.

'Look.' He opened his hand.

'How can something that titchy take photos?' It lay in his palm, sleek, beautiful, and nothing like my Box Brownie.

'It's a Minox spy camera. See the focus?' Victor slid the silver gadget open. The close-focusing lens was ideal for copying documents, apparently. 'This little chain here is for measuring how far away you are.'

What documents? formed in my mind. 'Who are you going to spy on, Victor?'

'Wouldn't you like to know?' He slipped the Minox into the pocket of his shorts and patted it.

NOW

Victor once showed me tiny grey photos from an envelope in the pocket of his baggy shorts. I tried so hard not to be impressed that I can now remember nothing of them. Simone, meanwhile, showed extreme disappointment in my photos of her. A Brownie was cumbersome to hold still. That was my excuse for the series of blurred images.

Something else I recall. Simone never bared her midriff when older men were around. Come to think of it, she avoided them altogether. Not Father. But she was tense around Uncle Selim, wasn't she?

An image flashes up in front of me. Selim and Alicia's father, standing together at Montazah. They'd stopped talking when they saw me, their usual self-assured expressions replaced by something less certain. The harder I concentrate, the less sure I am of anything. It's like trying to pluck at a cloud.

I go back to the iPad, but the wi-fi won't oblige. The new patient on the special diet moans about the wi-fi, too, so it's not just me being a she-donkey.

'You can use my hot spot if you want,' the woman mountain tells her. She doesn't extend the same offer to me.

Now the new patient is laughing helplessly at a Facebook video. Maybe it's the one with the cats who looks after ducklings along with her kittens. Her mirth is all at odds with how I feel. There's nothing good in here.

13

ALEXANDRIA, OCTOBER 1961

The night of the dinner at the Tawils' house, I had the most violent headache of my entire life. That's what I told Mother, anyway.

Although most of Alex was due to be there, Tewfiq hadn't been invited. I had seen him once more at Montazah since our first kiss. Emboldened, he had kissed me again, this time so enthusiastically that I had to wipe my mouth with my sleeve. Then he sucked my neck, which was quite nice, though I had to wear a scarf for the next few days.

Victor, alas, was expected at the Tawils', so I definitely didn't want to go, especially with Simone away with her friends. Ever since he had first begun to plague my existence a decade ago, Victor had not improved. Being overweight was not considered a drawback in a man, and people continued to rave about his qualities. *Comme il est beau. Comme il est gentil. Comme il est intelligent.*

When the evening of the dinner came around, I pleaded a migraine. I'd never had one, but had heard people complain at length of these crippling headaches. Mother observed me sceptically. I therefore got myself a flannel from the bathroom and ran it under the cold tap, twisting as I squeezed it out. I added a drop or two of *eau de cologne* and applied it to my forehead before stomping off to bed to groan dramatically.

Mother peered around the door. 'Which side is your headache on?'

'Both,' I moaned.

'You do know migraine is only on one side?' There was triumph in her voice.

'It started on the left before moving to the right. That's why I said *both*.'

I missed the big dinner and spent the evening in the kitchenette listening to the radio with Rashida, who promised on her mother's eyes that she would say I had been flat out in bed all evening with a cold compress on my head.

I pretended to be asleep when my parents got in, and learned the next day that it had been a wonderful party and that Mother's dress had drawn many compliments.

Later that day, Simone returned from Marsa Matrouh, about 200 kilometres east of Alex. Simone and her friends often went there to camp in the desert, and it was all innocent, so she said, though it sounded dangerous and exciting to me. I liked to think that anything could have happened with a group of five girls and five boys, even if the heavy ex-Army tents took hours to erect and smelled of damp socks.

'What happened to your tooth?' I asked her.

'Stop staring. It's only a tiny chip.'

True, but it was quite obvious, being on one of her front teeth.

'Remember I said there were no toilets? But there's a café

nearby and the nice café owner let us use the washroom and even have a shower, for only a few piasters. Well, I slipped on the floor and chipped my tooth. It'll be fine, though.'

'It'll be fine,' I agreed.

NOW

There was something important about Simone's tooth. I feel it in my bones, though I can't say which ones. I feel things all over my body at the moment, mostly pain. Did I once see Simone with a cut lip? Her bottom lip, I think, though I don't know when. A memory rises part of the way to the surface, then sinks back into the depths.

Now that the wi-fi has put in an appearance, I look for people called Tawil. There are so many! I try Amin. There are even more of them because the name appears to be Indian as well as Arab. To make things more complicated, some people spell it Ameen.

Three community groups have accepted me. I study the faces of the thousands of other members without recognising a single one. Now I'm so giddy I have to put the iPad down. Does this mean I have that Lyme's disease they like so much?

After a moment, I go back to the other Alex groups. *Damn.* My internet has vanished.

The woman mountain sits up, shakes out her greasy curls, and says in the general direction of the new patient, 'You want to think about something nice, dear. Take your mind off your lumbar puncture.'

'Think about Brad Pitt,' a throaty voice from a distant bed calls out.

There's the rattle of a trolley towards the new woman, a

swish of curtains being pulled, and the murmurs of a doctor and a nurse manoeuvring her into position.

The woman mountain seems to read minds. 'The internet will come back later,' she tells me. Why she's in hospital, I've no idea, but she is the authority on everything. 'They want to offload you,' she continues. 'Did you know that thousands of people die because they can't get a hospital bed? They can't bring them in, see, until they get rid of you.'

Fresh panic grips my chest. 'What will happen to me?'

Woman mountain arranges her blanket regally like a cape. 'There's places. I expect the social worker will come and sort all that out. Why are you staring?' she asks me. 'Do I remind you of someone?'

The wag down the end shouts out, 'Yeah. You're a dead ringer for that Elle McPherson.'

No, the mountain reminds me of nobody, except perhaps a witch in *Macbeth* prophesying doom. She then emits a giant burp before settling down again and covering herself with her blanket.

Nobody's watching. Behind a curtain, the staff are busy with the lumbar puncture woman. I tie my dressing-gown belt and slip my Nokia into one of the pockets. Didn't the physio say I could do corridors soon? Gingerly, I find my slippers. They feel like they're the wrong way around, but no matter. I shuffle my way to the top of the ward. It's less effort than picking my feet up with every step.

At the desk there's someone in a tunic, bent over her paperwork. I slip past, keeping close to the wall of the corridor. Here's the main door of the ward. I tug. Nothing. I push. Ah. There's a green button for getting out. It says *Push Once*. The green paint on its dome is worn. Bet it's been pushed a lot more than once. I press it and go through.

I'm outside the ward, just yards away from three lift doors.

The dizziness is back and my legs are uncertain. I hold on to the rail by the lifts for a moment and watch them open and close at intervals. The nearest lift door opens. I peer inside. There's only an old woman in slippers and a tatty blue dressing gown, with grey hair like a Brillo pad. When I smile, I swear she smiles back. I give a little wave, and at once she waves at me.

Oh, shit.

What am I doing here? I'm not dressed to go out, I have no money on me or any idea what to do. I've got nothing except the determined face that I've perfected to convince people I know where I'm going. With this sobering thought, I make my way back to my bed as inconspicuously as possible. Nobody challenges me, not even the nurse pushing a trolley into one of the side rooms. That's good. My little stroll was not a failure but a — what do you call it? Rehearsal, that's it. One day I really will get out of here.

Once back in bed, blood still roars in my ears, in my brain, in every artery and alley of my body. I take some deep breaths and force myself to settle down to my postcards. This card shows a museum. It has a seahorse on it, and Simone's message reads:

It's not all about Abukir and bagpipes.

Abukir. Bagpipes. That's A and B sorted, but what about C, D, and the rest of the alphabet? Or is it another of those codes? *INAAAAB* makes no sense. Must be about Abukir, then. Or rather, as Simone says, not. It's impossible not to think of Abukir. I've lifted some memories out of my head and put them back in so often that I must have changed them along the way, rendering them ragged and useless. But Abukir is exactly the same, as vivid in my mind as ever.

ABUKIR, OCTOBER 1965

Stars sprinkled across the sky. A dead seahorse. Giant shrimp in garlic. Bagpipes on the shore. A breeze across Fouad's hair. Our fingers intertwined.

Abukir is twenty-three kilometres from Alex, but it seemed like the end of the world. In 1965, its main features were a collection of rocks and fishing boats, and a long low restaurant facing the sea. The shellfish at the Zephyrion was legendary, but I wasn't paying attention to the food.

When first introduced to Fouad in 1964 at one of those endless buffet dinners, I'd regarded him merely as an escape from Victor. Much later, I saw him in his tennis garb at the Sporting Club one day with Androulla and Zeinab. Simone had gone for a swim, so she'd missed him, but I was at a table with my friends when Fouad appeared in Ray-Bans, swinging a racquet over his shoulder to tell the world that his session on the court had been effortless. We all swooned, albeit in a most subtle manner. Androulla played it so cool that her chair tipped over backwards, spilling Zeinab's Fanta into our laps.

Tonight Fouad wore a lightweight jacket with the usual cigarette packet bulging from its pocket. I had already been out with him several times in a group of friends. This time it was just the two of us, though that wasn't exactly what I had told Mother and Father. Almost as worrying as the secret police and Nasser's spies was the possibility of my parents hearing I'd been out on my own with a man, and in the middle of nowhere, too.

The Zephyrion gave us a table by the window. Outside, the moon danced on the water while, inexplicably, a Bedouin played bagpipes by the shore. In this romantic setting, we managed to spend our precious time talking about my parents, the Amins, Zouzou, and all the other people we had fled.

'Your father is a man of integrity.' Fouad stubbed out his cigarette. 'Everyone knows that.'

'That's what they say.'

'Zouzou is very vain.'

I agreed. 'Isn't she just?'

'She likes having something over people. Typical case of narcissistic personality disorder.' Fouad hadn't long qualified as a doctor. I'd already noticed his habit of making an impromptu diagnosis wherever we were.

We had finished our shrimp in garlic and rinsed our fingers in bowls of cool water, but that hadn't got rid of the smell.

'Simone is very pretty,' he said.

I was used to hearing that. 'She certainly is.'

'Like you. But different.' Without taking his eyes off me, Fouad moved his lighter and his packet of Cleopatras to a corner of the table. He reached across and held my wrist. The hairs on my suntanned arm stood up as I realised he wasn't going to let it go. I noticed a lion's head ring on his little finger. 'Who do you like best, Cary Grant or Gary Cooper?'

Emboldened by his hand, the darkness of the night, and a large glass of Stella, I dismissed film stars from my mind. 'You, of course.'

'And you are my favourite leading lady.' He kissed my hand. I had no idea he would follow this up with, 'Would you marry me?'

I replied without even considering what Simone might have advised. At that moment, an almighty crash came from the kitchen. I repeated myself to make sure Fouad had heard me. Of course he'd heard. He was grinning widely.

As the waiters had all disappeared, perhaps on account of the crashing sound, we stretched across the table to kiss briefly on the lips. All at once, I felt I was swirling in the middle of those Egyptian songs I heard so often, with their lyrics about eyes and dreams, hearts and souls. He took the gold ring off his little finger and put it on the chain I wore with a cross around my neck. 'There. Will it do for now? Until I speak to your father.'

On our way back to the car, an old man with one white eye proffered a handful of odds and ends from the beach in the hope that we might be interested. I chose a seahorse. Only later did I wonder how it had died.

'It is delicate,' the old man said as he handed me the spiny little creature.

'The young lady will look after it.' Fouad gave him far more money than he had asked for.

The old man thanked Fouad, calling him *ya basha*. Although titles like *Pasha* had been abolished long ago, they were still used to flatter people, especially those who'd never had a title. As we walked back to the car, the man implored Allah to shower us with blessings, keep us healthy, and grant us many children, before he finally shuffled away with his tattered robes and the rest of his wares.

'Trachoma,' Fouad said.

'What?'

'It's a bacterial infection of the eye. That is why he is blind.'

14

ALEXANDRIA, OCTOBER 1966

Tante Zahra was there on my wedding day, belching away as she surveyed the scene to check who was here and who wasn't. She wore a fancier turban than usual, while Tante Magda had a gigantic hat plastered to the side of her face. It was, as Alexandrian weddings went, a modest affair with about 100 of my relatives and a similar number of Fouad's. The crowd included Uncle Selim, Victor, and my friends from El Nasr Girls' College, with Androulla and Zeinab as bridesmaids.

Simone had taken me aside to dispense last minute advice. She had a boyfriend, a university student in her year, but I was pretty sure they hadn't done it yet because she told me, 'If you need to know anything about S-E-X, don't ask me. Ask Zouzou.'

As it happened, Zouzou had already slipped me a paperback called *A Woman Doctor Looks at Love and Life*. The title perplexed me. Of course she looks for love and life. What woman doesn't? It took me a while to realise that it was *AT*, not *FOR*. What would Miss Appleton have thought of me for getting my prepositions so hopelessly muddled? There was an official present too, a silver serving dish from Ralph and herself. Zouzou wore a purple moiré silk dress, with panels on each side that served no purpose other than attracting attention, like a tropical bird. It is strange what details you notice when your nerves are jumping.

Once, I'd have loved nothing more than to have Alicia there too on my big day. Truth was, I hadn't seen her for a while. According to Simone, Alicia was in a rest home. 'She's had a breakdown,' she explained as she fiddled with my chignon. It sounded like a flat tyre on the desert road. Alicia was having strong drugs to make her better, Simone added, compressing her lips. She said no more, and I didn't give Alicia another thought.

There I was, in a fashionable empire-line lace dress made by Mademoiselle Violette and a massive headdress that soared above my head as if it too had been back-combed. I had butterflies in my stomach and Ma Griffe perfume down what I optimistically called my cleavage. When Simone finished with my hair, Rashida declared that I was as beautiful as the moon. She gave me a present of a rosary wrapped in a scrap of cloth and then fiddled with my hem so I couldn't see her face.

Neither Rashida nor the *suffragis* could come to the ceremony as they had to prepare for the reception, but she was here beforehand, when it mattered, and would be there when I returned in the afternoon as a married woman, ready for another blitz of kisses.

An Aspro might calm me down. I looked for Mother and found her standing tearfully by the toaster in the kitchenette. Nervous as I was, I knew I was doing the right thing. What must my thirteen-year-old great-grandmother's wedding day have been like?

In the incense-heavy church, my aunts sat shaded by oversized hats. Mother's was pale blue, the best colour against the Evil Eye. Victor grinned like a monkey with his camera. He sat next to his mother, who was miraculously still with us despite her lethal heart condition.

Over there was all of Fouad's family, including his uncle, also called Fouad. Once tall and imposing, he disappeared deeper into his wheelchair each time I saw him. He'd paid his weekly visit to his Greek mistress when the lift cable broke, sending the car plummeting down four flights at literally breakneck speed. Now all he did was slobber. My Fouad was different. My Fouad was full of life. His hair shone as much as his patent leather shoes, and his face made me melt. To hell with Zouzou's advice. How could I ever cheat on Fouad?

As per Greek Orthodox tradition, the priest blessed the rings. I glanced at my parents. My father, his eyes unusually bright. My mother, her nose in a handkerchief. Tante Georgette and Tante Joséphine weeping steadily, like English rain.

The priest explained that weakness of one half of the couple could be compensated by the strength of the other half. A peculiar little cord between the crowns on our heads gave me the urge to giggle. Was this fragile string that linked our heads capable of binding us together forever? We each held a candle and drank from the same cup. Finally, we had our public kiss. Fouad must have been chain-smoking his Cleopatras.

A hailstorm of rice landed on us as we left the church. I brushed grains off Fouad's sleeve. Off my husband's sleeve. I had to get used to that word.

Tante Zahra burped. 'They won't be lacking babies. Not with all that rice.'

'And not with Fouad being a gynaecologist.' This, along with a filthy laugh, came from Zouzou's husband Ralph.

I glanced at Fouad's hands, the lion's head ring back on his finger. He was just five years older than me, but surely those hands would have explored many women. I hoped everything would be normal *down there*. Was I going to be inadequate as well as inexperienced?

NOW

Zouzou. She liked having something over people. Fouad had said so, along with narcissistic something. Some people disliked her. Maybe it was because of the affair she had with her own cousin. Or was it her brother-in-law? *Maalish!* The world forgave her for it. Besides, it made for excellent gossip at the time.

'Hello, Mrs,' Deirdre says. 'I've brought you a Pepsi for your dry mouth.'

'Thank you very much. I haven't found anyone yet.'

'You can use Google to look for people,' she says before she has to dash off.

I use the searching thing on the iPad that Deirdre showed me. It's called Safari, which makes me feel there's quite a trek ahead of me. I start with people who came to my wedding, but fail to find a single one. Before I know it, it's night-time. My headache is back, but for once the thirst is bearable. Miraculous stuff, that Pepsi. Now that the ward is in semi-darkness, the light from the iPad is shockingly bright. Deirdre didn't say how to dim it, so I fashion a shield from my pillows.

A silhouette rises from the woman mountain's bed. 'You. With that iPad.'

'Sorry.' I add my cardigan to the bank of pillows.

Apparently that's not enough. She grumbles and refuses to lie down till I put the iPad away. If she's going to moan every night, I'm never going to be able to find Simone. In this light, I can barely make out postcards. This one here is, I know, a London bus. It reminds me of the trips we took with my parents, marvelling at Buckingham Palace, the parks, and the pigeons. I already know that the message is:

Fouad is a good man. Be careful. S x

Is it a message about hurting Fouad, or is it something else entirely? Yes, he was a good man. I'd known nothing of men before my wedding day. Apart from a startling statue somewhere in Italy, I had only once seen a man without his clothes on. How strange that seems nowadays, when naked bodies are everywhere. The thought amuses me, and my laughter annoys the woman mountain, which makes it even better.

ALEXANDRIA, JUNE 1953

The door was open. I wandered into my parents' bathroom, hoping to persuade Mother to mend my doll's dress. Father stood at the double handbasin, holding a razor that looked like a penknife. He was concentrating so hard on scraping his face that he must have forgotten he had nothing on. I stood for a moment, frozen in study of his hairy buttocks and equally hairy back before I heard my squeaky voice say, 'Where's *Maman*?'

Father turned around. Half his face was covered in white lather, but that wasn't what caught my attention. A broad furry rug extended all the way from his chest down to his crotch, and there my astonishment stopped. 'She's with Rashida.' He returned to his shave.

Unable to erase what I had seen, I scampered off to report to Simone. 'Papa has no *zizi*! He's only got a bunch of mushrooms.'

15

EGYPT, OCTOBER 1966

Lace being the height of chic, my trousseau was dripping in it. In my nightdress of ivory lace, I looked out of the Cecil Hotel on to the darkening Corniche. The breeze was stronger now. Much too late for the green flash, for my wish that everything would be all right. Fouad and I had not discussed intimate matters, but he was a man, a gynaecologist, and older than me. Those three things meant that he must have had experience.

Subdued light from the lamp in a corner of the room.

A sheet with the scent of rose water.

My husband flushing the toilet then turning the light out.

His kiss, fresh with toothpaste. His pyjama bottoms coming off. Not a mushroom in sight. Just a huge column of flesh like a pillar from Abu Simbel.

My nightdress lifted up by its hem. Gentle kisses on my breasts. Trying to relax, because he told me he loved me.

A cold jelly then a tight entry. He loved me. He said so

again and again. But how could this be lovemaking? I didn't cry, but I didn't smile either.

'God bless you, my little one,' he said.

Was that it, the thing that the whole world made such a fuss about? I eventually fell asleep, a man by my side and an alien wetness between my legs.

The next day, a teeth-jarring journey to Luxor. Carriages from Hungary not quite compatible with the rails made in Egypt. Russian tourists everywhere. Talk of the High Dam.

Darkness outside the train window. Just enough space in the sleeper. Fouad in my bunk. His arms around me. The tube of lubricant jelly again.

I snuggled into his chest and clung on through the shaking.

Fouad wasn't just a smart gynaecologist. He knew about things above the waist, too. The following week, as we waited for a train at Sidi Gaber station, he explained to me how people learn.

'Don't they just study?' I said.

'That's true, *habibti*, my beloved. The question is, what is studying?'

'You go over and over something many times, until you know it by heart and don't need the book anymore.' It was what I'd always done.

He nodded then lit a Boston and described how the brain made new connections. 'Everything you see, hear, or touch—'

'Or smell?'

'Or smell. Every single experience you have makes a subtle change to the brain. It creates new connections between brain cells. Like this.' Holding the cigarette between his lips, he brought his palms together and interlinked his fingers. 'The more you repeat that action or that experience, the stronger the connection becomes.' He squinted at me through the smoke.

'I see. What happens when you stop doing that thing?'

'As time passes, the connections become weaker and then break.' He grinned. 'It is called forgetting.'

'It sounds simple.'

'Well, there are other elements, too, for retrieving memories. Like the hippocampus. It's a small part of the brain shaped like a seahorse.'

'Like the one from Abukir?'

'Just like that. Only smaller.'

ALEXANDRIA, FEBRUARY 1967

I could not fathom how I resembled a broad bean, but Mother found the similarity obvious. 'You'll go on growing until you're married,' she had said. 'Like a *fasoulia*.'

I had been married over three months, and we had climbed the two flights of increasingly rickety stairs up to Mademoiselle Violette's workshop. Although I had plenty of clothes, our little dressmaker had few clients these days, and Mother couldn't resist a charity case. So there I stood in front of the cheval mirror that had lost even more of its silvering.

Simone had come into town with us because she wanted a lift to the bank, and now she was waiting, I supposed, until the time of her appointment. That was all she told me. My sister was even less open these days than she used to be.

'Now that you've stopped growing,' Mother said, 'you could use a nice, new cocktail dress.'

'Tout à fait, tout à fait.' Whatever Mother said, Mademoi-

selle Violette agreed. She'd already cut the red fabric at a table that was laughably high for her.

In the mirror, I saw Simone leafing through an ancient magazine. Meanwhile, Mademoiselle Violette knelt on the floor beside me with a collection of pins gripped between her lips. 'Ruby is definitely your colour,' she said, despite the pins in her mouth.

Before I knew it, I was covered in pieces of blood-red cloth. The fabric felt silky smooth if I ignored the pins.

'A little snip here, another snip there,' Mademoiselle Violette said as scraps dropped on to the floor. '*Et voilà!*' I didn't think there could possibly be room for yet another pin, but Mademoiselle Violette found a way to slide in three more.

'V-neck. Don't you agree?' she continued.

From the threadbare armchair, Mother nodded approval. No wonder I possessed not a single decolleté dress.

I checked Simone's reflection. She was picking at her cuticles. From this angle, I could swear she had boobs.

'The V elongates the neck.' Mademoiselle Violette folded the neckline and added a pin on each side. '*Comme ça.* You see? And the hem, perhaps there.' Crouching down, she festooned the loose end of the dress with metalwork at about mid-calf.

'Can you make it a touch shorter? We're in 1967, you know.' I tried to catch Simone's eye. My sister wouldn't have put up with this without a full-scale war.

I swear Mother and Mademoiselle Violette sighed simultaneously. 'Nice girls don't go around with these ridiculous short skirts,' Mother said.

'I'm sick and tired of being a nice girl.' Wouldn't it have been better to make a minidress and send the spare fabric to charity? Besides, I was a married woman now. Not a girl.

'*Mais* Nadia, you hardly want to look like one of those degenerates,' Mother said.

'I don't want to look like a nun on her day off, either.'

With the reservoir of pins still squeezed between her lips, Mademoiselle Violette took ages shortening the hem, after which it was, give or take a millimetre, exactly where it had been before. 'In any case,' she said when she stood up, 'you can decide at the final fitting.'

It would still end up being someone else's decision, I knew. Who was I? Not my own person, that was sure. There were always others to please. Such was the fate of a nice Arab girl. And why wasn't Simone backing me up as she once used to?

'Nadia is miles away,' Mother said.

'Not at all. I'm hanging on every word.' I had no idea what they were talking about.

'Mademoiselle Violette suggests next Monday at four.'

'Fine,' I said.

Simone made to get up.

I shot her a glance. 'Meet you later at the Sporting?'

'Okay. I'll try not to be late.'

She was being lofty and mysterious again, all for no reason. As she walked past Mademoiselle Violette's dilapidated mirror, head held high, I saw. It wasn't my imagination. She'd had breast surgery. But when? Perhaps she'd sneaked off to some clinic in Cairo when she was meant to be in Marsa Matrouh with her friends.

Simone pushed a strand of hair off her face and ordered a Sinalco from the waiter. 'Don't stare.'

'Sorry. Do they hurt?' I asked.

'Do what hurt?'

'Your bosoms. From the boob job.'

'I didn't have a boob job.'

'Then what?' Everyone knew exercises and creams didn't work.

'Just a new bra.' Simone dropped a straw into her fizzy drink, leaving the paper wrapper in a concertina on the table.

I studied her but read nothing. The wintry sun was bright enough to justify sunglasses, at least if you were Simone. She smoothed out the paper tube from the straw before folding it up again. 'Do you suppose you'll spend the rest of your life in Alex?' she asked.

I pulled a face. 'We might move to Cairo at some point. If Fouad gets a job there.'

'Open your eyes, *ya ukhti*. There are many other places.' She leaned forward and lowered her voice. 'Where they treat women a lot better.'

I glanced at the table next to ours and at the table beyond that. Ladies enjoyed themselves, laughing, probably at the same old jokes, repeating aged gossip with a little additional embroidery, but *maalish!* Even in today's more egalitarian times, other people looked after the house and the children, freeing the women to play bridge or pass the time however they pleased.

'Such as where?' I was perplexed.

Simone's sigh suggested I was an imbecile. 'There's Lebanon, Canada, England, South Africa, the United States, France, and Australia. People have left Egypt to go to all those places, and many others besides. Especially if they speak English or French.'

'I suppose.' None of the countries sounded as nice as here.

She gave me the eyebrow above the rim of her sunglasses. 'Where's your sense of adventure, Madame Wissa?'

I shrugged. Of course, what I should have done was ask *What about you?* Before I knew it, she was gone. I was left contemplating an empty Sinalco bottle and a little strip of wrinkled paper.

NOW

I drain my jug of water. Simone never said what she was doing at the bank. Here's another thing. Mademoiselle Violette had offered everyone coffee, but Simone hadn't wanted any.

As I replay that afternoon in my muzzy head, my brain connections practically fizz. How is it that I remember some things only now, when, according to what Fouad taught me, the brain cells must have been connected all along?

I'd never thought of it before, but it's obvious now. Simone was pregnant! The woman mountain stares at me because I exclaim despite myself.

Ignoring her, I open the iPad and jab the screen like someone demented as I go back to the community groups I joined on Facebook and post messages asking if anyone knows Simone Khoury, now aged seventy-two, who used to live in Alex and go to El Nasr Girls' School followed by university. Too bad I have no photo to include. Still, it's got to be easier to find my sister than it was before the internet.

Woman mountain rises, her blanket still around her like a cape. Her pale face is as full as the moon, and not in a good way, as Rashida used to think of the moon. 'Having trouble?' she asks.

'No.' I feel myself blush. I couldn't have found the words to explain anyway.

Brainwave! I will simply Google *Simone Khoury*.

Oh. There are so many. I decide to concentrate on images. Sweat breaks out on the back of my neck as I search the pictures. Some of the people aren't even called Khoury and some aren't even women, as if Google deliberately wants to derail me. Still, I study each face, hoping the next one will be Simone. I'm sure she's not far. Didn't she tell us herself back then that she was going to Europe?

16

ALEXANDRIA, MARCH 1967

'I'm going to spend some time studying in Europe,' Simone said at lunch at our parents'.

She didn't ask what I wanted her to bring me back from her travels. Since studying literature at Alex University, she had become even more detached. Secretive, I might have said.

I bit into another pickle and aimed to sound nonchalant. 'When will you be back?'

'Soon, soon.' It was the same tone *Mugamma'* officials used when stalling, instructing you to return tomorrow for your exit visa, and the day after, ad infinitum.

'We'll miss you at Montazah.'

'I'll miss Montazah,' she said.

She didn't say she'd miss me. That should have told me, loud and clear, that our relationship had changed.

. . .

We got occasional postcards but no sign of when she might be returning. The Six Day War broke out that summer, and I hardly blamed Simone for keeping away. Although the atmosphere had taken a solemn turn, people still went to Montazah, played *tawlah* in the daytime, and partied at night. In between times there was always the simple joy of recounting a story in meticulous detail, never mind if it had been told hundreds of times before or if most of the elements had been made up.

Ralph was showing his age, but Zouzou paraded in a new swimsuit of a green so bright that it pierced the eyes, Mother declared, just as surely as if it had been made from metal kebab skewers. She had worn a turquoise costume the previous day, with its front slashed right down to *here* – Mother pointed at her navel – and held together with a plastic clip of unparalleled tackiness. And earrings the size of chandeliers! '*Très vulgaire*.' Be that as it may, Zouzou's outfits were much admired by other people's husbands.

Many Alexandrians disappeared in the 1960s. Some left to live elsewhere, as Simone had said, even if they had never known any other country but Egypt. Madame Amin had braved another plane journey and moved to her daughter's in Chicago, but they didn't all leave for good. Some came back, declaring that there was no place on earth like Alexandria, just as I had known all along.

I'd been married over six months and Fouad worked long hours, so I was often on my own at Montazah. Uncle Selim complained that it had been ten years since he'd last had proper English brogues. He lounged in a deckchair next to a gentleman I didn't know and made *tsk tsk* noises in the direction of his feet. '*Maalish*,' his companion said.

After the June war, the Egyptian economy got worse, though people only referred to politics obliquely. More often, they shook their heads before concluding that a beer was in order. Whisky was for parties and still widely available, though frankly – and here voices would be lowered – we were all heading for hell in a *hantour* exactly as Madame Amin had predicted.

Judging it safe to make a joke, the man with the eyepatch leaned forward in his deckchair and said, 'You know the military defeat was all because of the Russians?' He was taking a risk even referring to it as a defeat.

'How?'

'I will tell you,' he continued. 'The Russians gave Egypt the most excellent tactical advice: keep retreating until the enemy gets lost in the snowstorms.' With that, he slapped his hairy thigh and his audience laughed, though not too raucously. Nasser's socialism went hand in hand with paranoia, and we all knew about spies, informers, and the dreaded secret police, called the *Mabaheth*. Despite doing nothing wrong, ordinary citizens could be harassed and interrogated. There might be late-night phone calls or a midnight summons to go to *Mabaheth* headquarters. Most were allowed home after interrogation, though many, we heard, had been beaten or worse. A few were never seen again.

There were whispers that an army general had suicided himself, as reports had it. Abdel Hakim Amer was a field marshal who had been hopelessly unprepared for the June war. Rumours like these reminded us all why the police and the military were so feared.

The secret police were not that bad, according to Zouzou, whose apartment overlooked *Mabaheth* HQ. 'The other night, so many lovely people we knew went in and out. Georges and Monique arrived first then the Tawils and the Awads. And Yakis, of course. You must know Yakis. Don't you know Yakis?

Chérie, everyone knows Yakis. It was exactly like a cocktail party.'

'Aren't you afraid they might interrogate you?' someone asked Zouzou.

'Of course not. I'm far too dumb to be trusted with secrets.'

Sometimes conversation at the beach turned to methods of smuggling money out. People had tried false-bottomed suitcases ('*Ayoo!* How stupid!') and even a fake plaster cast on a limb. In at least one instance, the person had planted misinformation and got money out thereafter via the simplest of methods, according to the man with the eyepatch. Everyone pressed him to say more.

'*Mes chers,* I couldn't possibly tell.'

While many foreigners had left, a handful of others had arrived, including an Austrian contingent and a batty Scottish woman who reeked of the cats she rescued. Zouzou introduced everyone and told them which films they should see at the Rialto or the Amir. A woman in a wide-brimmed hat complained of gyppy tummy. I informed her that boiled rice stopped the trots even more reliably than Entero-Vioform tablets.

By October, a Belgian attaché had arrived in town. A tall man with a Donovan cap and binoculars, Alain was often a little apart, wandering under the trees behind the cabins where people parked their cars, or else gazing out to sea, especially in the early evening.

He was down by the rocks at the water's edge when I returned from a dip. 'I'm birdwatching,' he said, though I hadn't asked. He pointed to a distant speck that only he could see and gave it a fancy name that I promptly forgot. He never said much about Belgium, but he did talk about birds, and the only time I saw him without cap and binoculars was when he went for a swim.

There was no point in leaving the beach too early. Fouad wouldn't be home for hours. Once dried, I took myself under the trees with my book. I was still learning Spanish with the help of a lady from the consulate. Each time I looked up from my page and stared out to sea, I remembered that Cyprus was straight out there. I missed Simone. She would be home soon, I told myself, despite the lack of evidence for it. Not that long ago, I'd have spent time with Simone or my friends from El Nasr Girls' College, but Androulla was at university and Zeinab had moved to Cairo with her husband. *Howa kida*. That was how it was.

NOW

What had we discussed at Montazah, apart from cures for the runs and getting currency out? Did people smuggle money late at night after the *sawahel* and their camels had finished their patrol? In bricks hollowed out and shipped to Saudi, possibly. Something along those lines comes back to me. And who were the men who had sat for so long with Uncle Selim, doing nothing much, not even reading the newspapers that lay on their laps? There was his notebook, too. It had vanished along with its columns of words and numbers. The figures might have been sums of money. I don't know.

I massage my aching temples and resume my Google search. Not one of the pictures resembles Simone, even allowing for her to have aged fifty years.

Wait. I'd heard something that afternoon on the Corniche long ago, when Uncle Selim had been walking with the woman in yellow, the one Mother had called a *poupoule*. Despite my parents hastily dragging me away, a snippet of conversation drifts back. Selim reminded the woman that she was supposed to give him the money. That was it. And the woman had replied that it was her work, not his. *I'm the one who sweats and grinds.* Or words along those lines. I assumed that she'd been preparing coffee beans, as Rashida once showed me in the kitchenette with the ancient brass grinder that protested when you turned the handle. Coffee at Mademoiselle Violette's, of course, is how I now know Simone was pregnant. Now, who could have been the father? Even though I rack my brains, I can't recall meeting many of her friends, let alone a boyfriend. I can only think of Selim, but that doesn't feel right. It's no use. The harder I think, the more I lose myself in the past.

ALEXANDRIA, SEPTEMBER 1967

It was the second time in ten minutes that Mother had looked up from her *petit point* and asked, 'What is Fouad doing all this time?'

'Stitching up hymens, *ya mama*.' I added another pinch of cumin to the bean soup on the hob. In reality, my husband was still a junior surgeon learning his trade.

Mother took an elaborate look at her watch. 'At this hour?'

Why couldn't she go home and take her embroidery with her? 'Well,' I replied. 'As it's Tuesday, it must be Lina in Rushdy. Or is it Sonya in Ramleh? I've forgotten his rota of mistresses. Maybe Lina is Wednesday?'

'*Yiy!* Not even in jest,' Mother replied. 'You've not been married a year.'

People sometimes said that gynaecologists turned their profession into a hobby, but my husband, I knew, was most definitely not running around. Fouad was often late, hungry, and tired, but he always came back, invigorated by entering the door of our apartment in the Greek Quarter. Whether he'd been at the hospital or away at a conference, our passion only grew with time. I wanted him every bit as much as two years ago when he'd sauntered off the tennis court at the Sporting Club and into my life.

If marriage wasn't always what I had expected, *maalish!* I loved Fouad so much. I loved his head on the pillow, touching mine. I loved all his clothes hanging in the wardrobe, redolent of the Cleopatras he chain-smoked, and his toiletries lined up in the bathroom next to mine. All of it enchanted me: the shaving brush, the razor, the spare Gillette blue blades in the cupboard, and the small pair of scissors with which he trimmed the hairs up his nostrils when he thought I wasn't looking.

Mother finally rolled up her canvas and took herself home after kissing me goodbye. I arranged one of those nets over the bean soup to keep the flies off, then, in case Fouad was home soon, I applied pale pink lipstick and straightened the throw cushions on our sofa. I wasn't obliged to cook for him, wear make-up, or keep a nice home. I did it all of my own free will. If Simone were here, she might have argued with me, as she often did, but I now had my husband, my own home, my own life.

Women's lib was alive and well. Since 1956, Egyptian women could vote, and even stand for public office if their husbands agreed. Imagine that! Simone had not thought that enough. 'In the West, you only have S-E-X when you want to, and with whom you want,' she'd said over a Sinalco at the Sporting. 'Here, it is a luxury to sleep with the person you really want.' I didn't ask what she meant.

The women's movement hadn't caught on with everyone.

'You want *lib*? Here,' a podgy lawyer told me at a party as he draped a sweaty paw around me and offered me a bowl of *lib*, the seeds vendors sell on the Corniche. I pulled away, but that didn't stop the man laughing at his own wit and distributing halitosis.

Our apartment was perfect for Fouad and me, with the second bedroom still unfurnished. Back in the living room, I poked a stray wodge of kapok into one of the cushions and repaired it with a running stitch. A bit like repairing women *down there*. That was going to make Fouad one of the richest and most sought-after specialists in town. If people could afford the operation, that is. The cost of living kept soaring, and there was little sign of the good times expected under Nasser. Our grocer ran out of coins again today, and gave me change in the form of matches. We all knew the country was poor. It was only thanks to the Soviets that the Aswan Dam was being built. The dam was vital, said the government, as it would enable crops to be grown all year round.

Still, virginity remained highly prized in Egypt, almost as much as crops, and there would be always be people willing to pay for it. As Zouzou always said, you shouldn't ever do it before you got married. But, after you got married, you could do it with anyone you liked, including your own brother-in-law.

ALEXANDRIA, OCTOBER 1967

Father Christmas went to hell sooner than I'd expected, and he didn't use a *hantour* to get there.

Uncle Selim had a boyfriend, and the boyfriend was a policeman. That was all I knew at first. Not a high-ranking policeman, apparently. Opinion was divided as to whether or not that was a good thing.

'*Chérie*, if he is an important man, it will be hushed up,' Zouzou said. On the other hand, more people would be likely to know about the liaison. And to care. Had he been a humble traffic cop, nobody would have batted an eyelid. It was a common situation, after all. A straight man, often happily married, could support his entire family by being a rich old man's concubine.

I imagined my favourite *shaweesh*, the policeman who presided over the crossing at the top of our hill in his white helmet and long white cuffs. Try as I might, it was hard to picture him with his *zizi* sticking out of his uniform, let alone while handling someone else's.

Nobody was meant to die on a pleasant autumn afternoon at the beach, yet that was exactly what Selim did, and without warning, when I was right there, on my way back to the cabin from a walk along the shore. The immediate problem was what to do with the body. The second challenge was to pretend he had died at home. In the midst of all this, I noticed that the policeman in question had zipped himself up and evaporated from the scene.

Selim's body was prepared for the journey back to his apartment. First, the cigarette was extinguished, then two men struggled to get his jacket on. Someone's *suffragi*, who'd been busy rinsing plates, located Selim's panama and placed it at a jaunty angle to cover his eyes. Someone else thought to drape his worry beads on his hand and a *Journal d'Egypte* over his lap as if he'd dozed off over his paper. Looking vaguely alive once propped up in a car, Selim was then driven past the sentries at Montazah back to his home, at which point the doctor was called and informed he had died.

I wondered what possible fun the men could have been

having if only their *zizi*s were out. Surely homosexuals had other erogenous zones? I'd have asked Simone, but she was still away. All the news I'd had in the past three weeks was a postcard from Geneva.

NOW

Selim had beads of sweat around his mouth. And someone had wrung their hands behind a cabin. But who? I will myself to visualise more, and fail.

One of the patients sits in a chair, knitting. The woman mountain is lying down again. She has had some kind of procedure, on her bladder judging from the bag hooked on to her bed at the end. The liquid in the bag is as dark as whisky. Dehydration, I expect.

Now the floor is being cleaned with a method involving minimum liquid and maximum noise. How very different from the way floors used to be washed. With the hem of his *galabeyya* gripped between his teeth, Abdou would get down on his hands and knees, sloshing litres of soapy water on to the marble tiles. He scrubbed with a brush before rinsing it with another deluge of water that was on a par with a Nile flood. By contrast, the ward cleaner's contraption massages the floor in a circular motion that makes my head spin to look. The giddiness is so bad that I must cling on to the bedframe. Gingerly, I examine another postcard. It's a pretty clock made of flowers. Geneva once again, though it's not posted from there.

Don't worry about US.

I can't tell if it's capitals or little letters. It could be the United States, Uncle Selim, or us, as in two or more people. *Uncle Selim is. Be careful at Montazah.* That's what her other messages said. What had happened to his notebook when he died? Had I seen it in the other man's hand that day?

As if the machine weren't enough, the cleaner decides to chat at full volume with the patient who's knitting, so as to be heard above the din.

Next, the cleaner weaves his machine around between the beds, the furniture, and the woman mountain's bag full of whisky. A sick feeling rises up my chest. I've learnt what whisky can do when you're not used to it. For years afterwards, I couldn't bear the smell of the stuff.

ALEXANDRIA, NOVEMBER 1967

Arguing with Fouad was utterly senseless, I realised even at the time. Yet I couldn't help myself. I shouldn't have mentioned that another family's *suffragi* had helped fold Uncle Selim's corpse into the car. Later, I wondered how differently things might have turned out had my account been less precise.

Fouad had just got in from work and lit a cigarette. Subsiding into the armchair, he asked, 'So whose *suffragi* was it?'

'I'm not sure. Perhaps the Maggars'.'

He blew smoke sideways out of his mouth. 'Since when do the Maggars have a cabin at Montazah?'

'I don't know, but I often see them there.'

'Ah. But seeing them there is not the same as them having a

cabin. If they don't have a cabin, their *suffragi* wouldn't be there, would he? Do they have a cabin or not?'

'I don't know. Am I in property rental now?'

'Well, you seem very sure of your facts.'

'I'm not. I'm saying that he could have been their *suffragi*.'

'Ha,' he said triumphantly as he got up to pour himself an *arak*.

'You're so arrogant,' I snapped. Big mistake. He was grumpy only because he was tired. The poor man even had to go back to the hospital tonight. I'd have done better to assume he'd had a bad day and just said, *Maalish, ya gozi, whatever you say, beloved husband, light of my eyes*, or any other subservient claptrap.

What annoyed Fouad most was that the cook had heard our raised voices, or, more specifically, mine. Fouad retreated to the bedroom, and, instead of leaving well alone, I followed.

'How could you humiliate me in front of him?' he barked once he'd shut the door.

'I never humiliated you. You're being unreasonable.'

Simone used to speak her mind with Father when she was just a child, while it seemed that I, a grown woman, couldn't even have a discussion with my husband. I flounced out of the room, calling him *ibn el kalb* as I left. It was an atrocious insult, and I didn't even mean it. Fouad was hardly the worst husband and far from being the son of a dog.

I grabbed a bottle of whisky off the bar in our living room and stormed out of the apartment.

17

MONTAZAH BEACH, ALEXANDRIA, NOVEMBER 1967

Hands shaking, I shoved the sticky back door open. I walked through the cabin, pushed open the front door, and gazed towards the sea. I had missed the green flash on the horizon by some time.

Most of the people had already gone home. One of our neighbours was folding away the last of his chairs. He greeted me with a quizzical look and asked if I was all right.

'I'm fine, thanks be to Allah.'

I was far from fine, but no matter. I had a bottle of whisky for company and time to reflect. I found a tumbler from the cupboard, knocking over a can of Flit and stubbing my toe on the Butagaz cylinder in the process. After evicting a spider from the glass, I poured myself a lavish measure. Then I installed myself on a cushion on the outside ledge facing the sea and let the whisky hit the back of my throat.

I'd done nothing wrong. Maybe I had raised my voice a

fraction, but I hadn't humiliated Fouad. Couldn't I occasionally up my volume when I was pointing out to my own husband something that he was too slow to appreciate? This phrase pleased me so much that I repeated it aloud even if it wasn't clear what, if anything, Fouad had been too slow to appreciate. *Maalish!* It was time I was allowed to express my own opinion. To be myself.

Fouad was older and more educated than me, but that didn't mean he was always right. It seemed to me that the whole world was more respected, more listened to, than I was. The whole of the male world, certainly. Poor me, never allowed to say a word in contradiction of anyone. I had to be seen and not heard, like a little girl. Was that ever going to end? I slipped off my sandals and took another mouthful of whisky to consider this.

The *sawahel* passed. Camel hooves make hardly any sound on sand, but voices carry across the beach. Now the night was deep navy. Fouad hadn't come looking for me, but I wasn't afraid. If I wanted to, I could stay here all night, maybe write poetry or go for a swim by moonlight. I had never done either of those in my life, but no matter. I could do anything, as my new friend Johnnie Walker told me. I refilled my glass.

It was turning chilly on the ledge. I covered my legs with one of the spare cushions, which wasn't entirely effective. No point in going home yet. Fouad probably wouldn't be there anyway. He'd already said he had to go back to the hospital to help his boss. Besides, I needed to think. Not that I was going to think about Fouad, the bastard. Did he not even consider the fact that he was telling me off within earshot of our cook? I slugged some more whisky. It went down more easily now.

He thought he was so superior. Doctors lorded it over everyone else, especially nurses, I had no doubt. At the moment, I could only remember one nurse, the one who'd been there when I had my diaphragm fitted. A hideous experience, full of indignity and talcum powder. I wriggled on the concrete seat in recollection. A necessary thing, however, if we were to postpone having babies until we were ready, which was to say until Fouad was ready. I found it hard to assess my own views on the subject, given that Fouad's career was all-important. Even though the rubber contraption was far bigger than I'd once imagined it would be, I'd become used to it and to the spermicide cream with a smell so reminiscent of a chemical plant near Nouzha airport. It became second nature to apply two lines of the stuff on the dome before spreading it out evenly with my fingers. Then there was the insertion up to an hour before conjugal activity, as the doctor had called it. Initially painful, the process was now merely awkward. More than once, the slippery thing had sprung out of my hand to skitter across the bathroom floor and flop behind the toilet bowl like a dead frog. However, it was worth it for our precious moments of intimacy that I had begun to love. Although as of this evening, I reminded myself, I hated Fouad.

I had never drunk neat whisky before. It scalded my throat with every gulp and had failed to keep me warm after all. Wasn't there a cardigan in the car? And somewhere in the cabin there must be candles or an oil lamp. By the feeble light of the overhead bulb, I located a hurricane lamp and a dented-but-dry box of matches.

Clutching the lamp in one hand and the doorframe in the other for support, I stepped out of the cabin into the night. It was pitch black under the pines. Not pines. Casuarinas. I swung the lamp around to appraise my surroundings. Should have parked closer. I let go of the safety of the doorframe to negotiate my way. The cool sand was littered with needles from the trees. Stooping to extract them from between my toes, I lurched sideways and let go of the lamp. It promptly went out. With the next step, I stumbled and fell.

'Hello?'

I recognised the voice before I saw the cone of light.

'Are you all right?' He touched my arm. The Belgian attaché. Alain, his name was. 'Let me help you up, Nadia.'

With the aid of his torch, he retrieved my lamp and steered me back to the cabin. I would not have got far without him.

'Would you like a whisky?' I asked when we reached the door. It seemed merely hospitable to offer a drink. I never asked what he was doing at Montazah at such a late hour with his Donovan cap and a pair of binoculars. Weren't birds already asleep with their heads under their wings?

He found another glass and wiped it on his shirt. We sat with our whiskies on the ledge at the front, listening to the waves.

'You're cold,' he remarked as he put an arm around me. The words struck me as bad Hollywood dialogue, even if I was actually cold.

He got up, motioning me to stay quietly where I was. He had seen a *ghafeer*. *Ghafeers* were employed to ensure nobody stayed overnight, a regulation that could be relaxed by the exchange of a few coins. 'The man has gone,' he said when he returned to the cabin.

'Another drink?' My voice was husky. I didn't use his name. To me, he was just the Belgian attaché.

I can't remember what he said or how much more we drank before he placed his hand on my thigh and inched up beneath my skirt. Nor have I any idea how we found ourselves — only moments later, surely — fused together for several minutes or for as long as it took, that thing which, for the first time in my life, was not with my husband. We used the swimming towels afterwards and he held me close, calling me

Nadia over and over again. Through my drunken haze, I felt both powerful and guilty.

It was going to be a problem getting home after all the alcohol, but he said he would drive me back in my own car. 'After that, I can easily get home to Bulkeley. Tomorrow my wife can bring me back for my car.'

So the Belgian attaché was married too. What had we done?

It was after midnight, and Fouad had yet to return. My head thudded, my tongue was raw, and my mouth had become a felt factory. The bathroom wall began to spin, making a zigzag pattern of the black and white tiles. I needed Aspro, but first this.

It took a few moments to locate the equipment in the bathroom cupboard. I had no idea whether a *lavement* was an effective contraceptive, but what else did I have at this stage? Better hurry. Unless he had a dire emergency, Fouad could be back any minute.

There. The rubber tubing was connected and the reservoir filled with warm water. Now all I had to do was squat in the bathtub with the perforated nozzle poked up inside me and let the *lavement* do its work. The *Inglizi* call it a *douche*. I had discovered this years ago, in front of a group of nice English girls from school, one of them my friend Catherine from Tunbridge Wells and some others several years above us. It being the norm to mix one's languages, I'd gaily announced after sports that I would have a douche. The nice English girls emitted a collective gasp.

All became clear when a giggling sixth-former told me that a douche was not a shower as it was in French. At the age of ten, I did not quite grasp what a female hygiene procedure was, though the general idea seemed to be a warm lathering like the one Father's Ford got every week, only on the inside.

Leaning against the bathroom wall for support, I watched the liquid gush out of me and down the plughole, hopefully taking all the treacherous sperm with it. Then I dried myself and put the equipment away. As an afterthought, I squeezed a dollop of spermicide cream on to two fingers and inserted them as high as I could before rinsing my hands of the tell-tale smell and double-checking the bathroom for any traces of evidence.

Once in bed, I lay on my side facing away from Fouad's bed and forced myself to breathe slowly and deeply despite my racing pulse and the mess of emotions whirling round my head. I mustn't give him the chance to smell spermicide or whisky when he came home. If I pretended to sleep, I might eventually nod off, leaving conversation and everything else for another day.

NOW

Unbidden, a missing memory of Simone flashes up. Where had that one been hiding?

It was raining, that time when I went to lunch at my parents. Fish. It might have been a Friday, then. Abdou rarely complained of anything, but that day he had jaw ache. Ibrahim replied by slurping his gums cheerfully and advising him to have all his teeth out, as he'd done years ago.

After Abdou had descended back to the kitchen, we discussed getting him a dental appointment.

'Why not a doctor's appointment?' Mother said. 'After all, we don't know if it's his teeth or something else like a *sinusite*.'

'I could look at his mouth,' Father offered.

'*Mais non, chéri.* As if poor Abdou would want you to fill his mouth with the contents of your toolkit!'

Simone had been unusually quiet. I had sensed that she was out of sorts even before she wiped her lips on her napkin and excused herself without finishing her mango.

When I went to the loo later, I heard water running from the bathroom next door. Simone was shuffling around in there. Then I saw her exit, her face paler than I ever remember. I'm pretty sure I glimpsed a pinkish stain in the bath, which I assumed meant she had had the curse. But what if she didn't?

ALEXANDRIA, DECEMBER 1967

The art deco interior of Pastroudis dripped elegance and, whether lunching or sipping coffee, I invariably felt sophisticated here. Ladies talked with their hands and made a point of checking out everyone else, as did men, especially the kind who couldn't bear not to be the centre of attention. They shook hands ostentatiously, kissed each other on both cheeks, and slurped their coffee with exaggerated gestures while they gawped at everyone.

Pastroudis was the place where many things began, notably affairs and rumours, but today I was here to end something. I couldn't pretend the baby was Fouad's. For one thing, I used a diaphragm religiously at home. For another, the Belgian attaché didn't look one bit like my husband. Here, then, I was to meet Omar, on the basis that staying in plain sight can be less conspicuous. All the same, I hoped to see nobody who knew Fouad or me. When a waiter in a *galabeyya* approached, I ordered one coffee, *mazboot.* He bowed and swanned off before returning with a tiny cup and the customary glass of iced water on a tin tray.

When was Omar going to show up? I didn't want coffee. That morning I'd felt particularly bilious, though nothing had come up. Did nausea mean it was a girl, as people said it did? No, I mustn't think like that. It wasn't a proper baby yet.

Eventually he appeared, this contact of Zouzou's who was allegedly discretion itself. Omar was about forty-five with thinning hair and a prominent belly. It proved impossible to avoid chit-chat. Even before he installed himself at the table, he vowed on the Prophet that I was as beautiful as jasmine.

'Thank you.'

He grinned, showing crocodile teeth, too many for a human mouth. 'Business later, eh?' His nostrils flared, and a network of small veins on the side of his nose fanned out like the Nile delta.

'Fine,' I said, meaning the opposite.

'I hear you have a sister as well.'

'Do you know her?'

He stared at the wood panelling for inspiration before answering. 'Me? No, I don't think I do. So you need some help?' He assured me that, whatever I said, it would be safe with him. '*Madame, je suis un tombeau.*' He would be as silent as a tomb. That was reassuring. 'My lips are sealed,' he added as he passed a finger over his mouth. Although he wasn't a doctor, he told me he could have been. 'I have practically taken za Hibbocratic Oath.' He chuckled and spread out his fingers.

I'd rehearsed. 'My husband and I are not in a position to become parents at this stage of his career. It may sound wrong, but I don't even want to tell him about my condition. He would be too upset as he is doing some very important exams soon. Imminently, in fact.'

I felt myself blush as Omar leaned back in the chair and regarded me. He explained that it wasn't such a terrible thing, really. People did it all the time. 'It is za Alexandrian way.' He spread his hands again.

I asked if it was possible to see a woman doctor, because she would understand better, but, as I suspected, Omar shook his head. Fouad often mentioned that gynaecology lacked females, which always puzzled me, as I'd thought that more of them would want to advance women's health as well as their pitifully low status in society. Instead, Omar suggested a doctor he knew in Cairo, one who would not know Fouad. 'But really, you don't need za doctor for zis.'

I dreaded the thought of a backstreet operator wielding a barbaric metal spike.

'There are many ways,' Omar continued. 'It can be done wiz a plant.'

I didn't want to die with a stalk of *molokheyya* sticking out of me either. 'I prefer to see a doctor. I'll see the one in Cairo.'

'*Tayyeb*, okay. I will fix that for you.' I would have to meet him again on Monday evening, he told me.

'Do you know much it will cost?'

He mentioned a figure then waved it away with his hand. 'No money yet.'

'Please tell me when.'

'Not everything needs money.' Omar's crocodile teeth made another menacing appearance. 'Remember, Monday.'

18

ALEXANDRIA, DECEMBER 1967

My stomach churned constantly, and I wasn't sure it was just my condition. I was all at sea without Simone. Why wasn't she here to help me? Of course, my sister would hardly have been stupid enough to get pregnant, but she would have had an opinion all the same.

I saw Omar again the following Monday. Instead of meeting me inside Pastroudis, he was pacing the pavement a few metres away. 'Good news.' He approached and stood too close. 'I have za abbointment.'

'When is it?'

'Let me see.' He made a show of patting all his pockets. Hadn't he brought the appointment details with him? His plan soon became clear when he gestured with his thumb. 'My apartment is just in San Saba.'

A fountain of acid surged up my gullet. 'Is it?'

'Yes. It is where I left the paper with the abbointment.' He displayed his entire collection of crooked little teeth. 'Unfortunately.'

'I'll wait here. Or in Pastroudis.'

He put a hand on my arm. 'But we are nearer my apartment.'

Leave me alone, you gargoyle, I shouted inside my head. I needed that appointment, so I forced myself to accept his proffered arm without making a scene.

'Zis is my building.'

'I'll wait here. I have the payment for you.'

He waved this unseemly thought away, though we both knew that he would take my money in the end. *'La', la'*. It's not like that. I have money. But in my life there is not enough beauty.' He fixed me with his eyes and sighed.

I'd done it the once with the wrong person, and now it seemed I had to do it again to undo the damage. 'I'll wait here,' I repeated.

'I have *amar el deen*,' he wheedled.

The mere thought of apricot paste brought the acid feeling back with a vengeance. 'Very kind, but no thank you.'

He went inside, and I tried not to look like a *sharmouta* as I waited on the pavement. He was gone some time, during which several cars slowed down and honked. I put on a totally superfluous pair of sunglasses and made a detailed study of the stonework on the nearest building. Feigning interest in the niceties of construction, I stroked the mortar and admired the colour and texture of the stones. Where the hell was the man?

Eventually Omar emerged with a scrap of lined paper that he must have folded and refolded many times. The appointment was in ten days. I read that much before handing over the envelope containing the cash I'd drawn from the bank.

I wasn't quick enough. Before I could make my escape, he

gave me a kiss on the cheek and squeezed my bottom, right there in San Saba street.

NOW

Pregnant and humiliated. I bite my lip at the memory. What else had Omar said? A sort of proverb, perhaps. What do I really recall? Maybe this is one of the memories I've altered, just by shuffling through them too often.

Simone had been pregnant, even if I'd always thought her too smart for that. Maybe Victor has photos of her or knows something. I can't bear the thought of contacting him, so it's something of a relief that the wi-fi won't oblige.

There's moaning from a side room. A phone rings. I see the Laura Ashley doctor leaning against the nurses' station in electric-blue Crocs that give feet all the elegance of bags of cement. She's on the phone. Probably hatching a plan to transfer me to one of those care homes. The nurses said so.

My mouth is too dry for thinking. I reach for what's left of my water.

Blood is thicker than water. That's what Omar had said! It's a – what's the word? Motto? Slogan? Long ago, I read a book filled with things like this, and now I can't figure out if it's important.

ALEXANDRIA, DECEMBER 1967

Nausea hit me like a cup of vinegar as soon as I arrived. My parents' salon was filled with flowers. Worse, people milled around, talking with their hands while their elbows stuck out at precisely the right height to whack me in my tender breasts.

It was my parents' pre-Christmas lunch, with all the aunts, uncles, and cousins of assorted ages. Here was Tante Zahra, giving an animated account of her *aérophagie*, despite the fact that everyone present must have known all her symptoms by heart. With Fouad working again, it was hard to find an excuse to miss this lunch. I yearned to go home for a *siesta*, which had become a necessity ever since I'd missed my period.

Tante Joséphine called me *trésor* as usual, and Tante Georgette wondered if I was eating properly. *'Tu as l'air fatiguée, chérie.'*

I unwisely admitted I was a little fatigued, whereupon Joséphine panicked. *'C'est une anémie! Elle a besoin de B12.'*

I had to reassure her that I needed no injections of B12 or any other vitamins.

Victor ambushed me by a poinsettia and studied me with that squint of his that nobody else seemed to notice, then launched into all the details of his new job. It would have irritated me even if I'd felt well.

'Why don't you want to talk to me?' he whined.

'Let's be honest, Victor, since when have I ever wanted to talk to you?'

'Where's Fouad?'

'At work.' I gave a glacial smile and headed for the drinks cabinet. What kind of world was this where a woman of nearly twenty-two needed the protection of a husband against her own cousin? I took a glass of *arak*. I'd never much liked the stuff, but it was something to fiddle with until lunch was ready. As I sipped, I noticed Victor's father standing too close to one of my pretty cousins from Cairo. I hadn't realised how often he did that.

When we went into the dining room, Abdou brought in a

salver of rice. In honour of the large gathering and of Christmas, he wore a red sash around his best *galabeyya*. When had his temples gone grey? Ibrahim, the older of the two by far, hadn't aged nearly as much. His face had been a river of wrinkles and his mouth devoid of teeth for as long as I remembered.

I delighted Tante Magda by sitting next to her. She adjusted her fuchsia hat and said, 'Such a shame Simone isn't back yet.'

I fiddled with a fork and managed, 'A great shame.'

'You must miss her very much.'

Instantly my vision blurred. I missed my sister terribly. Or were my tears due to my hormones?

'Such a lovely tablecloth, isn't it?' Tante Magda said.

I gulped hard, seeing not a thing.

NOW

As the thunder of the lunch trolley recedes, carrying uneaten meals back to the kitchens, I reflect how little I really knew Simone. If I'd known her, perhaps her disappearance wouldn't have surprised me as much as it did. Now, though, I need her as never before. She's the missing piece of everything.

Someone moans. This brings a nurse to do her obs and give something for pain. When the nurse goes, the woman's visitors talk to each other with forced jollity. The jollier they are, the graver the prognosis, it seems. There's nothing graver than a grave, is there?

Now the wi-fi has resurfaced. I've had no responses on those Facebook groups I messaged. Should I google Victor?

With his photos and his insatiable curiosity, he must know something, but I can't. I just can't.

The big news on the internet is that a body has been found near Thurrock. I don't know Thurrock, and nobody seems to know the woman. She's thought to be in her seventies, it says. My gut twists on itself. Suppose it's Simone? The iPad shakes in my hands and the crack across its screen feels like a bad omen.

I'm still trembling when Sheila arrives to see me. Her jumper has lots of those tiny pearl dishes stuck on to it. I can't think of their name.

'How are you, old thing?'

'Oh, Sheila. I'm not feeling myself.'

Sheila's eyes widen. 'Ooh! Then who are you feeling?'

I respond with the obligatory smile before telling her about the latest dead body.

'Oh, sweetie. Don't worry. There are lots of bodies that can't be identified, sometimes for months. Or years. Thousands are found every year.'

This doesn't reassure me in the slightest. 'But one of them could be—'

'Now you mustn't talk like that.'

'But I can't help thinking it, can I?'

'Take some deep breaths. In through the nose, out through the mouth.' She says it's something called Hash Tango. Whatever that means. 'Anyway,' she continues, 'I didn't know you had an iPad.'

I tell her about Nurse Deirdre and what I've found so far, including the Egyptian Facebook groups.

'Why don't you just search the electoral register for Simone instead?'

'What do you mean?'

'Tell you in a minute. I need to make a quick call.'

While Sheila is making her call, I watch the nurses set up a blood transfusion on the patient who has stopped moaning. Once again, my mind goes out for a stroll without asking permission or letting me know where it's heading.

Blood is thicker than water. Omar said so. He claimed not to know my sister, and I had believed him. A man who's a liar. Well, that's hardly a first.

Simone wasn't drinking coffee, was she? And her boobs. I should have realised ages ago. Zeinab gave me coffee, that year. Impossible to erase that bitter taste from my memory. It's with me now, and that awful visit to Cairo is forever branded on to my brain connections.

CAIRO, JANUARY 1968

The air, stiff with dust, hit me as soon as the train door opened. Nobody can pretend that Cairo is a city on the fringes of Europe. Palpably different from Alex, it has the heat and the beat of Africa.

My friends sometimes went to Cairo to enjoy themselves, and they kept raving about the fabulous nightlife, the chic Gezira Sporting Club, the polo, the museum, the superb Mena House Hotel, the camels, the *feluccas* sailing on the Nile, and those silly Pyramids.

There was no point reminding these friends that Alex had hotels, camels, and a sporting club that was equally chic. We had *feluccas* on our Mahmoudieh canal, too. And had nobody spotted that the polo had stopped in 1956, and that the best stores in Cairo had long gone, too? No more Grands Magasins Cicurel. Too capitalist, too Jewish. Cairo was just a melée of traffic, vegetables, dust, honking horns, music blaring from cafés, pale puffy Russian faces, overladen donkey carts, shops spilling on to the pavements, concrete government buildings, and *shaweesh* vainly trying to control the flow of cars, of bicycles, of humanity.

There were no half measures with Cairo. You were either for it, or you were against it. For my family, a trip to Cairo meant some unpleasant duty like queueing for hours at the *Mugamma'* building in Tahrir Square for an exit visa that might or might not be granted the next day, if at all. Officials often used the word *bokra* which technically means tomorrow, but then again might mean the day after, or not at all.

This time, I got off the train and headed straight to Zeinab's via an erratic taxi ride that took in overflowing bins, broken pavement slabs, and plucky little lawns struggling for existence. I resolved to be brave, as if Simone were with me. *Don't be a she-donkey,* I told myself.

My friend was putting me up, but she wasn't going to get the whole story, even if we'd been at school together and her brother Tewfiq had been the first boy who'd given me a love bite.

'How was your journey?' Zeinab asked when I arrived at the apartment that she and her husband rented in Salah el Deen Street.

I didn't need to describe anything. Zeinab's smiles and nods suggested that she knew already. She brought me coffee that was sickly sweet but mercifully tiny. I chased it with iced water.

'Tewfiq asked after you.' Zeinab gave me a sideways glance.

'How is he?'

She told me proudly that he had a government job, which greatly pleased him and the family.

I hinted that I was in Cairo for a cosmetic procedure. 'A little adjustment.' I made a pincer with thumb and index finger. 'I haven't told Fouad, but it will surely delight him.' Here I winked in what I hoped was a convincing manner.

Zeinab smiled as her gaze dropped to my chest. Everyone knew someone who'd had a boob job. As I recalled from our school days, Zeinab had a famously knowing look even when she was clueless, such as when tested on her nine times table, which was one of the easiest.

She inverted our coffee cups and tilted her head coquettishly. 'Shall we read our fortunes?' As we waited for the grounds to settle, she enquired about mutual friends who lived in Chatby, Ibrahimeyya, and other parts of Alex. 'And how is Simone?'

The question pinged an elastic around my heart. 'She's away for a while.'

'*Insha Allah* she'll be back soon,' Zeinab said.

'*Insha Allah*.'

On inspecting my coffee grounds, Zeinab gave me that look and said, 'You'll be very happy.'

'I'm happy now,' I managed to lie.

'Then you'll become even happier, you and Fouad.' She pointed into the depths of the cup. 'Look. There's a bird, and a letter, and here's a number three. Three children, probably, and quite soon.'

'All in good time. Let's see your cup now.' I improvised about a present coming her way.

'That's right! You just gave me that lovely jewellery box.'

I peered again into the grounds. 'And a job, maybe?' As she was training to be a teacher, it wasn't exactly far-fetched.

Zeinab giggled and said I had always been very clever.

It was nearly time for my doctor's appointment by then. Getting up from the sofa, however, I became aware of something warm and sticky between my thighs.

19

CAIRO, JANUARY 1968

In Zeinab's dimly lit bathroom, I discovered where it was coming from. It was heavier than any curse I'd had before. I sat on the toilet until I felt less faint.

Luckily the bathroom cabinet housed a pack of sanitary towels. I grabbed two of them and shoved them inside my pants, hobbled to the guest room for fresh underwear from my overnight bag, and stumbled back to the bathroom.

I ran cold water as Simone had taught me, and the blood came out easily. There appeared to be a number of thicker fragments as well. That happened sometimes, didn't it? I rinsed them down the drain before patting my underpants dry with a towel. I was lightheaded. Trying to read on the train had probably contributed to that. But no problem. I could easily get back to the guest room.

A volley of cramps stopped me from reaching the bathroom door. Each one gripped like a vice, squeezing the life out of my pelvic organs. Lightheaded, I slumped on the edge of the bath, still clutching my damp underpants. Another pain came, and, with it, the thought that I might not need the abortionist.

NOW

I'm still dizzy from the memory when Sheila returns, beaming. 'Did you have a little doze?'

'I don't know.' I take a sip of water. 'Now explain how you think I can find Simone.'

'As I was saying, you could try the electoral register.' She says there's a website called 192.com. 'I don't know how they put it together, but basically it's information from the list of voters.'

'Does that mean anyone eligible to vote in the UK?'

'That's right. And if Simone has been here a while, she should be on that list. It's worth trying.'

'One nine two dot com,' I repeat.

When Sheila leaves, however, the iPad refuses to show the three curved lines that tell me I'm connected, and no amount of shaking the thing or invoking St Anthony makes them appear.

Blood is thicker than water. I keep going back to that.

CAIRO, JANUARY 1968

I was weak, thirsty, and late when I arrived for my appointment.

The doctor had an Armenian name and a squashed nose like a bulldog. He made me stick out my tongue, checked my pulse and blood pressure, then took me behind a curtain to place his icy hands on my breasts. 'You are no longer pregnant,' he announced.

How could he tell just from feeling my bosom?

'It is because of the hormones.' He gave me an explanation that I was too muddled to absorb.

'Will I need to go to hospital?'

He hesitated, but he thought, on balance, probably not. I wished he sounded more certain. 'This injection will help.'

The needle in my buttock was relatively painless. He then put his arm around my shoulders and instructed me to rest.

A taxi took me back to Zeinab's, speeding past a florist in Zamalek. As a child, I'd assumed the water cascading down the windows was on the outside of the glass until I'd tried to lick it one hot day. But the woman from the shop had rushed out to scold me. The water was to stop plants from getting parched, not naughty little girls.

I told Zeinab that my period was too heavy to risk any kind of procedure. She gave an understanding smile. '*Maalish.* But of course it's safer to postpone your operation. Go and lie down, *habibti*. We'll have something light to eat, a bit later.'

'Thank you.' I shuffled down the corridor to the guest room, relying on the wall for support.

The cramps worsened that evening. I downed a couple of Aspro and lay on my side in the bed, knees pulled up. I needed something stronger to soothe the physical pain in my belly, and the other pain inside my head. Where was Simone now that I really needed her?

NOW

Blood is thicker than water. My heart races as I realise what it means. Simone had been to Omar too, when she was pregnant.

Now that my internet is back, I will find her. Here's that 192.com with details of people, businesses, and places. Ah. It wants money. I lunge for my wallet, and I don't even care if the website is dodgy. With fingers shaking it takes several goes to key in the long number on my credit card.

I discover two Simone Khourys in London, and six others not far away. And here are their phone numbers! The banging in my chest is fiercer than ever and my legs have turned into rice pudding. I take deep breaths Hash Tango style, just as Sheila said to do, in through the nose and out through the mouth, but my head still spins. I must try those phone numbers from the electoral thing. My Nokia, however, is being useless. I punch in two, four, two, four, in quick succession, the sure way of summoning a dialling tone in Alex, but there's still no sign of life. Disgusted, I practically hurl the mobile off the end of the bed.

The woman mountain observes me with interest. 'No signal then?'

I shake my head.

'It's better downstairs,' the mountain says.

Deirdre is off duty today, but there's another nurse. 'What shops are there downstairs?' I ask.

'There's a newsagent. And a Costa coffee shop, a fruit stall, and a hairdresser.' She pauses to assess me. 'Fancy getting your hair done?'

I'm past caring about my hair. 'No. Just after a change of scene and maybe a coffee. Could I go to Costa, do you think?'

'You could,' the nurse says. 'Terry can take you. He'll be here later.' Terry's a volunteer, apparently, and he's really nice. I don't care what he's like as long as he can push a wheelchair.

While I wait for this Terry, I check that my phone is charged, and I note down the numbers I need to ring. As he's not here yet, I dip back into the postcards. This one shows a bridge in Cambridge. Simone had drawn a butterfly in the corner, labelling it *Butterfly*. Why? The Simone I knew wasn't one for superfluous statements. Below the doodle she'd written:

All well. I'll be in touch. Love & kisses, S x

I can't focus on that now. Didn't the nurse say Terry would be here soon?

ALEXANDRIA, FEBRUARY 1968

Energy had drained from me along with the blood. The tall Armenian doctor in Cairo had advised rest. 'You can tell people you have *le foie fatigué*.' It sounded plausible enough. Practically everyone I knew had claimed to suffer at some point from a tired liver. 'Take iron tablets. And eat nourishing dishes like chicken with rice and white sauce,' he added.

I wasn't used to resting. 'What shall I do with myself?'

'Try jigsaw puzzles,' he replied.

While I stayed for a few days at my parents', waiting for my fatigued liver to recover, I plundered Mother's cupboards and found a 5,000-piece puzzle that might, days or weeks hence, become a Cunard ship with its many funnels.

'*Ayoo!*' Rashida stroked the box. 'Pretty, pretty boat.'

'Yeah. So what?' I found it hard to summon enthusiasm for putting the pieces together when there was a perfectly good photo on the box.

'Don't get angry, my heart,' Rashida said.

'Sorry, Rashida.'

Simone would have ordered me to snap out of it with one of her killer lines, and I was equally sure I'd have obeyed. Months now since she had left with only a vague promise to return, and so little information since. I tipped the puzzle out on to the breakfast table and half-heartedly sorted through it. The blue pieces all looked the same, though suppose that the piece in my hand wasn't part of the sky or the sea, but something more significant that I should be looking for?

'Simone's sent another card,' Mother called out when the postman had been.

Her postcard from Lucerne showed a covered wooden bridge next to a tower growing out of the lake. Rashida fussed about making coffee so we could all study Simone's message properly.

All's well here, alhamdul'Illah.

The fact that all was well, thanks be to God, was hardly enlightening. I imagined her studying — she hadn't even said where — and learning new things, but why didn't she care for us enough to tell us more? I couldn't imagine why Mother and Father hadn't pinned her down about her plans. She got away with a lot, did my sister.

The card read and reread, I made my way back upstairs to my room, using the cool iron handrail to haul myself up. My weakness annoyed me. Hadn't I wanted to get rid of that pregnancy? I refused to call my repulsive condition a baby. That would be for next time, when it would be a child for Fouad and me. Once back in bed, my tears came. I had a need for my sister to call me names and tell me to buck up. I just had a need for my sister.

Mother padded in with *eau de cologne* and a facecloth. 'The liver takes four weeks to recover,' she said as she patted my brow. 'I remember from when my own mother had *la jaunisse*.'

'I don't think one can put a definite time on it,' I replied.

'Funny that you're not yellow at all. When my mother and my sister Georgette had it, they turned yellow.'

'Not everyone with a tired liver goes yellow.'

'Perhaps we should get Doctor Tadros to have a look at you.'

'I'm sure I'll be fine. My friend Zeinab's doctor did all the tests. In fact, I'm already feeling better than yesterday.' I gave what I hoped was a persuasive smile.

'Well, that's good.' Mother finally left me alone.

Only one thing would be good. Simone's return. Every postcard surely meant she was still alive and well, but my parents and I needed more. We'd spoken to her classmates from school, of course. Father had also asked Hamza and various other well-known characters around Alex. Involving the police was out of the question, but when Simone had been gone for a few months, he called on an ex-journalist he knew to help track her down. Monsieur Jean, we called the man. It wasn't his real name. I wondered if he'd ever been a real journalist. Rashida made him the usual coffee when he arrived, but she, too, saw his frayed cuffs and made her disdain plain.

'Who knows why she left? After all, the brain is a mysterious box, especially a female's.' Monsieur Jean spread his hands and laughed at his own wit.

How dare he speak about my sister like this, and what did he know of the brain, anyway? He was just some retired journalist in ragged clothes.

The man extended his little finger and sipped his tiny coffee with huge noises. 'She hasn't disappeared completely,' he said when he'd put down the cup. 'That is good.'

True, she hadn't, but there was no denying she was missing in the sense that she was no longer here in Alex, with her family – Mother, Father, and most of all me, her biggest fan, even if she did have a tendency to say I was a *humara*. Well, she could call me a she-donkey all she wanted if only she'd come home.

'What is her name again?'

'Simone. Would you like to see the postcards she sent?' Father asked the man.

'Of course.'

Father handed him a small bundle of cards.

'No letters?'

'No.'

Monsieur Jean should have realised that letters took longer to reach Egypt, arriving many weeks late, if at all, with a printed strip down one side of the envelope where the censors had slit it open then sealed it up again. Under Nasser, nobody wrote letters if a card would do.

'Let's see.' The man picked up one of the postcards and held it up to the light coming through the only window. We were sitting in the basement, the one room that we were fairly sure wasn't bugged. He examined the card at length. If he was looking for invisible ink, he was more naïve than I imagined. 'Her handwriting is interesting.'

Father gave a polite smile. 'In what way?'

'Well, I am something of an expert on calligraphy.'

Of course he was, according to his own assessment. 'What do you make of the writing?' I ventured.

'It's very mature,' he said.

Since Simone was twenty-four, this was hardly a revelation.

He took off his glasses and twirled them in his fingers. 'I suppose you have spoken to her friends?'

Mother fidgeted in her armchair. 'Most of them. Of course.'

'In cases like this, there's always something the family overlooks. But I have my methods,' he assured us.

As a well-behaved young woman, I had to mind my manners, but it was hard to hide my impatience.

Father asked what he proposed to do, and the man outlined his plans. His account clearly aimed to impress, but it was just a long-winded way of telling us he would use the network of contacts he'd made over a thirty-year career in newspapers.

My parents thanked him courteously, and he left, doffing his battered hat and promising to be in touch.

'*C'est un pauvre con*,' Father said as soon as the front door had shut.

Mother glared at him because *un con* is the height of vulgarity, and not at all the same thing as *con* in English, though he was probably one of those too. 'But,' she added, 'he's the only chance we've got.'

If that was the case, then we were never going to find my sister.

Mother raced to answer the phone. Every call, especially when heralded by the trunk-call ring, held the wonderful possibility that it might be news of Simone. It wasn't.

I walked into the bathroom I had shared with my sister. Here we would try out make-up, practise walking like Zouzou, and imitate the most memorable teachers from El Nasr Girls' College. I'd undo my school shirt and pretend to point at a blackboard of conjugations to mimic Miss Appleton who always left a crucial button undone in the middle of her flimsy blouse, and we'd then laugh until we cried. Rashida often came in and shared in our hilarity, though she had no idea why.

I should investigate Simone's room. Perhaps there was something I missed.

Her blue Olivetti portable sat on the desk. The E on the keyboard was worn. Could the carriage or the ribbon tell me anything? I turned my attention to the blotter, with equal lack of success. Inside the top drawer, I found writing paper along with a few envelopes, a couple of ball points, and some airmail stickers. The writing pad was a standard one with a picture of Nasser on the front. I examined the ruled page intended as a guide to writing in straight lines. It bore a forest of indentations from letters written with a biro. In the top left corner, I made out the word *Alicia* among the jumble of hieroglyphs. Well, the fact that Simone had written to Alicia was hardly enlightening.

The next drawer down housed a drawing pad with a good sketch of Hassan in his misshapen white hat, head bent over a piece of paper as Rashida dictated a letter to her brother. On another page, Simone had drawn a Bedouin woman beaming at the infant on her lap.

A number of *pantalons cigarette* hung in the cupboard on padded hangers made by Mother. Propped up on the chest of drawers was a picture of a lotus leaf, created out of different-sized holes punched in a piece of leather. Father's work, no doubt.

Was she happy, wherever she was? Relishing a freer environment than in Egypt, wearing a miniskirt wherever she went, and kissing and being kissed anywhere at all, even the middle of the Via Veneto in Rome? According to pictures in *Paris Match,* people did this a lot, especially if they were famous. Simone probably had a Mary Quant haircut, took the Pill, and was teaching her lover a few choice Arabic words.

It wasn't cold today, yet I shivered, my legs weak and my head full of ill-defined but unwelcome thoughts. Outside the window, the sun shone, and Hassan was sweeping the path with a palm branch. I ducked before he saw me, though I had every right to be in my sister's room.

Most of Simone's warm clothes still appeared untouched. Funny. I'd have thought she'd have needed them in Europe. There at the back was a well-loved teddy bear. So much for her claim of having got rid of all soft toys by the age of ten. The yellow ribbed cardigan next to it was actually mine. A cigarette burn went through the right elbow. Well, that would explain why she had never returned it. I sniffed the cardigan and picked up a faint scent of Femme de Rochas, which, in Mother's opinion, reeked of *sharmouta*. I returned the cardigan to the drawer alongside a stack of monogrammed handkerchiefs and Mother's ubiquitous cotton bags for socks and tights.

Inside the white painted bedside table, I found various nail varnishes, a Mary Quant lipstick, and a lipstick brush. In the drawer lay a few 45 rpm records. Bobby Azzam's big hit would never be the same again now that Simone had gone. I sang 'Ya Mustafa' softly to myself, willing the tune to work its magic and bring her back.

NOW

Was Simone's sketch of the Bedouin mother significant? I flick through the postcards in the metal box. No Bedouins, of course, but here's Buckingham Palace.

Children are so precious.

I do know that.

The doctor with the Laura Ashley glasses is now at the bed of the redhead opposite. She'll be round to me next, with talk of Lyme's disease, nursing homes, or something else to terrify me. I don't catch the whole conversation she's having with the other patient, but I hear her say that less operations are done these days for something or other.

I put down my postcard. Less operations? Every El Nasr Girls' College schoolgirl would have known that, for operations, or anything else that can be counted, the correct term is always *fewer*.

The woman mountain is padding up and down the ward without a urine bag. ''Ere. Want a read of this?'

Terry still hasn't materialised, so I accept her magazine. 'Thank you.'

There isn't much in *RightHere!* apart from pictures of women showing off their living rooms or draping themselves over men's arms at society events.

'I'm finished with it now,' I say, but the woman mountain has lain down in the shape of the Pyrenees.

Here comes a man with a shaved head and an earring. He smells of cigarettes as he leans over, demanding my name and date of birth. He's got a bloody cheek, this Terry. All I want from him is a ride downstairs in a wheelchair.

20

ALEXANDRIA, SEPTEMBER 1970

My upstairs neighbour Yvonne shrieked as she kissed me. 'How are you, *chérie, habibti*?' Both words mean exactly the same thing, but no Alexandrian uses one word when they could use two or more. 'It's been simply ages.'

'Absolutely.' After all, we had not seen each other since the hairdresser's yesterday.

There were ten of us at dinner that night, including friends from our building and several colleagues of Fouad's. This was my life now, without Simone. In our modest apartment, we had flowers in crystal vases, Motown on the new cassette player, and a full cocktail cabinet. Fouad offered a whisky soda to each new arrival, and we picked at slices of *batarekh*, the fish roe delicacy that people raved about, plus the cheese and pineapple chunks I'd prepared. Apart from myself and one other woman, everyone smoked, flourishing silver filigree cigarette holders that served no purpose except to look chi-

chi. Long before 1970, research had firmly linked smoking with cancer, but nobody in Alex was much bothered.

Fouad related a crude joke while admiring the cleavage of Mimi Tawil. As he always told me, it meant nothing. 'It's expected, *chérie*. Women like to feel appreciated,' he had once explained, drawing out the penultimate syllable in true Egyptian style.

The time now being right, according to Fouad, I was expecting, though my belly was still flat in my imitation Pucci miniskirt. I waved away a cloud of smoke and refused a glass of Clos Matamir. I had gone right off alcohol.

Fouad refilled glasses and continued with one of his stories about a couple's wedding night. 'They were both virgins, and they were clueless. Really clueless.' There were titters while Fouad paused to reach for a cigarette. 'Finally, after three nights of lying patiently next to each other in the bed without anything happening, the wife goes to her mother for advice.'

'Ah, *kida*. And what does the mother say?' someone asked.

'She said to her, "My darling daughter, all your husband must do is put his hardest part into where you pass water. You understand?" "I understand." So the girl goes back to her husband.'

'Then what happened?'

'I will tell you.' Fouad took an extended drag from his cigarette. 'That night, when they are once more lying side by side in the bed, she carefully repeats her mother's advice. "*Ya habibi*, my darling, all you have to do is put your hardest part into where I pass water." And do you know what happens? The next morning, the husband is found with his head jammed in the piss-pot.'

The resultant laughter called for another bottle of Clos Matamir, and Nessim embarked on a story that he swore on his mother's eyes was 100 per cent true. 'This friend of mine,

Guirguis, he goes to Luxor on business, but the only hotel room available is one he has to share with another man.'

'*Howa kida*,' Fouad said. That's how it was. In smaller hotels, it wasn't unusual for strangers to share rooms.

'The next morning, the other man gets up before Guirguis and goes to the handbasin. There he washes his face. And then, would you believe it, he takes Guirguis' toothbrush to do his teeth!'

'Not possible!'

Nessim continued. 'But Guirguis, he says nothing. He does not move one single muscle. He waits in bed with one eye open until the man finishes. Then he gets up. He goes to the washbasin, pulls down his pants, and uses the toothbrush to scrub his backside. Of course, the other man is horrified.'

'Of course.'

'The man says, "Do you always do that?" So Guirguis says, "Always. Doctor's orders. I have piles."'

Fouad smacked his forehead with his palm while Yvonne from upstairs convulsed with laughter.

'Of course, that is hardly the correct treatment for piles,' Nadim pointed out. 'Even a neurosurgeon like me knows that.'

The doctors then regaled one another with tales of difficult cases, grateful patients, and heroic operations. 'Did I tell you about the huge woman with appendicitis?' Nessim asked. 'A real *balooza*, at least 130 kilos. She overflowed the operating table, *kida*.' He stretched out his arms.

As the men continued with their stories, the women and I shared anecdotes of cooks, recipes, and shopping.

'Your perfume is exquisite,' my neighbour said.

'Thank you. It's Rive Gauche.'

Despite surveying the room, I found it hard to tell what meant nothing and what meant something. I watched the people in our apartment, leaning in to get a light, or sharing a wink over the table. A compliment about a dress. A lingering glance by the cocktail bar. A hand on someone's buttock. Did these things all mean nothing?

NOW

Terry apologises because I am not Mrs Valerie Something. And he, it turns out, isn't even Terry. He is a blood-taking person looking for another patient entirely.

The real Terry is still not here. To occupy myself, I find the card with Big Ben.

> *So here I am, well enough, and hope you are too. Take care, little sis. Don't worry about me. S x*

Of course I worry. I've worried for years. But what's this code? Taking the initial letters, I get *SHIAWEAHYAT* and *DWAM*, neither of which makes sense. With palimpsests in mind, I scrutinise the writing and the surface of the card for signs of an underlying inscription. Nothing.

'Where is Terry?' I ask one of the nurses again.

'I don't know,' she replies with a hint of irritation.

'People keep talking about this Terry. Does he even exist?' After all, nobody believes my sister is real.

The nurse's glare is enough to kill me.

ALEXANDRIA, OCTOBER 1970

The shock came the day after our little dinner party. I hadn't known about Nasser's heart trouble, and neither had anyone else. Even so, he died immediately after the Arab League Summit. On the fifth of October, the populace piled into the streets for his funeral and convulsed with grief. While much of the Arab world sobbed and wailed, Fouad and I shed no tears. We looked forward to having a baby who would not be born under Nasser.

A few days later in rue Cherif, a boy came steaming around the corner in his bare feet, his hard little head at the exact height of my belly. 'Sorry, *ya sitt*. Sorry, sorry,' he mumbled.

'*Maalish*,' I replied, though it had been quite a knock. No wonder my muscles tightened and I felt faint. Cutting short my shopping trip, I went straight home. I hadn't lost even a speck of blood but, to play it safe, I lay on the sofa for the rest of the afternoon, my pulse flying at around 100 a minute. I knew because I kept checking it.

When Fouad came in, he kissed my lips and my still-flat stomach before taking my pulse. 'You and the little one will be okay,' he assured me.

'Can you use your stethoscope?'

'No point. It is too soon.'

The next day, the ache in my lower belly was back. Exactly like the curse. It meant nothing, apparently. Pregnant women often get that in the first few weeks. 'It's only round ligament pain,' Fouad pronounced after feeling my tummy. 'Don't worry, *habibti*.'

I had no idea where the round ligament was until Fouad showed me a diagram in one of his books. Turned out I had two round ligaments, right and left.

Despite the pain meaning nothing, Fouad rang me from work twice daily for the next few weeks.

NOW

I still have no signal. 'Is Terry here yet?' I ask a passing nurse.

'No, dear.' She is off before I can ask more.

A cleaner is here with a rag on a stick that redistributes dust around the ward. I see bits jiggling in the light, like chalk in a classroom. The cleaner is now jolting my bed and knocking into that thing beside it. She does exactly the same at the next bed, but the woman mountain sleeps on.

There's still no sign of Terry or anyone who offers to take me downstairs. However, Laura Ashley appears. She pushes her glasses up the bridge of her nose and gives me that half smile they all seem to learn at medical school. 'Tell me. Have you had children?'

'You asked before.' This I remember.

'Sorry.' She makes a face. 'I don't think I wrote it down. So, did you have any children?'

I rotate the hospital ID bracelet around my wrist before answering. 'It's a long story.'

ALEXANDRIA, OCTOBER 1970

I grabbed a towel and climbed out of the bath while Fouad scraped foam off his chin.

'You know, I don't mind what we have.' He twisted his face in front of the mirror. 'But maybe it will be a boy.'

There was nothing unusual in that. Every Arab man wants a son. Having a girl or, worse, being a girl, didn't bear thinking about, even in the early 1970s. My preference was for a baby that was healthy and, if I dared wish for more, it would be for Simone to be back for the birth.

'If we have a son, I could teach him to play football.' He examined his upper lip at length in the mirror. 'Maybe he will become a doctor too?'

'Or maybe our daughter will?'

Fouad dried his chin in silence.

My hopes continued for another five days. At about ten o'clock in the morning, I had just got up from reading a Spanish book when I felt it. I automatically squeezed my thighs together against the flow, though I knew it was hopeless, even before the pain built up to a crescendo that had me clenching my jaw and gripping the arm of the chair. I crawled to the phone in the hall and called Fouad at work.

'Are you sure it's a miscarriage?' he said.

'Yes,' I replied through gritted teeth.

'How do you know?'

'A woman knows these things.'

When I'd had my miscarriage in Cairo, the Armenian doctor had assured me that one miscarriage didn't mean there'd be another. Many women miscarried, he'd told me. There was nothing whatsoever to worry about. This time, I went into hospital to have my womb evacuated. The doctors there, like Fouad, all gave me the same story. Chances were the next pregnancy would be fine, *insha Allah*, and surely we'd be blessed with a son very soon.

'*Insha Allah*,' I repeated, even though a daughter would have done me perfectly well.

I went home the next day, clutching Fouad's arm for support. Still groggy from the anaesthetic, I headed straight to bed to rest, as Fouad said I must. As everyone said I must.

. . .

After that second miscarriage, or, as I remembered to call it, my miscarriage, we didn't share a bed for six weeks. Fouad said it was better not to. Then we started again. It was a hot night in spring and we had been to a long Alexandrian dinner with a first course served around eleven o'clock. Many drinks. *Chin-chin*. Flirting. I was convinced Fouad had been studying the *derrière* of one of the few British women in town that did not look like a horse from both back and front.

'How was Patricia Farquhar?' I asked Fouad afterwards, over a glass of water in our living room.

I expected a coarse pun about the woman's surname. Instead, he stubbed out his Belmont and said, 'I'm not in the least bit interested in Patricia Farquhar.' He lunged at me with a stubbly chin and wanting lips, delivering kisses that left a smoky taste in my throat. Then, to the background of feral cats yowling outside, we were soon entangled on the bed in a knot of sheets. I had missed him so much.

'*Chérie*,' he moaned. 'I have loved you all my life.' Not strictly accurate, maybe, but enchanting none the less.

It wasn't long before I conceived. This time, I was allowed to take no chances. Bed rest and abstinence were the order of the day, and *petit point* was the most energetic activity allowed.

'But *habibi*,' I asked Fouad, 'didn't you once say that you can't dislodge an embryo any more than you can shake an unripe mango from its tree?'

'I did. But still.'

By August 1971, Anwar Sadat had been in power for the best part of a year. His so-called corrective revolution had trimmed back the dreaded secret police and relaxed currency controls. People talked more openly, and the austerity of the Nasser era was behind us, too. Happier times ahead, I hoped.

However, my womb proceeded to reject our second much-wanted pregnancy.

'It's only your second miscarriage,' Fouad said.

I mentally crossed my fingers. 'I know.'

'Many women miscarry.'

'I know, *habibi*.'

'You believe me, don't you?'

'Of course.'

Maalish, people said. Some added *maktoub*, as if it were written that we would not have a baby. I told myself and anyone who asked that we were absolutely fine as we were. With Fouad as my husband, I lacked nothing.

Privately, it was a different story. I shut the door of the empty nursery in our apartment, yet it was still there, impossible to ignore. Simone's presence would have helped, but where was she? Without her, I had nobody to confide in. I still dressed up for parties, smiled when anyone glanced in my direction, made small talk about films, and admired people's handbags and hairdos. I pretended to have fun, as people called the endless merry-go-round of Alexandrian activities. Doctor Tadros prescribed vitamins to lift my mood, and Fouad also got me some pills from the hospital. He pushed the tiny glass bottle into my palm.

'What are these?'

'They are very special,' Fouad said. 'Take one daily.'

A lot of people, like Zouzou and Ralph, never had children and they were okay. A child would have been a distraction, I consoled myself. Alongside being the good wife that I had vowed to be, I had a little Spanish translating work. *Thank you, that was going very well*, I always answered, to which everyone replied they'd always known I was clever.

What I did the following year was far from clever, but it was very much the done thing.

NOW

I won't think of that. Instead, I will concentrate on my plan. My phone is doing nothing, but I will get on with it the instant I can.

'Is Terry coming in today?' I ask a nurse. I know, I'm repeating myself.

She hasn't even heard of him. I bet he's one of those made-up animals that look like a horse with a horn sticking out of its head.

But here is Sheila. I clap my hands with joy as soon as I see her.

'You're looking jolly. How are you, *bellissima*?'

'Fine.' I explain my plan.

'*No problemo*. But how will you get into the wheelchair?'

'A nurse will help,' I reply loftily.

It is a mammoth effort even with the nurse. My legs are too wobbly to keep me upright for long, and my arms are equally pathetic. Eventually I'm installed, my list in one pocket and my Nokia in the other. I'm praying there'll be a signal somewhere downstairs.

'Let's go,' I say.

Sheila has strong arms from all her gardening, but I wish she wouldn't keep ramming the wheelchair into walls. 'Sorry,' she says every few metres.

Once the lift reaches the ground floor, we are in an atrium crammed with businesses that will make money. There's the Costa coffee along with WH Smith, various little shops, and a salon that gives off that special hairdresser smell. I'm focused on my little Nokia. It's vastly more powerful than the bulky Bakelite phones of my youth, but only if it can catch a signal.

'Here.'

Sheila fails to hear me at first.

'Here!' I repeat. We're between a cash machine and the pharmacy, which is not ideal, as some people are in a long queue for medicines and the others are racking their brains for their PIN numbers.

'Let's try over there,' Sheila says.

We stop by some recycling bins and I check my phone. 'Okay. This is good.'

My heart thumping somewhere in the vicinity of my tonsils, I squeeze each of the eleven digits for the first contact. A phone rings somewhere in East London.

'My name is Nadia. Sorry for calling out of the blue, but is it possible to speak to Simone Khoury?'

21

EGYPT, OCTOBER 1971

The sea at Sidi Abdel Rahman was the most turquoise blue ever, as I remarked on each of the three days Fouad and I spent there. This time, however, it stirred my soul in quite the wrong way. Instead of filling my lungs as I ran on the shore, I sat and contemplated the horizon where deeper waters painted an ultramarine band.

Fouad took my hand. 'Are you warm enough?'

I nodded, pulling the crocheted shawl around me. It was a dazzling multicoloured web that had caught my eye when I went downtown, so Fouad had bought it for me along with a necklace set with precious stones. After my latest miscarriage, he had been even more attentive and generous, but nothing he could say to me, or buy by way of bright accessories, had helped. Perhaps this short break would relieve us both of stress.

Fouad had been doing his best to distract me ever since we

got to Sidi Abdel Rahman. 'Let's get some sea urchins.'

Riccio was here with his basket. Although he was Egyptian like all the fishermen, people called him Riccio which is Italian for sea urchin. As usual, he was selling sea urchins that he'd caught with the dinner fork that was attached where his right forearm used to be.

'Propeller accident,' Fouad muttered.

Riccio brought over his basket. 'They are fresh, *ya basha*,' he told Fouad. '*Shouf*, look.'

We looked. The things were still moving.

Fouad cut one open and squeezed lemon juice on to the peach-coloured flesh. It made the spines wiggle. I turned away. 'Urgh. It's still alive.'

'Not really,' Fouad said. 'It is only a reflex.'

We talked on the beach at Sidi, mainly about Simone. While strolling on the sand, I asked him point blank. 'Would you tell me if you found out anything at work about Simone?'

'Of course.'

'But what about doctor-patient confidentiality?'

'My beloved, I would find a way.'

That's when we discussed Mousa, the university student Simone had been seeing. 'It's been years. Why haven't we spoken to him already?' I wondered. The journalist was right. This family, too, had missed something.

'I don't know, but we should,' Fouad said. 'I will talk to him man to man.'

'But she's my sister.' Either he didn't trust Mousa with me, or me with him. 'What's the problem? You think I will attack him in rage?'

Fouad didn't answer, but he agreed Mousa might know something, especially if he and Simone had been close. After tracking Mousa down through the university, the plan was that I'd arrive first to meet him for a coffee at Le Trianon downtown, making it clear that my husband hoped to join our table half an hour or so later.

NOW

'We may have to think of something else,' Sheila says. 'Back upstairs?'

I nod, unable to find words. The first Simone turned out to be twenty-two. Another one was at work, but, from her flat-mate's description, she's not my sister. Three did not answer. One had an answering machine. I started to leave a message but couldn't finish it for stammering.

We return to the ward in silence. Mine, not Sheila's. When she's not apologising for her poor steering, she is blatantly trying to cheer me up. 'I can try the other numbers for you later.'

'Thank you.'

'We'll have to think of something else, too,' she says again.

I'm too disheartened to imagine what.

'Let's think,' Sheila continues. 'What was Simone really like?'

'*Is* really like,' I correct as she carves another hole into the wall.

'Well, indeed. But you don't necessarily know what she's like now. Only what she was like then.' She is smart, this Sheila, I'll give her that. 'So have a little think,' she continues as she parks the wheelchair by my bed. 'It all helps.'

I don't bother asking how many missing people she has

tracked down. Even the private eye and that ex-journalist couldn't find Simone.

Undeterred, Sheila continues. 'Nicknames, for instance. And hobbies. And friends, of course.' As if I've not already thought of all this.

Once I'm back in bed with the help of a nurse, I say, 'Thanks, Sheila.'

'*No problemo.* Sorry, but I have to go.'

'When will you be back?'

'I'm not sure. But I'll ring the other numbers for you and let you know right away.'

I hand her the list. 'Promise?'

Her phone pings with yet another message. 'Promise. Now, chin up, Nadia.'

I watch her leave. I think I've always known that Simone wouldn't come back, and wouldn't be found. Yet I can't allow myself to feel low, like all those years ago. It was the early 1970s. I remember exactly what went wrong.

ALEXANDRIA, OCTOBER 1971

'The lovely Simone's sister,' Mousa said. He had unnecessarily thick lips and a gossamer-thin shirt that hugged every curve.

'You must be sad,' I began.

He studied the ceiling fan as he combed his fingers through his short curly hair. 'Very sad.'

'Have you heard from Simone?'

He shook his head in an equally unconvincing manner.

I had been with him for no more than ten minutes when Fouad burst into the Trianon with a grin and greeted Mousa like an old pal. He probably did the same to patients or relatives worried about their forthcoming surgery. Right away, he asked when Mousa had last seen Simone.

Mousa rubbed his earlobe. 'Long time ago now. I think at a seminar, one morning.' He thought it might have been their last term at university.

Fouad wanted to know if she had make-up on. 'And what was she wearing?'

'Jeans, for sure. I don't know about make-up. I suppose she was wearing lipstick. Girls normally do, don't they?'

'Was she in the same clothes as earlier that week?' It didn't take a genius to work out that Fouad was asking if Simone had slept with him, or with someone else. Perhaps it hadn't occurred to my husband that people could do it without spending the whole night together.

Despite consulting the ceiling again, Mousa remembered no more about clothes, but he did vaguely recall something Simone had mentioned in reference to Milton at the seminar. 'It was strange, though not necessarily stranger than some of the other things she came out with.' However, he failed to recall the words she'd used.

Fouad glanced around the room and leaned forward. 'Did she ever say things about the government, the army, the police, that kind of thing?'

Mousa was shaking his head before Fouad finished asking. 'She was clever. She never made political remarks. Ever. Other than to say Castro was a good man and an interesting one. She told me he slept in his uniform.'

I might as well leave. Perhaps Mousa would say something useful when I'd gone. I waited for Fouad around the corner at the agreed spot and watched palm branches sway. A tram rattled past with passengers inside and out. A couple of boys jumped off without glancing behind. By the time Fouad emerged, I had bought two jasmine necklaces from a vendor.

Fouad lit a cigarette. 'What did you think?'

'I'm not sure. I didn't trust him.'

He blew smoke towards the palm trees. 'You can't mistrust someone just because you don't like their shirt. Or their lips.'

I wasn't sure why not. 'Well, what did *you* make of him?'

'Don't know, really. Did we learn anything significant? Probably not. I wondered if Simone might be pregnant? But I don't know that either.'

'She's too clever to get pregnant.' I brushed stray jasmine petals off my dress. 'But do you think they slept together?'

'Definitely. One hundred per cent.'

'He actually told you?'

'He didn't need to. I can tell when people have been screwing.'

As it turned out, however, Fouad couldn't tell.

22

ALEXANDRIA, JULY 1972

Gilbert was quite the ugliest man I had ever seen. I'd never intended to sleep with him, still less with his cousin from Marseille, but it happened anyway. Like bobbins rolling down a staircase, as Mother might have said, had she known of my activities.

Gilbert was a friend of a friend of Ralph's. He had a squat body and a lopsided jaw. However, if viewed in a certain light, such as the semi-shade outside the Brazilian Coffee Stores, he could be described as delectably hideous.

After a coffee at the Brazilian, he walked me towards my car. The road turned out to be blocked by a broken-down truck piled high with vegetables. While men in ragged singlets argued at full volume as to the cause of the breakdown, little boys in pyjamas helped themselves to onions and tomatoes from the truck. Whatever was wrong with the vehicle, I couldn't get my own car past the obstruction, no matter how much *baksheesh* I offered.

'We could pass by my apartment,' Gilbert said. 'It's right here.'

'May as well,' I said.

He placed a hand on my lower back as he ushered me through a wrought iron and glass door into his building. His apartment had a shiny parquet floor. 'Would you like a coffee?'

I'd only just had one in rue Cherif. I accepted anyway.

As the *suffragi* was out, Gilbert went through a beaded doorway to the kitchen and made the coffee himself. I glanced from the *petits fours* on the cracked plate back to his asymmetric face. He exerted an earthy attraction balanced by a potent repulsion. We chatted about politics and he predicted another war with Israel. When he made for the zip at the back of my dress, I said, 'I'm sure the truck has moved by now.'

The second time that we happened to meet at the Brazilian Coffee Stores, attraction conquered repulsion. We needed no vehicle to block the street, and I made only token resistance. He reached for a cigarette box with a smile, displaying the condoms he kept there.

'You don't smoke then?' I asked.

'Nobody smokes these days.'

I didn't tell him that Fouad did. Somehow it seemed a greater betrayal to mention my husband a moment before writhing frantically on another man's sofa. There was no sense in it. There was no pleasure either, nor was there guilt. I felt only the transient frisson of doing it with someone who oozed a simian masculinity.

As he helped me zip up my dress, Gilbert said, 'My cousin is coming to Alex next month. You should meet him.'

'Is he like you?' I asked for want of something better to say.

'Not at all. Robert is from the handsome side of the family.'

I demurred politely.

'You'll see,' Gilbert said.

Although I had no intention of making a habit of *le cinq à sept*, I agreed to meet the cousin. Throwing parties in people's honour being very much the thing, I was invited to a gathering on a Tuesday night, *un petit cocktail, chérie*. Fouad was working late again, but didn't people keep saying I had to go out and cheer up?

As the whisky flowed, I found I knew a few people there, including Zouzou and Ralph. A French woman dressed completely in black asked Zouzou what she'd thought of the latest film at the Amir.

'The interval was excellent,' Zouzou replied. All the best people had been there, *le tout Alexandrie, chérie*. She reeled off a list of names along with descriptions of their outfits.

Robert was, as Gilbert had said, an Alain Delon to his Cyrano. He was studying economics, he told me over a whisky.

'I've never met an economist before.'

'That's probably because there are so few of them. Egypt has a dire shortage of economists.'

'As is obvious.' I instantly regretted my reply. Despite Sadat's more relaxed style of running the country, Egypt remained a police state and free speech was still an alien concept. What if informers or government spies had heard me?

'Many economists have been put in jail,' Robert remarked.

'Really?' I lowered my voice but feared I had already said too much. If Robert was an *agent provocateur*, a mere nod might land me somewhere cold and dark. Nobody could be trusted. One charming elderly lady, a prominent member of the community, was said to wear a microphone in the depths of a magnificent mink stole from Sistovaris. I studied Robert.

He was only wearing a shirt and trousers and, as he leaned in to hear me, I realised there was little scope for hidden microphones.

'I shall try to behave while in Alex.' The twinkle in Robert's eyes said the opposite.

I permitted myself a smile and, later that evening, managed to discard my doubts on the floor along with my underwear.

Robert eventually went back to Marseille and his PhD, but there was Loutfy, a handsome lawyer of Lebanese origin who preferred to be called Louis. He wanted a fling for just one reason: his wife had had an affair and had now moved back with her mother, taking the children. Neither Louis nor the grapevine, usually so bountiful with information, would say who she had cheated on him with. Could it have been Fouad? That would make, I thought as I climbed out of my fake Dior dress, a horrible symmetry.

What Loutfy lacked in tenderness was more than outweighed by enthusiasm, leaving us both sweaty and thirsty. While he went to fetch me a glass of water, I studied the framed photos in his bedroom. Sometimes flanked by children, sometimes not, a genial woman was at ease in all of them.

'You still love your wife. Maybe you should forgive her and try to get her back.'

He gave this solemn thought. 'And you should go home to your husband.'

He didn't need to tell me I loved Fouad. Zouzou believed sleeping around made people happy. It made me realise I was happiest with Fouad.

NOW

I stare at the paper pot with its blue pill, pink pill, and tiny white one. 'They've changed my medication.'

'They haven't,' the nurse says.

'But the pills look different.'

'That's because there are different manufacturers.'

I'm not sure I believe her. 'Are these antidepressants?'

The nurse doesn't think so. Whatever they are, she won't go until I swallow them. There are no capsules of St John's wort or ginkgo, that much I know. I haven't taken any for a while. The woman in the shop had said not to stop them, but I must say they're a touch overrated.

Sheila is back and her tone is serious. 'Sweetie. I've tried all the numbers.' She doesn't need to finish her sentence. 'None of them is your Simone. I'm sorry. Come on now. Cheer up. You'll find her.'

I wipe my eyes with my sleeve. 'How?'

'Let's think. What was Simone really like?'

'I don't know.' I wouldn't have said I'd ever cheat on Fouad, but people do strange things. Was it because the miscarriages messed with my hormones, or because of the drugs Fouad got me from his hospital? I've no idea. All so long ago. 'Do you know, sometimes I can hardly remember Simone.'

'Have a little think.' Sheila pats my arm. 'I've just got to check my voicemail.'

While she's gone, a woman changes the curtains around the beds. They did that only the other day. Paper curtains, they are. No wonder there are no trees left in that place in South America. But I must focus, as Sheila says, on what Simone is like. My head is thumping again, plus I haven't seen my sister for years. There's one thing I know, though. Simone felt awkward around older men. It's obvious to me now. What else? Simone was — no, *is* — kind. She once offered Hassan a pair of sunglasses. He thanked her but refused, insisting his hat was all he needed. Then Simone had made him accept two blouses as a gift for his wife instead. And she had comforted Mariam, that day over the laundry. It wasn't just about her legs. Mariam was complaining about someone who was good for nothing. Her husband, no doubt.

When Sheila returns to the ward, I tell her, 'Simone was generous with those in need. I missed it at the time.' I can't imagine how this is useful. It's hardly as if kindness is a job qualification, but Sheila says everything is significant. I sigh. She's one of these people who find meaning in everything. I know that from reading her coffee cup all those years ago.

Eventually, Sheila has to leave. I'm not surprised, given the number of times she's looked at her phone in the last five minutes. Hope that new man of hers is nice, whoever he is.

The postcard at the top of the pile is about Father.

Not everyone has such a wonderful father. S x

Perhaps the message is about a bad man fathering a child? Haven't a clue who.

Now a doctor I don't know is talking loudly to the mountain. His arms are bare below the elbow, not like our Doctor Tadros. He came in a suit, day or night, whenever anyone in the family was ill, whether it was typhoid or just a cold. Unlike *Inglizi* doctors, he would have listened, and he would have eased my pain whatever the cause. He might have given me intravenous vitamin B12 to restore my energy. Nobody in here has even suggested injections.

Still, Doctor Tadros couldn't save my pregnancies. Nowadays, a miscarriage is a proper bereavement. People name their lost babies and give due weight to their brief lives. Back then, yes, it was sad, but *maalish*. Despite prayers and tears, nobody in Alex mourned as if they'd lost an actual child.

I will cheer up and put my thinking cap on, as Sheila says. I can't get a minute's peace in here, especially with that doctor and the woman mountain still in full flow. I grab one of my pillows and cover my head, moulding it around my ears as I used to do in Alex to muffle the shouts from Father and Simone.

Now I remember. One morning, Simone had shrieked and said she wouldn't go if *he* was going to be there. I didn't catch who *he* was, but Father had insisted that she was talking about a respected member of the community. Infuriated, Simone had shouted back that the man was dangerous. What had Papa replied? Ah yes, that he was the parent and she was just a little girl.

Simone's retort is clear in my memory. *'Exactly!'* she'd howled. *'You can't possibly understand, because you're not a little girl.'*

Something else emerges through the haze. Father said he would find out something. Whatever it was, I hope he did. One could usually trust Father to keep his word, yet people and things don't always live up to their promise. I of all people should know that.

23

ALEXANDRIA, OCTOBER 1973

The government claimed that all was well. Once dubbed Nasser's little black poodle, President Sadat had become his own man, but the economy was still fragile, and Sadat needed more backing for his reforms. In a distraction technique little different to Mother's *petit point*, though considerably costlier, he came up with the brilliant notion that a military victory could boost his popularity. The snag is that victory is rarely a foregone conclusion, especially if you're Egyptian. I could have told his generals that.

Once again, the sixth of October was an important date for Egypt, as well as being both Yom Kippur and Ramadan. Egypt and Syria together launched a surprise attack on Israel. The war did not entirely go Sadat's way, but at least he remained in office.

By that time, Fouad had a job offer in England. 'It will be the perfect chance for me to learn from the *Inglizi* doctors.

And when my contract is finished, we'll come back.' He proudly showed me the letter from the Queen Elizabeth II Hospital.

'Does the hospital belong to the Queen?' I asked.

'I don't know. Maybe they all belong to the Queen.'

'And where is Welwyn Garden City, exactly?' I had yet to learn that the second W was silent.

'Almost in London.' He lit a Cleopatra. 'It's a very good hospital. You'll see, *habibti*.'

My thoughts turned to the London I knew, with buses whooshing and hissing on wet streets, and places I had not seen since childhood: Buckingham Palace, Trafalgar Square, Piccadilly, a hotel with ample windowsills on which to sit and watch people scurry with umbrellas on the street below.

NOW

'You're looking glum, Mrs,' Deirdre tells me.

I explain that the phone numbers from that 192.com came to nothing, and I've no ideas left.

'Let's be practical now. Where in the UK might your sister be?'

'Piccadilly.' I know that's wrong as soon as I say it.

Sure enough, Deirdre snorts. 'It costs a fortune to live there! What could your sister be doing, though? Is she retired?'

'I expect she's still working.' Simone is bossy and knowledgeable. 'Maybe she's teaching.' Or working as a nursery nurse or in a hospital. Maybe this one. No. That would be a ridiculous coincidence. Even someone with their brain crammed to the brim with Alzheimer's and Lyme's should know that. Then it hits me. 'She must be an artist.'

'Swish!' Deirdre says.

'But where should I look?'

Deirdre suggests I search Google for Simone's name followed by *artist* or *gallery*.

Once Deirdre goes, I do precisely that. There I discover many artists called Simone, though none called Simone Khoury. What if she has a married name, though? With that in mind, I look through all the Simone artists to find something that recalls my sister. Maybe a resemblance in their artwork. Some sites have photos of the artist, too. The task is complicated by the fact that *artist* can include musicians. I end up spending hours squinting at the iPad with nothing to show for it except dizziness and disappointment.

WELWYN GARDEN CITY, NOVEMBER 1973

Fouad put a cigarette to his lips before removing his deerstalker. The tweed hat, bought immediately on our arrival in England, didn't make him look as British as he'd hoped. 'There was a girl today with a bun in the oven.'

'What does that mean?'

'Pregnant. She was fifteen years old, and she arrived in established labour. Guess what she said in Casualty?' Fouad blew out a lungful of smoke. 'She said the baby couldn't possibly be born, then she showed me her navel. She had stuck Elastoplast over it to keep the baby in.'

How we laughed at her naiveté as we hugged each other to keep warm. It was freezing in autumn 1973 when we arrived in England. The overcoat that had felt so thick back in Alex gave me little protection against the icy dampness on our train journey to Welwyn Garden City. The Queen Elizabeth II

Hospital was not, as it turned out, that near London. It was in Hertfordshire and famous for being the first hospital to be entirely built by the NHS. Her Majesty the Queen had opened it ten years previously. It was the least she could do, in my view, it being named after her. Even if it wasn't the more celebrated Queen Elizabeth Hospital in Birmingham, Fouad would benefit from working here. The QE Two, as everyone called it, had a busy maternity unit thanks to the town's young residents. 'Copulating and populating,' Fouad said, with the accent on the third syllable of each word.

Fouad and I installed ourselves in Walnut Grove about half a kilometre from the hospital. Our apartment was in a square white block, cold and utilitarian, in exactly the same style as the rest of the town. The metal-framed windows in our bedroom never quite opened and never quite closed, and the thin curtains were of a yellow that, Fouad reckoned, couldn't decide if it was bile or urine. The main problem, though, was that they were marginally too short for the windows.

We did indeed have a lot to learn about *Inglizi* hospital staff and the names they used for patients, such as *me old fruit, me old duck, pet,* and *my lovely,* especially when they weren't. This was also my first experience of Europe as an adult. People I met while shopping called me *love* and *dear,* and sometimes asked if I thought it was brass monkey weather. I agreed. It was easier than showing my ignorance.

There were many other bewildering phrases like *taking a pew* which meant sitting down, exactly as we did at the pub one evening with a Portuguese anaesthetist and his wife. Gusts of tobacco and beer hit me as soon as we opened the door. Everything in the pub had turned ochre. In the corner sat a man with long frizzy hair and sideboards the size of loofahs, frowning into his drink.

The barmaid poured from pumps with china handles and

banged the dripping glasses down on towelling runners on the counter. We carried our drinks back to a sticky table.

'See that man's nose?' Fouad indicated the loofah face.

His colleague Manuel nodded.

'Rhinophyma,' Fouad whispered.

I stared at the fleshy red protuberance. 'What causes that?'

'Alcohol,' Fouad replied. 'And that woman at the bar has an overactive thyroid. You can see from her eyes.'

Our beers were sweet, vinegary, and yeasty all at the same time. That didn't stop Fouad and his friend Manuel 'sinking a pint', as they called it, while sharing a packet of pork scratchings.

'I didn't know you people could eat pork,' Manuel's wife said.

You people? I stiffened.

'We are not Muslim,' Fouad explained. 'Or Jewish. Nadia is Greek Orthodox and I'm a Copt. Copts are the biggest Christian group in the Arab world. We became Christian when St Mark came to Egypt in 62 AD.'

Our Portuguese friends did not know that, and neither, I suspect, did anyone else in Welwyn Garden City.

'But we were around long before that,' Fouad continued. 'My family is descended from the Pharaohs.'

From then on, Manuel and Eva called him King Tut. It wasn't long before the entire staff of the QE Two followed suit. Thanks to an exhibition at the British Museum, Tut mania had arrived in the UK, and it wasn't leaving any time soon.

None of us overdid the drink. Manuel said he was studying for a forthcoming exam. 'I mustn't get Brahms.'

'Brahms?'

'Brahms and Liszt. Pissed, you see?' Eva and Manuel had already been in the UK six months.

Now that we were in England and King Tut was busy, I had time to look for Simone. She was close by, I felt it. But where? I had hardly seen my pen pal Sheila since she'd visited Alex all those years ago, but now we had long conversations on the phone, in which I learned about magazine and newspaper columns with titles like *Where are they now?* I tried several of them, with no luck at all.

Once he got home, Fouad sank into the plastic armchair and took off his deerstalker. 'Guess what a patient said today.'

'What?' I always enjoyed hearing about his day.

'I began to examine this woman's abdomen, and she pushed my hand away.' A vertical line appeared between his eyebrows. 'She said she wanted a white doctor.'

That was awful. It was also puzzling. Like most Egyptians, Fouad wasn't dark, unlike President Sadat, for instance, whose face was routinely lightened in newspaper photos, though they usually forgot to bleach his hands. 'Maybe you should work on your accent, *habibi*, my beloved.'

He shrugged and lit a cigarette. 'What can I do? You have a gift for languages. I do not.'

My so-called gift lay fallow. Before I realised that I wouldn't be allowed a job, I'd tried a few translation agencies, but there was little work going.

'There's no call for Spanish,' they told me with the same cheery defiance that local shop assistants used when they said they didn't stock Ma Griffe perfume.

It was amazing what they didn't have in 1970s Britain. I hankered after proper lemonade instead of the fizzy concoction from bottles, but the only lemons on sale were in the form of a plastic replica. When I unscrewed its tiny green lid, the fake lemon dispensed a thin liquid that was nothing like the fruit that Rashida used to squeeze to death with a fork. I sat with the synthetic lemon at the kitchen table in Walnut Grove and fought off tears.

The key turned in the lock. Even before Fouad got through the door, I detected the aroma of tobacco alongside a vaguely clinical smell and a hint of BO, as the English called it.

'Have you been to the doctors' mess, King Tut?' Now and again, I encouraged him to go to the bar where junior doctors met for a swift pint. I had been once. It was just a room with beer, a dartboard, and a hubcap for an ashtray.

He shook his head. 'Emergency.'

'You've got dried blood on your eyebrow,' I said, picking at it.

He displayed the Elastoplast on his left index. 'And here.'

'What happened?'

'Cut my finger.' The scalpel had sliced through the glove and into his fingertip while he and the consultant battled an aggressive tumour.

'What kind of tumour?'

'A rare one. Uterine,' he replied, with the stress on the last syllable. 'And very large. Sadly I think the patient will crump quite soon.'

'*Crump?*' It sounded more like baking pies than practising surgery.

He reached for a Silk Cut and his lighter. 'It means to die. I think suddenly.'

'Like collapsing?'

He nodded. 'I heard it in the doctors' mess.'

I avoided his touch that night. He assured me cancer couldn't be caught like that. Still, nobody knew what had caused the woman's tumour. I didn't want to crump.

NOW

Crump. That's the word. Pamela had crumped. The term sounds far too jolly, but then doctors joke about the most serious things. I expect Fritz is joking about me now.

I go back to the postcards. This one has a West London postmark and is from long ago.

We'll meet one another one day.

Nothing special about that. Wait. She didn't say *again*. Wouldn't it be *again* if it was a reunion with her own sister? The grammar is odd, too. If she and I were to meet, it should be *each other,* not *one another*. Unless there was someone else with her. A man? Her child? I am pretty sure she had a bun in the oven. If Simone was pregnant when she left, perhaps somewhere I have a niece or nephew.

There's a pain I'm trying to blank out, something that has hurt since forever. I can't think about Simone having a child without reflecting on all my miscarriages. Each time I had one, Rashida retreated to her attic room, a sanctuary where she kept pictures of St Anthony and *el Adra,* the Virgin Mary, along with a burning wick floating on a glass of oil. St Anthony didn't return lost babies as readily as misplaced keys and pink handbags, but that never stopped Rashida praying with increased fervour every time I miscarried.

I cannot allow myself to be jealous of my own sister.

WELWYN GARDEN CITY, DECEMBER 1973

Although the Ramadan War in 1973 lasted under three weeks, it affected Britain too, sending oil prices soaring as supplies dropped, following which there was trouble with the coal miners. The story wasn't wholly clear to me, but the miners went on strike sometime before we arrived in Welwyn Garden City. The working week shrunk to three days for most people. Power cuts were another problem, because it made the heating in our apartment 'pack up', as the English put it. I had no idea where it went once its bag was packed, but it was freezing. The English books I'd read as a child showed pictures of cosy open fires, not windows that never quite opened and never quite shut.

A paraffin heater stood tucked away in a kitchen cupboard. We'd never used it, but instructions were on a label on the back of its bright orange cylinder. I found a knob to elongate the wick, then lit it with a self-satisfied smile. Maybe I should move the heater to the corner near the chair.

The fire went out with a bang. Of course. The safety cut-out operated whenever the heater was lifted. I tried again and, until the paraffin level dropped, I enjoyed a meagre warmth, barely equivalent to the thin winter sun in Alex, let alone the summer heat I craved.

'I'm keeping my vest on,' I told Fouad in bed.

'I love you even in a thermal vest, *ya habibti*.'

It turned out that a thermal vest was no bar to conception. This time, I told myself, all would be well.

24

WELWYN GARDEN CITY, JANUARY 1974

There was a new moon and my pregnancy test was positive. Knowing the powers of the Evil Eye, I did my utmost not to look at the crescent through glass, and I definitely didn't tell anyone that I was expecting again, not even my parents or Sheila.

We saw Sheila once, on one of Fouad's rare weekends off. On the long journey to Surrey, he dozed on the train. Sheila's garden was embellished with footballs and bicycles, courtesy of her two sons. I had all this to come, or so I hoped.

'Drink?' her husband Henry said. He barely uttered another syllable all day.

I only got a snatched moment alone with Sheila. The roast dinner had her dashing about from pans to plates and back again, all the while trying to rectify lumpy gravy. 'Oh, well. It tastes all right, doesn't it?' Sheila held out a spoon for me.

'Delicious.'

'Now what about your sister?' she asked, her mind mostly on cutlery.

'I'm running out of ideas. Short of scouring the whole country, what can I do?'

Sheila threw an oven mitt over her shoulder. 'Private dick.'

My old pen pal was so coarse. 'Dick?'

'It means detective. I'll give you a couple of addresses.'

After lunch, Henry sprawled in his armchair while Sheila cleared up and then harangued the boys about tidying their toys and washing behind their ears, which they had zero intention of doing. 'Come along then, you two. Up the wooden steps to Bedfordshire.'

Another new phrase for me.

I contacted the people Sheila had mentioned. One of the private detectives was in Barnet, a part of North London not far from Welwyn Garden City. He was ex-police and a cheerful soul who claimed excellent results. I handed him a photo of Simone.

'Leave it with me. Gosh. She's a right stunner, isn't she?'

When the next power cut came and the heating gave up the ghost (another fine English term), I thought it no big deal. Pregnancy provides inbuilt central heating. I also had the pullover Mother had bought me from Hannaux. Pulling the cuffs right down over my hands, I felt warm for a few moments, but it wasn't long before a chill crept into my bones. I was homesick as well as cold.

Soon, the dick from Barnet gave up the search, having spent all the money I'd given him. The next day, I miscarried. I resisted hospital treatment at first, but the trouble continued over several days, like Nasser's coup, only bloodier. Fouad eventually persuaded me that I was risking infection and possibly any chances of having children.

Transported by trolley up to the same ward where Fouad had most of his patients, I passed signs indicating that the maternity unit was on the top floor. Would my oven ever keep a bun in long enough for that?

The gynae ward looked out on to a lawn with a melancholy backdrop of trees. As the woman in the next bed explained, the hospital had been built the wrong way around. The woods and the land I could see had been intended to provide a grand approach to the hospital entrance but, in the event, the nearby landowner refused to sell, so there was no choice but to make do with the back of the hospital as its main entrance. It sounded entirely possible. Everything was topsy-turvy to me.

I was taken to the operating theatre. Just a quick trip, the doctor said, nothing to it, though that was not how it felt to me. Fouad saw me immediately after I returned to the ward. 'You look pale, *habibti*.' He kissed me and lowered his voice. 'I checked the hospital records in the basement. Just in case. But I didn't find Simone.'

'Is that allowed?'

'Of course not.'

I cried all night, as much for Simone as for our baby. Alas, having a doctor in the family didn't produce solutions to all your health problems, and having a gynaecologist for a husband hadn't stopped yet another miscarriage.

As we got back to our apartment in Walnut Grove, I cut the plastic bracelet off my wrist. 'Don't you have patients like me?' I asked Fouad.

He shook his head, looking, for the first time, perplexed. A long moment later, he reached for a Silk Cut.

. . .

We went to an expensive clinic to see a specialist. The learned man wanted to know about my periods, my history of miscarriages, and any family history. Throughout the consultation, he addressed Fouad, barely glancing in my direction, until he invited me to hop on to the couch, there's a good girl. After examining me with cold hands and an even colder instrument, the consultant pronounced me to be a fine young woman, almost certainly as fertile as the day was long. It struck me, on emerging from the clinic at five o'clock into wintry darkness, that the day was not so very long.

NOW

I have an idea, so I flag Deirdre down and grab her arm. 'Do you think you might be able to check the medical records here?'

Deirdre shakes her head. 'Sorry, Mrs. It's more than my job's worth.'

'But my sister could have had a baby here. In this hospital.'

Deirdre still won't relent. 'Please don't ask me again,' she says as she leaves.

I understand her predicament, though it doesn't help me at all. But what would? Simone's baby would be more like fifty years old now. Imagine that! They probably don't even have records going back that far. Fifty is ancient. I remember being thirty-five. Even that is a venerable age, or so I thought at the time.

ALEXANDRIA, OCTOBER 1981

I was old, as I told the mirror.

'I don't think so, *habibti*,' Fouad said.

The strong Alexandrian sun shining into the bathroom said otherwise. 'But I'm thirty-five. Thirty-six in January.'

'Maybe so, but only a very small part of you is thirty-five. That is the beauty of cell renewal. Look at your fingernails. And your hair.'

He was right. Those were definitely not the same bits I'd been born with.

'Your red blood cells are four months old,' he continued. 'Your stomach lining is just four days old.'

I was thinking more of the bits I could see, like my sagging jawline. 'What about my skin?'

'Your skin is about a month old. Even bones, that everyone thinks are strong and permanent, renew themselves.'

'How about my brain?'

'About thirty-five.'

'And my ovaries?'

He was forced to admit they were thirty-five, too. Ovaries and brains never get any younger.

Men with moustaches grinned as smoke drifted across the gathering. Plump matrons wrapped in evening gowns and yards of pearls swapped gossip, while old men cosied up to women too naïve to escape. I was thirty-five. I was no longer one of the bright young things attracting moths to my flame, though lighters still flashed when *la comtesse* twisted another cigarette into her silver holder. Perhaps some believed she really was a countess after all.

'Do you think Simone will be back soon?' asked Madame Something, whose fur-draped neck might once have concealed a microphone.

I focused on my *arak* instead of responding. Madame Something soon got distracted by a man with a huge gut who was as ugly as a cockroach until one learned how many *feddans* of land he owned.

A woman with eyebrows plucked into oblivion beckoned me behind a hideous vase. '*Chérie*, he wasn't supposed to have any land left. But one or two little parcels were somehow overlooked in the land reforms, so there we are.'

Here was *le tout Alexandrie*, and it had a lot to discuss. Much had changed since the Nasser era and some property had been redistributed. Many who'd fled Egypt had returned, especially *shawam* who'd discovered that Beirut, Geneva, or New York fell far short of life in Egypt, but not all returned to Alex. Fouad and I had been to Cairo. The city now had fine restaurants that rivalled many in Paris, and, after a particularly good meal, I'd been forced to agree that Alex had been left behind when it came to fine dining.

Naturally we talked of the biggest news of all. Sadat has just been assassinated at a victory parade in Cairo to celebrate the success of the Ramadan War eight years previously. To many, Sadat was a hero, especially compared with Nasser. Some even believed that Nasser's precious Aswan dam had increased the number of cases of bilharzia, a water-borne infection that went back to Ancient Egypt.

'The new man must be given a chance,' said the man endowed with spare tyres and many *feddans*. The new man was Mubarak, formerly Sadat's vice president.

'They call him The Laughing Cow, like that cheese,' said the woman with no eyebrows.

The man of many *feddans* wobbled like jelly. 'He is the biggest cheese of all now.'

'I think he needs to get to grips with bilharzia. It's endemic.' I knew from Fouad that the parasite lived in water, was carried by snails, and still killed thousands every year.

Zouzou sidled into view. 'Bill who, *chérie*? Is he a fashion designer?'

It was she who instantly noticed the tarnished clasp on my new handbag. 'Such a shame. It's a pretty little bag.'

It was the one Fouad had just bought me. With two more miscarriages recently, Fouad bought me more presents than ever, though no amount of navy leather, however prettily stitched, could compensate for the things we didn't have. Mortified, Fouad said he would complain to the shop.

At the beach, Victor was often there with one of his cameras. He also spent a lot of time in Cairo, doing nobody knew quite what, though people remained convinced it was very clever. *Comme il est intelligent.* When I saw him, his squint seemed worse. *One eye in Cairo, one eye in Alex*, I imagined telling Simone, if she were here.

Zouzou pouted next to her cabin. Although her toenails were still a shiny crimson, bunions now protruded from her mules. Ralph sat some distance away, his bald dome visible above his deckchair.

The Belgian attaché, having gone back to Brussels, was once again in Egypt with his binoculars and his cap, looking older than I recalled but still intent on scanning the horizon.

Nobody was surprised at the attaché's return. '*Habibti*, you know what happens once you drink the waters of the Nile,' Zouzou said.

'Yes,' Fouad replied. 'You get bilharzia.'

He was a successful gynaecologist now, with more leisure time. 'Why don't you ever sit in the sun, *ya habibi*?' I asked one afternoon at Montazah.

'Do I want to look like that Mrs Morris? Her shoulders are like a baboon's backside.' As usual, visitors from Europe were apt to underestimate the Egyptian sun. He lit another cigarette. 'Besides, *ya habibti*, ultraviolet rays cause skin cancer and cataracts.'

I never told him about the stupid game I used to play with Zeinab and Androulla, daring one another to look straight into the sun for as long as we could. I still had the memory of the after-burn. How was I to know, until Simone told me, that my friends cheated by shutting their eyes?

Reasoning that Fouad was too busy, I took the handbag back myself. The shop was downtown, near the old pigeon restaurant and a place that sold mainly socks. I passed a car-repair workshop with tyres piled high outside. The air rang out with the *thwang* of someone bashing metal and, in the intervals between the blows, the mechanic yelled at his workmate, calling him an imbecile and a donkey.

The manager of the leather shop said he would happily rectify the problem with the clasp. He spat on a rag and wiped it, then, when that achieved nothing, he accused me of having taken the bag too close to the beach. I said I hadn't, whereupon he produced another dozen excuses for the rust.

NOW

I have this memory as clear as a glossy picture fallen from an album: Simone downtown, possibly in Saad Zaghloul street, in front of a store that sold mainly socks. She was about to dive into an alleyway between the shops. I reckoned she had a secret lover, which was why I'd followed, Instamatic in hand. Down an alley I went, between the pigeon restaurant and a shoe repairer. There were cobblers all over Alex, which seemed superfluous considering how many people went barefoot. I had passed a place festooned in old tyres. Next thing I knew, I'd tripped over a skeletally thin cat with a kitten dangling from her mouth. And Simone had evaporated from view.

I try to see more, but the harder I try, the less there is left.

Deirdre's here. I've just seen her with that new patient who has liquid trickling into her arm. She's avoiding me, though. I must have offended her. Now I wish I'd never mentioned the hospital records.

My jug is empty. I wait for a passing nurse before asking for more water.

'In a minute.' There's a strong whiff of cigarettes about her.

When the nurse comes back with the water, I get her to plug the iPad in. Better do what I need to do before Deirdre decides to take it back.

'Thank you,' I say, but the nurse must have a diploma in moving quickly. Off for a cigarette break, no doubt. I still find it hard to take a neutral view of smoking.

ALEXANDRIA, JANUARY 1988

Fouad lit another cigarette after dinner. 'Do you think we should go and live abroad again?'

'I guess we might find Simone there,' I replied.

'But we might not, *chérie*. Would you want to live abroad regardless of that?'

'What, now, when everyone else is coming back?' Mubarak had raised living standards, released political prisoners, even opened dialogue with the opposition, though he hadn't gone so far as to have more than one candidate on the latest ballot sheet. Was there a need for other contenders when people liked the president for working hard, living modestly, and having the populace's interests at heart?

'Still,' Fouad said. 'Egypt is hardly a democracy. It is an empire, and he is the Pharaoh.'

'I suppose.' Mubarak had huge powers of detention and imprisonment. He was also paranoid about being murdered, another reason why he'd strengthened the security forces and imposed a state of emergency.

Fouad and I never made progress on the question of going abroad, and the issue, like so many in our country, remained unresolved. I did, however, have something I very much wanted Fouad to do. 'Fouad, *chéri*,' I often said. 'Have you thought of giving up smoking?'

'No. Why?'

'It's bad for your health.'

He'd blow out a lungful of smoke. 'I know.'

I persevered. 'Cigarettes will kill you.'

'One has to die of something,' he pointed out. 'Besides, I'd rather live a short life and be happy than a long one and be miserable.'

'Have you thought that I might become a widow and have to move out of our lovely apartment? You're so selfish.' Even as I said it, I knew it sounded petulant and spoilt.

'I think about you all the time, *chérie*. Even when I am at work. Even when I'm on the toilet.'

Smoking was addictive, people said, yet not everyone got hooked. I'd only smoked once, the time Zeinab and I giggled over a shared cigarette on the Corniche, barely able to light the match in the breeze. Still in our uniforms, we tucked ourselves below the wall for shelter while men went by in billowing *galabeyyas* and women begged, their babes in arms.

The first puff merely tasted hot and musty. Zeinab explained that I wasn't doing it right. 'Inhale like this.'

I obeyed. Instantly my head went into orbit and my legs jellified. That wasn't all. 'I'm going to vomit,' I announced as a wave of nausea rose into my mouth and a simultaneous urgency announced itself at the other end.

Zeinab's mouth stretched into a telling smile as she took the cigarette from me. 'It's always that way the first time.'

I had grabbed the sea wall for support until I could rush to the nearest café for a toilet. Why did people bother to smoke if it made them feel like this?

25

ALEXANDRIA, NOVEMBER 1990

Another round of surgery was out of the question. There isn't much left to chop out after you've had one lung removed.

'Why is this happening to me? Why, in the name of all that's holy?' Fouad beat the medallion on his chest as another fusillade of coughing intervened.

Mentioning cigarettes would have been pointless. I stroked his bony back through the loose folds of his vest. 'Would you like some tea?'

It was our *suffragi*'s day off. The tea I made, with added honey and brandy, had a soothing effect, but it was purely temporary. Nothing could cure someone this grey, this gaunt. Fouad gripped the cup along with the crumpled handkerchief he carried everywhere, and cleared his throat. 'Perhaps they should have given me a different kind of radiotherapy. Or maybe chemo.'

I glanced up only briefly. *Petit point* was good for avoiding eye contact. 'But you've had the best treatment available for lung cancer.' That wasn't saying much. Fouad had had a lung cut out when the cancer was first diagnosed, followed by radiotherapy to zap some of the lymph glands. The burns on the front of his chest showed exactly where the rays had been aimed.

'The pneumonectomy was terrible,' he reminded me with a shake of the head.

'It took out the tumour.'

The tea-cup rattled in its saucer as he put it down. 'But it's made me so breathless.'

I couldn't argue with that. The specialist agreed that Fouad had hardly any of what he called respiratory reserve. That was why his breathing was laboured after even the slightest effort.

Silver ashtrays still dotted our apartment. We also had a Queen Anne-style lighter, cigarette boxes that gave off an aroma of cedarwood mingled with tobacco, and the pocket lighter engraved *All my love, Nadia* that I had given him. Fouad had used none of this paraphernalia, however, since a few weeks before the diagnosis.

'I'm a bit out of sorts,' he had informed the bathroom mirror one morning. He scrutinised his chin and his tongue, then his lower eyelids.

'You should see the doctor.'

'I'll wait and see.'

'Why wait and see? You already feel awful and you cough all the time.'

'But I haven't lost any weight.'

By the time Fouad finally made an appointment to see Dr Abdel Nour, he'd coughed up blood twice.

'Just a small burst blood vessel,' he said. 'That happens with bronchitis.'

Originally from Aleppo, Doctor Abdel Nour had worked

for years in London before returning to Alex. On the day of the appointment, Fouad had reinvented himself as a non-smoker.

'Do you smoke?' Doctor Abdel Nour asked.

'Not at all.'

The doctor appraised Fouad's stained fingertips. 'Have you ever smoked?'

'I used to.'

'When did you give up?'

'Two weeks ago.'

The doctor's grey eyes flashed meaningfully at me. I turned my gaze to the certificates on the wall, the photos of children on the desk, the tram stop outside, a flag in the distance.

X-rays revealed a sizeable shadow on Fouad's left lung. He went to hospital for a biopsy, then breathing tests, lung removal, and a protracted convalescence. Now it was winter. Rain and sea spray kept him home for weeks. '*Insha Allah* you'll be better tomorrow,' I said over my *petit point*.

Tomorrow came and went. If anything, Fouad was worse, with a cough that racked his body while he thumped his breastbone in a bid to make it stop. We had days on which he planned outings like a little walk on the Corniche or a coffee in town, then failed to find the energy.

'It was my patient's fault,' he said.

'Which patient?'

'The woman in Welwyn Garden City. With the rare uterine tumour.'

'I don't think that's possible, *habibi*. How can a man catch a tumour of the womb?'

He wiped his mouth. 'And you're a doctor now?'

I resumed my needlework and resolved to be patient. He only had one lung left. Perhaps there wasn't enough oxygen flowing to his brain.

NOW

Deirdre is still not talking to me. I glimpse her coming down my end of the ward, striding past the woman with the drip. Well, I won't even glance at her. I'll focus on my Google instead. Here are some people I could search for:

Mimi Tawil. Guirguis. Yvonne. Nessim. Nadim. Zouzou. Hassan. Alicia. Cousin from Cairo. Mousa. Victor.

Now I'm forced to look at Deirdre, because she's right by my bed.

'Right. I'm going to do it,' she mumbles. Her voice is so soft and her departure so swift that I can scarcely believe she was here. I gaze at the place where she stood before returning to my list. Victor is the only family member on my list. There's nobody else left, not since 1992. Another year that was hell in a *hantour*.

ALEXANDRIA, OCTOBER 1992

'They should have given me chemo,' Fouad said. 'Then we'd have been sure that the tumour wouldn't come back.' He coughed and wiped his lips and stubbly chin with the hankie. 'Professor Fakhry said he might be able to look into my case.'

I made a non-committal noise. There was no easy way to tell him that the doctors had given up. Breathless and wheezy as he was, Fouad was on the phone to one of his medical contacts practically every day. Fakhry was the latest in a long line of specialists whom Fouad begged for another opinion. Each of them said the same, albeit in slightly different words. There was nothing more that needed to be done. Some left a sliver of hope by adding *at this stage*.

At night, Fouad would get up and pad around the apartment, examining objects as if he had never seen them before. He fiddled with the things on my dressing table, even though he knew they were sacred.

'Come back to bed, *chéri*,' I said.

It was as if he hadn't heard me. 'What's this?' He opened the metal box in which I kept Simone's postcards.

'Please leave them alone, my beloved, *ya habibi*. They're from Simone.'

'You should give up your obsession over Simone.'

'But she's my sister.'

'Then why doesn't she come back?'

'I don't know! Sorry. Didn't mean to shout.' I finally gave the box to my aunts for safekeeping.

Now chemo was Fouad's refrain. It was the only way, he insisted, to get rid of the remaining cancer cells circulating around his body and thereby restore him to full health.

Doctor Abdel Nour had a private word with me. 'Essentially, your husband is terminal.' It was now a case of palliative care, and nobody could do anything more. 'It is about keeping him comfortable.'

'Did you tell my husband he was terminal?'

The doctor nodded. 'But, essentially, he's in denial.'

I used to believe that, when we got old, Fouad and I would sit in companionable silence in our sitting room, perhaps with an outsized air-conditioning unit blasting away on hot days. If it wasn't to be, I would do my best to keep him — what word had the doctor used? Comfortable. That was it. I loved him. I had always loved him, and it had grown without my noticing into a love strong enough to tear out my heart.

The rest of my world was also turning upside down. All over Alex, new blocks sprouted at an alarming rate, annihilating period buildings in the process. I welled up to see treasures of the last century tossed aside as rubble. Monstrosities replaced them without regard for common sense or regulations, let alone heritage. With socialism gone, nothing was controlled. Residential blocks sprung up cheek by jowl, and balconies from one building practically touched those next door. Where Alicia's home with its enviable pink roof had once been, three concrete eyesores had taken root.

'Vandals,' Father spat. 'Did you see the building that had permission for eight floors? It now has fourteen. Fourteen, imagine that!'

'They're nothing but pirates. Throwing new homes up like children's toy blocks,' Mother said.

I wasn't sure how pirates came into it, but Mother was right about oversized blocks going up despite serious structural flaws. As a result, they often came down again just as quickly. *Maalish!* The less well-off needed homes, and to hell with the hazards.

There was one consolation. As old constructions made way for new, riches sometimes emerged. The archaeologist Jean-Yves Empereur was the moving force behind excavations beneath both soil and sea. Under his direction, the waters yielded ancient columns, obelisks, and statues. No reason to visit Cairo for that crumbling old Abou el Hol in Giza when we now had more than thirty of our own sphinxes right here in Alex, barely metres under the waves.

On land, rescue operations raced against the frenetic pace

of destruction and construction. Drilling for foundations uncovered ceramics and artefacts that went, in reverse chronology, all the way back to Alexander the Great. It gave me hope, somehow, to hear of relics emerging layer by layer from ten metres of soil crammed with two millennia.

The earthquake came on the twelfth of October. Tremors began a few minutes past three in the afternoon, judging by the saucepans rattling on our kitchen shelf. I rang my parents to check on them. Abdou said they'd gone out.

The hospital phoned me later. Destiny turns on the slimmest axis, and, for one fraction of a second, I believed disaster could be unsaid and undone, but of course it couldn't. A concrete balcony had crashed on to my parents as they ambled arm in arm towards avenue Horreya. They had been cruzzed.

They were put in adjacent hospital rooms, along with their multiple fractures and intravenous drips. Their bruising shocked me. Father had a broken pelvis and a bag bulging with blood-stained urine. Mother had been started on antibiotics for her critically crushed leg.

'We will save the limb, *insha Allah*,' her doctor told me.

The doctors were kind, though the nurses required constant *baksheesh* just to fetch a glass of water. '*Izay el Butagaz*,' explained one of them when I was a little slow in finding my purse. As with a gas cylinder, you must pay to get anything out of it.

I brought my parents the usual chicken and rice with white sauce, but they had no appetite. Mother was flushed and her skin was dry. I smeared Vaseline on to her parched lips and fed her slivers of ice to suck.

Her leg didn't improve. Worse, her kidneys began to fail, the doctor took Fouad and me aside to explain. It was all to do with her damaged muscles releasing harmful toxins.

'Is there nothing you can do?' I asked.

They'd already tried everything.

The toxins seemed to have reached Mother's brain, too. 'Simone says she's coming back,' Mother muttered after I dabbed more Vaseline on to her lips. 'Just to visit.'

'Really?'

'Of course.' She had written the other day, Mother said, a proper letter in which she had asked after everyone. 'I forgot to tell you.'

'Is that the first time she sent you a letter?'

'I think so.'

'May I see it?'

'It's somewhere in my bag. She has a son. Now that he's better, she can think of travelling. He has been very ill, you know.'

It sounded bizarre. 'I didn't even know she had a son. How did you hear about him?'

Mother made a nondescript sound.

'How old is her son?' I persisted.

'How should I know?'

'Right. Where's your handbag?'

Her shoulders slumped. 'I remember now. Rashida took it home for me.'

Rashida? But she had retired to her brother's village in Lebanon years ago.

Later that day, Mother spiked a fever and grew restless. 'Don't lose the photo,' she muttered as she plucked at the bedclothes.

'What photo?'

'Simone's, of course. It's right here.' She waved an emaciated arm festooned with those purple spots old people get. I looked through the bedside cabinet and found no letters or photos, just a fabric pouch containing one stocking.

Mother spiked another fever the next day and became even less coherent. Her urine bag remained empty and her mouth was so dry that I could barely catch her ramblings. I wiped her lips with a wet flannel as she murmured, 'Like a marmalade spoon. A cute one.'

'What did you say?'

There was nothing more. Those were her last words, and I had no idea if the rubbish about marmalade spoons meant anything. And now that Mother lay flat, her face marbled, I wondered if I had imagined her saying anything about Simone writing a letter, let alone visiting Alex or having a son. I searched my mother's things at home. Once again, I found no letter, no photo, not a thing from Simone. With Mother in such a confused state, and with no evidence to back it up, I couldn't believe she had a son. Still muddled, Father could tell me nothing. He hung on for another six days before he too died.

I needed to reach Simone, but how?

'Maybe you could try the university,' Zouzou suggested.

'Would they really know anything after all this time?'

'I suppose not. I did have one idea, but …'

'But what?'

'Nothing, really.'

'Can you think of anything that might help? I really am desperate.'

She couldn't.

Despite his own weakness, Fouad tried to console me. 'Concentrate on the good things, *habibti*,' he said in an increasingly hoarse voice.

'What good things?' Both my parents had died, and I feared losing my husband soon.

'The happy memories.'

'I'll try.'

I really did. In my head, I gathered together an assortment of Mother's bonkers similes and irrational fears, laced them with Father's grins and his inept repairs, and tried to keep the lot centre stage. Yet I was lost. With the death of my parents, a piece of my identity had disappeared as surely as if the *Mahabeth* had confiscated my papers. Who was I now, without my sister, my mother, and my father?

Who are we?

26

NOW

I'd discounted most of what Mother had said in hospital, especially that peculiar thing about marmalade. Yet there could have been a letter and there could have been a son. Someone could have stolen Mother's handbag. Even in this hospital, multiple signs warn patients and visitors to keep their belongings safe. I guard my box, obviously.

Looking back, I'm hardly surprised my parents were killed by a crumbling balcony. Despite what people liked to think of as Mubarak's progress, everything in Egypt was actually going wrong. When had things ever gone right? Probably sometime during the Ptolemaic era. That makes a lot of centuries of going wrong. I pause to calculate. Twenty of them, give or take.

A son. Simone had a son. Simone *has* a son. I say this to myself, trying it out to see if it has the ring of truth, and I'm still not sure.

'Is Deirdre here?' I ask the nurse who reeks of cigarettes.

'She may be in later.'

'Maybe she's lost her job,' I offer.

Finding this funny, the nurse displays her yellow teeth. 'What are you talking about?'

I shouldn't have mentioned sacking. Luckily the nurse has gone. Off to have another smoke, I imagine. She doesn't know what happened to Fouad, and I doubt telling her would make any difference.

ALEXANDRIA, MARCH 1994

I'd have to return the morphine syrup to the pharmacy. This was the stuff I'd spooned into his mouth, and often down his chin, to supplement injections from the nurse. Her needle seemed to me to scrape the bone of his wasted thigh as it went in. Then he would nod off before the nurse had even pulled up his pyjamas.

Every time he coughed, he'd have to clutch the arm of the sofa with what was left of his might. It worried me even more when he stopped coughing, because I'd think he'd gone already.

One day in March, he did. I was watching a flag on a nearby building. The pretty green flag of my childhood had long gone, replaced by the eagle of Saladin on a tricolour, the bands of red, white, and black symbolising blood, purity, and darkness overcome.

'Fouad, *chéri*, can you remember what year the eagle on the Egyptian flag became all gold?' I turned towards the sofa, and I knew.

Two lives ruined by tobacco. Other people smoked but had

not all got cancer. Why Fouad? It had to be the Evil Eye. Hadn't dozens of people told me I had a wonderful husband and a perfect marriage, even without children?

NOW

These days, medical advice pops up in every newspaper alongside tales of disgraced celebrities and sleazy politicians. There are special tests for lung cancer and trials for new cures. No wonder posters advise you to see the doctor if a cough lasts longer than three weeks. That has to be better than gasping to death with only one lung.

I force myself to think instead of brooding, but that brings me little comfort. One name keeps popping into my head, just as he always used to pop round when he was least wanted.

It proves easy to find Victor online. While I can't recall how I know he's in public relations, it's fitting to find him minding other people's business and getting paid for it to boot. He's about seventy, of course, and quite the statesman of his field, it seems, with offices around Europe.

Not the least bit bald. Or is that salt-and-pepper thatch a wig? While I wouldn't go as far as to call him handsome, he's not bad. Not bad at all. To my mind, he still has a slight squint, but his ears seem fairly normal and, all told, he looks more like George Clooney than he does a chimpanzee. Victor knows everyone, according to the web pages boasting of important clients and embellished with their compliments. One eye in Cairo, one eye in Alex. I remember that from somewhere. I must say, the site, or whatever you call it, is all very sleek. Made by AK Design, it says. There's a link on which to email him, but I am not that desperate. Funny that he too ended up in London.

ALEXANDRIA, JULY 1994

Zouzou put down her coffee cup. 'You should go to London. *Pour te changer les idées.*' She was a great one for changing ideas as often as swimsuits and lovers. A trip to London was, in her opinion, exactly what I needed after Fouad died.

She had a thin bent spine these days and was, by my reckoning, nearly eighty. While she still sauntered around in high-heeled mules, her collection of eye-catching swimsuits was less often on display. The rise of fundamentalism, Zouzou claimed, made anyone with exposed flesh feel out of place, even on a beach. It may also have had to do with a recent bout of shingles. Last winter, the virus had attacked her viciously, leaving searing pain and a long scar across her torso. 'From here to here.' She pointed with a gnarled finger. 'At least I'm still alive.'

Her poor Ralph had died in a hospital bed rather than a deckchair. Their apartment block was now surrounded by piles of rotting garbage, and the new building next door nearly touched hers. Whisky was increasingly expensive, and she didn't much care for the current clientele of the Brazilian Coffee Stores. *Maalish!* That wasn't enough to stop her going there every day.

I wondered if her advice might be right. There was less and less to keep me here and, while I told myself to stop living in hope, if I went to Europe there was probably a better chance of finding Simone.

'So have you ever thought of leaving?' I asked over our espressos.

'Leave Alex?' Zouzou spread her hands. 'Where would I go?'

That was a dilemma. She wasn't Italian, French, Lebanese, Greek, Austrian, or anything but Egyptian, and had only ever lived in Alexandria. I had two aunts in London, but Zouzou had no family outside Egypt.

Although I didn't need her to take me to Cairo to catch my flight, it was a kindness on her part. By then, I hadn't heard from Simone for a while, perhaps only a couple of times since our parents had died. She couldn't even have known of her deaths, but there was a chance that she might write again. I asked Zouzou to look after my post when I left.

'Of course.' She put a skeletal hand on my arm. 'You know you can trust me.'

NOW

Fritz strides in with Laura Ashley in tow and a nurse hovering behind both of them. 'Right,' he begins. They still seem unable to pinpoint what's wrong with me, but he gleefully reels off a list of diseases that I've now been tested for and categorically don't have. 'In summary, then, we'll need to transfer you to another facility.'

I shrink into the pillows. 'Not a care home?'

'Well, not necessarily.'

I don't believe him. In fact, I don't believe any sentence starting with *well*. They need more beds and their plan is surely to dump me in one of those places where I will fester until I'm incapable of any movement, including breathing. I watch Laura Ashley for clues. All she does is push her glasses up her nose and give me one of those smiles that means nothing.

'I don't know if she is even entitled to NHS hospital treatment,' the nurse pipes up.

Of course I am entitled! I would explain it to her exactly, if I could find the words for all the stuff I had to sort out and the hoops I had to jump through. My visa was all by the book, with the help of my aunts. Seriously, must I be an outcast wherever I go?

Fritz shrugs and, after a few moments, the doctors amble away. My head's in a spin and Deirdre's not here to help me, but somehow I have to avoid ending up in that facility that they pretend isn't a care home. I've no idea who can help get me out of this fix, and Sheila is hardly on the right wavelength at the moment.

I find my way back to Victor's website easily. It's quite artistic, I'll give him that. A red London bus goes careering across the screen, to show that he is oh-so-British. Obviously, he didn't make the website himself. Where does one go to get those things made? A ping goes off in my head. Right away, I open another tab, as Deirdre showed me.

Website designer Simone Khoury. Go.

I am instantly lost in page upon page of results. Honestly, I can't tell if there's anything related to my sister here. Would she have the skills to send buses whizzing across a website? When I last saw her, nobody we knew even dreamed of having a computer.

LONDON, OCTOBER 1999

My aunts had left Egypt, too, after my mother died, and now all I had to do was take the number ten bus virtually to their door. Tante Georgette had owned the apartment in Pimlico since the days of Farouk, though she and Harold had lived here for a only few months as a couple before Harold's death.

Although I was over fifty, my aunts still considered me to be a treasure and a love, greeting me with, '*Trésor, amour*,' and noisy kisses, after which they would feed me to the point of stuffing me like a Strasbourg goose.

'*Chérie, on est très bien à Londres*,' Tante Georgette said, depositing the remains of her crimson lipstick on the rim of her teacup.

Georgette's perfume was still rose-scented, though today Joséphine reeked of Vicks VapoRub as she was warding off a chill that could yet prove to be life-threatening in this dreadful weather. 'It rains every other day, you know. At least.'

'Some days are sunny, *chérie*,' Tante Georgette said. '*Yom 'assal, yom bassal.*' *One day honey, one day onions* was still a saying in perfect keeping with my aunts' love of food. 'At least I don't need to fan myself all the time.'

I couldn't understand why they had waited so long to leave Alex. With assets and accommodation in Europe, along with right of abode, they could have moved here decades earlier, when people were desperate to leave Egypt.

'But Egypt is our homeland,' Tante Georgette said.

'And we couldn't leave our dear sister. You see that, don't you?'

I saw. The rest of the world might have forgotten Simone, but her family hadn't, and Mother had needed her sisters.

'Now, *chérie*, tell us what you're doing these days,' Georgette said.

Translating wasn't as lucrative as I'd hoped. 'I'm teaching colloquial Arabic to small groups of adults.'

Joséphine clapped her hands. 'I always said you were clever.'

'Are they good students, *chérie*?' Georgette asked.

My students kept stumbling over the simplest words and looked blank when I bid them *sabah el kheir* each week. I'd hoped that, after six months, they'd have grasped *morning of hope*, the most common Arabic greeting of all. 'They're a delight.'

'I'm so pleased, *chérie*. Have a palmier biscuit.'

'Wow. Better than the ones from Baudrot.'

Georgette tutted modestly.

'She made them,' Joséphine said. 'I hope you can stay for her galantine of chicken.'

'The recipe is so easy,' Georgette claimed. 'Even a simpleton like me can follow it.' My aunts had never had to find jobs in the end. Instead, they had become accomplished cooks.

They had heard nothing of Simone, but were still in touch with people from Alex and had some news to share. 'Do you remember a Belgian attaché called Alain?' Tante Georgette asked as she slid a slice of galantine on to my plate and offered me pear chutney.

'Belgian attaché, my foot.' Joséphine sniffed. 'He wasn't an attaché at all. Probably wasn't even Belgian.'

'Surely you know him, Nadia?' Georgette said.

'We may have met once.'

'Well, *chérie*,' Georgette said. 'He was Belgian, but no diplomat, as Joséphine says. I don't know how he fooled people for so long.'

'He's in jail now,' Joséphine said.

'Stop it, you.' Georgette batted her away. 'Let me tell her. Apparently, he had been smuggling for years and years. Drugs in, money out. Maybe people, too. In or out. I don't know about all these dreadful things that people get up to these days. But the Belgian was a complete fraud. Did you know he pretended to watch birds at Montazah when he really had his eye on little boats that came in after dark?'

'At Montazah?'

'Yes!' Georgette continued. 'It was your dear cousin who discovered this.'

'What dear cousin is that?'

'*Le cher Victor!*' Georgette crowed.

'*Comme il est gentil! Comme il est beau!*' Joséphine went.

'Yes, and Victor took photos that proved it. After that, the Belgian was arrested.'

'And now he's in jail,' Joséphine repeated.

'As you know, *chérie*, Egyptian prisons are an absolute hellhole.' Tante Georgette was overjoyed.

'Victor is in public relations. He's very clever,' Joséphine added. 'He was always clever, of course, even as a young child. *Comme il est intelligent.*'

I yearned to contradict her, but then Victor did help bring the Belgian to justice.

'*Et comme il est riche!*' Georgette waved a hand back and forth to indicate the extent of his wealth. 'His own business and everything. He's doing so well for himself. Isn't that perfectly wonderful, Nadia?'

I grudgingly agreed. 'Did I already mention that your galantine is exquisite?'

NOW

Of course. That's how I heard about Victor's work. And now I know exactly where to find him. The imminent threat of being sent to a facility, whatever it is, makes me desperate, so, with some effort, I locate a biro and draft this on the back of a menu.

Dear Victor

He's never been dear to me before, but men love flattery. I remember that much.

How wonderful to hear of your stunning success. They always said you were brilliant. I know this is a long shot, but I wonder if you have any news at all of my sister. As you remember, Simone left Alex in 1967 with only vague plans of returning. I am in hospital and would love to get in touch with her.

No, that's all wrong. I want information from him, not a get-well card.

It would be very useful to get in touch with her as soon as possible, so anything you know would be much appreciated. Look forward to hearing from you.

I transcribe it laboriously. There. Send.

It's late, so I close the iPad and connect it to its plugger. Maybe Alain did smuggle people. I think of jails in Egypt. They may be vile but, here in the UK, torture takes place in care homes. Something or other abuse, people call it. They'll pull me about like a ragdoll and won't care if I fall apart at the seams. I have nobody left to protect me.

LONDON, JUNE 2003

In the darkened apartment, I chased traces of powdered sugar around the glass bowl, the last remains of the Turkish delight, then I licked my finger. It was an easy decision to keep most of the crystal, the portraits, and the brightly coloured silk scarves, still redolent of Georgette's rose perfume and Joséphine's musky scent.

My aunts had died in quick succession, leaving me with an apartment to my name and a hole in my life. The property had to be sold, of course. I couldn't have afforded the upkeep, even with the money my aunts had also left me.

I earmarked a few photos to keep, including two of Simone as a teenager at Montazah, and of course there were the precious postcards my aunts had looked after for nearly ten years, in the tin box with faded French writing.

27

NOW

I tense and consider hiding under the bedclothes as two doctors stride towards me. One is my regular Teutonic medic and the other is a young man with a sizeable whitehead sprouting from his forehead. It hardly inspires confidence when doctors can't cure their own acne.

Fritz has found a new topic. 'How many miscarriages did you have?'

'I think it was seven in all.' When I'd told them before, they'd shown not an ounce of interest. Same as when I mentioned the list I couldn't find at the chemist.

'And did your mother?' Fritz tilts his head.

It's doubtful whether Mother would have shared such details. 'No idea. I don't know about my sister, either.'

Their eyes meet. 'She says she has a sister,' Fritz says.

'I do have a sister.'

They ignore me as they confer over a clipboard. 'What

symptoms did you say she had on admission? There was a seizure, wasn't there?'

'Seizures!' The spotty one's face suggests he's just won the lottery. He and Fritz deliberate for a moment. 'Could it be antiphospholipid syndrome?'

Fritz nods. 'I'd say so.'

'But I haven't had a seizure since I've been here. What are you taking about?'

'You could have APS, also known as antiphospholipid syndrome or Hughes syndrome.' His volcano threatens to erupt from excitement as he explains that APS can cause still-births as well as miscarriages. 'Or, indeed, the entire spectrum of fetal loss,' he finishes with a jubilant flourish. It's scary how inappropriate a doctor's expressions can be. They're deadly serious when sharing good news, and relentlessly upbeat when someone's going downhill.

'Is there a treatment?' I don't know why I ask. It's too late for me now.

Fritz nods. 'Well, aspirin can help, as can heparin.'

'It's an anticoagulant,' adds the spotty one.

I'm taking this in. So my miscarriages could have been prevented. Fouad should have known, being a gynaecologist. How could we all accept that such violent expulsions from the womb were normal events to be endured again and again? I can't bear to think of all those repeated losses over the years.

'We'll know more when we've run some tests,' Fritz says.

I'm not sure I want to know after all. This APS is hardly going to help me now, when I should have had the treatment decades ago. So many lost opportunities. There could just be one silver lining. 'How long did you say the tests might take?'

'Couple of days, probably,' the spotty one says. 'Why?'

Hardly long enough to delay my transfer to a facility. 'No reason.'

Before they leave the ward, they fire off a final salvo of questions about thrombosis, rashes, nose bleeds, cigarettes, the Pill, and headaches. My head is bursting now, that's for sure.

When Sheila comes in, I tell her I emailed Victor.

'You always were in love with Victor. Is he married?'

Typical Sheila. She doesn't know the first thing about love. Although quite a lot about lust. I can tell she has a new man from her sparkly top and the spring in her step.

'No idea. I just hope he has some news of Simone.'

'Me too, sweetie.' Sheila gets up, promising to be back soon.

Is Victor going to answer? I wouldn't put it past him to ignore my email, just to drive in the fact that he is the important man he always wanted to be. By contrast, I'm barely capable of getting out of bed unaided. If I'm to escape from this downhill slide that ends in that facility, I have to do something, and soon.

And I will, *fuck him*. I say it under my breath, but why shouldn't I be allowed to swear out loud? At seventy, I'm entitled to say *fuck* whenever I want. Fuck. So there.

I wake up the iPad, because I have things to do. Advertisements tell me I can buy powders to make me stronger, but I ignore those. Here's what I need. Exercises. There are all kinds. Unfortunately, most of them seem designed for people who are already gymnasts.

Ah-ha! Exercises to strengthen the legs. These can be done sitting on the floor. Or presumably on a bed. It says here that the idea is to make the quads muscles work. I peer under the bedclothes. My quads are nowhere to be seen. The video, however, shows exactly what to do. Keeping the knee straight,

I must lift up each leg by just a few centimetres off the horizontal. Reckon I could do this without anyone noticing. I study the video with the sound off.

'Keeping yourself busy, I see,' the woman mountain says.

'That's right,' I reply.

I watch the iPad again as I lift each leg off the mattress in turn. After a few repeats, I only get a useless trembling above the knees, but it must be in my brain connections now. I've learned the exercise and can do more later. Right now my legs are wobbly and they hurt like fuck. Yes, like fuck.

LONDON, FEBRUARY 1996

Oh Lord, how that hurt! I was as dry as a disused gate. Also like a rusty gate, there was a hint of red fluid.

Norman and I met at a dreary event at the public library where we sat on hard plastic chairs and endured an author droning on from his latest book. I wished I hadn't bothered braving the onset of snow flurries, because the first chapter was dire and the second chapter worse. Bored and trapped, I gazed about the room. Another person, I saw, was equally unimpressed. We shared conspiratorial glances and waited until our author stumbled on to an end.

Norman met me before I reached the door. 'Hello,' he said by way of a stunning opener.

My response was no less original. 'Hi.'

A quick look over his shoulder, then he said, 'I haven't been this bored in a long time.'

'Me neither.' I was on sparkling form.

A few more witty repartees, and we'd shared names and

discovered we were both famished. 'There's a little place to eat nearby,' he said. 'I forget what it's called.'

'Sounds good to me.' It had been a long time since I'd been out for a meal with someone, *tête à tête*. This was before I discovered that it was one of those places that specialise in burgers, fried chicken, pizza, and kebabs, none of which was particularly appetising. Egg and chips seemed the safest option, though the chips turned out to be overdone and the lukewarm egg white wobbled on the plate. I had a mug of tea and tried not to swallow the teabag.

Norman had blue eyes and good teeth. When he offered to walk me home, I let him take my arm, which resulted in my losing a glove. We got to my building, and I knew he would come up. Just for a coffee, we agreed. He gave me a dazzling smile. They might have been dentures.

I was fifty and hadn't seen the curse for a year. For longer than that, there'd been drenching night sweats and, by day, hot flushes that could be mortally embarrassing in public. I was curious, I suppose, to know whether things still worked.

I cried in bed later, and not just from the physical pain. It was Fouad's birthday, and I knew that this could never be love or even pleasure. The blood was on the paper when I went to the bathroom. I gripped the basin to steady myself.

After Norman left my apartment, promising to keep in touch, I cried again at the thought of something being wrong. That was before Sheila informed me the following day that I'd been jolly silly and might have caught an STI.

'STI?'

'You mean you don't know what that is?' Sheila said.

I duly went to the private clinic she recommended near Regent's Park, where the doctor interrogated me at length about oral sex, anal sex, and everything in between. And had I ever paid, or been paid, for sex?

'No,' I replied yet again. Sheila had told me they routinely did all the tests, so why did he have to ask such intimate questions, unless he was enjoying the embarrassment of a foolish, middle-aged widow who had not considered even the simplest precaution?

He had a thousand more questions. Was I on medication for blood pressure or anything else? I was not. Did I take herbal medicines? When I made an impatient face, he pointed out that there were many interactions and side-effects linked with all kinds of medicines and supplements, whether prescribed or not. I supposed he was trying to justify the hefty clinic fee with a ton of irrelevant queries.

The whole thing cost over £200, more than I had earned that entire week from teaching. When the results came by phone later, I cried once more, this time with relief.

NOW

I crane my neck but Deirdre isn't here. She hasn't been into work in I don't know how long. What if she's lost her job on my account?

There's still no answer from Victor. He's deliberately making me suffer. Well, I can just get on with my exercises. When I follow the routine as per YouTube, I tremble less, but my legs feel unbearably heavy before I come anywhere near completing all those repetitions.

I take a breather and, while nobody's looking, I get my handbag and take my St John's wort. I'm fiddling with the plastic lid when it hits me. What had the sex-infection doctor said? I'm not sure he mentioned particular medicines, but the thought is enough to stop me. I shove the container back in the locker before a nurse catches me. I'd better ask the doctors, even if I don't entirely trust them.

It isn't long before Fritz and Laura Ashley are on the ward again, putting some other patient through her paces. I literally lie in wait for them to amble over.

'Hello, Ms Wissa,' Laura Ashley says. 'How are you?'

I save time by ignoring this. 'Can my symptoms be due to herbal things?'

They resume their study of some papers in Fritz's hands.

'Because I've been taking ...' I turn to the locker where my tablets are, but the words won't come.

Fritz looks up, irritated. 'What?'

'Can herbal tablets give you headaches, dizziness, and make you tired and weak?' I blurt. 'Because I've been taking some for a while.'

Fritz has already been bleeped away, and Laura Ashley makes to follow him. 'Try not to worry, Ms Wissa. The new tests will help sort things out. Someone will be along shortly to take blood.'

'Are you coming back?' I throw after her, but she's already gone.

28

ALEXANDRIA, SEPTEMBER 2004

'I don't want to see the building that killed my parents.'

'You won't,' Zouzou assured me. 'There are so many new places that you can't even see where it used to be.'

There'd been a population explosion since I was last here, and a construction boom to match. My city had grown into acres of motley apartment blocks, some half-finished, many barely started, others crumbling into ruin, and not one of them recognisable.

It was September 2004, and I was here for some legal documents which, I'd been repeatedly told, had to be signed in person. Alex bubbled with noise and confusion, with clanking metal, pulses of music, mounds of horse droppings, eternal klaxons, shouting from windows, yelling from everywhere, a broken donkey cart, a reversing lorry disgorging oranges, and people gesticulating wildly while hollering into mobile phones.

Zouzou and I decided to meet at the coffee shop. My sense of direction befuddled, I took several wrong turnings, navigating past stinking mounds of garbage and women thrusting their fly-covered babies at me in the hope of a few piasters.

When I got to the Brazilian, Zouzou was already there. I bent down to kiss her. She still had gaudy lips and impeccable carmine nails, but age had shrunken her despite the towering mules that went *click-click* when she walked. Each bone of her bent spine protruded through her thin dress, giving a good impression of a stegosaurus. As expected, she asked, 'How long has it been?'

We made several guesses and failed to agree on the answer. Zouzou's jaw still moved rhythmically.

'Still chewing your beloved mint Chiclets?'

She shook her head and confided that she was struggling to keep her dentures in place. 'I need a new top set, but my dentist has died. *Maalish!*'

Zouzou must have been nearly ninety now. I didn't ask, and she'd have lied anyway, but I did remark that her complexion was still smooth.

She patted her cheek. 'Botox in Beirut.'

'What happened to Madame Amin?'

'She's still in Chicago, and her suitcase is still missing.' Zouzou always knew everything and everybody. If Alex was the capital of wagging tongues, Zouzou reigned as its queen.

'I hear the Belgian attaché got caught smuggling and ended up in prison.'

'He did. They're probably torturing him now,' she added brightly. 'Do you know that they hang people up in a large sack, along with a couple of stray cats? Then they beat the sack with a stick. The cats get scared and tear the prisoner to ribbons, you see.'

I saw.

'Did you know he tried to seduce me?' Zouzou said. 'Not every man likes them young, you know.' She drew herself up as straight as her spine allowed.

Zeinab still lived in Cairo, but I had lost touch with many other friends. 'Do you ever hear anything of Alicia or her family?'

'Not a word. Her parents are dead, of course. They'd have been about 100 now. I suppose Alicia is still in that place. If you give me a moment, I might remember the name.' Zouzou rapped the side of her head with her knuckles as if knocking to be let in.

I asked if she had any news of Simone.

'Simone?' Zouzou echoed. 'I'd forgotten all about her, *parole de dieu*. Do you remember Neguib who had a cabin near the Amins? I went to his funeral a couple of months ago. It was an excellent funeral. One dresses up, of course, though that has become harder now that Mademoiselle Violette is no longer here.'

'Where is she?'

'The cemetery at Chatby, poor soul.'

'Poor soul.'

Zouzou consulted her rhinestone-encrusted watch. 'Khairy should be here any minute.'

Sure enough, a young man turned up in a crisp white shirt and dark trousers. His thick glasses evoked goldfish bowls, and his beaming face suggested a knack of looking on the bright side of everything. Zouzou hailed him as the best friend she'd had since her darling Ralphie had died, God rest his soul.

'At your service, *ya madame*.' Khairy kissed her hand.

'Khairy *mon amour*, my friend Nadia has been away for a few years, so I want you to show her as much of Alex as you can.'

Khairy pronounced himself delighted and said his car was

around the corner. Zouzou folded into the back of the little Peugeot, while I installed myself in the front, pushing aside a spring that had worked its way through the seat. Despite blue nazar beads against the Eye, Zouzou felt it advisable to cling to the back of Khairy's seat while simultaneously clutching her faux Chanel bag.

Khairy manoeuvred the car capably, given that he had a random approach to gears and barely gave the road a cursory glance. I drank in my surroundings. Many once-familiar streets had vanished altogether, while others had been transformed into dual carriageways. The kerbstones were still black and white, and the breeze coming off the sea was as stiff as ever, but the road was now an eight-lane highway hugging the shore. This had meant trimming back many of the beaches, which were impossibly crowded as result, even in late September.

'What's the point of that?' I gestured towards a hideous structure spanning Stanley Bay. With a square turret at each end, it looked a cut-price Montazah Palace.

Khairy fixed his goldfish bowls on me. By now, he had given up all pretence of observing the road. 'The point of the bridge is to relieve congestion. It is also a tourist attraction. And courting couples like to stand just there, and gaze into the sunset.'

I allowed myself a little snort. The congestion didn't look much relieved to me.

'It is beautiful, is it not?' he asked.

I made a face. 'Not really.'

He broke into a hearty Egyptian laugh, the kind that tells you nothing, least of all whether the person agrees with you.

My childhood home had gone, replaced by two mismatched blocks of some fifteen storeys. I pointed. 'Is that building leaning?'

'A little,' Zouzou said.

In a side street that used to be near our house stood a parked car, battered and dusty, with one of its headlights knocked out. A couple were making out in the back, the woman traditionally cloaked in a black robe, not pretending to conceal what was going on.

'People used to pay the Belgian to use cars. Do you remember?' Zouzou said. 'That was one of the things he did.'

I didn't remember.

Khairy double-parked at Zouzou's request. Three storeys taller than before, the block where Fouad and I had lived was adorned with sheets hanging from the windows, fridges and chicken coops on balconies, and satellite dishes stuck on everywhere. The front entrance of the building was open. People huddled in the lobby, glued to a football match on TV. A frenzied commentator harangued both teams at full volume, invoking Allah the merciful at every kick of the game and scolding each of the players as if they were naughty children. I had forgotten what Egyptian sports programmes were like.

We drove on. 'So many buildings gone,' I whined. Only one passageway downtown seemed untouched, between the pigeon restaurant and a shoe repairer. The name of the alley escaped me, but there it was, along with a memory that lay just beyond my grasp. I rapped the side of my head as Zouzou had done. Nothing came to me.

'There's another McDonald's.' Khairy pointed.

'It's better than the building next to it.' I was being a curmudgeon of the worst kind, a cosmopolitan Alexandrian who could not accept that the olden days, *ayam zaman*, were gone. Yet how could anyone be indifferent to the obliteration of culture that went hand in hand with a rocketing population and a frantic pace of construction?

'*Eh da?*' I gestured towards yet another concrete eyesore

with rusty iron bars poking their way out of the masonry and errant electric cables hanging over the doorway.

'It is someone's home,' Khairy replied.

He was right, of course. Rents had been frozen at ridiculously low levels. That made it impossible to maintain older buildings properly, so they were left to decay until they were demolished to make way for new. People needed homes, and the new ones went up quickly. Those shoddy blocks, too, rapidly went into disrepair. That much I knew. I waved my arm hopelessly. 'And all these new buildings collapse.'

'Not all,' Khairy pointed out with impeccable logic as he changed from first to fourth without troubling the gears in between. 'There are more buildings standing than have fallen.'

The dazzling Bibliotheca, at least, did not disappoint. Every single cliché about it is true. It is upward and outward looking, the essence of Alexandria as I wanted to remember it. Momentarily uplifted, I suggested driving out to Agami and its dazzling white beaches.

Zouzou made a choking sound. 'God, no! Four lanes of cars where there was once nothing but palm trees. And the ugliest buildings in the world. Nobody goes to Agami anymore.'

'On the contrary, *ya madame*,' Khairy corrected her. 'Everyone goes there. That's why it is crowded.'

Zouzou gripped Khairy's seat tight with bony hands. 'Trust me. You don't want to go to Agami.'

'What about Montazah?'

'Well, people do go there,' Zouzou conceded. 'People nobody has ever heard of, naturally. Do you want to see what's become of Pastroudis? We can go, if you like.'

I preferred to forget Pastroudis.

NOW

Blood is thicker than water. I've already worked out that Simone had sought Omar's help. But, if Mother was right, she had a son. I don't know what to make of it. That she didn't have an abortion?

The alleyway by the pigeon restaurant bugs me. Maybe Victor knows something about it. He was always hanging around, shoving his nose and his camera into other people's business. One eye in Cairo, one eye in Alex. Now I regret that my email only asked him for recent information on Simone.

Hadn't Simone muttered something about Alicia before setting out that day? *Alicia and the others.* How is it only coming back to me now? Sometimes brain connections are so strong that I recall things perfectly, while at other times there's nothing there. Perhaps the connections work loose now and again, as in Father's appliances. What had Simone meant? On the back of my menu, I jot down *Alicia and the others,* in case it becomes significant.

A cleaner is here, wiping under the beds with a stick thing. I get her to plug in the iPad while she's here. 'Got any rubbish?' she asks.

I toss the bottles of herbal supplements into her bin bag.

There are a couple of nurses by the desk at the top of the ward. When one of them passes to do someone's dressing, I try to intercept. 'Excuse me.' I have to say this twice before the nurse notices.

'Yes?'

'Do you know when Nurse Deirdre will be here again?'

'She's off sick.'

I don't for one moment believe it. 'Do you know what's wrong with her?'

'Couldn't say.'

Fuck. Deirdre's lost her job, and it's my fault. I sit brooding until I realise it won't help anything. Turning on my — no, Deirdre's — iPad, I see Victor has replied. My elation subsides when I read his email. He would be happy to help, he says, but he knows nothing of Simone. *It seemed you two often kept yourselves to yourselves,* he adds.

Truth be known, Simone excluded me, too. Half the time I had no idea what she was doing. I reread Victor's short message. At the bottom of the email, there's a logo and something about a new project. Seems he is involved in some charity that I've never heard of. I hadn't expected that. Victor must have changed. My thoughts turn again to what Simone was like. Standoffish when she felt like it, but compassionate and generous, too.

I sit bolt upright. Could she be working with a charity? Not one to do with animals or Arabs, I don't think. Maybe Sheila can give me ideas when she comes in. I've lost track of when visiting is. Here in hospital, I'm in a strange version of reality where my pulse is too fast, my headache is eternal, and nothing is normal. Sometimes time leaps from one moment to another. Next thing I know, it limps and staggers, then sits itself down for a breather before setting off again. I lie against my pillows as I recall a clock doing exactly that.

CAMBRIDGE, JUNE 2009

A cluster of visitors had formed on the corner of Bene't Street to gawp at the monstrous winged apparition perched atop a golden disc. I too observed the clock at length, comparing its moving blue lights against my watch. It was indeed accurate only once every five minutes. The massive gold pendulum was irregular in its journey from left to right, and right to left as well. How? Its designer must have had considerable talent to create a timepiece so reliably unreliable.

The sinister creature at the top, part grasshopper, part dragon, moved its hideous jaws and blinked its gothic eyes at random. It's called the Chronophage because it eats time, though nothing eats time quite as much as standing there in a pack of tourists, forcing bicycles and everyone else to detour around you.

No less than three tour guides in waistcoats tried to interest me in a walk around the colleges or a trip on the river in one of those flat-bottomed boats they call punts. I shook my head and they went on to accost others, calling out, 'Hi guys, are you here for the punting?'

From here, King's College Chapel loomed over my shoulder, and it was only, I'd read, a few steps to the Backs, the grassy open part where some of the oldest and most magnificent colleges meet the river. Within a couple of hundred metres, I could also visit Trinity College Great Court or any number of other iconic tourist destinations.

I preferred to scan faces. Simone, with her intellectual tendencies, would have loved Cambridge. A wisp of a woman manoeuvred her huge baby buggy up on to the pavement. When she turned, I saw what made it unwieldy. Her toddlers appeared to be twins thrashing their chubby legs with delight.

I wondered what made a child happy or miserable. Would I have worked out how to look after a baby, a toddler, and then maybe another baby, because, after all, most women have more than one?

Weary, I stopped at the Copper Kettle for a coffee, after which I made my way down to the river where people slopped the beers they'd bought from a postcard-perfect pub. The bridge in Simone's postcard was another bridge entirely, though, wasn't it?

It turned out to be a slow trudge up to Magdalene Bridge, which, I discovered, is pronounced *maudlin*. I passed ancient courtyards, majestic buildings, and eternal souvenir shops. Tourists paused on the narrow pavements to take photos or to snack from Styrofoam containers. I had to walk in the street until a bicycle bell virtually in my ear forced me to leap back on to the pavement.

Magdalene Bridge, when I got there, was something of a disappointment. I wondered why, of all the resplendent sights in Cambridge, Simone had chosen a card of this place. Leaning against the railings, I gazed at a weeping willow trailing into the Cam and punts gliding beneath the bridge. Was Simone here? I studied the murky waters and failed to see through to the bottom.

29

NOW

There's a huddle by the nurses' station. 'Old people get institutionalised,' says a nurse in a darker blue than the others. Her head movements suggest that she's talking about me.

I need to escape. Now they're talking about EMI this and EMI that.

The woman mountain reads my puzzled face. 'Elderly mentally infirm,' she chips in. 'That's what EMI is. Places for the mentally ill.'

If I'm already elderly mentally infirm, it's too late. I shut my eyes and pray, infusing my whispered words with Rashida's voice.

When I open my eyes again, the staff have gone, my mouth has turned into a wad of blotting paper, and there's a newspaper at the foot of my bed, its headline screaming about something else that gives you cancer. 'Where did this paper come from?' I ask.

The woman mountain stirs. 'Woman in bed three left it before she went home.'

Sure enough, the redhead has gone, and her bed lies flat and tidy. 'That was nice,' I say. 'Do you know when lunch is?'

'We've already had lunch,' the mountain says. I detect the shadow of a smile.

Three doctors arrive. It's Fritz, Laura Ashley, and the one with the eruption on his forehead. I leaf through the newspaper while keeping an eye on their progress down the ward. On the bottom of the page, an article says that over ten per cent of hospital patients are admitted because of drug side effects. This is my chance. The arteries pound in my temples as Dr Laura Ashley approaches.

'Look.' I hold up the newspaper. 'And I've had lots of tablets. I've been taking—' In my excitement I've once again forgotten the names of the pills. That's okay. I'll show them the containers.

'Let us know when you remember, okay?' Laura Ashley says. She looks at some charts before returning to her discussion with the other two, and they all set about *umming* and *ahhing* about different tests until they leave.

I will jot down everything that's bobbing about in my head. Apart from herbal pills to tell the doctors about, there are knee exercises to do. And what's happened to Deirdre? Magdalene Bridge is the odd one out. I'm confused and my tongue is like the Sahara. Could Simone be working with a charity? Will Deirdre ever come back? I know I've got a mountain to climb, but that's nothing to the lengths I've already been to. I thought I'd find my sister in Cairo, that famous spring. The pounding inside my skull echoes the thump of tanks on the tarmac.

CAIRO, JANUARY 2011

Waves of young people. The air thick with tear gas. Tanks on the bridge. Police in riot gear. A fusillade of water cannon. Molotov cocktails from protestors. A hailstorm of rubber bullets into the crowd.

Blood throbbed in my temples as we approached Midan el Tahrir. I grabbed Zeinab's hand. 'Let's go the other way.'

The only recognisable part of Tahrir Square lay to the South. From its chunky, Soviet-style building, the *Mugamma'* handles ninety per cent of Egypt's extensive bureaucracy. That day, the *Mugamma'* might have been shut, but Tahrir was very much open. Zeinab and I slipped into the square alongside a family who seemed set on a jolly day out.

Despite some unease, it felt the right place for me to be, and there was the chance I might find Simone. This was, after all, the country in which I'd last seen her. If she was in Egypt, she'd be right here, taking part in the demonstrations with this motley crowd dotted with faces painted in black, white, and red, their placards and banners aloft. I asked around. 'Do you know a woman called Simone? About my age.'

An old man shrugged. 'Nobody cares what age you are. We are all the same here.'

Scuffles broke out again. The police were here. No. Wait. They popped up over there.

My sixty-fifth birthday was on the Day of Anger, which I took as a sign, though I had missed the first two days of protests. Once in Tahrir Square, Zeinab and I soon made friends with a Cairene of about forty. Wedad had long black hair and glitzy earrings. As she explained, she was one of thousands who had sworn not to leave the square until Mubarak did the decent thing and left office.

'When do you think that will be?' I asked.

'Soon, soon, *insha Allah.*' Until then, Wedad would be here along with a gigantic poster that read *My new address: Tahrir Square*.

The number of women struck me. Here, veiled Egyptians mingled with young women in jeans and sunglasses. The chants, the banners, the graffiti all sent out the same message. *El sha'b yureed, isqat el nizam.* The people want the downfall of the regime. The banners and placards said so, not just in Arabic, but in English, French, Spanish, Hebrew, even Chinese.

'Is it for the TV cameras?' I yelled.

'No, my sister.' A demonstrator gave me that Egyptian nod that means *No*. 'It is to make absolutely sure the president understands.'

The curfew made no difference. Zeinab and I came every day, along with thousands of people in *galabeyyas,* headscarves, T-shirts, blue jeans, bringing open-mouthed children, too, all of them chanting and waving flags. This was a world in transition, but to what, exactly?

Another wave of action. People leaped on parked cars. Water cannon and tear gas pushed back a line of protesters. Demonstrators responded with stones and slogans and made helmets out of cardboard boxes. Blood stains on the tarmac. A bonfire. Police cars aflame. Fire engines. More sprays of tear gas. A young man handed out vinegar and onions as protection. People also used sunglasses, scarves wrapped around the nose and mouth, sleeves held up against the face, and sweaters pulled up as far as they would go.

Then calm. Midan el Tahrir became a village, complete with TV screens, football teams, and loudspeakers rigged up to palm trees. Above first-aid posts and sleeping bags rose flags of many nations. I wasn't the only one who'd felt the pull back to the homeland. No Simone so far, but the neighbourhood was as cosmopolitan as the multilingual banners. Christians side by side with Muslims. All of us Egyptians.

Wedad flicked back her hair as she related tales of cruelty far worse than anything under Nasser. She declared that the long state of emergency had just been a smokescreen for intimidation, persecution, arrests, imprisonment, and worse. Everyone knew someone who'd been made to vanish. 'The United States thinks this is capitalism,' Wedad yelled. 'So it has supported Mubarak. But it is not capitalism.' She wagged a finger. 'It is brutal dictatorship.'

Zeinab agreed with a nod. She knew.

Protestors bellowed across the square as they grumbled about the economy and the sky-high cost of food and rent. Self-righteous men declaimed. Mubarak's reign, throughout which there had been a state of emergency, had been a thirty-year saga of oppression and poverty, of non-existent services, and mass unemployment. Twenty-five percent! No wonder the Muslim Brotherhood were on the way back. Banned under Nasser, the *Ikhwan* had emerged at long last from the shadows. The Brotherhood was a force for good, many said. I so wanted to believe it.

Every day, I went round the square, dodging fellow protesters and food vendors. Still no Simone in the crowd. Was she here? Then it occurred to me. She might even be injured, and I'd have no way of knowing.

I tried to talk to Wedad about my sister, but her mind was on other things. 'Do you realise, after all this, Mubarak refuses to stand down?' Wedad spat. 'The idiot.'

'We will beat him with our shoes,' Wedad's medical-student son said. Footwear is the Egyptian weapon of choice for insults. Hadn't Nasser threatened to hit the British with a shoe over Suez?

I asked Wedad's son if he knew how to find out about casualties.

He shrugged. 'Just wait. One hears eventually.'

Helicopters chuffed overhead and the fluttering in my chest kept time at twice the pace of a normal heart, I was sure. Then the atmosphere turned festive again, and my nerves unwound. When we weren't talking or chanting, we sang the songs of Umm Kulthum to the beat of *tabla* drums. In the square, barbers gave free haircuts. People danced. Couples married. We were a million people now, they said. Who was going to stop a million people?

We are all Egyptians.

I joined in, even if some would still call my family *shawam* or *khawaga*. Wiping my damp palms, I bought a couple of pretzels. Along with vendors, musicians, novelists, and poets had also appeared. The folk hero Ahmed Fouad Negm was too frail to attend, but the crowd recited his poems again and again. I knew only the title of one of his poems, the one that always resonated for me, 'Who Are They and Who Are We?'

They said Omar Sharif was standing on a balcony, over there, look! The only person I wanted to see was Simone, but I too looked, of course, and saw nothing. Rumours erupted and made their way around the *midan*. Singer Amr Diab wasn't here yet, but Bruce Springsteen was definitely coming.

'No, really. On my mother's eyes,' one man swore, gesticulating into my face.

A woman mocked him. 'And tomorrow we have Elvis, *mish kida*?'

More rumours flew. Mubarak had already fled, some said.

People embraced, cried, jumped for joy. Turned out it was wishful thinking. Tahrir had it all, pro-Mubarak rallies and looting included. Vigilante groups sprouted, many composed of Muslim Brotherhood. Young women were harassed, jostled, intimidated, cornered, and possibly worse. Even at the age of sixty-five, I feared that Zeinab and I might become prey too. The people, we heard, had burnt police stations and unlocked jails, freeing thousands of prisoners out on to the streets. Was that true? I had no idea, but, on our route back to Zeinab's after that news we felt safer tagging along with a married couple we had met.

On the tenth of February, Zeinab and I made our way to our now usual spot in Tahrir. The air was heavy with thunder before sunshine dispersed the clouds. We bought falafel sandwiches from a man who swore on the Prophet that Mubarak would be going very soon and the people would finally get their wish. Zeinab shook her head sadly. 'It's not possible.'

But the falafel man was right. Mubarak relinquished power the very next day. People leaped up and down, kissed and hugged, posed with tanks and soldiers, and chanted over and over.

Thus, the pharaoh was toppled. I gazed past the fireworks towards the museum where so many earlier pharaohs lay. Mubarak escaped to Sharm el Sheikh by helicopter, leaving the Supreme Council of the Armed Forces in charge of eighty million people. Eighty million! But where was my sister?

NOW

My pulse races in my temples. Even here in this bed, the memory of Tahrir persists, loud and lethal. I smell the tarmac, feel tanks pound the ground. How naïve I'd been to think I might find Simone in that melée! How naïve the world had been that spring.

Still, there's something I retain from it. Everything you experience, Fouad said. Everything you hear, see, or feel. I forget what it is, but I think this thing is important.

Look, Deirdre's here. 'Hello, Mrs. It's my first shift back from sick leave.'

Maybe it's the truth. 'You were missed,' I say. 'Are you better now?'

'I'm fine. Just a gallbladder attack.' Her voice is subdued, and her face is what Mother would have called peaky. 'Now I'm sorry, but I didn't find your sister.'

'Nothing?'

'Nothing at all.'

'Thank you for trying.' I attempt a smile. 'Maybe her name is no longer Khoury. She could have married.'

'Very likely,' Deirdre says. 'How are you feeling, anyway?'

'I think I poisoned myself.'

She titters. 'You Egyptians always exaggerate.'

'All right, I don't mean like that poor Russian who was killed so cruelly with whatever it was. I did it with tablets from the health shop.' I remember polonium now, but not the names of my pills. 'I know they were for my memory.'

'Did you take ginseng?'

'I don't think so.' Stupid me. I threw the containers out, didn't I? Now I have only some mad jottings on a menu.

'Evening primrose oil? Flax seed?'

'Definitely not.'

'Could it be ginkgo ?'

'That's it! And St John's wort.'

'Well, now,' Deirdre says. 'You'll need to tell the doctor.'

'I told them. They don't care.'

Deirdre has to go, leaving me to my tangled thoughts.

Ginkgo and St John's wort. Despite the multiple cracks in the iPad, I manage to look up St John's wort. The side-effects are uncanny. Headache. Dry mouth. Fatigue. Dizziness. Anxiety. Upset stomach. And seizures! I have all of them except sensitivity to the sunlight, probably because I've hardly been outside. As for ginkgo, it can give you headache, dizziness, stomach bleeding, nausea, vomiting, diarrhoea, restlessness, palpitations, and seizures. I scribble most of this down. Still, I'm a bit better recently. Is it because I stopped taking so many of the tablets? I could be a doctor, I tell myself. This makes me chuckle.

The internet says nothing about St John's wort causing trouble concentrating or finding words, though. Is that something different? At least I realise a cow doesn't have five legs.

I know who would make the doctors listen. Simone. She would give them all hell. But now it's down to me. There's a lot to do if I'm to avoid that EMI facility. Knee exercises. I can't focus because my mind is all over the place. Chanting. Molotov cocktails. Crowds and chaos. Banners and bonfires. Flags and falafel. What else? Wedad.

CAIRO, FEBRUARY 2011

'Wedad doesn't want to go home,' Zeinab told me as we trudged back to her apartment.

'I know. She's waiting until Mubarak resigns.'

Zeinab gave me that face. 'Is that what you think?'

'Well, what?'

'It's because of her husband, *ya humara*.' It had been a long time since anyone had called me a she-donkey.

'What's wrong with her husband?'

Zeinab rolled her eyes. 'He beats her.'

I tried to digest this. 'But she's an educated, emancipated woman. Look at her. She's confident. She has a job. She wears whatever she wants.'

'Doesn't make her immune from a man's violence,' Zeinab said grimly. 'No woman is.'

'Oh. You too?'

'No, thanks be to Allah. I'm just saying you mustn't judge on appearances. Look a bit deeper, my sister.'

30

NOW

Look deeper. Zeinab said so.

I start with the iPad and look at charities. There are so many! A hundred and sixty thousand, it says. At least I think that's what all the noughts mean. It's going to take me forever to go through all these. The top one is Cancer Research, and that's where I start. Before I get muddled, I need to jot down the charities I've looked through, so I don't go back over myself.

All this scrolling makes my eyes go funny, and all I've discovered is that Simone probably doesn't work for Cancer Research. Unless it's in one of their shops? They have shops everywhere. She might easily volunteer in one of those and I'd never find her.

I look up at the wall and tell myself not to give up. I've got to find the needle in the haystack before the doctors pack me off to EMI. But there are so many haystacks, and no guarantee that any of them has a needle in it.

Deirdre comes to do my obs.

'I reckon my sister works for a charity,' I tell her as she wraps the blood pressure thing around my arm.

'Ooh, which one?'

'That's the thing. I don't know.'

'Perhaps it'll come to you.'

I doubt that. If there's one thing I've learnt, it's that you can't rely on your nerve connections.

ALEXANDRIA, LONG AGO

I never liked the dark, so, as usual, my bedroom door was ajar as I awaited the sandman. A rectangle of light poured in from the kitchenette where Mother and Rashida were whispering again. I was perched between sleep and wakefulness when I heard them.

'Poor thing.'

'It's not fair.'

'*Maalish.*'

'A good woman.'

I turned on to my side to face the wall. As cars came up the hill, their headlights played on the wooden shutters at my window, creating shifting patterns of ladders on the wall. But this wasn't as interesting as the voices from next door.

'Money, of course. You know exactly how it is.'

'Of course, *ya madame, ya sitti.*'

'What else can one do?'

'Life is short. May Allah protect her.'

I peeled back the bedclothes. Mother always went on about

splinters, so I put on my teddy bear slippers before padding into the kitchenette. 'What are you talking about?' I asked.

'We weren't saying anything, my heart,' Rashida said. 'Were we, *ya madame*?'

'But I heard you.'

'I was only saying my rosary.' Rashida held it aloft as proof.

'Come on, *chérie*.' Mother shooed me back to bed.

NOW

Simone was such a puzzle. Still is, of course. She was so superior most of the time, and yet so kind and caring, especially to Mariam, like that day she had cried over the laundry. Hadn't Simone also given the gardener two of her brand-new blouses for his wife? Perhaps she works at a charity for women or young families? I really should follow this idea. The iPad doesn't tell me how many of those charities there are, but it looks like there are masses of them all over the country.

I throw myself into the search. The first few are huge operations and, as with Cancer Research, there's no easy way to figure out who works there. I try under *Our Team* or *About Us*, where sometimes they list people's names. With each new charity I research, I get a tingle, which then turns to an ache as I realise Simone doesn't work there.

I drink the last of my water from the jug. It's nearly evening and I have barely stopped. Fourteen charities so far. The wi-fi is holding out, but I'm flagging and my headache wreaks havoc with my concentration. Doubt creeps in. I felt it strongly, that Simone would work with a charity that helps women, but I have no evidence for that, and now the idea seems increasingly stupid. Anyway, my head is thumping so violently that I have to stop. There's just this one here called Awning. Last one I'll look at before I give up.

The AWN stands for All Women Now, apparently, and the ING is for In Need Group. Their website is so massive that I may as well be an ant inside the pyramid of Cheops, but I've got to try. No Simones work here, alas, let alone a Simone Khoury. How much more info is there? My eyes are already going goo-goo when I see there's an annual report tucked away on the website, forty-four pages with nothing but financial statements and other dry documents.

Wait. Is that a group photo at the end? A row of smiling people lined up below a banner that's meant to look like a shop awning. The photographer has cut everyone's legs off at the knees so I can't examine any ankles, but there's something about a woman in a white top and chunky necklace. She's near the middle and the crack in the screen goes right through her face. Captions help me work out that the woman in the white top is called *S Fairclough*. I enlarge the photo with my fingers as Deirdre showed me, and I'm still none the wiser. This *S Fairclough* has short grey hair. No glasses. Her front teeth may not be quite straight and, with a lot of imagination, one eyebrow is potentially higher than the other. It could be Simone, I suppose. I hold the iPad at arm's length, then bring it in close. Nah.

I always imagined that I'd recognise my own sister immediately, that seeing her photo would send every single nerve cell jangling, but that's not happening. I guess that means it can't be her. I let the iPad go to sleep.

'Hello, Mrs,' Deirdre says when she wanders over after the medicines round. 'Still think you're being poisoned?'

'No. I mean yes.' My headache's proper thumping now.

'How are you getting on?'

'I don't know. I've got as far as a charity called Awning.'

'Awning, eh? I've not heard of it.'

'It's a women's refuge. And there's a photo of this woman in their annual thing. Sorry. I closed it now.'

'Did you take a screenshot?'

'I don't think I did.'

'Or bookmark the page?'

I've no idea what that means either. 'But I can find it. Hold on a minute.' A few moments later, there's *S Fairclough* again with her necklace and short hair.

Even though Deirdre's never met Simone, she studies the image forensically. 'Where's your phone?' she asks.

Looking at Awning's details, I see only an emergency number for victims of domestic violence. 'I've no signal anyway.'

'I can ring the emergency number for you.'

'But it's wrong to do that,' I say. 'I'll email.'

'If you're sure.'

'I'm sure. There's an office email here.' Honestly, I doubt it's my sister. S is such a common initial for a first name. The woman's teeth may not be perfect, but they don't look like Simone's. Besides, don't most people of this age have uneven teeth?

Deirdre leaves. I hardly need to draft my email on the back of a menu.

I'd like to get in touch with S Fairclough as we may be related.

Send. There.

I'll do those knee exercises by way of a break. My quads muscles feel like they're coming on without the help of that physio, wherever she has got to. After a few more repetitions, I can't resist checking my mail. A reply already! Oh. It's only an auto-response informing me that Awning aims to respond to non-urgent queries within seventy-two hours but cannot guarantee doing so.

By the time I get an answer, I could be locked up in that facility Fritz mentioned. If I haven't crumped in this ward like Pamela. Life is short. Rashida had said so, may Allah protect her, and it has taken me all these years to realise it. Blood is thicker than water. A bird in the hand is worth two in the bush. No time like the present.

31

NOW

What harm can a little phone call do? I said it was wrong to phone the charity's emergency number. But if I do nothing, I could be the emergency. The Nokia is fully charged. No signal, though.

No matter. I have a plan. If Deirdre were here, I'd talk it through with her, but her shift has ended. I jot down the number on my precious paper.

As soon as I discard the blanket, a nurse materialises from nowhere and warns me not to cause trouble. 'Don't you go falling about again,' she says as she tucks me back into bed.

I give her my best smile. Butter wouldn't melt.

Visiting time begins any minute. There'll be a stream of people, and the nurses will retreat somewhere for a cup of tea until there's only one nurse wandering about anywhere near the beds. The women around me have visitors now. That's good. Most important of all, the mountain is busy with her two granddaughters in their skimpy tops.

I'm giddy when I first stand up in my slippers, so I take a moment to hold on to the bed. My fingers tremble as I tie my dressing gown belt and check the pockets. The number is in one pocket and my phone in the other. Steadying myself with a hand on the wall, I make it to the door of the ward. Someone holds it open for me without any need for me to bash the big green button. I smile a *thank you*.

Now I'm at the lift. I press the call button as if I know exactly where I'm going. It's a look I've perfected in the last few months. I get light-headed as I watch people get out of the lift. Then I shuffle in. To stop myself swaying, I lean against the mirror at the back of the lift car. I'm not the only patient going down to the ground floor. Some are taking a stroll with their relatives. Numerous signs show me the way out. I'm wobbly, but nobody asks if I'm all right. Good. Now I mustn't fall over or attract attention.

Oh. Revolving doors. I choose the disabled exit instead so there's nothing heavy to push.

It's London and the air is not that fresh outside, plus there's a band of smokers and vapers outside the entrance. Those vaping things make them look like a bonfire.

A middle-aged woman with a scary perm is attached to some machine with the aid of a tube that snakes inside her dressing gown. She smokes as she clings on to the machine stand. After each puff, coughing spasms rack her body. The woman is just one of several hardened addicts loitering with their backs to the *No Smoking* sign so they can pretend, if challenged, not to have seen it. They're standing on the edge of a strip of earth that could be a flower bed if people bothered to use the bins. A young man with those white things in his ears takes an elaborate detour around the woman with the drip stand. Why does he look familiar? It's not just his short dark hair. I think it's his purposeful stride and the confidence in the tilt of his chin. My memory is playing tricks. The man looks nothing like my Fouad, though he's doctorly in his demeanour. There's something about them that tells the world they're doctors. *Them.* Always *them.*

I, too, navigate around the woman with her machine and her cigarette. Truth be told, I'm a bit woozy, as if my head is nothing but a giant marshmallow. There's a railing to grab but nowhere to sit. I have to let go of the railing to reach the phone in my pocket and turn it on. I do that before finding the paper with the number. Should have keyed it into the Nokia while I was still upstairs.

My fingers quake, as does the rest of me. Before I know it, I'm sprawled on the concrete, and my shoulder feels like someone ripped my arm off.

''Ere, love. You awright?' the woman with the drip stand says.

I nod, by which I mean *No.* The pain in my right shoulder is too fierce for me to speak.

She points with her cigarette towards a phone lying a couple of yards away. It looks like a broken Nokia, but that's hardly my priority right now. I support my arm with my other hand, but it's no help. I can't move. People arrive and heft me into a wheelchair, which doubles the pain.

Next, I'm in A&E, and a nurse is telling me off.

'It's not my fault.' I try to explain that the smoker with her machine is in everyone's way.

After that, I sit in the wheelchair for ages, hanging around to see a doctor and have x-rays. I cry from the pain, right there in the corridor where everyone can see. My right arm is a hideous drainpipe of agony from shoulder to forearm. It's no surprise to hear that my shoulder is dislocated.

'But your arm isn't broken,' a doctor informs me in a jolly voice. Clearly this news is supposed to cheer me up and make the pain vanish.

'Dislocation has followed me everywhere,' I say, but the doctor doesn't get it.

Once I've had a mega sedative, my shoulder joint is put back in place, *bish, bash, bosh,* exactly like last time. After another X-ray to check it was done right, I'm finally back on the ward with my arm in a sling, and I'm being ticked off again for venturing downstairs on my own.

'Been in the wars?' the woman mountain asks.

I groan by way of reply, though my shoulder is marginally easier since the *bish, bash, bosh.*

The woman mountain doesn't give up. 'What you done to yourself then?'

I pretend not to hear. I need to see Deirdre, Sheila, or anyone who's kind. Sheila didn't say when she would be in, and I can't exactly ring and ask her.

'Have a little doze now,' says a nurse who does my obs.

Sheila breezes in, wafting alcohol. 'You poor old thing,' she trills.

My head is clearer now that the sedative has worn off, and I manage to explain about the photo of S Fairclough. Sheila promises to bring me another phone, though I doubt I could use it with my arm in this sling.

'I think you should try emailing the charity again,' she tells me. 'Mark it clearly for the attention of S Fairclough this time.'

'Oh, Sheila. It's probably not even her. Besides, what am I going to say after fifty years?'

Sheila insists. She even does the keying in for me.

Dear Ms Fairclough,

Am I right in thinking that your name might have been Simone Khoury? From the picture on the Awning website, you bear a close resemblance to my sister, last seen in Alexandria.

'Should we add anything else?'

'No,' Sheila says. 'Keep it short and simple.'

I'll keep this short and simple in case I am wrong, but I very much look forward to your reply, even if it's a negative one.

Kind regards? Best wishes? Love? We opt for *Nadia Wissa, née Khoury.*

The email has barely launched into outer space when Fritz and Laura Ashley are back. Sheila slips away, leaving me to face them alone. Fritz looks put out, though it's not his shoulder that's out of joint.

'I remember the names of the herbal pills,' I begin.

The only thing that bothers him is that a care home might not take me until my shoulder is better. He runs his fingers through his non-existent hair. 'What's the plan here?'

The nurse who's been loitering nearby pipes up. 'She has assessment for Rosemount Park. They have EMI unit.' I won't forget that in a hurry. That's Elderly Mentally Impaired. Or is it Infirm?

'When's the assessment?' Fritz asks.

The nurse says it's tomorrow. I think I might throw up.

'And how long after that till they can take her?' he asks.

'It depends,' Laura Ashley says, without explaining on what.

'Excuse me,' I try, but they're occupied with their own concerns as they disappear down the ward.

If my assessment is tomorrow, there's no time to lose. But

I've no idea what to do, and, to cap it all, I suddenly feel ill. It's anxiety about the care home, I'm sure. Now I've got the shakes as well, along with waves washing over me like seasickness. Should I press the buzzer with my good hand before I pass out? I feel I'm about to crump.

I grip the buzzer tightly and squeeze it twice. As well as nausea, there are now vicious cramps, the like of which I've not had since the time I gorged on *amar el deen*, the apricot paste I stole from Mother's cupboard. I'd better buzz again or I'll mess the bed.

In the nick of time, someone turns up with one of those fancy dress hats and manoeuvres my bottom into place. Even with the nurse to steady me, I struggle to stay on it. I'm practically lying down, and I'm sure the seal between cardboard and *teas* can't be perfect. Soon there's a second nurse here to help. When I've finished, the nurses inspect the cardboard hat. 'We have to tell Doctor about the blood.'

Blood? I take a peek and instantly feel faint. Maybe it's the shock of seeing a red lake like this, after so many times when I'd lost babies. This is not from *there*, of course. I'm not that much of a she-donkey.

Now I'm shivering. The nurse assesses my forehead and believes I have a fever. How can that be possible? I'm freezing. Even when I retreat under the bedclothes and cover my head, my hands and feet stay icy cold. One of the nurses says she'll do my obs. I'm light-headed as their voices become indistinct and my vision blurs. Everything blends into one while a current drags me under, pulling me back to another time.

ALEXANDRIA, LONG AGO

Day or night, Doctor Tadros came whenever we needed him. A little round man who arrived in a big car, he'd been our family doctor for as long as I could remember. As he was always jolly, you couldn't tell if he was going to give an injection. It was best to hide, just in case, ever since that first polio jab he had given Simone and me, taking us unawares with a horrid needle that went right into our backs near the shoulder blade, of all places. Most of his needles went into the *teas*. I didn't know which was worse.

From behind the curtains, I heard Doctor Tadros struggle up the marble staircase with barely enough breath to carry himself, while Abdou followed behind with the medical bag.

I was quickly found, of course, and marched back to my room. Then Doctor Tadros would sit on a chair by my bed, intermittently wheezing and asking Mother for every detail of my illness. Only then would he extinguish his cigarette and examine me. His stethoscope was a cold metal pyramid that travelled all over my chest then ventured to the ticklish bits near the armpits. I sat still and breathed ever so quietly, not wanting him to find anything that might require one of his needles.

'Will she need an antibiotic injection?' Mother asked.

I then cringed into the bedclothes to make myself as small as possible.

He mused. 'She has a fever. I suppose it can't hurt.'

But it did hurt. I tried not to cry as the needle stabbed me in the bottom, followed by the slow cold pain of penicillin inching its way down my leg like freezing oil. Then he and Mother would retreat to talk in another room. Once, the door swung open and I heard Doctor Tadros say, 'That leg. Poor woman.'

I made out no more.

NOW

The nurse is right. She pulls me out from under the blanket, and I do have a fever, though she doesn't let on how high. Now I must have blood tests and stool tests. Having one arm in a sling isn't exactly convenient. I turn my face away so the other patients can't see me weep.

When Fritz returns, he looks disgusted. Neither he nor Laura Ashley will touch me without gloves.

'What's happening?' I ask.

'Well,' Fritz says. 'You might have C diff.'

'What's C diff?'

'An infection that's rather common in the elderly in hospital. And in those with a poor immune system.'

I want to protest that I'm hardly elderly compared with Tante Zahra, and that my immune system was perfectly fine when I arrived. There's more to tell them as well, but my head is too jumbled.

They're glancing at each other and plotting further attacks. 'She needs a drip,' Laura Ashley says. 'And a side-room.' I'm led to believe this C diff is catching.

I get one of those sharp tubes in my hand with a plastic bag of liquid going in. I know about those. Sometimes the bag runs out before anyone gets around to fetching a new one. Once, my hand ended up cold and puffy when the liquid went where it shouldn't. There are words for all those things, but I've mislaid them for the moment.

I'm wheeled into a room all to myself. It's nothing like a private hospital, though it has an *en suite* shower room and the bedside light works. I know that because it's been left on.

More cramps. And the room stinks. Is that from me and my C diff? When I consider that I am further than ever from leaving hospital, I cry again. With one arm in a sling and the sharp thing taped into the other hand, I can't reach the tissues, so I use a corner of my sheet. At least this time there's no woman mountain judging me.

Despite the thing in my hand, I'm able to hold one of the postcards. It's extraordinary the detail that I can see of St Paul's Cathedral now that I have decent lighting. Oh, look. Simone seems to have written on the picture side of the card with a biro that has no ink. When I hold it up to the lamp, faint grooves come into focus like an ancient engraving.

Avoid Alicia's F

How did I miss it before? The message may have been longer, but time has evened out the marks. I can guess it says *Alicia's Father*. Someone should have warned me before that day, the day he put his fingers where I knew they shouldn't go. It was horrible, but nothing more had happened, and it was all so long ago. I don't know why Simone bothered to mention him in a postcard. Now my brain throbs and I need to rest. It's hard to believe I'll ever feel better.

32

NOW

My mouth is dry, my eyes have gone sticky, and I've woken up to a numb arm. On the plus side, I've remembered that the thing in my hand is called a drip.

When I press the side button on the iPad, I make a discovery. The iPad is dead. It needs its plugger to bring it to life. Stuck in here with a drip in one hand and my other arm in a sling, there's not a lot I can reach. Although people keep walking past, nobody has been in for hours. Seems to me that once the nurses shut the door, they forget all about this room and me inside it. Deirdre hasn't been in to see me. Maybe she doesn't look after this part of the ward. Or maybe she thinks I crumped. I've no idea what time it is, and I'm even beginning to miss that woman mountain.

Next thing I know, a nurse is here fiddling with my drip. I observe her gloved hands for a moment and hope she's adding the right stuff to the liquid.

'Do you think you could help me please?'

'What do you need?' She seems cross at being distracted.

'My iPad is empty. I need to reach the plugger.'

'I'll come back shortly.' It's hard to tell through her mask whether she means it.

There's nothing to do but wait. I have a buzzer, but it's behind my right arm which is in a sling. The buzzer digs into my elbow, my pillows have gone flat, and the blanket slipped off ages ago, so nothing about this bed is comfortable. Yet things could be far worse in that Rosemount Park they keep talking about. The minute I'm better, they'll whisk me off there. I start feeling sorry for myself and soon I'm patting at my eyes with my gown.

Then something good happens. A different nurse comes in to check my obs. She's not wearing a mask either. Maybe I'm not that ill.

'Do you think you could help me reach the plugger for my iPad?'

Just like that, she does it.

'Thank you very much.' I pause. 'You're not wearing a mask.'

'That's right, but we have to wear gloves and an apron, and wash our hands with soap and water. Not sanitiser, as it doesn't kill C diff spores properly.'

'Ah, spores.' I nod, hoping to appear intelligent. 'Is Nurse Deirdre about?'

My nurse has already gone.

I check the iPad. The wi-fi seems to be working, and here's an email from the charity! I hold my breath as I click it open.

Ya ukhti? My little sister? I can hardly believe it. I had no idea how to find you. Yes, I am Ms Fairclough, as you cleverly discovered, and married to Ken. We have three children and two grandchildren. I'm one of Awning's founders, but I'm sure you know all that. What about you? Are you well? Are you in the UK now, too? Tell me everything. I asked Zouzou a while ago. She said she had no news of you, and now she's dead.

Can it really be Simone? I clutch the iPad tight, as if it literally holds us together like one of those brain connections. After all this time, I've found my sister. I can touch her through this iPad. She's almost as close as when I trotted behind her on the beach, walking in her shadow on the wet sand. A hot feeling grows behind my eyes until it spills out. I dab my face with the sheet. Then, although it's awkward with my left hand, I begin my reply.

Dear Simone,

Cramps stop me before I can compose another word. Worse, dizziness overtakes me, and a sour water floods into my mouth. I know what that means. As I press the buzzer, the iPad slides from my grasp and hits the floor.

ALEXANDRIA, FEBRUARY 1972

When I developed a fever after my miscarriage in 1972, Mother called Doctor Tadros again. That time my only fear was that I might never have a child.

He wheezed his way up the stairs, stubbed out his cigarette in the ashtray that Rashida held out, and mopped his brow with a handkerchief from his pocket. For the first time, I noticed his surprisingly small feet. I supposed he had a small *zizi*, too. Sheila said that the two went together.

Like the whole of Alexandria, Doctor Tadros already knew I'd lost another baby, and there wasn't much to tell him except for my temperature. 'The pain went before I left hospital,' I told him. 'But a fever started in the night.'

'*Trente-huit trois*,' Mother added, furrowing her brow. She had perfect recall for the hourly readings that she'd insisted on ever since the mercury hit thirty-eight.

Doctor Tadros gave a solemn look, studied my tongue, and checked my pulse. Then he pulled down my lower eyelids to check for God only knows what. Finally he examined my belly, his voice rasping as he explained that I had an infection. This time, he needed no prompting to produce his syringe and needle. The icy pain of penicillin trickled down the back of my leg as it always did. He prescribed tablets as well. They smelled like benzene. I took them four times a day, and I survived, so they must have worked.

NOW

Well, a nurse did get here, and she brought one of those kidney dishes for me to be sick in. She also picked the iPad off the floor for me. New cracks have grown all over the screen like a spider's web, and it seems a hopeless case, but the thing still powers on.

'Let's get you cleaned up,' the nurse says. Once my bed is tidied up, she helps me hobble to the bathroom. 'You've lost weight,' she says. 'But you look better.'

I'm not sure I feel it. Washing is a monumental business when you have a sling on one side and a drip on the other. Once I get my breath back and the nurse leaves, I finish my reply to Simone. It's just a couple of lines to ask where she lives, to tell her where I am, and to say that I hope to see her soon. Should I mention it had better be before they cart me off somewhere? I can hardly see what I'm typing, but I add *very* in the hope of making it read *very soon*. It takes all my energy to write that, so it's just as well that I decided to leave out the care home, the shits, the drip, the sling, and the fact that nobody can visit unless they tog up as for an Ebola patient.

Suppose Simone has changed? Apart from getting older, that is. Suppose she doesn't actually want to meet? Another thing: why didn't *she* look for *me*? Maybe she doesn't want to do any more than send me a pleasant little email calling me *ya ukhti*, then get on with her important life. And there's that thing she said about Zouzou, the woman I had trusted. I'm too lightheaded to make sense of it.

The next thing I know, Fritz is here. He seems most put out, as if I caught a gastro-thingy on purpose to avoid my assessment. He studies the chart, then says, 'You're on the mend. Depending on your test results, you can have that assessment for Rosemount Park.'

'I'm not EMI,' I tell him. 'The tablets are the missing link.'

He understands nothing and swans off. Then a woman called Pippa turns up wearing a fluffy jumper and carrying a big notebook. I think she says she's a social worker. I've no idea what a social worker is meant to look like, but Pippa has a fish tattooed on her ankle. There's a special name for that fish, though I can't bring it to mind. I'm sure there was a film about one. A huge fish. It chewed into boats and bit people in half.

Pippa starts raving on about all the lovely facilities in a place called Something Lodge, which confuses me as I expected Rosemount. They have a hairdresser and an art class. 'And sometimes a dog comes in,' she says. 'It's like a lovely hotel.'

I don't know any hotels with art classes or dogs. 'Is it EMI?

Because I'm not EMI, you know. And I can prove it.' Of course I can't, but it's worth a try.

'Let's just get that assessment, Nadia. Then we can decide.' Pippa pats me on the arm before she goes.

I'm not going to be the one who decides, am I? I need my sister to help. I compose another brief email to Simone.

Hope it's soon. I dint know what's happening in this plaec.

I begin to ramble and make mistakes that I have no energy to correct. There's no time, either. I bring my email to a stop and send it.

ALEXANDRIA, JANUARY 1953

Seven years old at last! I had a big party in the basement, and I didn't even mind Victor being there or having a bandaged arm after my fall in the garden, because I now owned a biro that wrote in four colours, as well as a toy camel that I loved at first sight. It wasn't all that cuddly, as it was made of lead, but that didn't stop me clutching it to my side most of the afternoon.

The *gala-gala* man arrived. He spread a bright green cloth over the table and proceeded to make bright yellow chicks appear from his pockets, his sleeves, his hat, and even from behind Androulla's ear. They were real chicks, soft and warm with little feet that tickled my palm.

Everyone sang 'Happy Birthday', including Rashida who knew none of the words, and I blew out all the candles by myself in almost one go. Each of us at my party got one of those clicky party favours. Simone and I had a shiny ladybird, but I lost mine. She passed her ladybird to me under the table and said I could keep it. I clutched it in my fist. I wasn't in a hurry to get to the next day anymore. I wanted this day to last forever.

'Just till bedtime,' she added. 'It won't be your birthday tomorrow.'

NOW

They took my sling off for the physio to see my arm, and today my drip is out as well. There's no answer from Simone, though.

Sheila turns up in the afternoon. '*Ciao, bella.* You look a lot better.' She's brought me a new mobile.

'How much do I owe you?'

'Forget it. It was under a tenner.'

'That's very kind.' I reckon I will need it in that place, Rosemount or the other one, so I nod sagely and pay close attention when Sheila shows me how it works. The new phone makes a different jingle to the Nokia, but it has the same number once Sheila does something clever to its innards. As predicted, I can't get the phone to function.

'That's because there's no signal in the room,' Sheila says. 'You could do a WhatsApp call using the internet, though.'

I've no idea what she's talking about, but I thank her all the same. I want to explain about the place they're taking me to and the fact that Simone hasn't answered and I may miss Simone forever, but my vocabulary keeps sliding away into the distance, and there's a warm feeling behind my eyelids.

Sheila hands me a tissue. 'I'll leave you to it, old thing.' Being ever so *Inglizi*, Sheila isn't good with tears.

. . .

It's a new nurse and she won't listen. 'I'm not going to that assessment,' I tell her again. I perch on the edge of the bed and cross my arms as best I can, considering the state of my shoulder. 'Anyway, wasn't it meant to be tomorrow or the day after?'

'Yes, but they had a cancellation.'

I expect someone crumped.

'The transport is here for you.' As if that's going to persuade me.

'I don't care. I'm not going.'

'I think you should give it a try.'

'Fuck,' I say.

'I'm going to get another nurse.'

She returns with a nurse I've seen before. I expect them to team up so they can manhandle me into my clothes. Instead, they talk patiently and say I should definitely give this place a try. It will be my chance to show what I can do, they tell me, and that I should think of it as a stepping stone to going home.

'Not fucking going.' I feel a bit sorry for them, truth be told.

'I'm going to ring Doctor,' the second nurse says.

The doctor is here. 'Now, Ms Wissa,' she says as she sits down on a chair opposite me with a sigh.

I start by staring her down right in the middle of those Laura Ashley glasses. I may not be in the best bargaining position in a hospital gown that's fallen off one shoulder, but I plan to stick it out. Simone is my role model and, if necessary, I will stamp my foot and shriek, '*Non, non, et non!*' until they hear me from the other end of the hospital. Still, I'm finding it hard to whip up a storm with someone who's sitting completely still, not saying anything. She doesn't even look angry, just tired and sad. After a long silence, she goes, 'There's not much options available, you know.'

I'm past correcting her grammar. 'You need this bed. I know how it works.'

'It's not just that. You can't look after yourself on your own, so ...'

'But I could try. I just need to be given a chance.'

She tilts her head. 'Then you can try at Rosemount Park, can't you?'

'Can't I try here?' That would make far more sense to me.

'No. That's how we do it in this hospital.'

In this hospital? How confusing, because it's not actually in this hospital, is it? It's in that Rosemount Park or that other place, Lodge something. Wasn't it the social worker with the fish tattoo who mentioned that?

'Which of the nurses do you get on best with?' she asks.

'Nurse Deirdre.'

'I'll go find her.'

Deirdre is all smiles, as usual. 'Now, Mrs. There's that assessment for you.'

'Not going. I already told them. Deirdre, please tell them about my being poisoned by the health shop.'

Deirdre nods. 'But you still need your assessment.'

'I want my sister.'

Laura Ashley glances at the ceiling. 'She doesn't have a sister.'

'Oh, yes she does,' Deirdre says. 'Her name is Simone Fairclough, and she works for some charity.'

'But she didn't answer my last email,' I add.

'Well, then, all I can suggest is that you go for your assessment today while you wait for your sister to get in touch,' Deirdre says, and Laura Ashley nods like crazy.

Reluctantly, I let myself be dressed.

I'm halfway out into the corridor when Laura Ashley says, 'One of the nurses will pack all your things up.'

That's when it hits me. They're not planning to let me back here. Well, I'm not leaving then. I plant myself as firmly as my wobbly legs permit and I shout, 'Fuck the lot of you!' That's when I see a woman in the corridor, right there in front of me.

'What's going on?' she says.

33

NOW

I know I shouldn't stare. The woman is seventy or more with short grey hair and a pair of glasses perched on top of her head, as if her eyes decide to manage without help after all. There's a scarf slung around her neck, and her slim trousers are of the type Mother called *cigarette*. I don't need to look down. I already know that her ankles are chunky and not nearly as elegant as the rest of her.

The woman beams at me. 'Nadia?'

'Simone?' My voice is wavering.

The woman stretches out to give me a hug. 'Nadia, *ya ukhti*.'

'Ow. My shoulder.'

She ignores this and addresses the doctor and Deirdre. 'I'm Simone Fairclough,' she says.

'I said I had a sister,' I tell Laura Ashley. 'Can I go back to bed now?'

Laura Ashley is stumped, but Simone takes charge. 'Have a rest, *ya ukhti*. Now, can I speak to the doctors about you?'

I nod, relieved. A nurse helps me back to bed, and off they all go.

Simone is back when I open my eyes. 'The doctor told me you had C diff.'

I didn't think to look that up. 'Did you find out what that is?'

'An infection called *Clostridium difficile*. C diff for short. They gave me this.' She waves an information sheet. That's what it takes to get proper answers from these people — a relative showing up.

'*Difficile?* I'll say it is.'

'Sorry I couldn't come in for a couple of days. They said it was safe to visit, but I had a meeting in Leeds.' She gives me a hug. 'My baby sister.'

Not such a baby now, but I let that go and allow her to envelop me in the haze of a fragrance I cannot name. The hug ends eventually, and I see Simone smile with a chipped tooth showing.

'You broke that tooth at Marsa Matrouh,' I tell her. 'A long time ago.'

'A very long time ago. Over fifty years.' She perches on the edge of the chair and takes my hand. I'm sure she has never done this before. Either I need the last rites, or she's going to give me a clicky ladybird toy.

'How did you figure out where I was?'

'You told me yourself, in a somewhat garbled email full of typos. The mistakes made me realise how unwell you must be.'

Simone still has a superior look and one highly mobile

eyebrow. But something has changed. I'm not sure what. 'You look different,' I blurt.

'You too.'

'Is it your fringe?'

After that, our words cascade out. I can't say it's as if we've never been apart, but there's something simultaneously alien and familiar about being with Simone again.

A nurse comes in to check on me.

'I told you I had a sister,' I inform her too.

'That's nice.' The nurse leaves the room before I explain about the fifty missing years.

Simone wants to know all about me and where I'm living. 'And what's that hole in your head?'

I touch my temple with my free hand. 'Oh. That's where I fell.'

I do know I never had a brain biopsy. My mind may be tired, but it's clearer, all the same, and I feel like a *humara* for having got confused over what did happen and what didn't. The danger of gaps in the memory lies in the stuff you find to fill them.

ALEXANDRIA, SEPTEMBER 1970

It was after dinner, after far more alcohol than I imagined ten people could possibly consume, that Fouad related, to riotous laughter, the tale about the newly-wed with his head stuck in a chamber pot.

'But tell us,' Nessim said. 'Did he have to go to hospital?'

There followed guffaws and thigh-slapping, after which they moved on to a discussion of their least favourite operations. 'I hate performing brain biopsies,' Nessim said. 'It is always bad news. Either it's a primary brain tumour, or a secondary, or one of those diseases that nobody can cure.'

'Then you shouldn't have become a neurosurgeon, *mish kida?*'

'Well, we can't all make a living by touching women.' Nadim paused for the inevitable laughter. 'Did I tell you about the time we lost the flap of skull that we put in the *talaga?*'

'*Ayoo!*' Cigarette still clamped between his fingers, Fouad smacked himself on the head. 'Don't you know never to keep anything important in the hospital fridge?'

Nessim stretched out languidly. 'For me, lung biopsy can be a pain in the *teas*. Did I tell you about the patient I had last year? I thought we had sampled the worst part of his lung. Then the lab came back and said it was so bad they couldn't tell what it was. We must have taken the wrong bit.'

'What happened to him?'

'He died,' Nessim said.

The room went quiet for a long moment.

'Anyone for a refill?' I asked.

NOW

It makes sense to me now. When I felt very ill, I guess I imagined not only the biopsy, but the doctor who came to see me about the result.

Simone is studying me through her glasses as if I'm a page full of sums. 'How are you feeling, *ya ukhti?*'

'Much better. I can't believe I've found you. Not imagining this, am I?' No, she really is here. There's her laugh, her wry smile, her famous eyebrow, and the curly hair which is almost the same grey as mine. 'May I?' Using my good arm, I untangle one of the earrings that caught in a lock of her hair.

'Thanks. You know, I don't think there's an accepted script for sisters who meet after this long. We'll have to play it by ear.' She's acting tough, but that doesn't fool me. Her eyes are moist behind her fancy glasses.

'You did say we'd meet one day, but I didn't dare believe that postcard you sent from, you know …' I wave my arm vaguely. 'Why did you leave Alex?'

Our conversation is halted by the arrival of Pippa and her giant notebook. I don't quite follow all the terms she uses, but I get the bit about rescheduling that assessment at Rosemount. She's already talking dates and times.

'But why does she need to go to this Rosemount? She could stay with us.' Simone's tentative voice suggests she needs to discuss it with the other elements of *us*, whoever they may be.

'I can't impose on you,' I say.

'For a while you can. As long as your C diff really is sorted.'

The social worker beams and slams her notebook shut. 'That's settled then.'

As soon as she's left, I pull myself up as straight as my iffy shoulder permits. 'That's very kind of you, Simone, but I'm perfectly capable of managing on my own, you know. I'm not a little baby.' As if to prove it, a fart erupts despite myself.

'Of course.'

'Why did you leave Alex?'

'Maybe tomorrow,' she says.

'So you're an official at the *Mugamma'* now?'

She ignores this. 'What happened to Fouad?'

'He died in 1994. Lung cancer.'

'I'm sorry. And did you have children?'

I gaze towards my feet and give my usual reply. 'It's a long story.'

'We have the rest of our lives, *ya ukhti*.'

'You don't know that.' I have a moment of great lucidity. 'Nobody can predict the future. Not even that clever Professor Hawking.'

'I never said how long the rest of our lives would be, did I?'

Always such a smarty pants. 'So, you have one daughter. And two sons. You were expecting before you left Alex, weren't you?'

Simone nods. 'I was pregnant with Maddy, the eldest. The boys are Alexander and Richard.'

Perhaps Mother was right about a son. 'And their father ...?' I leave the question trailing.

'Let's do this some other time.'

She's in luck. Fritz and Laura Ashley breeze through the door. After the briefest of greetings, Fritz asks, 'What supplements were you taking?'

I'm certain of the names this time. 'St John's wort and ginkgo.'

'Ah-ha,' Laura Ashley goes. 'When did you last take them?'

I shrug my good shoulder. 'Don't know.'

'Since you've been in hospital?'

'Maybe just once or twice. I don't remember exactly.'

'And when did you start them?'

'Right after I bought them. I got them on special offer.' This doesn't seem to be the answer they're after.

'Well,' she begins. 'St John's wort may do little harm in modest amounts, but there can be side-effects, especially if one takes too many. We think it may have triggered your seizure.'

'It was two for the price of one,' I remind her.

'That doesn't make it a good idea to take twice as much.'

She gives me a watery smile. 'The side-effects can be unpleasant. Headache, fatigue, dry mouth—'

'I know! Tiredness, palpitations, confusion. I've been trying to tell you. And I've had a dry mouth and headache from the start.' All that was my discovery, and now she and Fritz are going to claim it as their breakthrough.

Laura Ashley ignores me and continues her lecture. 'Not to mention dizziness, anxiety, sensitivity to sunlight, and upset stomach. Seizures too, as I mentioned.' She pushes those silly glasses up her nose and resumes. 'As for ginkgo , it is increasingly popular and a lot of people take it to boost their brain power. However, scientific studies have failed to confirm its benefits. In a randomised group of patients …'

I struggle to keep up at this point, perking up when Laura Ashley lists the unwanted effects. 'Ginkgo biloba has been linked with gastro-intestinal bleeding, nausea, vomiting, diarrhoea, headache, dizziness, restlessness, and palpitations. Seizures as well, as a matter of fact.'

'I know!'

'Supplements can also be contaminated with toxic heavy metals. There are no standards for purity, you see.'

'So is there anything else wrong with me?'

'We found nothing else. Although you did get C diff and manage to dislocate your shoulder.' She and Fritz find this priceless.

'What about all those tests and scans?'

'Well, we're pretty sure about the cause of your miscarriages. The plan is to review you in outpatients in a couple of weeks, when the supplements have washed out of your system.' The doctor shifts from one of her crocs to the other, a sure sign that she's ready to leave. 'You won't take any more of them, will you?'

'Of course not.' I would never have gone near them without Sheila and the special offer.

'I'm really sorry, Deirdre. I made another crack in your iPad.'

'Keep it, Mrs. I don't need it.'

'That is so kind. Thank you.' She's by far the nicest person here. 'When do you think they'll let me out?'

'Soon, I expect.'

I'm still light-headed and my mind wanders, but my obs are fine and, as far as I can make out from the scanty details they let me have, the C diff tests are now satisfactory. The physio has finally been back and she seems most impressed with my knees, though less so with my shoulder, which she says needs putting through its paces.

'Ow!' They are most definitely her paces, not my shoulder's. Left to its own devices, my arm and I would have a nice rest.

'You've got to keep using it,' she threatens. 'Or you'll get a frozen shoulder.'

So I do my best, and the physio finally says I'm getting the message. She leaves me with a sheet of instructions about the sling and exercise. There are movements that I must do to strengthen the muscles, and movements that I mustn't do because the shoulder could pop out again. Most of them seem impossible anyway.

Then Sheila comes in. She's wearing a mauve blouse, and I swear she's had her hair done.

'What's new?' I ask.

'Eric. He's a pilot.' The glint in her eyes suggests ability in the cockpit is relevant to his bedroom skills.

I'm sceptical. 'What kind of pilot?'

'I don't know, actually.'

'Maybe he's a crop sprayer.'

'Don't be such a snob,' Sheila says.

When Simone comes in, I tell her about the physio.

'Bravo,' she says. 'That's excellent news.'

'So why did you leave Egypt?' Simone knows I need a proper explanation. I don't think being pregnant justifies never coming back.

She changes the subject and asks if there's anything I don't eat.

'Nothing. Apart from lamb and *molokheyya*, obviously.'

It's another day before I get what the nurse calls my marching orders. 'You can leave as soon as you get your TTOs.' The nurse implies I should know exactly what she means. 'We are very busy now.'

The TTOs, I discover when I'm handed a blue and white paper bag, are drugs I am to take home. Maybe TTO is short for *To Take 'Ome*. I still have to wait for a letter. This arrives later, courtesy of a burly man with heavily tattooed arms and a grey T-shirt with a monogram. I stare at his badge. *TRUST VOLUNTEER.*

'Are you Terry?'

'Yeah,' he replies in a high-pitched squeak. 'Them's your letters.'

There's an outpatient appointment plus a letter for my GP. The envelope is sealed to keep all the doctorly info away from a patient's prying eyes, but I plan to open it anyway before I give it to my doctor.

Now Simone is here. 'Ready?'

In addition to my box of postcards, I seem to have accumulated quantities of other stuff and there's a jumble of plastic carriers with belongings that refuse to fit into the bag I arrived with. As I can't tell what's important, we take it all, which means that I carry one bag with my good arm while Simone lugs the rest.

I glance into the main ward before we leave. There's no woman mountain in sight, but that doesn't stop me bellowing, 'My sister's taking me home.'

34

NOW

'Here's where I live.' Simone wants to drop me off and park the car.

'How do I know you won't disappear again?'

'Trust me.'

'That's easy to say.'

The house turns out to be spacious by London standards. Simone takes my carrier bags and me up to a spare room furnished with bunk beds, presumably for the grandchildren she mentioned. On the shelves, the books and toys are practically antique. A jigsaw puzzle of York Minster catches my eye.

'Do you have a Cunard puzzle?' I ask.

'I doubt it. Why?'

'*Maalish.*'

We hug. Again, this is a real hug. I don't count fake hugs that accompany *mwah mwah* kisses.

'Simone, I don't know what to say.'

She smiles as she flings one end of her scarf over her shoulder. In the last fifty years, it seems she has taken to wearing scarves like Mother and her sisters. Her glasses are parked on top of her head again, so I stroke her cheek for reassurance, though I see her perfectly well.

'Why don't you have a rest and come down when you're ready? You can meet Ken and the family later, and have a bite to eat if you feel like it.'

'Ken. Your husband. Right.'

'Shout or text me if you need anything in the meantime. I promise not to make *molokheyya*,' she adds before the door clicks shut.

I stretch out on the lower bunk and cover up with a bedspread that has sailboats on it. This is too weird. I mean, the person downstairs is obviously Simone, but she's more amenable than I remember. Has she changed that much, or is she making a special effort because I've been ill?

As I stare at the wooden slats above me, I daydream. The hospital fog is lifting but new mists swirl around, and I have a thousand questions. And I'm still weak. I haven't done stairs in I don't know how long. When I attempt them later, it's a huge effort despite clutching the bannisters.

'You should have called me,' Simone says. 'I'd have helped. Coffee?'

'Yes, please. Why did you leave Alex?' I say again. 'What were you trying to tell me, and why did you only send postcards instead of letters?'

An eyebrow shoots up. 'That's a lot of questions.'

'Okay. Let's start with why you left Alex.'

'Can we start with something simpler?' She doesn't wait for my answer. 'I had things to warn you about.'

'Yes, I know some of it. Selim was a pimp, for a start. And gay, though that's hardly relevant.' I'll tell her later about his *poupoule* on the Corniche. And I'll keep his death to myself until I'm good and ready. Two can play at that game, as the English say. 'And you were pregnant when you left. I figured that you probably had the baby. The father was a no-gooder. Who was he?'

She stirs her coffee intently by way of a reply. I swear the spoon will wear through the bottom of the mug.

'And Alicia went to a rest home,' I continue.

She finally puts down the spoon and her cheeks flush. 'Actually, the story begins with Alicia.'

'Alicia?' I echo.

There is a crash at the front door followed by scuffles in the hall. The pictures on the living-room wall tremble as two boys and their laughter burst through the door.

'Who are they?'

'*Ya humara!*' Simone says. 'They're my grandsons. Jake is twelve and Max is ten. Boys, this is your great-auntie Nadia.'

Jake and Max say *Hi,* and one of them gives a dinky wave. They have burgundy-red uniforms, snub noses, and freckles, but Jake is fairer and taller. It's odd, to say the least, to have an instant family that I knew nothing about. 'I've only just become an aunt. Now I'm a great-aunt, too?'

A twitch plays on Simone's lips. 'It would appear so.'

I blow my nose discreetly. While I'm thrilled to be with Simone and her family — *my* family — it's hard not to feel the weight of the missing years. Will it always ache like this?

Max assesses me. I must have passed the test, because he becomes desperate to show me his collection of football stickers. Jake, meanwhile, is into something mesmerising on his mobile phone.

'Do they live with you?'

'No, but they're often here after school.' Simone rises and

claps her hands. 'Right, who wants to make pancakes with me?'

Despite the lure of football and iPhones, they both leap up. There's a whoosh of air as they lunge towards the kitchen.

Simone's husband comes in a little later. Ken turns out to be a thickset man who is going bald. We barely have a chance for introductions because the grandsons fling themselves at him.

He laughs. 'This is what I get for being away most of the week.'

'You're popular,' I remark.

Ken says he needs to get changed before he has a glass of his favourite gin with tonic.

'Tell us, Grandpa,' Jake asks. 'What *is* your favourite gin?'

'A well-earned gin!' Max hoots.

'I always say that's the best kind,' Ken says, as they troop into the kitchen.

Alone now, I rest back on the sofa cushions. Although the room is pleasant, there's something alien about it, and not just because it's my first time here. Ah. I have it now. There's nothing oriental apart from the solitary Persian rug. The side-boards are resolutely British in a style best called sturdy, and the ample green sofa I occupy is squishy verging on battered. The curtains have a William Morris design, and the lamps on the side tables are more shabby than chic. The room doesn't give much away, except the look of comfort. Simone has no blue beads, gilt chairs, mother-of-pearl boxes, fussy chandeliers, or *petit point* table covers. Beyond the French window, I catch sight of a garden with trees, a table, some chairs. So very *Inglizi*.

Supper is chicken and mushroom pancakes, which everyone seems to love, though one of the children has more ketchup on his plate than pancake. I daren't eat much since that C diff, and I struggle to keep up with the conversation bouncing around the kitchen table. Max describes a particularly desirable football sticker in meticulous detail. He worries that he won't ever get that one for his album. 'It's so rare, you see.'

Simone suggests a swap with someone who has spares. 'That's what we did with our stamp collections. Isn't it, Nadia?'

It's coming back to me. Orange and green stamps with King Farouk's face crossed out with heavy black bars. Metaphorical bars, since he never went to prison.

Max gives his grandmother a pitying look. 'There's never enough of the good ones for swapsies.'

Maddy will be here after supper to collect the boys, but I can't keep my eyes open. 'Do you mind if I go to bed?' I say before dessert.

'Course not. Here. Take some water up with you.'

'Good idea,' I say, though my thirst is less fierce than it was in hospital. Must be because it's cooler here. I accept the carafe from Simone and turn to go up the stairs.

'You're going the wrong way,' she points out.

'Right.' I stagger up to the first floor without spilling much water.

As I lie on the bunk that night, noises drift towards me and random thoughts ripple in my head. They're not quite random, though, are they? Every single thing you see or hear or do – or smell – makes brain cells join up. No experience passes without making its mark.

The morning light is red and yellow through the Lego print curtains. I wake early and lie for a while until Simone brings me a mug of tea in bed. I must say, this is a new turn of events.

'How are you?'

'Thanks. I'm all right.'

'What would you like for breakfast?' She reels off a list of offerings.

'Maybe later.'

When I've made my cautious way down to the kitchen, she tells me about the refuge. 'Ken's a fundraising whizz. He works there, too, but mostly off-site. As you can imagine, his presence at the refuge might cause problems for some.'

It's great to see her enthusiasm. 'What about your art, though? Did you never want to do something with that?'

'My art was *khara*.'

'It was pretty good compared with mine.'

'My art, as you grandly call it, was never going to support me, let alone a child as well. But I use it alongside my work with the women and their families. Let me show you something.' She gets up to rummage through a drawer in the kitchen dresser. 'We make a good profit from these. Here.'

The Christmas card shows the Virgin Mary holding her baby. Of course. Her Bedouin sketches. 'It's lovely.'

'Now tell me about Uncle Selim,' she says.

We're sitting at her kitchen table in London, which is far-fetched enough as it is. It's even more surreal as I describe Selim's death at Montazah and the young policeman who was with him.

Simone's eyebrow takes on a life of its own. 'Really? With his *zizi* sticking out?'

'Yes.'

'I tried to warn you about his *soi-disant* work,' she says. 'Did you know he wanted to recruit me?'

SELIM IS. 'To what?'

'What do you think? As a *sharmouta*.'

I bristle. 'How dare he?' Long ago, being a prostitute sounded impossibly glamorous. Little did we appreciate as teenagers that the role did not merely involve accepting lavish gifts and smoking Balkan Sobranies, but a life of sexual slavery and violence in order to feed a family or a heroin habit. 'Simone?'

'What?'

'Why didn't you come back to Egypt? You did say you'd tell me.'

'I considered it once it felt safer to go back, but then I worried that, if I did, I might never leave. The pull of Alex is very potent, you know.' She pauses to heave a sizeable Le Creuset pan off the shelf. 'I left under dubious circumstances.'

'I know you were pregnant. But still.' I want her to sit down again and talk properly, not clatter about making kitchen noises.

'I was in a hurry to leave, and it cost me a lot of money.' Now she's peeling onions. 'There was a fixer. Name of Omar.'

'Omar? The man with too many teeth for one mouth?'

'*Ya khabar!* That's him exactly,' Simone says. 'How do you know him?'

I raise my chin to make clear that I have secrets too. 'Perhaps I'll tell you sometime.'

'Omar fixed lots of things,' Simone continues. 'Unlike most Alexandrians, he also kept his mouth shut.'

'He knew where you were all the time?' The bastard was lying. I knew it.

'He knew that I had left. Not where I had gone.'

Despite this revelation, I'm stifling a yawn and my right shoulder aches.

'You're tired. Go have a nap, *ya ukhti*. There's always later.'

. . .

There are voices from downstairs. I've only been lying down for some twenty minutes, but I'm wide awake and feeling fine. Still, I make my way down the stairs ever so carefully. The last thing I need is a shock to the system.

Simone is in the living room with a woman. 'Nadia, come and meet my daughter Maddy.'

'Hello.' Maddy adds that she's heard a lot about me.

She's probably fifty, though she looks younger. Her face is pleasantly round, as is her shape, but she covers her mouth when she smiles. Probably has bad teeth, like a lot of people. 'I've only got a few minutes before I need to get back to Awning,' Maddy says. 'Anyone for tea?'

It's only when Maddy brings in mugs of tea on a tray decorated with kittens that I see her properly. She beams as she hands me a mug, and this time her mouth is visible. Surprisingly, her teeth are perfectly straight and not at all discoloured. The striking thing is her upper gum where it meets the lip. Bubble-gum pink. Just like a rabbit.

My heart takes a leap out of my chest and my lungs feel about to burst. Shaking, I put down my tea which now has a cloying hint of cherry.

35

NOW

Maddy has left, and I've composed myself as much as I can.

'Right,' Simone says. 'I'll tell you.'

I have a horrible hunch that I know already.

'Are you allowed alcohol?' she continues. 'Because I might make us a drink.'

It is about eleven o'clock in the morning, and I haven't had breakfast, so I must be sensible. 'Gin and tonic, then.'

'I'll make doubles.'

Once we're installed in the living room with our drinks, Simone plants her hands on her knees. 'Alicia had filled me in on the details, and Alicia's mother knew what her husband was like. She eventually refused to bring young girls into the house.'

I shiver, and realise I had a lucky escape. 'You mean she brought them especially for him? Do people do that?'

'You'd be surprised ... But I'm not sure. Maybe she did, or maybe they were friends of Alicia's on play dates, as we'd now call them.' No wonder Simone wasn't keen for me to go to Alicia's. 'Makes no difference anyway. Others found girls for him. Selim did, too, I suspect. The man also took out his hideous perversion on his own daughter.' Muscles knot themselves between Simone's eyebrows. 'She was abused, then discarded.'

'Ah. She went to that rest home' The country-house fabrics and the solace of the sofa are at odds with the discomfort in my belly. I hope it's not C diff making a comeback.

'Yes. It was a place for people with nervous breakdowns, as they were known. Most were women, of course.'

That pad of writing paper in Simone's room. 'You kept in touch with Alicia.'

The knot now covers most of Simone's forehead. 'I did. I went to see her. She sat like a corpse in an armchair.' She downs a glug of gin. 'Soon after I visited her, I decided to confront her father. I couldn't bring myself to go to his home, so I went to his office. You remember that old building in the alleyway past the pigeon restaurant?'

Something stirs, waving for attention. A place where I followed Simone. There's another shard of memory too, of somewhere that made me shudder on the day a man called Khairy drove me around Alex in his Peugeot, with Zouzou clinging on for dear life. The same place, I'm sure.

'He had abused you, too?' Later I'll tell her what he did to me, back then.

'No, no. I myself hadn't been *abused*, or *interfered with*, call it what you will. But he was always too familiar and too close, though, which was creepy. And of course there was all that sleaziness and superiority from most of the men around us.'

'I see that now. Our whole world was unfair, and we just accepted it. Men called all the shots. *Howa kida*.'

Simone is barely listening. 'It was what he had done to his daughter that got to me. So I planned to storm into his office and let him have both barrels.'

I wipe condensation from the glass and smile. 'I can imagine. You used to yell at Father every morning.'

Simone is not smiling. She focuses on the ceiling as if the light fitting is spellbinding. The air grows thick as moments pass. 'Nobody dares say *No* to a man,' she says finally, 'however unreasonable his demands. He reminded me of that very forcefully.' She turns her face away.

Surely Simone isn't crying? I've never had to dry my sister's tears. What should I do?

'He threatened me.' Her voice wobbles. 'He hit me and my chipped tooth cut into my lip. Remember the day I came home with a cut lip?'

I nod, remembering exactly.

'Anyway. I didn't scream, not then. Maybe I should have. Or, better still, kicked him in the *couillons*. Honestly, though, I don't think I stood a chance whatever I did. He was an important man, he reminded me. He made sure I understood that nobody would ever believe me. My parents would believe me, I said, but he laughed in my face and told me not to be ridiculous.' Simone shrugs. 'The balance of power, you know.'

I'm faint and my pathetic hands shake. She may be calm, but I'm not sure how much more of this I can take. I grab one of the chintzy cushions to hug.

'He had a sofa in his office. A ghastly thing, yellow with dirty grey bobbles. I screamed then, when —'

'Stop.' My chest hurts.

Moments pass before Simone begins again. 'I did think of telling you, but I was so ashamed.'

'He raped you.' I'm letting this sink in. In truth, it has already sunk like a stone inside me, obliterating all other thought and rendering me incapable of saying anything articulate.

'And I got pregnant.'

I can hardly imagine anyone carrying a rapist's baby. 'Couldn't you get an abortion?' I feel queasy as my brain cells join up the dots. She'd tried at home, hadn't she, doing something to herself in the downstairs bathroom that day when I saw blood in the water?

'I wasn't going to have a backstreet one and risk dying of an infection. But yes, I could have. I needed to leave because of the humiliation. He'd taken my dignity, my respectability. I'd achieved nothing by confronting him, except to make things much worse for myself. I managed to smuggle money out, and there was a clinic in London that Zouzou had told me about, supposed to be clean and good. I actually went to the clinic, but, in the end, I couldn't do it. I couldn't.' She pauses to down her drink.

My head reels as all these details collide. 'How did you get the money out?'

'In tubes of hair cream. Zouzou taught me. You unfold the bottom of the metal tube, take most of the cream out, put in banknotes tightly folded, then do up the end of the tube again. If you're careful, nobody can tell.'

Money. Clinics. Zouzou. Smuggling. Something else is sinking in.

'Obviously,' Simone continues, 'the bigger the tube, the better. I used toothpaste tubes, too. You have to wash the notes for ages afterwards to get all the sticky paste off, and to make sure they don't stink of mint.'

I toss the cushion aside. 'Wait a minute. Zouzou knew?'

She nods.

'You said in your email you were in touch with Zouzou. Then she knew about the pregnancy and everything?' My voice rises, I realise.

'She did.'

'She knew about it all, and she didn't tell the whole of Alex? Never mind that. She didn't even tell me?' I could bloody well kill Zouzou. Then I remember that she's dead already.

'Just a moment.' Simone goes to check on something in the kitchen.

My hands are steadier. All my shaking is on the inside now. My sister, raped by her friend's father. Worse, suffering for decades afterwards. Couldn't Simone have shared that with me sooner? As soon as she returns from her cooking, I suggest it.

She replies, 'I'd been shamed. That's a very powerful thing.'

'Couldn't you have even sent us a letter? Censorship had relaxed under Sadat. Postcards are all very well, but we couldn't reply.'

Simone leans back in the armchair and examines her knuckles as if they hold the answer. 'To begin with, I couldn't take the risk of even having a PO box. I wasn't ready to explain it all, not by a long shot, so I didn't want to be found.'

'But what about your family being ready to find you?' I think of all the love and support she could have had when she needed it most, though I can't find the words to say this aloud. 'And then you stopped writing altogether.'

'I did not!'

Chilli con carne smells come through strongly now, but food is hardly uppermost in my mind.

'What happened, then?' I'd love to hear what excuse she comes up with.

'I wrote you a long letter in 1992, about my son and his

cancer, among other things, at the same time as I wrote to Mother and Father. I gave you my address, but you never responded. Not once.'

She's making it up, obviously. 'I never got that letter. Why didn't you try writing again?' On the other hand, post going astray isn't exactly a rarity. Or else Zouzou lost it. She's the one who looked after my mail when I left Alex. She may even have forgotten about it, since she was properly old by then. I can't believe she did it on purpose. Although, as Fouad said, she always liked having something over people.

'I have a question.' Simone's voice has an edge. 'Why didn't you bother looking for me before, instead of waiting until you were ill and needed my help, like the little child that you always were?'

That's one hell of an accusation. I'm angry now, not merely flushed from alcohol. 'Of course I looked for you! I hired detectives. I did everything I could, as did our parents.' Father got that has-been journalist whose name escapes me. Simone says nothing and I continue. 'We loved you. We never stopped loving you. The rest of the world went on as if you'd never existed. Worse than that, you went on as if *we* didn't exist!' My palpitations are back with a vengeance.

Simone gets up. 'The chilli is burning.'

I nearly explode. 'The chilli is burning? Is that all you can say?' I feel like shouting *fuck* and throwing something at her, but I content myself with glaring through the kitchen doorway for a moment before going upstairs. I'm shaking so much that I can't stomp up the stairs. I have to go up on all fours. Once I get to the guest room, I slam the door, in vain as it fails to make the impressive bang I had in mind.

I lie on the bunk under the jolly little yachts. This isn't how I imagined our reunion. Half a century to find her, and just a couple of days to cause irreparable damage. How on earth could Tante Georgette and Tante Joséphine live together? Simone did rescue me, but, all the same, her altruism is limited. Why does she care more about those women and children under her awning thing than about her own family? Our poor, poor parents. It's so cruel of her to have left them in the dark all that time.

I clutch the edge of the bedspread and do those Hash Tango breaths that Sheila is so keen on, without much success, though I suppose I'm now calm enough to hear birds singing outside the window. Simone has bird feeders and bird tables and all that stuff. Yes, she cares more for little feathered creatures than for her family.

While I'm livid with Simone, I'm also furious with Alicia's father who began all this. Once I start on this train of thought, I don't know who to blame, who to hate. *Whom* resounds in my ears. I'm always with Simone, whatever age I am.

Fuck it. I'm going to escape. That'll show her.

First, my knee exercises. Those quads are coming on, though I'm a long way off growing bulges like that Olympic rower, something Cracknell. As for my shoulder, I hardly need my sling now. I take a painkiller and have a go at some of the exercises.

The chilli con carne smells amazing from here. There's no food in my flat. Well, now that I can use an iPad and pay for things online, I am sure I can work out how to order groceries. I should have known all along that I would need to manage on my own.

Simone stares at my shoes.

'I need a walk.'

'They said not to let you out on your own.'

'What do they know? I'm fine.' I don't let on that I took a tumble while putting on my socks.

'I'll come with you.'

'I'll be perfectly fine.'

In truth, my head swims, and I teeter on my spindly legs as I leave the safety of Simone's front door, then I hold on to the garden wall before I dare turn around and wave. Hopefully I'll make it all the way to the pillar box and back without falling or dislocating anything.

Despite attacks of vertigo, I manage to reach the corner with the post box. My little wander takes about ten minutes, all told, during which I'm sure Simone is watching from a window. I manage my little rehearsal. That's the main thing.

The front door is already open for me when I struggle back up the path. 'There? You see?' I try to act normal as I cling on to the door knob as if it's a life raft.

'Come and sit down,' Simone says.

She brings me a cup of tea in the living room. This nice, friendly stuff doesn't fool me one bit. Well, two can play at that. She'll see. When I've subdued the banging in my chest, I ask, 'So you didn't tell Mother and Father where you were?'

Simone shakes her head. 'Not until 1992. Before then, I assumed my postcards, bought from wherever, would tell you, in a roundabout way, what you needed to know.'

'Not exactly, though I figured out that you weren't alone. That postcard you sent about meeting one another. It meant there was more than one of you.'

'Of course. Remember Miss Appleton's lessons? *Each other* means two people meeting or whatever. *One another* means more than two. I had Maddy.'

'I thought it meant you had some man.'

Simone brightens. 'But surely you understood Magdalene Bridge? And the butterfly I drew, meaning new life?'

I don't answer. No point her thinking I'm stupid. 'I went to that bridge in Cambridge, you know. To look for you.' My eyes drive in my point.

'Then you must realise that the name of the bridge was a clue. Maddy is short for Madeleine.'

'It could have been Magdalene for Tante Magda.'

'Don't be silly.'

So that was why she hadn't chosen a more photogenic view. But still, I cannot imagine the horror of carrying her assaulter's baby. 'I don't get it. You decided against a termination.' The air shifts while I wait for her to speak.

'That's right,' she says eventually. 'You can't know what you'll do in a situation until you're in it. Another G and T?'

It's incredibly easy to say *Yes*. 'Dinner smells delicious, by the way.'

Two fresh glasses in front of us, and Simone says, 'Now I want to know about you.'

I wasn't planning to open up, but a swig of gin helps. 'I, too, got pregnant when I didn't want to.'

Up goes her eyebrow.

'I didn't do it to imitate you. As it turned out, I got pregnant easily, many times, but the miscarriages kept coming, one after another.' It's been years since I cried over my lost babies. They deserve every single tear, but I can't let myself go now. 'Could I have some water?' I'm a bit more composed when Simone returns with a glass. 'Anyway.' I take a sip. 'I'm glad you had your daughter.'

'Me too. Maddy completely changed my life. And my son's.' She bites her lip. 'When her brother was desperately ill, she donated bone marrow.'

'You mean she saved his life?'

Her eyes are abnormally shiny. 'Alexander is fine now.

And, while it may be hard for you to believe, family is everything to me.'

There's a silence. No matter how hard I try, I'm not sure I believe Simone about family being everything to her. Brain cells have their own agenda, and they don't do things to order. I avoid her gaze and focus on the window instead. Some flowers have opened since I last looked. Lupins, possibly. Or maybe snapdragons. Sheila would know. In the corner by the pergola stands a metal sculpture made out of cogwheels and levers. Thanks to Father, I know the names for all those things. Maybe someone enjoyed putting that sculpture together.

'Let's sit in the garden,' Simone says.

Before I can protest, she guides me outside. She actually brings me a stool for my feet and insists I have a bite to eat, muttering about the dangers of drinking on an empty stomach, though it seems a bit late to worry about that.

'Perhaps I will.'

I swear my sister has never been this solicitous. She probably feels guilty.

I balance the plate of cheese and biscuits on my thighs. There's a lot to take in. It smells of spring here, with an English dampness that hints at rain in the not too distant past, as well as in the near future. Just the sight of the flower beds makes me feel healthier, as if all things are now possible. I actually recognise one of the plants, but then even a she-donkey would know it's a rose.

Although I'm planning to escape, I still want answers. 'Why didn't you return to Egypt?' I know I sound like a broken record.

This time Simone gives a different reply. 'For a long time, it was fear. The man didn't just humiliate me. He threatened me. *Go away, and don't ever come back.* I'll never forget what he said. If I ever dared set foot in Alex after my smears on his good reputation, as he called it, he would have me dealt with. *Dealt with*. I couldn't take the risk. He may even have meant the secret police. They were very powerful, you know.'

'Of course I know. I lived there longer than you. But Alicia's father is dead now.'

'Okay. But, after our parents died, there was no point returning anyway.'

I give up the plate of cheddar. 'You could have come back for me.' I cross my arms, feeling another row bubbling up.

'*Habibti*, I was more likely to find you here.'

'You could have come back for our parents' funerals.' I immediately see it wasn't feasible. Funerals in Egypt always take place so soon after a death. With no direct flights, how could Simone have been in Alex the next day?

'I couldn't. And you know,' Simone adds, 'it was no longer my home.'

Now she's being idiotic. 'So now you only go to places that are your home?' My voice has an edge.

'You go to them in a different way.' Her tone is so haughty that no retort is possible.

Simone returns from another trip to the kitchen for refills. There is definitely something about the combination of plants and booze. If I carry on like this, I may turn into Sheila.

'So,' Simone says, 'did Mother did tell you I was hoping to return to Alex that year?'

Ah. The letter Mother said she'd got, and I never found. '*Maman* was very ill at the time. I thought she was imagining it.'

'I sent you a letter, too. I drew a flower on yours.'

'So you say. I never got it.'

'I postponed my trip because Alexander had leukaemia. A rare type, as it turned out.' Simone gives a long and incomprehensible name with acute myelo and mono and bits like that in it.

A phrase from long ago comes back to me. *Like a marmalade spoon. A cute one.* I'd assumed Mother's last words were another crazy simile, but now I suspect she meant this leukaemia. Acute one. Of course. 'And he's okay since the bone marrow?'

'Yes, he's fine. And he's married. Isn't that great?'

'It really is.'

'You'll meet him.'

I nod, but I'm not planning to stick around, am I?

'Another thing,' Simone says. 'It took me a long time to come to some kind of terms with the rape. Nowadays we'd call it PTSD, though we didn't understand post traumatic stress back then. Ken and I learned to cope with the trauma around Maddy's conception, but going back to Alex would have brought it all back, and I feared another breakdown.'

'Another breakdown?' There is so much she hasn't told me.

She makes a nondescript noise. 'By the time I felt brave enough, I had two sons, Alexander and then Richard. They live nearby. The family is just giving us some space for now.'

Space? That is so not-Arab.

'You're staring again,' Simone informs me.

'I am?'

I turn towards the flower bed. Nothing's quite in focus. Maybe I'm swaying. At any rate, Simone takes the plate away and persuades me to go have a *siesta*, which is fine. I can use the time to plot my escape.

. . .

What actually happens as I lie on that bunk bed is that my brain simmers before the sediment eventually settles, each tiny particle finding its place. I know why women may need a refuge. Once, I might have wondered why women in danger couldn't go back to their parents and relatives. Now I see.

When I next go downstairs, I find Simone in the living room, hunched over a laptop by the window.

'Are you working?' I ask.

'I was, but now I'm ready for a drink. What about you?'

'No more gin for me.'

'I meant tea, *ya 'abita*.'

As Simone bangs around with mugs and tea caddies, I ask, 'Why did you decide to open a refuge?'

'Growing up in one of the most sexist, most repressive nations makes you think. If it doesn't, there's something wrong with you. Do you actually know the number of sexual assaults in Egypt?'

'I know the vast majority aren't reported.' Here we are talking about Egypt when I asked her something entirely different, but that's Simone.

'And I'm not talking about pestering a woman at the station or groping her bottom on the Corniche,' she continues. 'I mean vicious assaults that are planned and orchestrated. Mobs out to wreak sexual brutality, and they're so well organised that there's no escape.'

'I know. I went back in 2011.' I'd tell her all about Tahrir and Wedad, if I could muster the energy.

'You did? Well, the UK isn't perfect either. At a rough estimate, over a million women a year in England, from all walks of life, suffer domestic abuse, and there isn't enough help for them. Two women a week die from violence in the home. Sorry. I sound like a lecture. But it's why I do what I do. Sugar?'

'Just one.' The nerve cells are sparking again, and another memory flickers into life. Someone's crying. She has the strongest arms in the world, but her legs hurt all the time. Today they're bruised because she walked into a table last night. That's what she says. Same as last Thursday. Her home must be full of tables. 'Mariam was abused by her husband, wasn't she?'

Simone shakes her head. 'Not by her husband.'

I hold up my spoon mid-stir as I make the connection. 'Oh my God!' Mariam preferred Simone and me to her own child.

'Exactly. Her son was a gambler. He would take all her earnings and squander them, then beat her when he wanted more. Mother helped by giving Mariam extra pay, but nobody actually addressed the problem.'

A good woman. Poor thing. May Allah protect her. That's what I heard that night.

'He killed her in the end,' Simone adds.

'No! Did he go to jail?'

Her eyebrow rises. 'What do you think?'

I've regained some of my equilibrium, when it occurs to me. 'Is all of that why you've kept absolutely nothing from Egypt?'

'Not quite.'

Simone leaves the room and returns moments later with a little Boules Quies tin, empty of its wax earplugs but still precious for the embossed hieroglyphs on its lid. In her hands she also has one single turquoise mosaic tile, a bookmark with the image of a saint, and a party favour. It's a small clicky tin thing in the shape of a ladybird. They're clean treasures. Exactly my sister's kind of treasure.

'I didn't take much,' she says. 'I thought I was coming back.'

'We're not going back, are we?' I said *we*. Shows how hard it is to stay angry with Simone.

She hands me the clicky toy just as she did back then. I fiddle with it a couple of times before picking up the tile to feel its rough edges and its smooth surface. As if alive, it becomes warm in my grip. Nonsense, I tell myself. It's heat transferred from my hand. I hold it up to the light. It is the colour of the sea at a place I will never see again.

36

NOW

A week on, and I've put my dramatic exit on hold. I need a couple of things from my home, so here we are, Simone and I, with a couple of empty holdalls in my stuffy apartment. The basil and mint on the kitchen windowsill appear completely dead, but Simone says you never can tell, especially with mint, so, to please my bossy sister, I give both pots a soaking. Other than that, we stay only long enough to collect a few clean clothes and my post. Amid a thousand pieces of junk mail and pizza offers, a letter confirms my outpatient appointment for tomorrow.

Now I'm ready in Simone's hall with bus pass, wallet, keys, and mobile phone. I check my bag. The hospital letter is there, too. Simone has already donned her jacket. 'I'm coming with you.'

There is no point arguing.

It's strange being on public transport again. A man whose teeth don't fit valiantly attacks a baguette regardless, distributing crumbs and grated cheese all over his lap and on to the hipster next to him. Two young men in paint-splattered joggers chatter in some Eastern European language. One of them gives a couple of banknotes to the other one and shoves the rest of the wad back into his pocket.

'Here we are,' Simone says as we get off the tube train.

We negotiate the smokers outside the hospital entrance and use the revolving door. Signs tell me to check in at one of the machines with my hospital letter. Simone helps me with the barcode reader, and we go up to Clinic Six, where I find a young man behind the counter, chatting up the other receptionist, in so far as anyone can chat up someone who is comatose.

I observe her. The woman isn't in a coma after all, because she is sucking a sweet. 'I have an appointment.' I hand her the letter.

By way of an answer, the receptionist points to a corridor where a dozen people are already waiting. There is just one seat vacant.

'I'll stay here,' Simone says.

Waiting in crowded corridors is normal in the NHS. It was never like this in Egypt, if you could afford *baksheesh*. In a strange way, I feel more at home here than almost anywhere else I've been lately. Institutionalised, that's me.

The passage here is too narrow for someone to pass if a patient is in a wheelchair or just crosses their legs. As it is, one wheelchair is jammed into the end of the corridor. The man in it has waited for over an hour, he keeps reminding everyone who'll listen and quite a few who won't. Eventually tiring of it all, he covers his head with a towel.

Visibly alarmed, a nurse orders him to remove the towel.

He refuses. 'The light stings my eyes.'

'I can't help that,' the nurse says.

A woman in a sari interrupts them to ask if there's wi-fi.

One of the consulting room doors is open. Inside, a doctor is swearing at her computer. Doctors always do this. Twenty minutes later, there has been little progress along the clinic conveyor belt, though someone has written an apology of sorts on the whiteboard.

When a chair becomes vacant, Simone moves next to me.

'Don't say anything to the doctor,' I tell her. As if she'll take any notice.

Eventually it's my turn.

'Hello Ms Wissa,' the doctor says. I can never retain her name, but she still has Laura Ashley glasses and pink hair down one side.

Fritz is there, too. Simone restrains herself admirably while the doctors smile at me as if I am senile. 'Now,' Fritz says. 'Do you remember what we said about the herbal supplements you were taking?'

'Of course. Now my head hurts less, and my mouth is less dry. I suppose it's because I've stopped taking them.'

'Hmm. Did you have a feverish illness when it all started? Maybe waterworks trouble or a chest infection?'

I did, as it happens. 'I had flu about a year ago. The worst cough and rib pain I've ever had.' I felt as bad as I had with the measles, the difference being that nobody called Doctor Tadros, and Mother didn't give me suppositories to bring down my temperature. 'I stayed at home for weeks, and I was disorientated for a long while after, when I finally got out and about.' I kept trying to tell the doctors about losing my list outside the chemist, but they hadn't wanted to know, had they?

'Ah-ha,' Laura Ashley goes. 'And when did you start taking those supplements?'

'I don't know exactly, but it was around then that my friend suggested I needed something for my brain.'

Laura Ashley says, 'I expect that was it. You had a confusional state from your flu, then you took all those expensive toxins, which gave you further symptoms.'

Of course, they don't commit themselves. Fritz makes me subtract sevens and repeat lists of words. I think I do better than before. There's so much less brain fog these days.

'We should repeat those psychometric tests,' Laura Ashley says.

Today's psychometric woman is nicer than Ms Smits. I do all right on them, too, but then my brain isn't trying to thump its way out of my skull any more. From the noises the doctors make afterwards, they also think I'm better, so they let me off and ask me to return in a month.

We're just through the revolving doors when Simone gestures with her hand. 'I had a lot of assessments there when I was in hospital. But mostly I had drugs.'

I'm shocked. 'When?'

'My breakdown. Well, both of them. I was in hospital a long while, then afterwards there was a lovely CPN. A community psychiatric nurse.'

We're right by the strip of waste ground where I dislocated my shoulder, and it's all I can do not to fall again. 'That's awful.'

'Far worse for Alicia,' she says. 'So, your condition. Was it really all down to those wretched pills you took?'

'Well, I was already not quite right before then. Otherwise I wouldn't have bought the pills in the first place.' Confusional state, I think Laura Ashley said.

'What do you mean, *not quite right?*'

'Not being able to count, for one thing. I still know my nine times table, but I can't do mental arithmetic like I used to.'

Simone gives that Arab nod that indicates disagreement. 'That's because of your flu or chest infection of whatever. Anyway, who needs to do mental arithmetic when they have a smartphone?'

'I got lost when I went out shopping. And I was sleeping pretty badly.' I was lonely and miserable too, but I leave that bit out.

'Stress, I expect,' Simone says. 'It changes your perspective and affects how you concentrate and how you think. And being alone is very corrosive.'

'I'm not alone anymore,' I say, as I trot alongside her to the tube station. *And neither are you,* I add under my breath.

When we get back, I'm exhausted. We sit with cups of tea in the garden and that question pops out of my mouth again. 'Tell me, really, Simone, why didn't you come back to Egypt?' I can't stay angry with her, but I want answers.

Sure enough, Simone comes up with a new explanation. 'It wasn't just me who'd changed. Egypt had. I could see that, even from here in England. That brand of Arab nationalism excluded people like us, the *shawam*. All that time, we had a foot in each camp but were at home nowhere. Don't you see?'

Of course I see. Persecuted in our home in Syria, we then became Egyptian but weren't fully accepted in Egypt.

'It wasn't our home,' she continues. 'It was only lent to us.'

'How can you say that? Our families lived there for over 100 years! The *shawam* did so much for the country. We founded that newspaper, *Al-Ahram*. And, well, lots of things.' I can't be expected to remember them all.

'You have to let it go,' Simone says.

It's not quite the weather for it yet, but we have a barbecue, mainly because Max and Jake pester their grandfather until he gives in.

Maddy brings her husband, a bearded man by the name of Dirk. Alexander, Richard, and their partners are also here. I might no longer be poisoning myself, but names are still a problem.

Max frets. 'Is there enough ketchup, Grandpa?'

Ken assures him there is.

I observe as Ken grills burgers and ears of corn. Although he doesn't fan them with a piece of cardboard, the corn tastes almost as good as the stuff cooked on the Corniche.

Max douses his corn in ketchup.

'Ugh. Like a road accident,' Jake says.

I wonder if Max will always love ketchup. How much do people change with time?

The evening is drawing to a close. Ken and Maddy's husband — Dirk, that's it — are animatedly discussing petrol lawnmowers while Simone and I, now in cardigans, finish off the wine.

I know I'm staring again, but it's hard not to. In front of the dying barbecue, Maddy and her sons are singing 'Walk Like an Egyptian', which they accompany with impeccable moves. To complete the look, each of them has draped a towel over their heads, the *Egyptian Cotton* label facing outwards.

'That's hilarious,' I say. Something about the ensemble takes me back to 1961, when we used to warble 'Ya Mustafa' into our hairbrushes. 'By the way, does Maddy speak any Arabic?'

Simone shakes her head. 'Not a word.'

'Really? Why didn't you teach her?'

'I didn't want to.'

If I'd had children, I'd have made sure they knew something of their heritage. 'But why not?'

'Stop asking me.'

'I could teach Maddy,' I offer. 'You know I give Arabic classes, don't you?'

Simone doesn't answer.

Cheeks glowing, the three singers subside on to the garden bench.

On impulse, I begin the story. '*Kan fi bint el nooneyya.*'

'Shut up,' Simone hisses.

Maddy continues the tale in English. 'She was only this tall and had everything that was teeny tiny. One day along came a thief and stole all her teeny tiny things.'

'You taught her that story?'

'Well, yes,' Simone admits. 'Oh, put your eyeballs back in their sockets. That story is, after all, a fine feminist parable. The finest one we ever heard at home.'

I correct her. 'The *only* one we ever heard at home.'

Simone and Ken are clearing up. Apparently, I can just about be trusted to carry a single plate into the kitchen before being ordered to sit down and rest.

'Maybe you and I should go to Egypt,' Simone says from the sink.

'No, we shouldn't.' I think of people who return to Alex from exile and spend their days moaning, and I can't blame them. Madame Amin was right about our city going to hell in a *hantour*. It's not just period architecture and cosmopolitan culture that have vanished. It's also the tolerance that everyone had enjoyed. Yet Egypt is in my brain and in my bones. For now, Simone and I can't agree on a return trip, but that's okay. I give her a sly grin. 'We have the rest of our lives to decide.'

'I think we will go back,' Simone says. 'You know what they say. Once you drink the waters of the Nile …'

'I know. You get bilharzia.'

Back to my apartment tomorrow. We're having a drink before bed, Simone and I, and I gaze around her kitchen as we sip mint tea. I've never had a fridge like hers, covered in lists, grandchildren's artwork, and the odd magnet. Never will.

Simone asks, 'When you got pregnant, that first time, was it rape, too?'

I shake my head. 'More like whisky and stupidity.'

For now, I leave it at that. You can't understand where you are until you understand what went before. That's what our history teacher taught us. But you also have to accept what's happened, even if you don't fully comprehend it. I still long to know how Simone got her exit visa, and what Maddy knows of her parentage. Maybe someday I'll ask that, too. Not now, though. I'm savouring this precious moment, as the present shakes hands with the past.

37

NOW

Home at last. It's musty. I open the windows and sniff the spring breeze. *Sham el nessim.* A sweet smell wafts up. Must be that man on the pavement vaping as he walks past.

I'm doing a lot better than the herbs on my windowsill. Neither the mint nor that other thing made it. Basil? Oregano? Okay, my vocabulary occasionally lets me down, my legs aren't as strong as they were, and my right knee is dodgy, exactly as I told them at the hospital, which is why I still veer off to the right now and again. All in all, however, I'm doing well. Look, I can boil a kettle and even lift it with my right arm. The physio would be impressed.

Recovery from illness brings a certain euphoria. Only those who've experienced it can understand. I see everything sharply yet calmly, even the leaves on the trees, and I'm enjoying things like my favourite CD of Umm Kulthum in concert. In between the hypnotic lyrics that she belts out over and over, there's clapping, cheering, and whistling, all hallmarks of a rapturous audience. I remind myself to turn down the volume. A neighbour complained last time, fearing Al-Qaeda had taken up residence in the apartment below her.

My GP, Doctor Patel, has been around to check on me, and actually seemed pleased with my progress. Even she appreciates that I'm less confused than a month or two back, though I'm less bright than I was a decade ago. Was I ever that bright, though? I must have been dumb not to realise something was wrong — *kan fi haga ghalat,* as we used to say when I kept miscarrying. But then Fouad had been stupid, too.

Bang on time, Sheila's at the door. 'How are you, sweetie?' she says, thrusting a bunch of tulips at me.

'I'm fine. And thank you very much.'

As Sheila arranges the flowers in a jug, she tells me she's seeing Eric again this evening. 'He's rather nice.' Her eyes flash.

'And he really is a pilot?'

'Well, he was.' It turns out he decided against renewing his light aircraft licence because of the expense.

The intercom goes again. Victor bears a showy bouquet of yellow flowers that come with their own vase. 'I thought it would be easier for you,' he says.

'That's very thoughtful, Victor.' This time, I don't recoil from the kisses he plants on both cheeks.

Sheila knows what Victor's flowers are called, and she reels off a string of complicated names.

Victor is as slim as a warthog. A prosperous one. With lots of hair, some of which may be his own. He's clearly had his nose fixed to look less Arab, and his ears were pinned back while the surgeon was about it, but the most obvious change is that he's an awful lot nicer than I remember.

I ask after him and his family. He's well, he's married with two children, and his mother is still alive. 'Thanks be to Allah, her heart condition turned out not to be the worst one in Alex after all.'

'So, this is the cousin that you've been hiding from me all these years,' Sheila simpers, her eyes fixed on Victor. To my mind, Victor doesn't look as good as he does on his snazzy website, but that doesn't stop Sheila wanting to know all about his fascinating work. It won't take her long to forget the pilot.

I go to boil that kettle and manage to drop the bag of granulated sugar. I'm as clumsy as I ever was with *shorbat el toot*. The grains are everywhere, including underfoot. *Fuck*, I exclaim, but it doesn't sound like me after all.

Worse things have happened than I ever imagined, but I also see that good things can happen, even at my age. I have few qualifications, have never held down a proper job, raised a family, or filled a house with *petit point*, but I speak several languages pretty well. Maybe I'll study another one to help stave off dementia a bit longer. German, perhaps. It's not as admirable as running those marathons that other seventy-year-olds seem to do, but it's exercise of sorts, isn't it?

Simone wants me to work at the refuge. As I wipe away the last of the sugar, I decide I won't. I've followed my big sister for decades. Should I follow her for the rest of my life? Finding her proves I can do things without her. Although it also shows how much I need her. Look, I'm confusing myself now.

Who are we? I'm still not sure, but I'm getting to know who I am. At seventy, it is about time.

A NOTE FROM THE AUTHOR

If you enjoyed this book, I'd really appreciate your taking a moment to leave a short online review on the site where you bought this book. Reviews help other readers discover books more easily, and they mean a lot to the author too. Thank you.

ACKNOWLEDGEMENTS

Huge thanks to my agent Sam Brace at Peters Fraser + Dunlop and her team who got this book off my computer and into your hands.

There was some earlier prep work. My developmental editor Benjamin Evans steered me towards a more coherent story, then my enthusiastic team of beta readers helped shape this book. Special mention goes to my author friend Jane Davis who went above and beyond in reading my manuscript twice and giving me insights that only a very talented novelist can.

My aunt Muriel Dubois-Ferrière followed my writing with interest and was an inexhaustible reference to all the things I had forgotten about Egypt. Nonetheless, any errors are my responsibility.

While the plot is fiction, every scene is steeped in memories that warm me as the summer sun once did. Even half a century later, I can taste the smoky corn on the cob grilled over charcoal on the seafront, the blood from licking my skinned knee as I'd tried to escape a visit to the doctor's, and sweet homemade lemonade that made everything better.

My mother's family settled in Egypt in the 1860s. They were shawam: my grandfather was from Lebanon and my grandmother's family came from Damascus. The Arabic words in this book are in the colloquial Egyptian dialect, so they're bound to disappoint classical scholars. All the same, I hope readers relish the tale of El bint el nooneyya as much as I used to.

The characters here are imaginary, except for a handful of well-known figures such as Gamal Abdel Nasser and Omar Sharif. Historical events are intended to be accurate, at least from the perspective of characters at that time, and the other events are made up. In general, the opinions reflect those of a bygone era. It's also worth noting that Nadia's recall becomes less reliable with age.

Much of the plot relies on my medical knowledge. There's only a small grain of truth in the dysfunctional exchanges between Nadia and the hospital staff, but, with apologies to fellow doctors, every story needs a villain or two. Besides, an attentive clinician might have made the diagnosis too soon for the purpose of the narrative.

On behalf of thousands of women, I am grateful to Professor Graham R. V. Hughes for discovering antiphospholipid syndrome. Also called Hughes's syndrome, APS can cause recurrent miscarriage, premature birth, and stillbirth. While there's no cure, treatment can improve the chances of a successful pregnancy, and it's now usual to test a woman who's had three early miscarriages or, in some cases, just two. Unfortunately for Nadia, APS was unknown until 1983.

I hope that the inclusion of several other medical conditions in this book will interest readers rather than disturb them. On the plus side, the present day in The Girls from Alexandria is around 2016, so it's a Covid-free zone.

Finally, I thank my husband Jeremy who has been unfailingly supportive of this writing lark. Having had to make supper every single night is the least of it. I owe him big time.

GLOSSARY

All words in the glossary are Arabic unless otherwise specified.

abadan never

âge de raison *(Fr)* age of reason

Al Ahram Egyptian newspaper founded in 1875 (literally: the Pyramids)

alhamdul'Illah thanks be to Allah

arak anise-flavoured alcoholic drink

ayoo oh wow (or similar exclamation), commonly used in Alexandria

balooza a large wobbly dessert

basha pasha (Arabic has no letter P)

batarekh bottarga, a salty delicacy made from mullet roe

beit el mayya toilet (literally: house of water)

bien *(Fr)* well, good, or okay

bokra tomorrow

c'est un pauvre con *(Fr)* he's a pathetic little man

caca *(Fr)* poo

cher, chéri *(Fr)* dear (to a male)

chère, chérie *(Fr)* dear (to a female)

cinq à sept *(Fr)* a lover's tryst (literally: 5pm to 7pm)

comtesse *(Fr)* countess

couillons *(Fr)* bollocks

eh da? what's that?

fi haga ghalat there is something wrong

feddan a measure of land based on the amount oxen can till within a given time (about 4200 sq m)

galabeyya ankle-length gown worn by men (sometimes called *djellaba* outside Egypt)

gala-gala magician (often called *gully-gully* in English)

ghafeer watchman

gozi my husband

habib beloved (if he is male)

habibi my beloved (if he is male)

habibti my beloved (if she is female)

hantour horse-drawn carriage

howa kida that's how it is

humara female donkey

Ikhwan Brotherhood

Inglizi English

insh'Allah or ***insha Allah*** God willing

kan fi bint el nooneyya, 'andaha kul haga noonoo there was once a teeny girl, and everything she had was teeny

kan fi haga ghalat there was something wrong

khamseen hot sandy wind from the desert blowing in spring for up to *khamseen* (Arabic for fifty) days

khara shit

khawaga a foreigner; can also mean gentleman

kida like this

kobeyba savoury dish made from minced meat

la' no

labneh creamy cheese made from yoghurt

le tout Alexandrie *(Fr)* the in-crowd or elite of Alexandria

maalish never mind

maktoub it is written; it is destiny

merde *(Fr)* shit

midan square or open space

millième a tenth of a piaster

mish kida? isn't that right?

molokheyya green soup made mainly from minced jute

Mugamma' name of a government building in Cairo

n'est ce pas? *(Fr)* isn't that right? (equivalent to the Arabic *mish kida*?)

parole de dieu *(Fr)* the Gospel truth (literally: word of God)

Pasha highest official title of honour throughout the Ottoman Empire; its usage continued after Ottoman rule ended

pâte de fruits *(Fr)* chewy sweet made from set fruit paste

petit point *(Fr)* fine canvas embroidery similar to cross-stitch

piaster currency unit worth one hundredth of an Egyptian pound

poupoule *(Fr)* prostitute

roba bikya junk or old things (originally from *It*)

salaam peace; also bowing to someone

samna clarified butter

savon de Marseille *(Fr)* traditional hard soap made from vegetable oils, usually sold in large cubes

sawahel people from the coast (generally of East Africa)

sham el nessim non-religious Egyptian spring festival dating from 2,700 BC, now celebrated the same day as Orthodox Easter Monday (literally: sniffing the breeze)

sharmouta prostitute

shawam people from Syria or Lebanon

shaweesh policeman, usually traffic

shorbat el toot mulberry juice

sitt or ***sitti*** madam/lady

soi-disant *(Fr)* so-called

soodani wa lib peanuts and watermelon seeds

suffragi waiter, butler or other male servant

tais-toi *(Fr)* be quiet

tarboush fez

tawlah backgammon

tayyeb good

teas bottom

tout à fait *(Fr)* exactly

trésor *(Fr)* treasure

ukht/ukhti sister/my sister

'abit idiot (male)

'abita idiot (female)

ya khabar! oh my God! (literally: what news!)

ya used when addressing someone, eg *ya ukhti, ya Nadia, ya humara*

yiy eek or similar exclamation

zizi *(Fr)* willy

Printed in Great Britain
by Amazon